Y

LAUREN CHILD

FORT

AND YOU DIE

CANDLEWICK PRESS

Copyright © 2016 by Lauren Child
Series design by David Mackintosh

First published in Great Britain by HarperCollins Children's Books, a division of HarperCollins Publishers Ltd

First U.S. paperback edition 2019

Library of Congress Catalog Card Number 2018944779
ISBN 978-0-7636-5472-6 (hardcover)
ISBN 978-1-5362-0863-4 (paperback)

19 20 21 22 23 24 SHD 10 9 8 7 6 5 4 3 2 1

Printed in Chelsea, MI, U.S.A.

This book was typeset in Eames Century Modern.

Candlewick Press
99 Dover Street
Somerville, Massachusetts 02144

visit us at www.candlewick.com

For **Lucy G.**

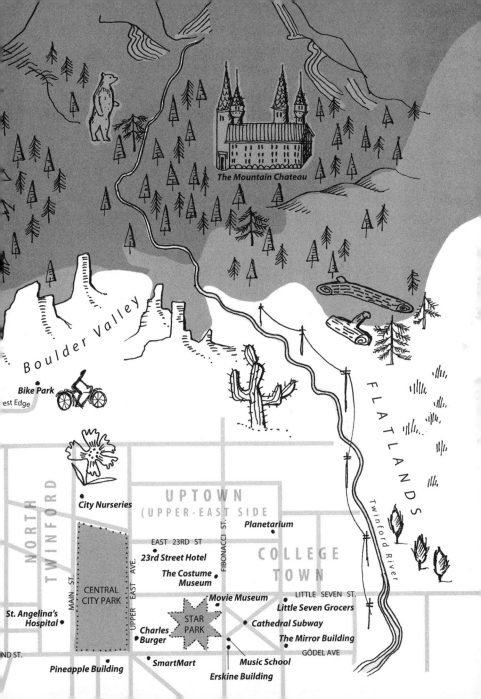

The Mountain Chateau

Boulder Valley

Bike Park
est Edge

FLATLANDS

City Nurseries

NORTH TWINFORD

UPTOWN
(UPPER-EAST SIDE

Planetarium

EAST 23RD ST

23rd Street Hotel

The Costume
Museum

COLLEGE
TOWN

FIBONACCI ST.

Twinford River

MAIN ST.

UPPER EAST AVE.

CENTRAL
CITY PARK

St. Angelina's
Hospital

Movie Museum

LITTLE SEVEN ST.

Little Seven Grocers

STAR
PARK

Cathedral Subway

Charles
Burger

The Mirror Building

GÖDEL AVE.

ND ST.

Pineapple Building

SmartMart

Music School

Erskine Building

N O R T H
T W I N F O R D

CENT...
CITY P...

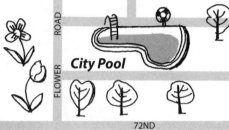

City Pool

ROAD

FLOWER

**St. Angelina's
Hospital**

STREET

**Pineapple
Building**

72ND

STREET

STREET

Bergwend-Nyle

STREET

BLEAKER

STREET

FLAUBERT

STREET

MAIN

ACER

STREET

AMBASSADOR   ROW

**Wilm...
Buildin...**

The Crews'

EVERGLADE

CHANCE   STREET

TWINFORD
SQUARE

BIRD

STREET

AMSTER

**Tony's Hair
Salon**

STREET

STREET

BIRCHWOOD

ROSE

STREET

CHATTER-BIRD
SQUARE

Photo Cam

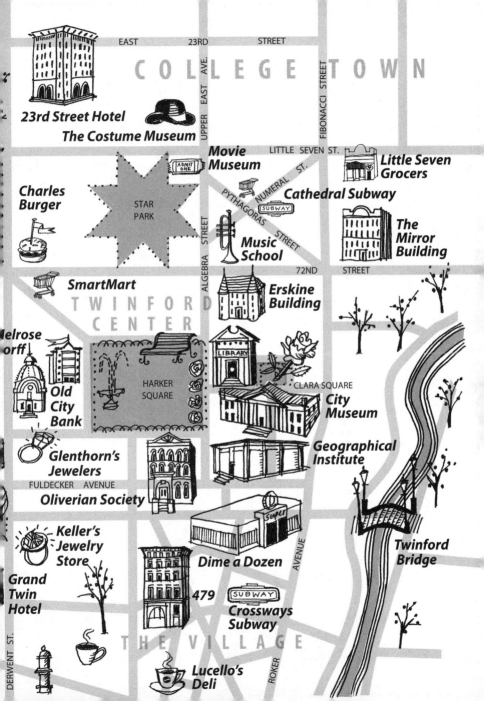

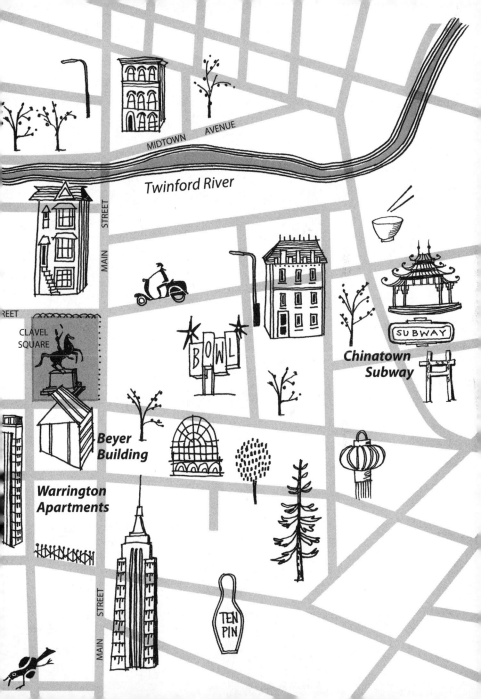

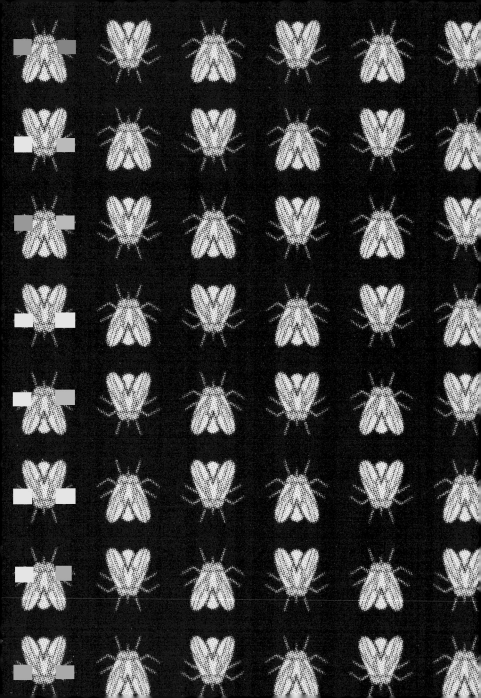

"Close your eyes and see the truth."

from The Indigo Code Breaker's Bible,

author anonymous

The Buried Fear

IT HAPPENED ONE BRIGHT APRIL DAY when the child, then barely five weeks old, was sleeping. The world crashed down and the baby opened her eyes, but there was only darkness to see. The walls were packed around her, almost touching, and the doors and the windows all gone. The baby cried out, but no one came. She screamed and clenched her furious fists, trying in vain to push at the tomb of rubble, but nothing happened. Her little mind began to panic, her eyes closed, and her heart began to hurt.

She was alone and no one would ever find her.

The baby had been left in the care of the housekeeper, who had just put some cookies to cool on the porch when, without warning, the ground began to shift and the buildings began to shake, trees creaked and then cracked. Some of them—the big oak on Amster Green—stood firm; others—the giant cedar of West Twinford—fell.

Sidewalks buckled and streetlights toppled. The earth tremor lasted just a few seconds and Twinford City escaped by and large unscathed—a few buildings needed repair, but remarkably no one, not a soul, lost their life. The townsfolk mourned their fallen trees but counted their blessings: no one had died. There was only one real casualty; the house on Cedarwood was completely destroyed. After one hundred years of standing just exactly where it was, looking out across the ever-changing townscape of West Twinford, this historic house was gone.

It was the housekeeper who dug the child out with nothing "but the hands God gave her." This woman had endured more than earthquakes in her time, and no mere earth tremor was going to have her standing by while an infant lay buried, perhaps dead, perhaps alive. By the time the baby's parents returned to their home, now a wreckage of wood and brick, their daughter was lying in the housekeeper's lap, quiet as a lamb and smiling up at them. Everyone was very relieved, their little girl saved, not a scratch to her perfect face, no damage done.

Or so they thought, for in that baby's head a tiny kernel of fear had lodged, a fear that would grow and grow until in her thoughts a monster lurked.

An Ordinary Kid

WHEN RUBY REDFORT WAS THIRTEEN AND THREE QUARTERS, she found herself confronting the biggest dilemma of her short life. On the desk was an apple split in two. In her hand was a tiny piece of paper.

On the paper were printed two small letters; small letters that spelled something so vast and so terrifying it made her eyes water.

The letters told of betrayal and murder.

It was the Count who had planted suspicion, posed the grim question, and introduced the poisonous thought that the untimely death of Spectrum's most valuable agent, Bradley Baker, might have been "arranged."

"The question is," he'd said, *"who pulled the trigger?"*

It was the apple, the messenger of doom, that held the answer.

If Ruby was to believe in its truth, then life had suddenly become dramatically more dangerous. She looked down at the paper inscribed with the initials of the woman who called the shots, who held the lives of so many in her hands.

The boss of Spectrum 8.

LB.

Ruby looked into darkness and wondered who she could trust.

Trust no one, she thought.

Some several weeks later . . .

CHAPTER 1
A Window on the World

RUBY REDFORT WAS PERCHED on a stepladder, looking out the high window that ran the length of her room. The window was designed to allow the light in rather than to provide a view of the street below, but today it was the view Ruby was interested in. She was looking down at the network of roads and alleys, contemplating the scene below. Mrs. Beesman was wheeling her shopping cart down one of the back alleys that ran between the rows of houses. The cart was filled with several cats and some jars, saucepans, and a whole lot of random junk. A few of the cats appeared to have socks wrapped around their middles, presumably to keep them warm. Mrs. Beesman herself was wearing several coats and a fur hat with earflaps, ski gloves, and an extremely long moth-eaten scarf. Mrs. Beesman tended to wear a coat in all weather, but today she was especially bundled up, suggesting that it was a pretty chilly morning. As the old lady trundled past Mr. Parker's yard, his dog, Bubbles, began to bark.

On Ruby's lap was a plate of pancakes: her second serving and it was still only 6:47 a.m. Ruby had been away from home for the whole of November, and the housekeeper had missed her more than she would ever say. The minute Ruby had walked through the door, Mrs. Digby had reached for the batter and the skillet, and while she flipped pancakes they chatted. Their conversation had been interrupted by an urgent call from Mrs. Digby's cousin Emily, and Ruby, knowing the time these phone calls often took, had carried her breakfast up to her bedroom.

The pancakes were lasting longer than usual because Ruby's eating was interrupted by her neighborhood observations. Every few minutes she would put down her fork, set aside her plate, take the pencil from behind her ear and make a note in her yellow notebook. It was surprising how much was going on out there given the time of day. Ruby had begun the yellow-notebook habit when she was four years old and she now had 625 notebooks full of the exciting, interesting, ordinary, and often dull happenings that had occurred in the world around her. She stored the 624 notebooks under the floor, the 625th she kept hidden inside the doorjamb.

Ruby had returned unreasonably early that December morning from what she referred to as the "dork pound" and what the organizers would call Genius Camp "for the mathematically gifted." As far as Ruby was concerned, it was four weeks of her life she would never get back. It had been no walk in the park, not because the work had been particularly hard, but because some of the kids enrolled in the course were, well, *not particularly nice,* and some of them were a whole lot worse than *that*, namely Dakota Lyme. Ruby had run into Dakota not so long ago at the October mathlympics meet, one of the less pleasant days of Ruby's (on the whole charmed) life. Ruby had found herself going head-to-head with the objectionable girl in the final round of the one-day competition, and for all the trouble it had caused her, Ruby would have gladly conceded victory and walked away from the whole stupid circus. However, she won and took the consequences, which were a lot of abuse and a nasty encounter in the mathlympics meet parking lot. One of the problems for Ruby was that her brilliant brain brought her a lot of attention, attention she really didn't want, or, given her status as an undercover agent, *need*.

Mr. Parker came out onto the lawn to shout at Bubbles. The sound of his voice was a whole lot more unpleasant than the sound of the dog's barking.

Ruby's life as an agent was no picnic, but then that was hardly a surprise given the kind of people one was inclined to run into during the day-to-day battle of good vs. evil. *Evil*, a much overused word in Ruby's opinion. Not every person who committed a crime was *evil*, and only rarely (extremely rarely) would one consider them through-and-through bad with not an iota of goodness in them. But when it came to the Count, Ruby would have to concede that if there *was* any good in him, it was too small to see. Blame it on a bad childhood, a life gone wrong, his ma's and pa's genes, blame it on the weather, but whatever the reason, it didn't change the facts—goodness had deserted him utterly, and his soul had gone to rot. Around this monster of a man swirled a murky soup of the vile and the unhinged, all eager to do his dirty work. The plots they hatched and cruelties they inflicted were dark enough to give Wonder Woman herself reason to keep the nightlight lit. So how did a thirteen-year-old schoolkid from Twinford hold her nerve? Well, no one had promised her it was going to be easy. But what scared Ruby more than the cruel ones, more than the Count even, was the force behind it all, the one who pulled the strings. Because there *was* someone, and according to the Count it was this someone who wanted Ruby dead and caused the Count himself to shudder.

And one should always, in the words of Mrs. Digby:

Fear the wolf that other wolves fear.

Ruby watched as a moving van turned the corner and made its way down Cedarwood Drive. It stopped outside the gray clapboard house, the oldest house on the street. It seemed it was about to become vacant once more. As far back as Ruby could remember, no one ever stuck around long enough to make the house a home.

Ruby Redfort was a girl who embraced change and was not fearful of a little adventure, but lately she wouldn't mind if the whole world stood still.

A car drove by. It stopped at the intersection; the driver wound down the window and threw a soda can onto the street.

October had been a busy month. Her life as an agent at the most secret of secret agencies — known only to those in the know as Spectrum — had been dominated by the growing sense that somewhere in Spectrum's subterranean corridors there lurked a mole. Ruby had felt the steely looks as the eye of suspicion was trained on her. She had been interviewed by the head of Spectrum 1, Agent Delaware, and it had not been a comfortable experience, particularly when with a steady gaze he had uttered the words *"I could be staring into the eyes of a traitor right this very moment and not know it."* But Ruby shouldn't have taken it personally — it was simply protocol. Every agent in Spectrum was under suspicion, every single one of them interviewed, investigated, and scrutinized. No one had been identified as the mole, no one had been cleared; the tension in HQ was palpable.

As October brought in the storm winds, the Spectrum investigation brought an uneasy atmosphere that crept through its halls, seeding suspicion and mistrust. And for Ruby everything was beginning to settle at LB's door.

A builder's truck maneuvered its way down the street and pulled up outside the Lemons' house, blocking part of Cedarwood Drive. An angry driver began honking his horn, but the truck didn't move. The driver got out of his car, the truck driver out of his truck, and they began shouting at each other. The shouts of the men in the street masked the sound of footsteps on the roof above her. It was only when the ceiling hatch opened that Ruby realized someone was up there.

"Who's there?" cried Ruby, the ladder rocking dangerously as she turned to look.

"Ah," said Hitch. "It looks like you're back."

"Jeepers! Ever think of knocking?" scolded Ruby.

"A bit weird isn't it—knocking on the ceiling?" said Hitch. He had a tool belt around his waist and a reel of cable slung across his shoulder.

"What are you doing up there, anyway?"

"It's a long story and I'll fill you in on it when I've got time, but I ought to get going."

"You don't want to hear the latest?" she asked.

"Itching to hear your news, kid, but it's a pleasure I'm going to have to put on hold." He dropped inside, then opened a window and climbed out onto the ledge.

"Doors too good for you, are they?"

"I hadn't realized you were so hung up on the rules," said Hitch as he disappeared from view. "Good to see you kid," he called.

CHAPTER 2
Long Distance

RUBY HAD BARELY REPOSITIONED HERSELF on the stepladder when there was a knock at her bedroom door. Her husky, Bug, got to his feet and ambled over.

"Is that you?" she called, slipping the notebook under her behind.

"Who else would it be?" came the reply.

"You may enter," Ruby called.

"One day you'll break your neck," said the housekeeper, walking into the room.

Ruby looked down to see Mrs. Digby, holding a tray and scanning the floor for empty mugs and dirty plates.

"That's not a very cheery greeting," said Ruby.

"It won't be a very cheering sight if it happens," said the old lady. "Nor if that butler falls off the house," she said. "Is he after squirrels again? Or is it window weevils?"

"Who knows?" said Ruby.

"What are you doing up there, anyway? Spying on folks, I'll warrant."

"Watching," corrected Ruby.

"Same thing." The housekeeper sniffed. "Never was there a child as curious as you."

"Did my folks have a late night or something?" said Ruby, looking at her watch. It was rare for them to sleep in; they were what Mrs. Digby called "early birds."

"If you want the answer to that question, then you're going to have to dial long-distance," said Mrs. Digby.

"Huh?" said Ruby.

"Paris, France," said the housekeeper. "That's where they are."

"They are?" said Ruby. "*Why?*"

"That butler friend of yours talked them into it."

"Hitch?" said Ruby, like the Redforts had a team of butlers.

"He thought they needed a vacation; *why* I don't know, since the only vacation they could use is a vacation from vacations." Mrs. Digby tutted. Just thinking about the number of trips that pair took could make her travelsick.

"So when are they home?" asked Ruby.

"Day after tomorrow. They wanted to be back in time for your return, but apparently all the flights were chockablock."

"I'm sure Hitch could get them home. He's pretty good at persuading airline people to do what he wants."

"Well, he failed this time," said Mrs. Digby, "but I guess even he doesn't have much hold over the weather."

"The weather?"

"Blizzards," said Mrs. Digby. "Paris is under several feet of snow."

"Is that so?" said Ruby. "How long are they expected to —" She broke off, her attention caught by something else. "Mrs. Digby," said Ruby, peering at the old lady, "something has happened to your face."

"Well, that doesn't sound quite polite," said the housekeeper.

"I mean you look different." Ruby stared hard at her. *"Tanned!"* she said, finally figuring out what had changed.

"Well, since you ask, I've been cruising."

"What?"

"I've been cruising around the Caribbean."

Ruby looked stunned.

"On a boat."

"I know what a cruise is," said Ruby. "I'm just interested to understand how *you* got to be on one."

"I won it fair and square."

"Won what?"

"A cruise."

"How?"

"In a competition. I won it and took Cousin Emily along with me."

"What competition?" asked Ruby.

"Well, that's the curious thing," said Mrs. Digby. "I don't exactly remember entering one, but I suppose I must have, and you know what they say. . . ."

"What?" said Ruby.

Mrs. Digby looked at her conspiratorially and said, "Don't ask too many questions or they'll find you out."

Ruby rolled her eyes. "You mean they might have made a giant mistake and given you a prize you didn't actually win?"

"I'm not saying it's impossible," said Mrs. Digby.

Mrs. Digby's view on keeping one's mouth shut was similar to Spectrum's number one rule: **KEEP IT ZIPPED.** Ruby herself had a little book of rules, eighty of them, to be accurate — it was a magenta book with the word "Rules" printed on it in red. While the housekeeper busied herself collecting the rest of the dirty dishes, Ruby was left to her thoughts, and she was surprised that one of her thoughts was *I wish my folks were home.* Ruby was an independent kid; she didn't *need* people around her all the time for comfort or security. She had what Mrs. Digby called *inner reserves,* by which she meant a strong sense of who she was, but for some reason today, sitting up there on that stepladder, Ruby just felt a strong need to see her mom and dad. The house felt not so much quiet without them as actually empty.

"By the way," said Mrs. Digby, "I hate to be the one to tell you, but that Archie Lemon busted into your room and ate some of your books."

"What? You're kidding!" said Ruby.

"Before you get all animated about it, I should just say, it wasn't while I was watching him."

"So who *was*?" asked Ruby.

"That would be his mother, Elaine. She was over visiting your mom, and neither of them realized he had made a crawl for it — up all those stairs too."

"How did he manage that?"

"They're overfeeding him is my guess," said Mrs. Digby. "Who would believe such a tiny person could cause such havoc, but don't worry, I cleaned it all up, wiped the dribble off your books and put 'em all back."

"Gross," said Ruby.

"I'm not disagreeing with you." The housekeeper turned to leave. "Glad to have you back, child."

"Thank you," said Ruby. "I've missed you a bunch, you know that."

Ruby returned to her musings.

As Ruby ran through all the various things that had happened since April, some eight months ago now, she began to see how time was running out, and maybe not just for Spectrum — perhaps for her too.

She was beginning to tune in to something that was driven by neither fact nor logic; it was more of a Clancy Crew hunch type of a thing. Just a feeling that whatever trouble was out there, it was now headed her way and about to come knocking at her door.

CHAPTER 3
Catching Up

AT THREE P.M. RUBY HEARD A SCRATCHING at the back door.

"Bug, is that you?"

She was answered by one short bark.

"OK, I'll be out in a minute."

She pulled on her boots, coat, and hat, wound a scarf around her neck, and climbed out of the window.

Bug was waiting patiently outside for her, and together they set off down Cedarwood Drive to the Donut Diner on Amster. She left the husky on the sidewalk and he settled down for a nap.

It was medium busy, not too crowded, but as usual there were plenty of customers. Marla, the owner, waved to Ruby as she walked through the door.

Ruby took a seat at the counter, where Clancy was already waiting: in front of him, two mugs of ginger tea and a couple of apple donuts.

Ruby unzipped her coat, to reveal a T-shirt that read: ***happy to be here.***

"What's with the tea?" asked Ruby.

"My sister Amy has a cold, my sister Lulu has a cold, my sister Nancy has a cold, my sister Minny has a cold, my dad has a cold."

"Jeepers," said Ruby, "sounds bad."

"Drusilla says due to the high levels of antioxidants in ginger, ginger tea can strengthen your immunity, warding off infection, and I'm trying to remain uninfected," said Clancy.

"But why do *I* have to drink ginger tea?" asked Ruby. "It's you Crews who are harboring the plague."

"Who knows who it will strike next? You get sick, there's more of a chance I get sick, and I don't want to get sick. Christmas is my favorite time of year."

Ruby sipped her ginger tea. When Clancy was in this frame of mind it was easier to fall in behind him than argue it through.

"By the way, long time no hear," said Clancy.

"I wrote you: you didn't get my postcards?"

"I got 'em," said Clancy. He thought for a moment. "How come you typed them?"

"I didn't want anyone to recognize my handwriting," said Ruby.

"Is that why you signed them Aunt Mabel?" asked Clancy.

"I was trying to keep incognito."

"Well, it brought up a few questions with my mom, I can tell you that."

"What was she doing reading your postcards?" said Ruby.

"People *read* other people's postcards," said Clancy. "They're *postcards,* no envelopes, the *mailman* can read them if he chooses to, I mean if he happens to be particularly bored."

"So," said Ruby, "what did she want to know?"

"Why this Aunt Mabel, who she didn't know even *existed,* was recommending thermal socks. I mean, if you were planning on using a code, then why didn't you use the regular one?"

"Because if I had written a postcard in gobbledygook, then that would have looked really suspicious. This way it looks like I am writing to you about normal stuff."

"Since when is it normal for an aunt who doesn't even exist to write me about thermal socks?"

"OK, you have a point; I went too much into character, but can we get back to the important part?"

"Which is?"

"I *did* keep in touch."

"But you didn't tell me anything, not really, only that *something* had happened and it was hard to explain in writing."

"Well, it was."

"In that case, why didn't you call?"

"It wasn't so easy," said Ruby, biting into one of the donuts. "They had this whole lockdown thing going."

"Since when was Genius Camp so high-security?"

"It was more like boot camp, if you really wanna know — anyone caught out of their study area or generally not complying with mathlympics rules was threatened with disqualification."

"Seriously?" asked Clancy.

"You bet seriously," said Ruby. "I mean, you had to ask to use the pay phone — you know it *actually* had a padlock on it."

"When did you ever take notice of petty rules? Or locks for that matter. . . . Plus I thought you would have *wanted* to be disqualified and get sent home early."

"I thought about it, believe me, but then you know I felt bad for my mom and dad. For some reason having a daughter who is a major dork brainiac *means* something to them."

"*That* was your reason for staying?" said Clancy. "Since when do you care so much about your parents' dreams of a show-and-tell daughter? I don't buy it."

"OK, so not *just* that. I had my reasons for sticking around, and one of them was the Pink Pixie. I swear I woulda walked had it not been for that *box of crackers.*"

"You mean Dakota Lyme?"

"Yeah, her," said Ruby. "Boy, she was so crazy for winning, her eyes almost popped out of her face — you remember how she tried to injure that kid Ward Partial?"

"Yeah, I read about that," said Clancy. "Don't tell me she did it again."

Ruby nodded. "Only worse this time. That poor Partial kid was at breaking point. You know, for a dweeb he's actually kinda OK, plus he's only eleven. He can't handle the pressure."

Clancy nodded. "So what happened?"

"I'll tell you some other time, but suffice to say, I stuck it out."

"You know what?" said Clancy.

"What?" said Ruby.

"You're all heart."

Ruby took a big slug of her drink. "Well, I couldn't abandon him, could I? Let her go ahead and make mincemeat of him while I swanned off back to Twinford. You know what? This ginger tea's not bad."

"What *is* bad is the hogwash you're spouting," said Clancy. "Would you quit feeding me this garbage and actually tell me *why you left town*?"

Clancy had a way of sniffing out the baloney, and he knew there was more to Ruby's little math vacation than the tale she had been telling him. Since when was it necessary for her, the brightest kid at Twinford Junior High, to go away for a four-week intensive math camp?

Ruby looked him dead in the eye, plucked a napkin from the dispenser, and carefully wiped her hands.

"You promise not to get all flappy?"

"Why would I get flappy?" replied Clancy.

"OK," she said, "if you want to know so bad, I'll tell you."

Clancy waited.

"It was all Hitch. It was his idea that I should go. He came up with the plan for me to hunker down at geek camp," said Ruby.

Clancy looked confused. "Hitch is interested in your mathematical development?"

"Hitch is interested in me continuing to breathe," said Ruby, "and I'm kinda interested in the same thing. The geek camp was just a way of getting me away and out of Twinford while he assessed the situation and made things secure back home."

"Assessed what situation?"

"The situation regarding who might want me dead."

Clancy let go of his donut and it splashed into his tea.

"Clance, are you OK?"

"Hitch thinks you're on some kinda hit list?" said Clancy, his voice unsteady.

"Well, maybe . . ." she said.

"That's why you were in the middle of nowhere for four whole weeks?" He paused. "But are you sure it's safe for you to be home?"

"Safe as it's *ever* possible to be," said Ruby. "So long as I stay inside the house for the rest of my life, everything should be fine."

"It's not funny, Rube."

"I know," said Ruby. "I'm not really laughing, you know that, don't you?"

"So is it the Count?" asked Clancy.

"Well, a month ago I would have said yes," said Ruby. "But the last thing he told me down in that crypt was that he had decided *not* to kill me."

"Why?"

"Apparently he changed his mind."

"He actually said that?" asked Clancy.

"He said it was in his best interests for me to keep on breathing."

"Well, that's kind of worrying, don't you think?" said Clancy.

"Why?" asked Ruby.

"Because it sounds like there might be some other crazed killer out there."

"Yeah, well, I think there is," agreed Ruby.

"Why didn't you tell me?" said Clancy.

"I'm telling you now," said Ruby.

"So?"

"So what?" said Ruby.

"So the other thing you're not telling me."

"What thing?" said Ruby.

"I don't know," said Clancy. "That's why I'm asking."

"OK . . ." she said, "but don't get all worked up. . . . You gotta —"

"I knew it!" he said. "Something happened, didn't it? It was just after I got out of the hospital, after the Halloween pageant, the day before you went off to camp, am I right, am I, am I right?" *Now* he was beginning to flap.

"Clance, you promised you wouldn't flap."

Clancy ignored her and continued flapping.

"Look, Clance, the thing is . . ."

But he wasn't finished. "Something spooked you, *really* spooked you." He was getting all dramatic now. Ruby hated when he got all dramatic — at least, hated when he got dramatic about things that were actually already dramatic.

"Then you suddenly took off without a word. I knew there had to be a bigger reason than hanging out with nerds at some crummy nerd camp and I knew there had to be a bigger reason than just the usual Count encounter."

"Just the usual Count encounter . . . ?" spluttered Ruby. "The usual —"

"So what was it that spooked you just after Halloween?" interrupted Clancy.

"Well, it wasn't any kids dressed up as ghouls, I can promise you that," said Ruby.

"That I figured," said Clancy. "But why didn't you tell me what happened, you know, after . . . that night in the crypt" — his voice was a little shaky now — "with the undead and . . . and, you know . . ." he paused, before whispering, "the psychopath."

"Just a regular Tuesday night in Twinford."

But Clancy was in no mood for making light. He was just looking at her, waiting for her to spill the beans.

She breathed in a long slow breath, exhaled, and stared back at him.

"Well, I *was* going to tell you, of course I was, but I needed time to think."

"About what?" asked Clancy.

"Everything," she replied. "It's a big deal what I know, and I haven't told a soul."

"No one? But you musta told Hitch?"

Ruby shook her head.

"Blacker?" asked Clancy.

"No one," said Ruby.

"So," said Clancy, "what is it?"

"Not here," said Ruby, looking around. "Let's move to that booth in the corner. I don't want to risk being overheard—you know, walls have ears and all that."

They slid off their stools and took their drinks over to the other side of the diner, where the lighting was dimmer and the customers fewer.

"So," said Ruby, "ever heard the phrase 'a bad apple'?"

CHAPTER 4
Baby Grim

CLANCY DID NOT HAVE TIME to answer Ruby's question, nor to wonder what apples had to do with anything, because they were interrupted.

"Hey! Ruby!"

The voice came from across the busy diner and belonged to Elliot Finch.

"You're back," he called.

Ruby peered at her reflection in the chrome napkin dispenser. She nodded. "It would seem so."

Elliot tapped his head and said, "I saw Bug lying by the diner door and I thought to myself, Ruby must be in here somewhere."

"Quite the little Sherlock Holmes," said Ruby.

Elliot slid into the seat next to Clancy. "So how's the fruit baby?"

"What?" said Ruby.

"He's talking about the Lemon," explained Clancy.

The Lemon was Archie Lemon, one-year-old son of the Redforts' neighbors Niles and Elaine Lemon, and a baby very lucky to be alive. Had it not been for Ruby's decision to use him as a prop in the Halloween parade, Archie Lemon would have been asleep in his bedroom and the Twinford Tornado would have taken him with it when it whirled into the Lemons' home, destroying Archie's room. However, Archie *had* survived, and his parents could not thank Ruby enough. In fact, it was getting to be a problem.

"It must be cool," said Elliot.

"It's not," said Ruby.

"Being a hero's not cool?" said Elliot.

"I'm not a hero," said Ruby.

"You saved that kid's life," said Elliot.

"I borrowed that baby because I needed him to play the part of Baby Grim in the pageant. I needed him because I wanted us to win. If we had won, we would have gotten prize money. That's not heroic, it's self-serving."

"But you saved his life," insisted Elliot.

"Luck," said Ruby. "Coulda been the other way around, coulda been the tornado hit the pageant and it would all have been my fault and they woulda hated me for all eternity."

"Life is fickle," said Clancy.

"People are fickle," corrected Ruby.

"Still, it must be great, his parents *thinking* you're a hero, even if you're not . . . technically, I mean."

"It's a pain in the butt," said Ruby. "Elaine calls all the time asking me how I am." She sighed. "*And* she keeps giving me stuff."

"She's giving you stuff?" Elliot's eyes grew big. "Like gifts and things?"

"Yeah," said Ruby.

"Oh, boy," said Elliot, "I would love that."

"Would you?" said Ruby. "Really? I got a whole bunch of super-ugly sweaters you can have: pink ones, purple ones, kitten ones . . ."

"That's what she's giving you? Sweaters? Why sweaters?" asked Clancy.

"Her sister owns a knitwear business," said Ruby.

"Too bad," said Elliot.

"Look, the point is not *what* she's giving me, but that I don't want her to give me *anything*."

The bell over the diner door jangled and in walked Mouse Huxtable.

"You're back!" she mouthed.

Ruby nodded. "So everyone keeps telling me."

"Well, you've been missed, that's for sure," said Mouse. "Mrs. Drisco's been really grouchy."

"Why's that?" said Ruby. "I would have thought she would be happy to see the back of me."

"I think she misses the banter," said Mouse.

"So what's school been like since I left town?" Ruby yawned.

"Well," said Elliot, "it's been a real hotbed of finger-pointing since you were cleared of trying to wreck Del's life."

"I don't think you can say 'hotbed of finger-pointing,'" said Mouse. "It doesn't make a lotta sense."

"No," agreed Clancy, "it doesn't sound right somehow."

"Like *you* can talk," said Elliot. "What was it you said the other day —"

Mouse broke in, "The point is, Elliot, Ruby's off the hook and in the clear; everyone thinks it was someone from the outside, i.e., not a student at Twinford Junior High." She shook her head and looked at Ruby. "Boy, I guess someone really hates you out there."

"My money's on Dakota Lyme," said Elliot.

"Don't be so sure," said Ruby, who knew for a certainty that it was not. "You gotta be careful making allegations against people, however objectionable they might be." It was actually the vengeful Lorelei von Leyden, mistress of disguise, who had set Ruby up as saboteur. Dakota Lyme was just a fall guy.

Clancy checked his watch. "Yikes, I'd better get going. I have to pick up cough syrup for my sisters or I'll never hear the end of it — and I mean literally: cough, cough, cough." He pulled on his coat. "That thing we were talking about before, Rube, we'll catch up on, OK?" He shot her a look and she nodded.

"OK," said Ruby.

Half an hour later, Ruby and Bug headed off. Ruby didn't feel like going home just yet, so she turned the corner at Green Street and headed to Ray Penny's secondhand-book store.

On a winter's evening, with its cozy lighting and tropical heating (Ray hated to be cold), Penny Books was a pleasant place to kill time. The store was unusually busy today. Perhaps due to the warmth, and the fact that Ray wasn't much bothered about making a sale, a lot of folks used the place like it was a library.

Ruby left Bug outside while she browsed the graphic-novel shelves; apart from shuffling footsteps as customers edged around book stands, all that could be heard was the classical music playing and the sound of turning pages. Ruby stepped past a bearded guy who was sitting on a stool, looking at a book with a beige cover. He wasn't browsing; he was most definitely reading. In another corner was a boy flipping through a comic while he snacked on some chips.

Ruby herself settled down with a pile of Space Creep novels and began working her way through them. A moment later she was roused from her reading by the sound of falling books. Through a gap in the shelving, she could see part of a face, serious and intense. It belonged to a young woman who was clutching a pile of poetry books and continuing to browse even though her arms were already full. Too full. Every now and again one of the poetry books would slide out from the pile and hit the floor, and she would mutter "whoops" or "darn" or "for flip's sake!"

After the fifth drop, the guy with the beard looked up and said, "Here, let me help you with those." He put his book down on the stool and took the stack of paperbacks to the front desk.

The young woman was very grateful. "Thanks a lot, that's so kind, thank you, real nice of you, thank you again."

Ruby was curious to know what had kept the bearded man so enthralled for the past forty-four minutes and sauntered over to take a look. The object of interest turned out to be a book entitled *Fascinating Fungi*.

Ruby didn't doubt that the study of fungi might be fascinating, but this book was not presented in a way that would entice the casual browser. With its old black-and-white photographs and dense text, you really needed to be a total fungus nut to want to pick it up. But, as Mrs. Digby would say, "It takes all sorts." Ruby had never been a big fan of edible fungi, and even when in a survival-type situation hadn't been overjoyed to see one. However, the poisonous kind interested her quite a lot.

Ruby knew a great deal about poison in all its various forms, and her knowledge in this area had grown in recent weeks due to a series of attempts on the life of the Mongolian conservationist Amarjargel Oidov, organized, it seemed, by the Count and presumably his employer. No one exactly understood why Oidov had become the target of a murderer, but it seemed likely that it was connected to the ancient and previously undiscovered species of snake she was seeking to protect. The reptiles were an incredible yellow and marked with delicate diamonds of color. The skins would fetch high prices in the fashion trade, and the venom might be of interest to toxicologists.

Coincidentally, one of the unusual things about the snake was that it feasted on mushrooms. Why the snakes were of interest to the Count, or indeed the Count's boss, was still an unknown.

Ruby checked her watch: it was getting late and probably time for her and Bug to head home. She thanked Ray, who merely raised his hand in a lazy "bye-bye," and Ruby pushed her way out into the cold night air.

CHAPTER 5
Snakes and Mushrooms

IT WAS ANOTHER COINCIDENCE that when Ruby returned home that evening it was fungus that was the main topic of conversation.

Mrs. Digby was staring hard at a very ancient-looking recipe book and appeared unusually flustered.

"So what are you looking to cook?" asked Ruby, peering over the housekeeper's shoulder.

"Your mother wants me to make this stew when they get back — she's got her mind set on it — but I'll be darned if I will ever find the ingredients."

"Maitake," Ruby read. "What are maitake?"

"Hen of the woods," said Mrs. Digby.

"Chicken?" said Ruby.

"Mushrooms," said the housekeeper.

"What's the big deal with mushrooms all of a sudden?" said Ruby. "They seem to be popping up everywhere."

"Everyone's gone mushroom crazy, including your mother, and I can't get my hands on a single one of these rarer breeds."

"Breeds?" said Ruby. "Do mushrooms breed?"

"My point is, there's been a run on them, and it's all to do with those darned vipers."

"What vipers?" asked Ruby.

"Those ones that were on the TV."

"You mean the yellow snakes?" said Ruby. "The ones that were exhibited at the Environmental Explorer Awards?"

"Those are the critters," said Mrs. Digby. "There's been nothing *but* chatter about them, all the while you've been away — on the radio, on the television networks, in the newspapers." Mrs. Digby reached for the *Twinford Hound* and slid it across the counter. "I don't mind telling you, I wish those slitherers had never been discovered."

"I expect Amarjargel Oidov feels the same," said Ruby, thinking back to the conservationist's almost-murder. Oidov had made a full recovery, but it had been a close call. Now Ruby could see, as she scanned the evening paper, that the prizewinning conservationist Oidov was working alongside the scientific institute, and they were together

```
studying the yellow snakes, their diet, and
their environment, which remain a closely
guarded secret.
```

It was their diet, which included a rare and unnamed mushroom with rumored life-enhancing powers, that had sparked this fad for unusual fungi.

Ruby read on.

The research program is being conducted in
secrecy. The scientists are working with a
highly qualified dietary expert from Seville,
Spain.

Ruby had a pretty good idea who this dietician might be.

Mrs. Digby continued to burble on about the snakes. "They
say those reptiles hold a secret, but if you ask me, the only secret
they hold is how to get you dead lickety-split — one bite and you're
a goner."

"Plenty of snakes will get you dead," said Ruby. "Though
you're right about the venom; it is unusual. The skins are
kinda spectacular too. I mean, there are plenty of people who
might want to bump off Oidov and turn her yellow snakes into
handbags."

"Just the thought of it makes me queasy." Mrs. Digby
shivered. "What I would kill for is a half-pound of these hen of
the woods."

"Have you tried the grocers on Green Street?"

Mrs. Digby rolled her eyes. "You think I was born this
morning?" she said. "If Green's stocked such a thing, then I
would go to Green's, but these are no ordinary mushrooms."

"So maybe the farmers' market would have them?" suggested
Ruby. "They have pretty exotic vegetables."

"These are exoticker," said Mrs. Digby.

"Exoticker?" repeated Ruby.

"More exotic," said Mrs. Digby. "More exotic than what the farmers' market sells. These you have to forage for and even then you gotta be lucky, and I don't have the time to be lucky or the inclination to go roaming through the forests of Minnesota trying to spot a hen of the woods."

Ruby shrugged. "So substitute."

"What with, might I ask?"

"I don't know," said Ruby. "How about button mushrooms?"

Mrs. Digby shook her head. "What you don't know about cooking is a lot."

Which was true.

The phone rang and Ruby picked up.

"Pest control, we spray you pay."

"Hey, Ruby, it's us! We're in Paris!"

"Mom?"

"*Oui,* but of course."

"*Ciao ciao,* Ruby!"

"Dad?"

"Yes, it's me."

"How are you?"

"Well, the weather here is *très froid,* you know, and there's *neige.*"

"What? You mean snow?"

"Uh-huh, lots and lots of *neige;* the airport is still closed."

"So when are you likely to make it home?"

"Ooh la la—heaven only knows."

"Would you like to talk to Mrs. Digby?"

"*Oui,* yes, if you please, *s'il vous plaît.*"

Ruby handed the phone to the housekeeper and left them to it.

Maybe she'd have a go at solving Mrs. Digby's fungus problem.

Ruby might not have known a lot about how to get her hands on a hen of the woods, but she knew someone who probably did.

CHAPTER 6
Larger Fish to Fry

IT WOULD BE BETTER NOT TO LET MRS. DIGBY know whom Ruby was planning to call; it would almost certainly put the housekeeper in a very sour mood.

Ruby climbed the stairs to her room at the top of the house and used her private telephone line to make the call. She had quite a collection of phones in all shapes and designs. From lobster to squirrel, donut to clamshell.

She picked up the squirrel and dialed.

"Hola," said the voice at the end of the line.

"Hey there, Consuela, it's Ruby as in Redfort," said Ruby.

"Don't tell me, you're sick because you're eating all that garbage food. I bet you have pimples."

"No," said Ruby, checking her face in the mirror.

"It's your eyesight; you're not eating your kale?" said Consuela.

"Well . . ." said Ruby.

"You got bad vision because you don't eat your kale," said Consuela.

"I have bad eyesight because of genetics," said Ruby. "I'm all with you on the good-diet theory, but eggs is eggs and facts are facts."

"Facts you *know,* and yet still you eat all that junk," said Consuela. "So why *are* you calling?"

"I just wanted to congratulate you on your new job."

Silence. Then, "What new job is that?"

"I read you are working for the scientific institute, so I guess you're looking at the diet of those snakes."

Silence.

"What snakes?"

"The yellow snakes."

"That was not in the paper," said Consuela. "What I am saying is it is not to be chitter-chatted about."

"I know," said Ruby. "I just sort of figured it out."

"Well, I hope you will figure out how to keep your mouth shut," said Consuela. "So why are you calling when I'm all busy and up to my eyes cooking?"

"I thought you might be able to help me with an ingredient."

Ruby explained and Consuela listened and then thought about it, clucked her tongue, and told Ruby she'd call her back and hung up.

While Ruby waited, she took the opportunity to look up in her encyclopedia just what might make these mushrooms worth the trouble.

Maitake: *(also known as Hen of the Woods or Ram's Head) a choice delicacy, known to have many health benefits, including boosting the immune system and improving blood pressure. Grows in large circular clusters of spoon-shaped caps at the base of oak trees, gray on top and white beneath. September– November. Spores when magnified are elliptical and smooth. Makes a nourishing and meaty mushroom stew.*

Twenty minutes later, Consuela called back with a name. "You have to go to Mo's store; he's . . . What do you say . . ."

"A mycologist?"

"A heart pounder."

"Say again?"

"Que guapo."

"Really?"

"I asked him out and guess what he says? 'Maybe.' What good is maybe! His store is Daily Supplies in Little Mountain Side," she said. "No one else will have them, not late in the year as it is."

"Where's Little Mountain Side?" said Ruby.

"Look it up," said Consuela. "I got larger fish to fry," and the call was over.

After supper Ruby did just that, first checking the map that covered the walls of the guest bathroom off the downstairs hall—no sign of Little Mountain Side.

Must be out of town, she thought.

She went into her dad's home office and found a map of the

surrounding area and spread it out on the desk. It was not, as she had expected, somewhere near Little Bear, nor was it to the northeast, in the Wolf Paw range. Little Mountain Side turned out to be quite a way south of Ridgepoint, which was probably why Ruby had never heard of it: to get there meant a detour off the Pine Forest Pass, as the town was tucked away on the far side of the second Sequoia Mountain.

Mrs. Digby had recently given up "getting behind the wheel of an automobile" due to the "volume of numbskulls on the roads" (her words), and so unless she could find someone willing to pick the mushrooms up *for* her, it was going to be a morning's bus ride for the old lady.

Ruby thought for a minute.

Maybe I'll do her a good turn, make that bus trip myself, discover a new part of the world, and clock up some Girl Scout points while I'm at it. To be honest, Ruby could use the good press; after she'd been caught up in a street brawl (not her fault) and had been issued six hours of community service, her angel status had waned. The chance saving of Baby Lemon had restored a little of her good-kid status, but topping it up would do no harm.

But really this was only part of the reason for making the trip. There were tales about the Sequoia Mountains that more than piqued her curiosity. Rumors of unidentified flying objects and little green men appealed to Ruby Redfort, and while she doubted any of them were based on fact, she wouldn't mind taking a look for herself.

That decided, Ruby went back to her room, kicked off her shoes, switched on the TV, and slumped into the beanbag, clicking through the channels until she reached Horror on 44.

A dark-haired girl dressed in a check shirt, jeans, and no shoes was sitting at home with her dog. She was listening to music on her record player, and the dog was asleep. The girl sipped lemonade while flipping through a comic. Then all of a sudden the hound began to howl.

"Hey there, Rex," said the girl, "what are you barking at?" She stared into the dark. "There's nothing out there."

The dog continued to whimper.

The camera panned out the window and into the woodland. Something moved in the darkness.

Ruby looked over at Bug. He was fast asleep, no howling, no whimpering.

Her thoughts strayed to the strange happenings of recent weeks.

She picked up her pencil.

To date there were three known dangerous criminals wanted by Spectrum 8:

The Count: a psychopath, thief, and murderer with no real motivation for his evil deeds, other than the prevention of boredom and the pursuit of pleasure. What Ruby now knew for sure was that he was working *for* someone else, and what he had recently imparted during their crypt encounter was that he wasn't particularly keen on the arrangement anymore. However, what wasn't clear was how he had come to be in the power of another, or who that individual could be.

The Australian: a close acquaintance of the Count and equally ruthless.

Ruby was not sure what drew these two together but guessed they had known each other for more than a few years. It would seem the Count had requested the Australian's assistance to help tie up *loose ends;* they trusted each other, and from the way the Count had talked, he had great respect for her.

Lorelei: estranged daughter of the Australian and sometime employee of the Count. Lorelei was a law unto herself; that was beyond doubt now. She had gone rogue, betrayed the Count twice (there would be no third chance), and was hell-bent on raining havoc and destruction on those who strayed across her path — which put Ruby well and truly in the firing line.

Then of course there was the mole, the double agent, the traitor, puppet master, bad egg, bad apple . . . Call it what you liked, *someone* was pulling the strings; the question was, who?

And the Count was scared.

Not exactly a soothing thought. What kind of soul could make a soulless monster tremble?

The girl on the TV was getting twitchy: she was beginning to feel sure something was lurking out there in the darkness.

Ruby got up and went over to her own window and stood there looking out into the black. Somewhere something evil lurked. It was a big wild world, and this dark soul could be a thousand miles away. They could be watching from Mars or they might be just around the next bend on the Dry River road. However, what seemed most likely of all was that this enemy was already within and stalking the corridors of Spectrum.

The sixty-four-thousand-dollar question was:

This dark soul, could it really be LB?

HQ was on high alert, Spectrum 1 was in charge of the investigating team, security had been ramped up to carmine level, protection at Spectrum 8 had never been higher, but it was hard to feel reassured. After all, how does one protect oneself when the evil lies on the inside? From the safety of her own Green-Wood House, Ruby considered her options.

When you are written large on a psychopath's hit list, do you:

A: Stay indoors, turn the locks, switch off the lights, hide under the covers, and wait for someone else to do something?

B: Brush up on your kung fu moves, wrap up warm, get out there, root out trouble, and save yourself?

She tapped her pencil against her head.

The idea of being a sitting duck until another agent pulled the clues together, identified the mole, and rounded up these murderers was not an appealing one.

"Sit tight" was a Spectrum watchword, but as far as Ruby could tell, this was no time to be taking orders from Spectrum.

She smiled sadly.

It could only be option two.

Death or glory, she thought.

**Some eleven and
a half years ago . . .**

the guy lying on the side of the road looked up at the old man and saw the fear in his face.

"Am I . . . alive?"

The old man nodded. "It would seem so."

"You . . . OK . . . ?" stammered the guy. "You . . . look . . . like you're . . . gonna . . . faint."

The old man was shrugging off his jacket. He pulled a penknife from his pocket and began cutting at the sleeve of his own shirt, tearing it right off and wrapping it around the bleeding guy's leg.

"My name, should you be wondering, is Lenny Rivers." He was working quickly but methodically, binding the wound tight, trying to stop all that blood from leaking onto the road.

"Pleased to . . . meet . . . you . . . Len . . ."

"So what hit you, friend, a truck?" The poor guy was a real mess, the worst thing Lenny had ever seen, except for that time when he'd found a hunter who'd been attacked by a bear. That fella hadn't made it. "Was it one of those haulage trucks smashed into you?" he asked.

The guy smiled faintly. "The fun . . . the funny thing . . . is . . . I . . . don't re-mem-ber."

"Musta been going at a fair old lick," Lenny tutted. "Either didn't see you or just decided to leave you for dead."

"I guess," said the injured guy, his eyes closing slowly.

"Hang in there," said Lenny, more to himself than to the half-dead fellow lying there on the ground. He'd do what he could, but this poor soul's ticket was punched, Lenny Rivers was sure of that.

"So what do they call you?" Lenny asked.

One thing Lenny Rivers knew for a certainty was, he'd want to hear his name spoken aloud one final time if he were about to float heavenward. But the wounded man was already slipping away, his focus gone. "Hey there, son, don't leave me, tell me what you go by." Lenny gently tapped the injured man's bloodstained cheek. "Stick with me, pal. You must have a name, right?"

The guy's eyelids flickered and opened one last time. He was staring beyond Lenny as if his eyes saw some other figure standing behind him. "Loveday," he said. "It was Morgan . . . Loveday."

CHAPTER 7
One Bad Apple or Two?

THE SOAP RANG IN THE BATHROOM the next morning, and Ruby spat out her toothpaste and picked up.

"So what were you going to tell me?" asked Clancy. Ruby could hear his little sister Olive in the background, talking to someone.

"Who's there with you?" asked Ruby.

"Olive," said Clancy.

"But who's she talking to?" asked Ruby.

"Buttercup," said Clancy.

Silence.

"Her doll," said Clancy.

Ruby listened for a moment. "Jeepers," she said.

"Exactly," said Clancy. "So what were you going to tell me?"

"Well, I'm not going to say it over the phone, am I, buster?"

"Of course you're not, bozo. I was wondering if you'd like the pleasure of my company. Plus if I have to listen to more of this dolly talk I'm gonna go crazy."

"Anyone would," said Ruby. "Is she like this most days?"

"Try every day," said Clancy.

"I'll meet you in a half hour, usual place."

The usual place was the tree on Amster. They met there when they wanted to be completely alone and out of sight. It was December, and the tree's branches were bare and so the oak would not provide any cover, but at least sitting high in its boughs meant they were a long way from eavesdroppers and interrupters. It was as they sat up in the oak that Ruby filled her friend in on everything she had omitted to tell him before.

"LB killed Bradley Baker?" said Clancy.

"That's what the Count told me," said Ruby.

"Are you actually serious?" asked Clancy.

"Serious as the look on your face," confirmed Ruby.

"But . . . I mean, really? I mean . . . kill him? How?" asked Clancy.

"What you have to ask yourself is why," said Ruby.

"Why?" said Clancy. "Why is *why* the question I have to ask myself? Why not—*Can you get me outta Twinford as quickly as possible?* Followed by, *Could you call the sheriff's office right away?* Because those are the questions I would be asking if I just found out that the boss of the secret agency I worked for had murdered her best friend, and not *just* some average Joe either, not that that would make it all right or anything, but we *are* talking about Bradley Baker, legendary agent of Spectrum 8. So if LB did that, then yes, *Can you get me to a safe house?* and *Could you call the sheriff?* would be my first two questions."

"Well, thank goodness you're *not* me, Clance, because both of those questions are dead ends. For one: Who's actually going to believe any of this? And for two: If LB is really his killer, then how far am I gonna get before I end up going the same way as Baker? I mean think about it, Clance; she runs a team of highly trained agents, *secret* agents who are capable of"—she drew her finger across her throat before adding—*"secretly."*

Clancy opened his mouth to speak but could not think of anything cheerful to say.

"So what you gotta look at," said Ruby, "is the whole big picture. My boss *might* well be a traitorous killer: she has the means, the power, possibly a motive, but before we absolutely totally conclude she *is* a traitorous killer, we need to examine the evidence. For example, what do we know about Bradley Baker?"

Clancy shrugged. "He was the youngest spy Spectrum ever recruited, *super* respected and well liked, *and* he was the most talented code breaker and agent they ever had." He stole a sideways look at Ruby. "No offense, Rube."

"Don't sweat it, bozo; I hear it all the time."

"And," continued Clancy, "he was killed in a plane crash."

"Which it seems was no accident," said Ruby. "Nor was it at the hand of the enemy, but rather by the hand of his most loyal ally."

"And let's not forget fiancée," added Clancy.

"So now what we got to look at is who exactly is feeding us

this information," said Ruby. "Who is the deliverer of this sad and bad news?"

"The Count," said Clancy. "At least, it was *his* apple."

"Yeah," said Ruby, "it was his apple, and he *wanted* me to find the note."

"So," said Clancy, "so you're asking, do you think we should consider him a reliable source? Maybe he just *wants* us to believe LB is a murderer. He could be just making the whole thing up?"

"Yeah, and the truth is, I can't say I know him well enough to know," said Ruby.

"You do know him well enough," said Clancy. "You know him well enough to know that you can never know him."

"What?"

"I'm saying he likes to move the goalposts, he sorta enjoys playing with people, creeping them out, just for fun, and also, you know . . . killing them." Clancy shivered.

Ruby stared into the distance. "Yeah, he *does* like to mess with people's heads; once he's planted an idea, you just can't shake it. He knows how these thoughts grow, how they take off in different directions — you don't exactly know what they mean or even what you're scared *of*, you just keep running with it."

"So what has he got you thinking?" asked Clancy.

Ruby paused before speaking. "What he's got me thinking is, what if Bradley was not all that he seemed; what if *he* was the so-called bad apple?"

"You suggesting he wasn't the super talent everyone thought he was?" asked Clancy.

"No, I think we can accept that Baker *was* the super talent that everyone drones on about, but if he was such a talented agent, then he may also have had a talent for espionage."

"Huh?"

"What I'm suggesting here is, was he leading a double life?"

Clancy was looking at her, his expression one of puzzlement.

Ruby spelled it out: "Do we know which side he was really on?"

"Oh," said Clancy, "that . . . that wasn't something I was even thinking about."

"So let's just say he was a double agent. LB woulda *had* to kill him for the sake of Spectrum, for the sake of this country"—she stretched her arms out wide—"the world, even."

Clancy let out a heavy sigh. "I'd feel a lot better if that's how it was."

"It could have been that LB knew what *nobody* else knew: that he was a phony, a fraud, an imposter."

"Like some kind of mole, you mean?"

"Yeah." Ruby nodded.

"Boy, it sure makes you think," said Clancy. "Imagine finding out that your best friend, most loyal ally, is a total fake, not to mention murderer." He looked at Ruby. "Though I have to say, Rube, if you turn out to be an evil genius, I can't see myself killing you. I kinda like your company."

"I appreciate that, Clance, I really do."

"Still, I think LB had guts to do what she did," said Clancy. "If Baker was a bad egg, she did the right thing."

"Yeah," said Ruby, contemplating this for a moment, "but what if he wasn't? What if it was the other way around?"

"Jeepers, I was just beginning to relax," said Clancy.

"Yeah, well, don't, because what if it was Bradley Baker who was the good news in this story and LB eliminated him so she could get on with her plot to take over the world or steal the moon or whatever?"

"The moon?" said Clancy. "Can you even do that?" He was pulling himself up, as if he needed to be ready for what might be coming.

"Geez, Clance, it was just an example. How should I know what she's got planned?" Ruby paused, sorting through the thoughts that were flickering in her brain: the cyan, the indigo, the ruby eyes of the Buddha, the 8 key, the yellow snake. "If I could figure that out, and how it all links together, the thefts and the murders, the mole within Spectrum, well, then I might know what to do."

"Yeah, right," said Clancy, "if you knew all that, then you could just amble downtown and knock on Sheriff Bridges's door and hand him the evidence."

Ruby sighed. "Like that's gonna happen."

"But meanwhile, you figure one of them has to be a bad seed?" said Clancy. "Either it's Baker or it's LB?"

"Or it's neither?" offered Ruby. "Unless of course"—she looked at him out of the corner of her eye—"they were both bad apples."

Clancy made a face like he wished she wouldn't say these kinds of things.

"Look, could you give me a break here, Rube? I can only cope with one double agent at a time."

She thumped him lightly on the arm. "Take it easy," she said. "Yeah, I think it's probably *either* Baker *or* LB, and let's hope it's Baker, right?"

Clancy nodded. "Because if it's Baker, then LB is on the level."

"Only thing is," said Ruby, "if LB isn't the bad apple, then who *is*? Who's the one pulling the strings?"

Clancy gave her the pained look again. "I don't want to think about that right now."

"Yeah, well, time's running out. Whoever is behind this whole series of events has a master plan, and I get the feeling we're heading toward the endgame."

"So what's your next move?" asked Clancy.

"I guess I need to find out more about Bradley Baker. I mean, I know precisely zero about him other than *what a great guy, what a smart agent, how we all wish he'd come back*. But if I could dig down to what made him tick, what thoughts were whirling round that super-brain of his, and of course exactly how and why he died, then I might know more about LB."

"So ask around," said Clancy.

"What, are you kidding? People don't talk about Bradley Baker. They sorta mention him, how brilliant he was, but they don't actually really *say* anything." Ruby shook her head. "No, if I started in asking a lot of questions, then I would have to explain why I wanted to know, and then I would have to get into the whole bit about LB maybe being a murderer, and I get the feeling that's not gonna go down too well."

"You mean it might get you dead. *If* she's a cold-blooded murderer, is that what you're saying?" said Clancy.

"That *is* the worst-case scenario," said Ruby, "and me dead is something I'm trying to avoid."

"You could tell Blacker," suggested Clancy. "You trust him, right?"

"Sure, but this is not the same, this is *me* telling *him* not to trust his boss, and if you were asking, do I trust him not to go right ahead and speak to LB about my concerns? That would have to be a *no*. Blacker is loyal to Spectrum, loyal to the core, and I would have a pretty hard time convincing him that his boss is a bad egg or apple or whatever. People don't like to believe they have been putting their trust in, and generally *assisting,* a dangerous psychopath."

"But her name was *inside* a bad apple," Clancy reminded her. "Blacker can't ignore that."

"And who put it there?" said Ruby. "The biggest bad apple of them all. Everyone knows the Count would be happy to see Spectrum destroyed."

"You have a point," said Clancy.

"I know," said Ruby.

"So you need to find someone who will talk."

"Who exactly?"

"What about Froghorn?"

"What about him?" said Ruby.

"Do you trust *Froghorn*?"

"I trust him not to push me off a cliff or under a bus, but that's about it."

"But do you trust him to tell the truth?" asked Clancy.

"Froghorn? Oh, he just loves to tell it like it is," said Ruby. "He's like a regular truth trumpet."

"So ask *him*," said Clancy. "I bet you he'll talk. He's dying to rub your nose in the whole Bradley Baker legend; I bet you *anything* he'll tell you whatever you wanna know, just to make you feel small."

"You know what, Clance? That's not such a terrible idea."

He smiled. "Really?"

She gave him another friendly punch to the arm. "Nice going, Crew." She looked at her watch and then began to climb down the oak.

"Where are you going?" he asked.

"Little Mountain Side," she said.

"*Where?*"

"It's in the Sequoia Mountains; wanna come?"

"Why would I wanna go to the Sequoia Mountains?"

"Are you kidding? The Sequoia Mountains are a UFO hotspot," said Ruby. "I'm hoping to spot one on my way through."

"You're looking for unidentified flying objects?"

"Mushrooms," called Ruby.

"Same to you," shouted Clancy.

**Somehow
Lenny Rivers got the dying guy
to the hospital in Ridgepoint before
the dying guy actually died. . . .**

The old man was relieved, not because he thought the fellow had a hope in Christmas of seeing Christmas, but because he didn't want to see it happen. It was too sad, the idea that this Morgan Loveday could just pass away without a friend to hold his hand, die all alone on a deserted road or in the back of some stranger's truck. Well, it was too tragic to contemplate.

It hadn't been straightforward getting to the hospital. There had been some kind of incident on Pine Forest Pass, a cordoned-off road that Lenny had ignored — he'd had no choice.

Drive on, he thought, *and have a chance of delivering a man with a pulse.*

Turn back and he might as well have driven straight to the undertakers.

When Lenny Rivers handed him over to the ER team, Morgan Loveday was still breathing, but who knew for how long? Lenny gave his number to the triage nurse.

"Would you mind calling me?" he asked. "When he . . . you know, when . . . if . . . well, call me; his folks might want to speak to the guy that found him."

"Of course," said the nurse. "I promise I'll call you when the time comes."

CHAPTER 8
Little Green Men

DESPITE HIS RESISTANCE, Clancy Crew did join Ruby on her mission to find mushrooms. It took her no more than ten minutes of persuading before he reluctantly agreed. It took a lot longer than that to reach Little Mountain Side, but the journey was not the tedious experience Clancy had expected. As the bus wound up high into the Sequoia Mountains, the scenery became more and more spectacular, the great red trees rising from the rock. As the woodland thinned, they were confronted by staggering views to the south and west, and far away in the distance one could just about see the ocean.

When at last the bus pulled up in Little Mountain Side, there was no missing the perfect prettiness of the town either, perched high up there on the south side of the mountain, the sun slanting through the trees. As they stepped off the bus, Ruby and Clancy breathed in the mountain air; it was pretty good.

"Sure doesn't smell like Twinford," said Clancy.

"You can almost taste the trees," said Ruby.

By the side of the road was a sign that read:

FRIENDLIEST TOWN IN THE NORTHWESTERN MOUNTAINS AND "FREE OF SERIOUS CRIME" SINCE 1951

"That's reassuring," said Ruby.

It didn't take long to find Daily Supplies.

The man behind the counter looked somehow familiar, but Ruby couldn't place him. She decided that he probably just had one of those faces, even-featured, *nice-looking,* a friendly kind of appearance (at least what she could see of it under the beard). He was older than her dad and perhaps a tad taller.

He waved at them as they walked in, but continued chatting with a customer at the counter and ringing up groceries.

Ruby and Clancy checked out the shelves while they waited. They were stocked with a lot of interesting and unusual things. However, they had no luck finding the maitake mushrooms.

The customer finally paid and exited the shop, and Clancy and Ruby walked up to the counter.

She looked at the storekeeper and then figured it out.

"Oh, I got it."

"Got what?" asked the storekeeper.

"Where I saw you before," said Ruby.

"You've seen me before?"

"Yeah, in the bookstore."

"In Mountain Books?" he asked, pointing in the direction of the bookstore across the street.

"Ray Penny's bookstore," said Ruby, "in Twinford — you were reading a book on rare fungi. I mean, you must have read the entire book while you were there."

"It was a cold day and I was waiting for my truck to be fixed," he said.

"You often in Twinford?" asked Ruby.

"Rarely."

"You ever been to Penny's before?"

"Never," said the guy. "At least, not that I recall." He paused. "You ask a lot of questions," he said. He looked at Clancy. "She always this curious, your friend here?"

"Curious is a nice word for what she is," said Clancy.

The guy smiled at that.

The bell above the door jangled, and a burly man strode in, a shock-haired baby on his back.

"Hey, Mo," said the man. "How's the old leg doing?"

"Limping a bit in this cold weather. You know how it is."

"You got those Brazilian beans in yet?"

The storekeeper reached behind him and took a package from one of the shelves and stood it on the countertop. "Anything else for you, Sven?"

The man took out a newspaper. "Seven down," he said. *"Mix cantaloupe citrus."*

The storekeeper frowned. "How many letters?"

"Five."

"I'll give it some thought."

"Thanks," said the guy.

"Anything besides the beans?"

The man shook his head. "Just the coffee, that'll do it."

"How are you there, Spike?" The storekeeper directed this question at the baby, and it gurgled and looked very pleased.

"See you around, Mo," said the man as he turned to leave.

"See you, Sven. See you, Spike. Don't be strangers."

When they reached the door the storekeeper shouted, "Lemon! Anagram of melon, from cantaloupe."

"Of course! Can't think how I missed it," called Sven.

The storekeeper turned to Ruby. "He's a cryptic crossword nut," he explained. "So what can I help *you* with?" he asked.

"That's your name?" asked Ruby. "Mo?"

"It's what everyone calls me." He looked at her. "So what do they call *you*?"

"Ruby," said Ruby.

The storekeeper shrugged. "I had you down for something more edgy," he said.

"What, like Spike?" suggested Ruby.

He shrugged again. "You could carry a name like Spike," he said.

"I'll take that as a compliment," said Ruby.

"That's how I meant it," said Mo.

"So this is my pal Clancy."

Mo nodded. "Good to meet you, Clancy — what can I do you two for?"

"Hen of the woods," said Ruby.

"You've left it a bit late in the season," said the storekeeper.

"I have?" asked Ruby. "Are you sure?"

"Pretty sure," said the guy. "It's one of the few things I know something about."

"You seem OK at crosswords," said Clancy.

He smiled. "Yeah, that's the other thing . . ." he said. "So the maitake season is from late August to late November, and I usually order in from my mushroom lady out in Minnesota."

Ruby looked disappointed enough for the guy to reach for a pen and paper.

"I'll make a note and see what I can do; you might get lucky. It's been a pretty weird season, weather-wise," he said, turning to the calendar hanging on the wall. "She won't be around until next week; can you hang on a day or two?"

"I guess," said Ruby, "but it's a long way to come for a bunch of fungi. I don't s'pose you're going to be visiting Twinford this week?"

"Not if I can help it," said Mo. "It's noisy and full of people."

"That's what I like about it."

"Each to their own," said Mo. "A nice quiet life is what suits me."

Clancy was beginning to think it might *also* suit *him*. He liked it up here with the trees and the condors and the lack of serious crime since 1951.

Ruby sighed. "I'll do my best to make it back, but could you maybe call me when you're certain you got them?"

"Sure," said Mo. "Give me your digits."

Ruby scribbled down her number, and the guy pinned it up on the bulletin board behind him.

"Is there anything to see in this town?" asked Clancy.

"More than you'd think," said Mo.

"My friend here is keen on UFOs and little green men from Mars," said Ruby. "Anything like that around?"

"Call in at the Little Green Diner. They do a mean Space Burger. Ask for a side of Mars fries and tell Silas that Mo sent you and he'll give you a deal."

As they were going out the door they heard the phone ring; Mo picked up. "How many letters?" he said.

Ruby could see that for Clancy, stepping into the Little Green Diner was pretty special. It had been wallpapered in space pictures: *Apollo 13*, the spacecraft that made the ill-fated third manned trip to the surface of moon, took up most of one wall and a possible UFO sighting filled another.

Ruby and Clancy walked up to the counter.

"Mo said to say he sent us," said Ruby.

"Oh, he did, did he?" said Silas. "So I guess you'll be getting a deal."

"Have you ever seen a UFO, Rube?" asked Clancy, not

waiting for an answer. "I think I saw one once, took a photograph too, but my sister Lulu says it was actually a Frisbee and to be honest there's no telling."

"I think you'd know," said a small thin guy sitting at the counter. "When I saw my first UFO, I was in no doubt about what I'd just been witness to."

"Well, hang on a tiny minute, Walter," said the enormous man who sat on the stool next to him. "The thing is, no one exactly knows what they are looking for, so it's easy to get it wrong."

"I'm not disagreeing with you there, Duke, but when you've seen one, you've seen one, and I've seen two."

"It's true," said Duke. "He's seen a couple."

Clancy was all ears. "So what did it look like?" he asked.

"How you'd expect," said Walter. "A craft unusual in appearance, moving pretty fast across the night sky, bright lights, no markings."

"How do you know it had no markings if it was dark and moving at high speed?" asked Silas, who had doubtless quizzed Walter about this many times before.

"I know what I saw," said Walter, crossing his arms.

"Why do you think Little Mountain Side attracted so many UFOs?" asked Ruby.

"Because of the space base," said Walter.

"Space base?" asked Clancy. "There was an actual space base here?"

"No," said Silas.

"Uh-huh," said Walter, ignoring him. "It was some kinda space operation? In the Sequoia Mountains."

"It was an energy plant," said Silas.

"Oh, yeah, so how do you explain all the comings and goings, all the activity?" said Walter.

"There were more than a thousand people working there; what do you expect?" said Silas.

"I'm not talking about any power plant," said Walter. "I'm talking about something covert here, you know"—he leaned in close—"to welcome the aliens."

"Really?" said Clancy.

"That's what they say," said Duke.

"Who says?" asked Ruby.

"No one," said Silas. "This is Walt talking garbage, as usual."

"He's not a believer," said Duke, pointing his thumb at Silas, "that's his trouble."

"Likes to cash in on it, though," said Walter, holding up a flying-saucer napkin.

It was actually all good-natured banter and clearly had been said a thousand times before.

"So if there was a space base somewhere here on this mountainside, then why doesn't anyone talk about it?" asked Clancy.

"It was all very hush-hush, if you know what I'm saying," said Duke. "Not for civilians to know about."

Silas shook his head. "You guys and your conspiracy

theories. It's a bunch of hogwash. Sven's father worked at the plant for a whole number of years and he never once mentioned little green men from Mars."

"Well, he wouldn't, would he," said Walter.

Duke nodded. "That's right, Walt. Sven's dad would have signed some official secrecy document — everyone who worked there would have."

Walter nodded gravely and Silas chuckled to himself.

"I promise you this: if a Martian ever walks into this diner, I'll shake him by the tentacle and give him a side order of fries on the house."

CHAPTER 9
Lucite

IT WAS DISAPPOINTING TO RETURN to Cedarwood Drive empty-handed, but Ruby had enjoyed a more than interesting day, and Clancy, with all this new information about spacecraft and aliens, could not be shut up. They caught the bus just as it was about to pull out of the stop and clambered on, taking seats toward the back, away from the other passengers. Not that it was crowded: there were only seven other people taking the Mountain bus back to Maple Falls.

Ruby had a small spiral-bound notepad and she was staring hard at a list of things set neatly out down the page. On one side:

WHAT I KNOW

And on the other:

WHAT I DON'T KNOW

Some of the things had been crossed out and moved from the *don't know* column to the *know* column.

Why Buzz was called Buzz, for example.

"Why *is* Buzz called Buzz?" asked Clancy.

"It's not as exciting as you think," said Ruby.

"What, it's some kinda nickname?" asked Clancy.

"Less exciting," said Ruby.

"It's her actual last name?" said Clancy

"Less interesting than that," said Ruby.

"I give up," said Clancy.

"It will disappoint you to know," said Ruby.

"Try me," said Clancy.

"They're her initials, Brenda Ulla Zane."

"Oh, that's kinda disappointing," said Clancy.

"I told you," said Ruby.

"It's just totally obvious when you think about it."

"I know," said Ruby.

"Mind you, there's only one Z," said Clancy.

"Yeah, but you would still call her Buzz, one Z or two."

"I guess." He looked back at her list.

One object, `The 8 key`, had been crossed out altogether and replaced with:

`The Lucite key tag`

"The Lucite key tag," read Clancy. "*What* key tag?"

"The key tag that was attached to the 8 key," explained Ruby.

"Why are you suddenly interested in that?" asked Clancy.

"I thought it was all about the Spectrum *security key*?"

"I figured it had to be the key tag that was of interest. I mean, the locks were all changed as soon as the key went missing. Unless the whole point of the theft was about rattling Spectrum by proving security was so weak that anyone could break their way in, then stealing the key served no purpose whatsoever."

"So what's the purpose of stealing a Lucite key tag?" asked Clancy. He frowned before adding, "By the way, what *is* Lucite, exactly?"

"You know, like Plexiglas — Lucite is just a trade name. It's acrylic. Or, if you want to get technical, polymethyl methacrylate, a transparent thermoplastic, shatter-resistant, lightweight alternative to glass."

CLANCY: *So it was light?*

RUBY: *Well, not light light, but not as heavy as glass.*

CLANCY: *Was anything written on it? A number? An image?*

RUBY: *Nothing I could see.*

CLANCY: *So what makes it interesting?*

RUBY: *Nothing.*

CLANCY: *Nothing?*

RUBY: *Nothing except for who it belonged to.*

CLANCY: *So who did it belong to?*

RUBY: *Bradley Baker.*

CLANCY: *Really? You know this? Like, for sure?*

RUBY: *Not actually, and not exactly for sure. I guess I'm guessing in a way, but it just stands to reason, since LB told me it was a memento, that someone gave it to her when she was a child, and I sorta figured the person closest to her was Baker.*

CLANCY: *Why not her dad, or her mom or maybe her grandpa? I mean, it could even have been her junior-karate master; he was important to her, no? Or her trombone teacher, if she ever learned trombone, that is.*

RUBY: *I don't imagine she did.*

CLANCY: *Whatever. My point is, it doesn't automatically follow that it had to be Bradley Baker who gave her the key tag. It could have been a person of influence.*

RUBY: *OK, you're right, it doesn't, but you see, well, I kinda have this strange feeling that it was.*

She looked at him.

RUBY: *Do you think I'm losing it?*

CLANCY: *Nah, you're listening to your gut feeling and . . .*

Pause.

CLANCY: *I actually think you're right.*

Another pause.

CLANCY: *Well, almost right.*

RUBY: *Almost?*

CLANCY: *You're saying that the boss of Spectrum 8 was given this key tag by her best friend when he was a kid?*

RUBY: *Yes, LB said it was sentimental.*

She stopped talking. And then her eyes widened like she was seeing something.

It was unusual for Ruby Redfort to feel like she was the last one in the room to see the gorilla. It was more unusual still for her to feel like a complete and utter chump, but this was that moment.

RUBY: *What a bozo! LB wouldn't use some old key tag given to her years ago to attach something as valuable as the 8 key, a coder key. Spectrum is a professional outfit, LB's a professional agent, she hasn't got time for this stuff.*

She looked at Clancy.

RUBY: *That's what you were going to say, right?*

CLANCY: *I wouldn't have called you a bozo, but yeah.*

RUBY: *How did I swallow that garbage?*

CLANCY: *Quit beating yourself up. Everyone screws up once in a while — if we're talking about me, that would be most days.*

RUBY: *Yeah, well, you saw through LB's lie right away; why didn't I?*

CLANCY: *Because why would you? You had no reason to doubt her two months ago. Plus, when LB told you this story you had just survived being dropped from a high building. Your mind was on other things, i.e., wow, I'm not dead.*

RUBY: *Life and death — being thrown from high buildings — I'm supposed to be able to deal with things like that.*

CLANCY: *Yeah, I'm sure it's all part of the job, but don't you see, at that moment, right at that particular instance, this whole key tag tale was just a detail. LB mentions it in passing, and why wouldn't you believe her? Like I said, back then you trusted her completely. If she told you the same story today, you'd probably question it.*

He was right about that.

"So how do you think she *did* end up with the key tag?"

"Beats me," said Ruby.

Silence.

CLANCY: *Just one thing I don't get: if LB is the overarching villain and she is the one commissioning the Count to acquire all these truth serums and cyan scents and stuff,*

then explain why she would go to all the trouble of stealing
her own key tag.

RUBY: *That's easy. She wants to throw Spectrum off the*
scent. You see, everyone gets paranoid about moles and
double agents. They're all busy wondering who it could be,
but no one's gonna point the finger at her.

CLANCY: *Seems kinda far-fetched.*

RUBY: *Everything's far-fetched.*

CLANCY: *OK, but what if LB isn't the bad guy here, then*
what?

RUBY: *Then I guess I'm right: there is more to that piece of*
Lucite than meets the eye.

Clancy took another look at the list of unknowns. "So what
do you think the deal is with the Jade Buddha? I mean, the cyan
scent and the truth serum make sense. What criminal wouldn't
want a scent that can lure anyone anywhere? Or a drug that can
make anyone blab the truth? But what does the Buddha have to
do with any of it? What's with that?"

"I don't know," said Ruby, "but I think that Buddha holds
one pretty big secret, and personally I think the eyes have it."

"Huh?"

"It's in the *eyes* of the Buddha," said Ruby.

"Isn't that just some old legend?" said Clancy. "Look into
the eyes of the Jade Buddha at midnight and halve your age

and double your wisdom. . . . I mean, what fool believes in that nonsense apart from your dad. . . . No offense intended."

"None taken, Clance. What I'm saying is, I have no idea what the Count read when he shone that light into its ruby eyes, but I'm guessing he was able to see something—a symbol or even a code, maybe."

"So can't you get someone to look into its eyes for you?"

"It's back in Khotan," said Ruby. "Who am I going to ask?"

"Can't you call someone in China?" suggested Clancy.

"What, just call China and say, 'Please take a look at the eyes of the Jade Buddha of Khotan'?"

"Not just anyone," said Clancy. "Obviously it will have to be someone working at the Khotan museum."

"It's not as easy as that. I still have to figure out what that laser light device was, the one the Count used to read its eyes. It wasn't any regular flashlight," said Ruby. "And then I have to convince someone at the museum to go and do it."

"Get someone else to call the Chinese, like Blacker or someone?"

"I'm not authorized to investigate anything," said Ruby. "If I ask someone to put a call through to the Chinese, then I'm basically involved in an investigation, and only senior agents are permitted to access anything."

"So ask a senior agent?"

"What, like LB?" said Ruby. "How many ways have I gotta say it, Clance? I don't want LB to know that I might be onto something if it turns out that *she* is the *something I'm onto.*"

"Right," said Clancy unsteadily, "I guess not."

"I need to know what happened between LB and Baker. If she killed him, then *why* did she kill him?"

"If only you could trust LB, then you could ask her."

Ruby sighed. "If I could trust LB, then I would feel better about a whole lot of things. I might even be able to sleep at night."

"So you're going to have to talk to Hitch. You trust him, don't you?"

"A hundred percent," said Ruby, "but I'm not so sure he'd give me the time of day if I asked, *So Hitch, you think LB might be a murderer?* And to be truthful, I'm not sure I even *want* to go asking that particular question, at least not until I have a whole lot more information up my sleeve and possibly a hideout or some sort of weapon."

"Are you scared?" asked Clancy.

Ruby looked into the darkness. "You bet I'm scared. If I wasn't, I'd have to be crazy."

"So what are you gonna do when you next meet her face-to-face?"

"Hold my nerve, I guess. The thing is not to let on; act normal."

This was actually a Ruby rule. **RULE 51: WHEN YOU DON'T TRUST THE OTHER PLAYERS, ALWAYS PLAY YOUR CARDS CLOSE TO YOUR CHEST.**

CHAPTER 10
The Stars Above

THE WANDERER RETURNS," said Mrs. Digby as Ruby walked in through the kitchen door. "Where have you been?"

"Trying to solve your hen of the woods problem."

"Well, knock me down with a feather," said Mrs. Digby, who looked genuinely astonished. "Any luck with that?"

"I got a lead on them," said Ruby.

"From whom?"

"You gotta understand, I gotta protect my source, but suffice it to say, the wheels are in motion and there's a good chance I can get the mushrooms to you by the end of the week."

"Nice work," said Mrs. Digby. "You earned yourself a cookie, cookie."

"Just one?" complained Ruby.

"Don't want to spoil your supper," said Mrs. Digby.

Ruby looked at the table, set for two.

"Hitch is coming?" Ruby asked.

"He better be; I've made enough stew to feed an army." She reached for a ladle but was interrupted by the ring of the telephone. "Well, howdy, stranger. . . . *What?* . . . I can't say I approve. . . . It's not good for you to skip meals; did your mother never tell you that? You'll be jumping into an early grave. . . . I'll leave it in the warmer, if the dog doesn't get to it first." She put down the receiver.

"He's not coming?" asked Ruby.

"He said he had to get off somewhere in a hurry, something about a friend of his with a broken-down car." The housekeeper sniffed disapprovingly. "He'll not be long for this world if he doesn't take the time to eat."

"I didn't know he had any friends," said Ruby.

"*Too many* friends, if you ask me," said Mrs. Digby. "He certainly didn't seem one jot put out by my going on that cruise. He couldn't pack me off quick enough."

"Yeah, well, at least you wound up in the Caribbean," said Ruby. "He packed me off to spend a month in the back end of nowhere."

The housekeeper picked up the dog bowl and served a generous portion to Bug. "Anyone would think he wanted to get rid of us," she said.

Ruby decided to make it an early night: she needed to catch up on her sleep, and if she hit the hay early, then she might clock up a round ten hours. That would have been nice, but in the end all she managed was an uneven five. First came the phone call from Paris.

"Hey, Ruby, it's us!"

"*Bonjour,* Mom. *Bonjour,* Dad. *Quelle heure est-il,* by the way?"

"Pardon?"

"What time is it?"

"Almost lunchtime; what time is it with you?"

Ruby reached for her watch.

"Three in the a.m."

"Oh, Rube, you should really be asleep," said her mother.

"Yeah, you might want to try calling a little later, six hours maybe, either that or a whole lot earlier; there's a nine-hour time difference — that's nine hours *behind.*"

"Oh, I thought Twinford was nine hours ahead," said her father.

"Other way around, Dad."

"In that case, sleep tight!" said her mother.

"*Bon appétit,*" said Ruby.

An hour later and she was woken again, this time by the sound of a fly. Judging by the insistent racket, it was in its death throes, making a noise like it might be buzzing about on its back, legs in the air.

Still caught in sleep, Ruby attempted to bat it away, but her hand hit the edge of something solid, and her eyes blinked open to find not a noisy upside-down insect, but her Spectrum Escape Watch vibrating on the nightstand. Words in green blinked at her from the face on the dial.

A message from Hitch.

>> CITY PLANETARIUM 04:35 ROW F SEAT 6

It was four a.m., really not a good time to greet the day. But if Hitch was planning on taking her into HQ to meet with her (possibly murderous) boss, then four a.m. was as good a time as any.

Ruby reached for her glasses, struggled to her feet, fell over, cursed, hobbled to the bathroom, brushed her teeth, and peered at herself with bleary eyes.

Redfort, you have to pull it together, she told herself.

Ruby decided the only way she could wake up would be to stand under the shower. This she did, and it did the trick. She peered out the window into the still-dark morning. *Cold,* she thought, *colder than yesterday.* The temperature was really dropping.

She dug out some thermal leggings and pulled her jeans on over them, found a thermal undershirt, a T-shirt with the words **don't wake me** printed across the front, a black hoodie, and a snow parka and earmuffs. Snow was not forecast, but the air had turned icy. When she was ready, she picked up her backpack and tiptoed down the stairs and out the front door. The only people riding the subway from Green Street were night-shift workers and early birds.

She arrived at the planetarium and was surprised to find the doors open and a guy selling tickets. She had been prepared for a little breaking and entering.

She went up to the booth. "What's the deal?" asked Ruby.

"What do you mean what's the deal?" said the young man in the ticket booth.

"How come you're open? It's four thirty in the a.m."

"It's to celebrate the anniversary of last year's moon mission, you know, *Apollo 17*?" said the guy.

"I hate to burst your balloon, but you know you're early?" said Ruby. "The anniversary is December seventh."

"Yeah, we do know that, but a lot of people want to come, so we're doing a whole month of events," said the guy, pointing at the huge poster framed on the wall. "There's a whole bunch of stuff going on. You might have heard, the Observatory on Meteor Island is building a new telescope.... It's been in the news, you know: Planet Twinford — 1974's City of Space?"

"But it isn't 1974," said Ruby.

"Yeah, but it will be in, like, four weeks," said the guy. "You really haven't heard anything about this?"

Ruby was looking blank. Then, "Oh, yeah, I think maybe my parents were invited to something spacey, what was it?"

"Could it be the Galaxy Concert? Or the Astro Lectures? Or the Deep Space Gala?" suggested the guy, before adding a little sarcastically, "What planet have you been on, man?"

"Planet Geek," said Ruby. "I guess you might have a ticket for me, in the name of Redfort."

The guy shuffled through his stack of prepaid tickets and handed her an envelope.

"Enjoy!" he said.

Ruby opened the door to the auditorium and tiptoed down the steps. All the seats in the middle section were taken, but toward the edges there were plenty of empty ones. She found F and began sidling along the row.

She sat down. All the seats around her were unoccupied, and there was no sign of Hitch.

Mr. Punctuality appeared to be late.

She began to watch the show and quickly became absorbed by the commentary.

"Hey," said a voice.

RUBY: *Jeepers! I didn't hear you arrive.*
HITCH: *You seem tense, kid.*
RUBY: *Well, now that you mention it . . .*
HITCH: *By the way, have you eaten breakfast?*
RUBY: *What, are you kidding? It's not even five a.m.*

He handed her a paper bag.

"Thanks," she said. She pulled out a donut.

HITCH: *From Blacker.*
RUBY: *What's he doing up at this hour?*
HITCH: *It's all hands on deck while there's a madman at large.*

Like every other member of the audience, Hitch had his eyes trained on the ceiling, where the night sky rotated slowly above them.

Hitch pointed up at a cluster of stars. "That's Hercules, right?"

Ruby tutted. "Orion," she said.

"You sure?"

"Course I'm sure," said Ruby. "I read up on all that stuff about a billion light-years ago when I was five years old. I can draw you every constellation going — blindfolded and with my hands tied behind my back."

"That sounds like quite a party trick," said Hitch. "Who could know when that talent might come in handy."

"Yeah, right," said Ruby. "What are we doing here, anyway?"

"Oh, you know," said Hitch, "it's very soothing contemplating the stars, don't you think?"

"I guess," she said, giving him a "what's gotten into you?" look.

"So how was geek camp?" he asked.

"Geeky," replied Ruby. "So you been busy?"

"Pretty busy, at least up until your parents flew to Paris. Boy, do they have a social life!"

"So what made you think they needed a vacation?"

"What makes you think it was my idea?"

"Mrs. Digby told me it was."

"Well, I have got to admit, they were driving me a little crazy. Do you have any idea how many parties they attend?"

"I've been living with them the past thirteen years—what do you think?"

"So you understand," said Hitch.

"More than anyone," said Ruby. "I also understand Mrs. Digby mysteriously won a free cruise around the Caribbean. What I don't understand is how."

"I know, who would have guessed?"

"Not her, that's for sure," said Ruby.

"Life is full of surprises," said Hitch.

"So, what, you felt like you wanted the place to yourself?"

"We needed to make some adjustments to the house, add some security features," said Hitch.

"For my sake?"

"For all your sakes."

"You think my folks are in danger?" asked Ruby. "Mrs. Digby even?"

"I wouldn't fancy anyone's chances if they were to go after Mrs. Digby." He smiled. "But yes, I just don't want any of them to become any kind of target."

"You think that could really happen? Really, I mean?" asked Ruby. "The Count *knows* that my parents aren't involved in Spectrum; they aren't exactly agent material."

"You're missing the point, kid. If the Count has a mind to rattle you, or *worse*, destroy your world, he knows how to do it. He knows where you live, he knows what makes you tick," said Hitch.

"Meaning . . . he might make an attempt on their lives?"

"Meaning, it's possible."

"Hence the safety upgrade."

"Hence the safety upgrade."

"So what are you going to do when they get back?" asked Ruby, "I mean, you can't stop them from going out."

"I'll do my best, kid, anything I can to ensure their safety, and I'll try my darndest to keep them from knowing anything about it."

"So what *did* you tell them? About the house, I mean?"

"I didn't want to get them all in a stew about it, so I got a friend of mine who happens to be in construction to persuade them that the windows needed replacing. He told them they had a bad case of window weevils."

"How did he convince them of that?"

"Sprinkled a bit of glass dust around the place and loosened one of the window panes; they got the picture."

"Glass dust?" said Ruby.

"They were very concerned," said Hitch.

"I'll bet," said Ruby. "Since when was it possible for a weevil to eat through glass?"

"I know," said Hitch. "Alarming, isn't it?"

"And Mrs. Digby?" said Ruby.

"It was a big job, and I didn't want her picking up on what was really going on. She has eyes like a hawk. I told her I had changed the locks and upgraded the alarm system because I had mislaid a set of keys, but I kept the real reason from her."

"Well, so far you seem to have succeeded at keeping her in the dark. Mrs. Digby thinks you packed her off because you wanted to have a high old time with your friends." She looked at him out of the corner of her eye. "I told her I didn't think you had any friends."

"One day I'll introduce you to one of them," said Hitch.

"Mrs. Digby probably thinks you sent my folks to Paris because you couldn't handle their crazy social life."

Hitch winked at her. "I'm a trained agent; I can handle any party they throw at me." He paused. "Speaking of training, right now we have to get our skates on."

"Our skates?"

"It's a British expression," said Hitch. "It means to hurry up."

"Why? Where are we going?"

"A date with LB," he said.

He caught the expression on her face. "Jeepers, kid, relax a little. Anyone would think you were about to meet with the Grim Reaper."

CHAPTER 11
Act Normal

THEY PARKED HITCH'S SILVER CAR down a side street and walked perhaps another two hundred yards.

"Here?" asked Ruby.

"Here," said Hitch.

"So you meant literally," said Ruby, "*actually* get our skates on?"

They were standing in midtown, outside the ice rink on Bowery.

"No, not actually."

"But this is the way into Spectrum?"

"It is today," said Hitch.

"So why did you get me crossing town to meet you at the planetarium when you coulda just told me to make my way to the ice rink?"

"I like that place," said Hitch.

"The planetarium?"

"Yeah, like I said, I find it soothing."

Ruby rolled her eyes. "Whatever floats your boat."

They pushed through the turnstile and headed to the skate room, a labyrinth of shelves and cubbyholes each holding a pair of skates, too many to count. At the far end of this room was a door without a handle, and pinned to it was a poster of a skater mid-twirl. The skater looked happy, unaware that her tooth had been blackened by the casual swatting of a fly now squashed onto her picture-perfect smile. Hitch pressed his thumb into a barely visible identity scanner and the door clicked open. The door led to some stairs, the stairs led to Spectrum.

Once in the atrium they made their way across the vast space to the place where the Spectrum coordinator sat.

Nothing had changed, at least nothing had changed as far as the *eye* could see, but the atmosphere was very different. Breathe deeply and one could practically choke on the tension.

Buzz was where she always was, seated in the middle of the great round desk just off the main hall. Colored telephones encircled her, and Ruby guessed that a web of wires and cables must trail around her feet. And though the administrator's expression was as blank and unsmiling as always, in some strange way it was a relief to see her. That said, Ruby had no desire to hang out with the woman—she could bore you to death, if nothing else.

There was no "How are you," no "We've missed you," not the briefest snip of small talk; all Buzz said was "LB will see you now."

And Ruby felt her limbs become heavy as she walked the short walk to her boss's door.

This time it wasn't the fear of failure or of getting fired that made Ruby Redfort dread coming face-to-face with LB—this time it was a fear of getting found out. What if LB knew what she knew?

Ruby was grateful to have Hitch with her, though she felt no certainty that he would take her side if he had to choose between *her* truth and his boss's.

LB was looking steelier than she had five weeks ago. The signs of fatigue and stress were gone and had been replaced by a cold, unwavering determination. Perhaps she was eating an iron-rich diet, as Consuela would no doubt recommend, or perhaps she had been working on her martial arts. Ruby had heard it rumored that the Spectrum 8 boss was no slouch in this department, having studied karate in Japan under the great master Funakoshi. It all seemed very unlikely to Ruby, who had never seen LB outside the walls of HQ, let alone out in the field. It might simply be gossip or it might be a very tall tale, but Agent Holbrook had told her that LB was the only Spectrum 8 agent to have mastered the deadly wrist grasp otherwise known as the "assassin's handshake."

None of these assertions were exactly comforting at this moment.

LB waved at her to sit down.

"Do you want me to stay?" asked Hitch.

Stay, thought Ruby, *for Pete's sake, stay.*

"No, that won't be necessary," said LB. "Would you give me and Redfort five minutes?"

"Of course," said Hitch, stepping out.

Ruby had a strong desire to jump up and follow him. But she kept her face composed and herself in her seat.

LB waited for the door to close behind Hitch before addressing Ruby.

"So you're back, Redfort," she said.

"Yes," said Ruby.

"How was it?"

"It was OK," said Ruby.

"I hear you kept your head down and your nose clean."

"Yes," said Ruby.

LB peered at her from over her glasses.

"What, no smart remark?"

Silence.

"I'm beginning to wonder if they sent you to Swiss finishing school by mistake. I know I should be relieved, but it's making me feel uneasy."

Redfort, you're acting weird. Pull it together!

LB leaned forward. "Is there something wrong? Something you want to share?"

"I'm not giving you half my donut, if that's what you're getting at."

"That's more like it. I thought for one horrible minute I was speaking with some Ruby Redfort doppelgänger—I don't know, Lorelei von Leyden in disguise, maybe."

"It would be a tough act to pull off," said Ruby. "I like to think that when they made me they broke the mold."

"So do I," said LB sourly. She cleared her throat. "As you might have heard, Spectrum 8 has handed much of its operations activity to Spectrum 1, just while we try to figure how far this contamination has reached, and which agent if any is responsible for leaking information to the Count."

"Right," said Ruby.

If LB was bluffing, then she was a seriously cool customer. "A large number of our department have been suspended until we have clarity on this issue. Spectrum 7 agents will replace them until we have located our mole."

"So am *I* being suspended?" asked Ruby. She paused, thought about where she had been. "*Was* I suspended? What I mean to say is, was geek camp really a way of getting me out of the picture? So you could check me out?"

"Yes, but if it makes you feel better, we were as much concerned for your well-being as we were that you might in some way be leaking information."

"You thought I might be leaking information?"

"You can see our point of view here, I'm sure. On the one hand, we were suspicious that the Count would keep you alive—we had to ask ourselves why—but on the other, we were concerned that he might change his mind. He doesn't always abide by logic. And besides, his employer presumably still wants you dead, assuming *that* story is true, though when it comes to the Count one should never *assume* anything. Whatever else he is, he is predictably unpredictable."

"So now what?" asked Ruby carefully. "Am I trusted employee or traitor?"

"Quit being so dramatic, Redfort, you're neither; no one ever thought you were a traitor—a blabbermouth, perhaps, there was always a chance of that."

Ruby opened her mouth to object, but LB raised her hand.

"I never said you *were*, Redfort. I said there was a chance that you had brought this whole craziness to our door, but I concede that's unlikely. There's no evidence for it."

Well, that was a relief.

Though what followed was not.

"You, like every other agent in Spectrum 8, will be taken off duty. Eight is effectively closed to all lower-level agents. For all but vital access to our departments, permission must be given by a senior agent. My feeling was that your training should also be suspended until we have this security mess under control.

"However," LB paused and sighed, like what she was about to say was a great effort to her, "Hitch has persuaded HQ that it might be wise to keep up the survival skills. He seems to think you need all the protection you can get, and though you are no longer a functioning field agent or coding agent, after much consideration, I am persuaded he is right. We have a duty of care, and I have to concede that it is our responsibility to protect you. Thus, you will remain in Spectrum as a trainee agent. Under our careful supervision."

Ruby tried to smile. "That's good to know," she said.

A month ago, she'd have felt that LB's office was the safest place on this earth. Now she couldn't help feeling she was a fly about to be swatted.

Problem was, she had no idea who was holding the swatter.

CHAPTER 12
Ghost Files

RUBY WAS JUST TRYING to figure out where Hitch might have gone when she spotted a note on the table in the waiting area.

Meet me in Froghorn's coding room —
he will be expecting you.

She was surprised that he had arranged for them to meet there, and it was odd that Froghorn had agreed to it. With the exception of Blacker, Froghorn generally made it clear that *no one* was welcome in his coding room. Seeing him so soon after she had stepped back into Spectrum was an unpalatable idea, but then she remembered Clancy's words: *"I bet you anything he'll tell you whatever you wanna know, just to make you feel small."* It was true; Froghorn couldn't resist bragging about all the secrets he knew. *And let's face it,* she thought, *he loves nothing better than to drone on about the late great Bradley Baker.*

All I gotta do is get him talking. That's not so difficult.

Knowledge was her only weapon, the only superpower she

really had. And if she was going to find out the truth about how Spectrum's most revered agent met his end, then Froghorn was her only option.

The door to his coding room was unlocked, so she was puzzled when she discovered it empty of people. Miles Froghorn was usually very careful about security. Ruby took the opportunity to have a snoop around, and she found a lot of interesting things.

There were numerous files stacked neatly on tables, and codebooks filled with bookmarks, and notes carefully written in ink. There were several books on data transmission, particularly error-correcting codes that allowed computers to know whether there were mistakes in information they received. It was a subject that fascinated Ruby.

She flipped open a book.

Parity bits are one of the simplest systems for ensuring error-free transmission of binary data. Note, though, that as they indicate only whether the information contains an even or odd number of 1s or 0s, they are vulnerable to bits in the chain being swapped rather than lost, which is something they cannot . . .

She stopped reading when she heard footsteps coming down the corridor. She moved away from the table and listened, but whoever it was walked right on by. She continued to peruse Froghorn's papers. There was a whole handwritten list of what must have been ideas for locking devices: swipe card, iris lock, thumbprint, keypad, image lock, bolt key, 5 key, pressure key, voice key.

It looked like he had been working on some sort of multicoded security system, because there was a diagram that was basically three squares arranged like an upside-down L, with letters and numbers marked at particular intervals, and to the side of each of the blocks: E1 E2 E3. In the middle of the third square he had written FC1 FC2 FC3. Next to these were six small pieces of colored paper; each one was labeled with one of the sets of letters on the diagram, E1, E2, E3, etc., and on each paper was written a word or words, some crossed out, some replaced. E1, for example, said: **MUSCA**. E2: **SWAT**; E3: **TRANSMISSION**, FC1: **THE SPECTRUM**. FC2 said: **ROTOR MACHINE**, and then this was crossed out and had been replaced with **CHROMATIC**. FC3 was just a **?**

It looked as if he had been trying to figure out the best method of securing each part of a building or series of rooms.

There was a beep on Ruby's watch and she very nearly jumped out of her skin. A YELLOW FLY, meaning ATTENTION! A message flashed across the screen.

```
>> HUGE MISTAKE, I MEANT TO SAY MEET ME IN
FROGHORN'S OFFICE! IF YOU HAPPEN TO HAVE MADE IT
          INTO HIS CODING ROOM, THEN GET OUT!
               P.S. MEETING CANCELED.
```

Ruby did as instructed and got out of there quick, just in time as it turned out, because as she speed-walked along the corridor she ran into Froghorn coming the other way.

"Oh, you're back," he said slowly, drawing the words out as if he'd just found something unpleasant on the underside of his shoe.

"Hey, Froghorn," she said, deliberately ignoring the silent *G* so the word "Frog" sounded out very clearly. His irritation could not be missed.

"What a shame, did kiddie camp not work out for you?"

"Genius Camp, you mean?" said Ruby. "Yes, that *was* fun, but you know what they say, too much fun can get you bored, so I guess it's good to run into *you*."

"I thought it was going to be a bad day," said Froghorn. "Viridian days are always a total drag."

"What are you bleating on about—viridian days? Jeepers,

Froghorn, maybe you need to leave the building for an hour or two."

"I would if there was anyone who could possibly handle my job, but since we lost Lopez we've had a tough job recruiting anyone with half a brain."

"I'm surprised you didn't bring up Bradley Baker again; you guys seem to think the sun shone out of him."

"The sun *did* shine out of him," said Froghorn. "That's exactly it — he was a sun ray. And even though he's dead and gone to gray, he never was and never will be some pale imitation of an agent, some little girl living a little pastel-pink life."

"Boy, Froghorn, that's a very colorful picture you paint. So if you're saying Baker was sunshine yellow and I'm insipid pink — which, by the way, I take great exception to — then what are *you*? Potato-head beige?"

"*I'm* someone authorized to be here. What are you? Some little girl who needs to go back to school?" He checked his watch theatrically.

"No one said that about Bradley Baker, and wasn't he just some little kid when *he* started out?" said Ruby. Her comment had the desired effect.

"Bradley Baker was *never just some little kid*. He was extraordinary, a talent the like of which we will never see again."

"What is it with you guys and Bradley Baker? I've yet to hear one actual thing that makes this bozo so different from anyone else."

Froghorn stepped back like he'd been slapped. "What?" he said.

RUBY: *You people talk about him like he's some kinda super-agent, but he took orders same as you, same as me, same as every agent in this building.*

FROGHORN: *Baker took orders because it was his job to take orders. It didn't mean that he wasn't capable of making his own decisions.*

RUBY: *So you're saying he did make his own decisions?*

FROGHORN: *Of course he did. He was highly qualified, lived by his own rules.*

RUBY: *So he was a maverick, a renegade . . . took authority into his own hands, that sorta thing?*

FROGHORN: *No! That's not what I'm saying, not at all! He never did anything to undermine the agency.*

RUBY: *I don't get it; now you're telling me he was a zip-it-and-toe-the-line type of a guy? Make your mind up, Froghorn; either he had guts and initiative or he was just another listen-up-and-do-as-you're-told team player.*

FROGHORN: *The sheer magnitude of what you don't know about Agent Baker's guts and heroism would fill this atrium. Baker was an agent in a million.*

RUBY (YAWNING): *Yeah, right, so everyone keeps telling me, but it all sounds like a lot of hot air if you want my opinion.*

FROGHORN: No one *wants your opinion.*

RUBY: *Yeah, and why is that? I'm guessing because no one is tough enough to hear the truth.*

FROGHORN: *And what is that "truth"?*

RUBY: *Simply that there are* other *agents just as talented as him.*

Froghorn narrowed his eyes. "Are you actually suggesting that you are even close to being in the same league as Agent Baker?"

Ruby made a face to suggest maybe she was. Froghorn's reaction was as she'd hoped — very gabby. "Come with me," he said.

"Where are we going?" They were heading in the opposite direction now, and Ruby had a job to keep pace with him. When he reached his office, he opened the door and waved her in with an irritated gesture.

Her visits to this room were rare and usually very brief, so it wasn't perhaps so surprising that she had never before noticed how everything was color coded, and not just in a Spectrum way, but in a Froghorn way. His calendar, for instance: Mondays green, viridian green, Tuesdays yellow. December dark blue.

Froghorn looked like he was wearing a brand-new suit. It was ever so slightly shiny, and he had a new shiny steel pen to match; it was attached to a silver cord that hung around his neck. *Who does that?* she thought. *Who actually wears a pen?*

OK, Mrs. Drisco does, but she's Mrs. Drisco, what else would you expect? But this guy should know better. Boy, is he ever a potato head.

FROGHORN: *You think that cracking a five-way-thought code that led us to prevent the leaking of secret government dossiers isn't of value?*

RUBY: *Of course it's of value. I'm just saying, is it remarkable? I mean, he was a code cracker, right, so wouldn't that be all in a day's work to someone of his agent rank?*

FROGHORN: *So how about confronting the Count when he was a junior agent, getting up close and personal with this monster and living to tell the tale? He was the first Spectrum agent to walk away with his life.*

RUBY (STUDYING HER NAILS): *What, you mean like I did? More than once, actually.*

FROGHORN: *You got lucky, little girl, hardly heroic. Baker was captured by the Count and rescued by the Spectrum special agent squad.*

RUBY: *I rescued* myself. *Surely that counts for something.*

FROGHORN: *State-of-the-art Spectrum gadgets are what allowed you to escape.*

RUBY: *Isn't that how Baker got himself out of trouble a whole bunch of times? I'm sure he would have been toast without the Escape Watch.*

FROGHORN: *He was issued with them; you took them without permission.*

RUBY: *So that's the difference between being a hero and not being a hero — a signature on a slip of paper?*
FROGHORN: *If you want to be a Spectrum agent, then you have to behave like one.*

Ruby had quite a few things she wouldn't have minded saying in reply to this patronizing remark, but she was aware that it might not serve her well to get Froghorn so mad that he slammed the door in her face.

RUBY: *So name an occasion where Baker actually went above and beyond his job description.*
FROGHORN: *You think that leaping from an aircraft without a Spectrum aero-pack in order to save a fellow agent from certain death doesn't make him a hero?*
RUBY: *Can I ask, was the plane moving at the time?*
FROGHORN: *Try fourteen thousand feet. And it wasn't a regular plane.*

Ruby shrugged. "I don't know, Froghorn; I mean, is jumping without a parachute really such a big deal?"

FROGHORN: *You should try it sometime.*
RUBY: *Maybe I will.*
FROGHORN: *I'd be thrilled to arrange it.*
RUBY: *If there was* actually *any evidence that Baker had*

actually *done it, then I would be only too happy to give it a try.*

FROGHORN: *You should read the files; what's contained in them would make your head spin.*

RUBY: *Oh, so there are files?*

FROGHORN: *Of course there are files!*

RUBY: *OK, so I'll read them.*

FROGHORN: *You don't have authority to read files, least of all the Ghost Files.*

RUBY: *Ghost Files?*

Silence.

RUBY: *Oh, come on, Froghorn, you're making this up. Ghost Files? I mean, Spectrum's not gonna use a dumb name like that.*

FROGHORN: *You know so little of Spectrum. You arrive here thinking you're some kind of wonder-child, but you're not even a shadow of Agent Baker.*

RUBY: *Show me the files and I'll devote some minutes to reading them.*

FROGHORN: *It would take you more than a few hours to read a list of his achievements.*

RUBY: *So point me in the right direction and I'll get started.*

FROGHORN: *Why would I ever tell you where the Prism Vault is?*

RUBY: *Why would you, when you don't know?*
FROGHORN: *Of course I know. I've just this week completed the task of updating the code lock system.*

So that's what he was up to.
But what she said was "So where is it?"

FROGHORN: *Like I'd ever tell you.*
RUBY: *You should. It might help me understand this little love-in Spectrum has with old Bradley.*
FROGHORN: *If you ever see the inside of that place, then I'll eat my hat.*
RUBY: *Really? I'll work on it, then. I've always wanted to see someone eat their hat.*
FROGHORN: *I'm sure one of your kindergarten friends would oblige — little kids are always eating things they shouldn't.*
RUBY: *You not concerned that someone might crack your new vault codes?*

"No, little girl."
"No, and why's that?"
"Because first you'd have to understand what code you are dealing with, and that's something you aren't ever going to know.

"Even if you made it there," continued Froghorn. "Even if you figured out the location, you would still require *permission* to get inside, and we both know that's never going to happen, *or* you would need to get hold of a Superskin."

"What's a Superskin?" asked Ruby.

"Exactly," said Froghorn. "Then you would need to hold your breath for at least three minutes, and we both know you have no talent for that, am I right?"

Boy, is this guy's color potato-head beige.

"Even if you punched in the correct door code and got inside the vault, even if you did all that, just how many layers of files could you reach? One? Two?"

"Um," said Ruby, "is there a three?"

"Layer three you might as well dream about because there's not a chance you'd make it into that." As he said "three" he gripped the steel pen and turned it around and around in his hand.

"Careful with that," said Ruby. "You don't want to strangle yourself with that little necklace of yours."

He suddenly looked awkward, self-conscious even, and he barked at her, saying, "All file layers are code protected. I set them myself. . . . Think about it, little girl."

"Oh, believe me, I am," said Ruby. "So you say breath-holding's involved; is this vault under water or something?"

Froghorn's mouth snapped shut. He had said too much. He began fiddling with his stupid neck pen, nervously wrapping his tie around and around it as he tried to backtrack. "Dream on, you'll never lay eyes on the Ghost Files, let alone read them." He was confident about that, Ruby could see it: the look on his face said *The Prism Vault is nowhere you'll ever go.*

"You sound very certain," said Ruby.

"I am," said Froghorn. "I spent a lot of time coding those files and I did an excellent job."

"I'm sure you did your best, Froghorn, but remember what they say: pride comes before a fall, or wait a minute, is it once a potato head always a potato head? I can never remember."

CHAPTER 13
Sprayed and Delivered

AS RUBY WAS EXITING FROGHORN'S OFFICE, an announcement sounded over the speaker:

RUBY REDFORT, REPORT TO RECEPTION.

When she reached Buzz's desk, she was told in a bored tone to report to the gadget room.

When she got there, she found Hal standing next to a bicycle.

"So here you go," said Hal, stepping aside. "I've been working on it for a while."

"For me?" asked Ruby.

"No one else in Spectrum rides a bike," said Hal.

Ruby smiled. "Well, thanks."

"It's got a few features you won't be used to," said Hal. "The tires are of course unpuncturable, and the frame super-reinforced, but it's the bike's ability to grip the road surface that makes it special."

"Meaning?"

"It's very hard to fall off. As with a motorcycle, you can lean pretty low to the ground and so long as the wheels keep turning, the tires grip the road and you stay on the bike."

"Well, that sounds cool," said Ruby.

"It is," said Hal. "Spectrum gadgets are 99.999 percent reliable, and this bike is no exception."

"So what about speed?"

"It has speed, that goes without saying," he said. "You just have to decide when you're going to use it. It won't be continuous, but you might get ten minutes of hyper-speed every forty."

"So what's this?" asked Ruby.

"That's a bell," said Hal.

"And what does it actually *do*?" asked Ruby.

"It rings," said Hal. He demonstrated.

"Oh," said Ruby.

"That's not one of its special features," said Hal.

"I guess not," said Ruby.

"Obviously we'll give it a finish, make it some pretty color."

"Green," said Ruby.

"Pardon me?" There was a deafening grinding sound coming from the workshop at the back. "That doesn't sound good," said Hal. "I better go check out what's happening in there. Look, we'll have the bike sprayed and delivered," he said.

When he was gone, Ruby found herself alone in the gadget room. Of course she took the opportunity to have a look around. There was something very particular that she hoped she might find, something that would be invaluable to a person seeking to break into, say, a file room.

As luck would have it, she spotted it almost immediately.

THE MICRO-READER.
Hold device five inches from document and press
red button. Up to 1,500 images can be stored. The
device doubles as a projector: press the green
button to view your images on a screen or any
suitably smooth wall or pale surface.

Checking first that Hal was still otherwise engaged, she pocketed the small object, no bigger than a large pencil sharpener.

She was just thinking of reaching into one of the other low glass drawers when she heard someone cough. She stood up quickly, which caused her to bump her head.

Ouch.

"Hey, Ruby," said Blacker, "are you OK? I didn't mean to alarm you."

"Oh . . . no, you didn't," she said. "I mean, sort of, but hey, yes, I mean, hello."

For a second she was afraid he'd seen what she'd done, but he smiled. "Nice to have you back, Ruby, though actually it's my job to wave you bye-bye, I'm afraid."

"What?"

"There's to be no wandering the corridors unaccompanied, so Buzz sent me to escort you on your way out."

"You're serious? You actually are kicking me out?"

He shrugged and smiled again. "Not me — a Spectrum command from the top."

Ruby gave him a puzzled look.

"LB," he explained.

"OK," said Ruby. "I'll go quietly."

Despite the fact that he was there to march her from the premises, Ruby was glad to see Agent Blacker: he was a reassuring presence, and there weren't so many living creatures you could say that about these days.

As she and Blacker walked to the exit, Ruby struck up a conversation about the Prism Vault.

"Have you ever read the Ghost Files?" asked Ruby.

He stopped for a moment and looked at her. "Who told you about the Ghost Files?" he asked.

"Froghorn," said Ruby.

Blacker frowned. "He's getting blabby."

"What I'm wondering," continued Ruby, "is if Spectrum doesn't want anyone to read these files, as in *ever*, then why not just erase them?"

"I'm surprised Froghorn didn't tell you," said Blacker. "Ghost Files *can't* be erased; they are triple secured and locked so far down in the Prism Vault that you may need a password from

God himself. But they cannot be deleted. Spectrum files are created that way."

"But they can be read?"

"They can be read if you are *authorized* to read them and if you have code clearance to enter the Prism Vault. Of course, if you had code clearance they'd fly you there in the Spectrum helicopter."

Why does one need a helicopter to get there? wondered Ruby. "What if you don't have code clearance?" was what she asked.

"Then you'd be needing flippers or some kind of submersible."

"It's located in water?" said Ruby.

"It's no secret that the vault's in a watery location," said Blacker.

"Would that be in a lake? Or in the sea?" asked Ruby.

Blacker cocked his head to one side and looked at her like he was trying to gauge where this conversation was going.

"So how does one go about getting hold of a helicopter?" asked Ruby.

"You're kidding, right?" said Blacker. He was laughing, but he wasn't entirely sure she was joking.

"Of course I'm *kidding*," said Ruby, flashing him the Ruby Redfort *I'm just a kid* smile. "Has anyone ever helicoptered *you* in there?" she asked.

"No, ma'am," said Blacker. "Don't like helicopters. And there's no way I'm putting a Superskin on, not unless I have to."

"They make you feel claustrophobic?"

"No, they're just a heck of a struggle to get in and out of."

"So what exactly *is* a Superskin?"

He smiled again and shook his head. "If you're lucky you'll never need to know."

When Ruby stepped out of Spectrum headquarters it was into an entirely different landscape. No more gray — this one was bright white, the sidewalks already an inch deep in soft snow. She pulled her hood up, zipping the parka so her face was framed by its fur. She looked toward the sky, mouth open, and felt the snowflakes melt on her tongue. By the time she reached home the snow was already an inch deeper.

As she crunched up the path to her house she thought about what she had learned.

It seemed she had two unknowns, two problems.

The first: *Where* was the Prism Vault?

The second: How to get inside it?

And what in tarnation was a Superskin?

The things she did know were that water was involved and holding your breath seemed to have something to do with it. This second thing was *not* a reassuring prospect, for, just as Miles Froghorn had pointed out, Ruby had never been very good at holding her breath.

CHAPTER 14
The Wrong Kind of Snow

RUBY WAS CATCHING UP on some of the homework her homeroom teacher, Mrs. Drisco, had thoughtfully sent over while she was at camp. If Mrs. Drisco's intention was to overwhelm Ruby with schoolwork, then she was to be disappointed. Ruby had worked her way through about a quarter of it and she hadn't yet finished breakfast. If she continued at this rate, she should have the rest finished up by the middle of the week, easy.

Hitch offered to drive her to school, but she said she could just as well take the bus.

"By the way, what was that all about, sending me in to talk to Froghorn and then not showing up?"

"Sorry, kid. I had a plan to bring about world peace starting with you two, but I got into an argument with Agent Lunberg and time got away from me."

"So much for world peace," said Ruby.

"It's a harder prospect than you might imagine," he said. "Have a good day and give Mrs. Drisco a run for her money," he said as he walked out of the room.

"You can count on it!" called Ruby.

She glugged down her juice and stared at the cereal box in front of her. There were some brainteaser puzzles printed on the back, and as she figured them out (which took her under a minute), she thought back to that day when she had found the code on the back of the Choco Puffles package. At first glance it had appeared to be just some competition aimed at little kids, but if you knew more than a lot about coding and code breaking, you could see what it really was. Ruby had been just four when she'd noticed it. She'd filled in the form, addressed and stamped the envelope, and passed it to her father to mail, but he had forgotten and that was that. Now, sitting here some nine years later, she wondered if perhaps this code might have been set by Spectrum recruiters — it wasn't impossible, she thought. *Her* route to this underground agency had been by invitation — a phone call from the boss. Not a straightforward "Would you like a career in code breaking" phone call, but then nothing about Spectrum was ever straightforward.

Ruby was so lost in thought that she didn't hear the back door open.

"Didn't I tell you there'd likely be snow?" said Mrs. Digby as she stamped her boots on the step. "I can't say I'm surprised these so-called weather fellas missed it. They don't know how to read a sky the way my old pa taught me." She unwound her scarf. "It won't settle, though."

"It won't?" said Ruby.

"Mark my words, it will be gone before noon."

Ruby looked out at the yard, with its pristine white blanket. It was impossible to make out the path or the lawn or the patio.

"Looks like it's settled," said Ruby.

"Wrong sort of snow," said Mrs. Digby. "It can't last. I'm telling you, by the time the school bell strikes twelve it will have all but disappeared."

"The school bell doesn't strike; it kinda clangs," said Ruby.

The first thing Del said when Ruby climbed aboard the school bus was "You know you missed Thanksgiving."

"I didn't miss Thanksgiving," said Ruby. "I *had* Thanksgiving, just not with anyone I felt very *thankful* to be with."

"Why didn't your mom and dad come visit?" asked Mouse.

"They were in Paris," said Ruby. "Not that I was allowed any visitors anyway."

"So who *did* you spend Thanksgiving with?"

"A few of the mathlympics guys."

"Sounds super dull," said Del.

"Yes and no," said Ruby.

Del gave her the Del Lasco look of *You must truly have lost your brain.* "You're actually saying you *enjoyed* hanging out with those geeks?"

"Not all geeks are boring," said Mouse, reasonably. "I mean, if you define a geek as someone who's good at school stuff and knows all about movies and comics, then *Ruby's* a geek, right? No offense, Rube."

"None taken, but actually this is not the point," said Ruby.

"What *is*?" said Del.

"I'm saying, if you go into something looking for boredom, then more than likely you're gonna be bored; it's about attitude."

"So I've got a bad attitude — is that what you're saying?"

"No, not *bad*, just you're going into it all wrong. I'm arguing that there's no *need* to be bored, *ever*, not if you've got inner resources, an upbeat way of looking at things."

Del wasn't buying it and probably never would. Del was like that: once she'd decided something, it could be near impossible to get her around to your way of thinking, and it was usually a thankless task to try.

RULE 42: DON'T WASTE TIME ARGUING WITH SOMEONE WHO WON'T IN A MILLION YEARS CHANGE THEIR MIND.

Though that said, there was always **RULE 45: NEVER STOP CHALLENGING SMALL-MINDEDNESS.**

Del Lasco was almost back to being her old self except for one thing: she had learned a lesson about evidence and how sure one should be of it before accusing a loyal ally and close friend.

Who to trust when the chips were down?

For Del Lasco now that was a no-brainer. As far as Del was concerned, Ruby Redfort was the only person you could one hundred percent count on, no questions asked — beyond that, how to know?

When they arrived at school and Ruby walked into her homeroom, Mrs. Drisco did not look especially happy to see her.

Ruby Redfort and Mrs. Drisco were never going to see eye to eye on anything. Mrs. Drisco did not like Ruby's smart-mouthed attitude, and Ruby was not a fan of Mrs. Drisco's pettiness.

"Just because you have been away at 'camp,'" began Mrs. Drisco, "does not mean I won't expect your schoolwork to be in on time."

"I didn't expect you would," said Ruby.

"Good," said Mrs. Drisco. "So I will expect it before the end of the semester."

"If you want to, you can expect it by Thursday," said Ruby.

The promise of getting Ruby's homework three weeks early did not, as one might logically expect, make Mrs. Drisco happy. In fact, it had precisely the opposite effect. She felt undermined by Ruby's ability to actually succeed in the task set.

The task was meant to be impossible, and here was Ruby once again challenging her authority by succeeding.

"Well," said Mrs. Drisco, "it sounds like maybe you need stretching."

"Sounds painful," said Ruby.

Mrs. Drisco's eyes narrowed. "I will sign you up for the school Christmas show. I'm sure we would all adore to have you entertain us."

The school Christmas show was Ruby's idea of extreme humiliation. There was no way she was going to embarrass herself by stepping up on that stage and tap-dancing or performing some lame magic trick. But her reply was restrained.

"Mrs. Drisco, I would like nothing better than to be a performing monkey, but I'm afraid my optometrist simply won't allow it."

"Really?" said her teacher. "And why would that be?"

"I have this condition," explained Ruby. "I'm sure you understand."

"And I'm sure you'll understand that without a note explaining your condition, it will be impossible for me to take your word for it." Mrs. Drisco flashed a tight smile.

"He thought you might say that," said Ruby, rummaging in her satchel, "which is why I took the precaution of bringing this with me." She handed a piece of white letterhead paper to Mrs. Drisco, who reluctantly took it.

DEAR MRS. DRISCO,
    I AM WRITING TO INFORM YOU THAT MS.
RUBY REDFORT SUFFERS FROM A CONDITION KNOWN
AS THE OPHTHALMIC JOGGLE. THIS CONDITION
PREVENTS HER FROM DANCING (PARTICULARLY
TAP), SINGING, RECITING, JUGGLING, OR INDEED
STANDING ON STAGE IN FRONT OF ANY LARGE,
MEDIUM, OR SMALL GATHERING OF PEOPLE WHILE
LIGHTS ARE TRAINED ON HER.
    I TRUST, NAY INSIST, THAT SHE SHOULD NOT
BE EXPOSED TO ANY OF THE ABOVE ACTIVITIES. I
AM SURE I NEED NOT EXPLAIN THE CONSEQUENCES

TO A PERSON OF YOUR STATURE AND INTELLECT,
NOR SHOULD I WANT TO MAKE REFERENCE TO
THE LIABILITY ISSUES YOUR SCHOOL WOULD BE
SUBJECT TO.
    YOURS SINCERELY,
    E. F. P. TOZLPED

Mrs. Drisco had never heard of ophthalmic joggle and she felt she'd been in the teaching profession long enough to have heard pretty much every classroom excuse and medical condition. There was something about the name of this optometrist that made her uneasy, but she could not put her finger on what it was. So Mrs. Drisco gave another tight smile and said, "Fine," in a tone that suggested things were not fine.

En route to class, Mouse and Ruby passed Vapona Begwell coming the other way. Mouse was surprised when Vapona and Ruby did not exchange their usual insults of *bozo* and *dork-squirt*, but instead sort of nodded at each other. It was the nod of mutual respect — grudging, but respect nonetheless.

Mouse looked at her friend. "How did you two end up so close?"

"We came to an understanding," said Ruby, without elaborating further.

Only Clancy knew the *whole* story. It all had to do with Ruby keeping her mouth shut when it really counted, and Vapona repaying the favor by stepping in on Ruby's behalf and holding the baby, quite literally, as it happened. It did not make these old enemies friends, but for now at least they were not looking to trip each other up — a truce of sorts.

At recess Del was looking pretty excited.

"Are you coming snurfing?"* she asked.

"You mean hop on a wooden board and head on down a snow-covered mountain? You have to be kidding," said Clancy.

"You *skateboard*," argued Del. "What's the big difference?"

"What, are you nuts?" said Clancy. "Skateboarding takes place on a sidewalk. Snurfing is about throwing yourself down a perilous incline on a plank of wood, no poles, no nothing."

"Suit yourself," said Del. "But I tell you, this is gonna become a thing."

"It *is* a thing," said Clancy.

"Yeah, but I'm telling you it's gonna become a *big* thing," said Del.

"I don't doubt it," agreed Clancy. "There's no end to what dumb things people will decide to do, but it doesn't mean I wanna join in."

"Your sister Minny's got a snurferboard," said Del.

"A perfect example to illustrate my point," said Clancy. "Just because Minny is willing to throw herself from a cliff riding a plank doesn't make it a good idea. Most things Minny recommends are *not* great ideas and should on the whole be avoided."

*BELIEVE IT OR NOT, SNURFING WAS THE ORIGINAL NAME FOR SNOWBOARDING WHEN IT WAS INVENTED IN 1966.

"You need to lighten up," said Del.

"I also need my head to remain attached to my body," said Clancy, "which is why you are not getting me snurfing."

"You can quit discussing it because no one's going snurfing anyway," said Ruby.

"Whaddaya mean?" said Del. "I'm going even if that chicken liver doesn't have the guts for it."

"Not without any snow you're not," said Ruby.

"Well, duh," said Del.

"So you're not going today is what I'm saying."

"You're crazy," said Del. "It's four inches deep already."

But sure enough, by the time the clock struck noon it was all gone, barely a flake on the ground.

"How did you know that was going to happen?" asked Del.

"I have my sources," said Ruby.

CHAPTER 15
Thirty Minutes of Murder

RUBY ARRIVED HOME THAT AFTERNOON to find a pale pink bike to the right of the front steps, next to the bamboo. She didn't touch it; she just looked at it.

"Pink?" she said out loud. "Pastel pink? Why in darn-it did he make it pink?"

She typed a message into the Escape Watch, a very short message for Hal:

>> PINK?!

Ruby went into the house, slammed the front door, and started up the stairs.

"Where are *you* off to at such a lick?" called Mrs. Digby.

"My room!" shouted Ruby.

"If you're planning to watch TV, then make it Channel 44 or Channel 17."

"Why?" said Ruby.

"You need to brush up on horror," said Mrs. Digby.

"Brush up on what?" asked Ruby.

"Or crime," said Mrs. Digby.

"Again, why?" said Ruby. She turned, walked back down the stairs, and stood in the kitchen doorway.

"We got a date," said the housekeeper, pulling an envelope from her apron pocket and handing it to Ruby.

"What's this?" asked Ruby.

Mrs. Digby looked heavenward. "Well, you're not going to know unless you open it, child."

Ruby pulled out a letter. On it was typed the following:

Dear MRS. MYRTLE DIGBY,

It is our great pleasure to inform you that you have been successful in your application to appear on the Crime Time quiz show, THIRTY MINUTES OF MURDER. We look forward to seeing you and your nominated TMOM partner, MISS R. REDFORT, in JANUARY 1974 (exact date to be confirmed). Recording will take place at 11 A.M. Please arrive four hours before to ensure enough time for hair and makeup.

Yours sincerely,
PERRY FARRELL,
PRODUCTION COORDINATOR

Coffee and light lunch will be provided. Please state any scalp and skin product allergies and food intolerances if relevant.

Thirty Minutes of Murder was a film quiz show aimed at the older television viewer. All the questions related to the movies of yesteryear, all in the horror, thriller, or crime genres.

Ruby looked up at Mrs. Digby. "So you have basically signed me up for a game show."

"That's about the size of it."

"They need *four hours* to do our hair and makeup? *Four hours!*"

"Is that all you have to say? I thought you'd be tickled," said Mrs. Digby.

"Tickled" was not the word Ruby would have used, but she didn't want to rain on the old lady's parade, so instead she just said, "OK, I'll go watch something horrifying."

Before Ruby had reached the stairs, the telephone began to ring. She picked up.

"Redfort madhouse; if we seem sane to you, then you're probably crazy!"

"Ahh ... Ruby?"

"Hey, Dad."

"Guten Abend."

"Are you sure about that?"

"What are you saying?"

"My point exactly."

"You've lost me."

"Dad, you're speaking German."

"Oh, yes, that's right," came her mother's voice. "Brant, wrong lingo, we're in France."

"Bonne nuit," said her father.

"Close enough," said Ruby.

"We're just about to hit *la ville*," said her mother.

"When are you coming home?" asked Ruby.

"Tout alors!" said her mother.

"What's that supposed to mean? You're not making any sense," said Ruby.

"It's your father's translation guide; it doesn't work."

"I think you must be on the wrong page," said Ruby.

"We'll call back when we have more vocab," said her mother. "Bye, bye, bye."

Ten minutes later, Ruby set down her glass of banana milk, plonked herself on the beanbag, and flicked on the little TV that sat there on the shelf between her trivia books and the lobster phone.

Channel 16 was showing a rerun of a not-so-funny sitcom. And on Channel 17 *What's Your Poison?* was playing. She watched for a minute.

Greg Valence, the quizmaster, asked: "What venom will cause the victim to repeatedly convulse?"

RUBY: *Tityus serrulatus scorpion.*

GREG VALENCE: *Which animal is widely considered the most dangerous in the world?*

RUBY: *The golden poison dart frog.*

GREG VALENCE: *There's a bonus point if you can tell me under what circumstances a poison dart frog can be handled without using gloves.*

RUBY: *When it's in captivity.*

The contestant did not know this unusual and interesting fact—that the frog's toxicity came from its natural diet of insects. Once out of the wild, it no longer posed a threat. *If that's what a change of diet can do to you, maybe I should consider it,* thought Ruby.

She picked up the remote and clicked on, leaving the quizmaster to his unchallenging quiz questions. She kept clicking until she came to Channel 44. Currently playing was a movie she didn't recognize. She was fairly certain that it was not one she had watched before. She had entered the story as it was reaching its final scenes; a young woman was tiptoeing down a very grand stone staircase. In the hallway was a shadow of a hand, the fingers long and bony; the shadow reached out to touch the woman's shadow.

The woman, unaware that she had company, walked into a dimly lit drawing room and began frantically searching the desk for something, pulling open drawers and rifling through the contents as if her life depended on it. And maybe it did, because when she found a little box with an amulet in it, she sank to her knees and sobbed theatrical sobs. The actress had real screen presence, and though the film was on the hammy side, Ruby found herself gripped. However, it was only when the woman caught sight of the figure, an elderly vampire, and the camera zoomed in close on her terror-stricken face that Ruby knew that she had seen her somewhere before. The film reached its inevitable conclusion, and as was the custom with old movies, there was no credit roll, just two words: *The End.*

Before Ruby could begin to wonder *how* she knew this woman, the smiling face of another appeared, this one elbow-deep in dishes and very happy about the soap she had chosen to scrub them with.

Ruby took a look down the periscope, something she had constructed a long time ago so she could check out the to-ings and fro-ings in the kitchen. Mrs. Digby wasn't there. So Ruby called the housekeeper's apartment.

"Can't an old lady get a little peace and quiet?" she complained.

"Are you watching TV?"

"Why shouldn't I be?"

"No reason, which channel?"

"Thirteen."

"Oh."

"Why?"

"I wanted to know what movie I just watched — you know, on Channel 44?"

"Ah, glad to hear you're studying. I'll look it up in the *Hound*."

There was a lot of rustling of paper and then . . . "*The Shadow's Touch*," said Mrs. Digby.

"Who was the actress?" asked Ruby.

"It's pitiful you don't know," said the housekeeper. "It's a fearful gap in your movie knowledge. I thought you took an interest in horror. You're going to have to pull your socks up or we'll never win the big money."

"*So* I'm taking an interest; just give me her name and I'll look her up."

"Marnie Novak," said Mrs. Digby. "Now, I gotta go because the commercials are over and the TV bingo is just about to start again."

If Ruby had taken anything on board during her thirteen years of life, it was *never interrupt Mrs. Digby if she was watching TV bingo.*

Ruby went over to her bookshelves and pulled out the volumes relating to film. She had around forty, and they covered various genres of movie, some dedicated to particular directors or studios, others to actors and movie stars, and quite a lot of them were technical: books on props, sets, makeup, and cinematography. It was in one rather dense book titled *Stars of the B Screen* that Ruby came face-to-face with the woman who had caused her so many sleepless nights.

Marnie Novak (*formerly Gretchen Ehrling*).

The name was familiar—horribly so. For though Ruby had never actually *knowingly* crossed paths with the woman who called herself Madame Ehrling, she knew someone who had, a person who hadn't lived to tell the tale. Agent Lopez had followed the woman to the Fountain Hotel in Everly, a town south of Twinford. There she had witnessed a meeting of sorts and managed to intercept a message intended for Ehrling's cohort. Unfortunately, Lopez had been spotted—and for that mistake she'd paid with her life.

The FBI had found no recent picture of Ehrling, unless one counted the image caught on the Twinford City Bank security camera, her face obscured by a veiled hat. When they'd tried to trace her, they discovered that she had been dead for a number of years. So who was she and *Why,* thought Ruby, *do I feel so sure I know her?*

As she stared at the film still of the young movie actress, the answer came to her, the answer to the question *Where have I seen her before?*

Answer: *On Wolf Paw Mountain.* It was the eyes Ruby recognized: cold steel blue, the eyes of the Australian.

So Gretchen Ehrling had reinvented herself as Novak, and Novak had gone to the City Bank playing the part of a Madame Ehrling. It seemed likely that Madame Ehrling had been an old relative, now conveniently deceased.

Things were beginning to join up.

There was a brief paragraph on Marnie Novak; a few facts about her short-lived career and a list of some of the films she'd appeared in, most of them thrillers and horror movies.

Marnie Novak had been set for stardom. Regarded as a great talent, she was the protégée of notorious film director . . .

And then nothing. The following page was missing.

Ruby leafed through the book. *Where is it?*

And then she remembered what Mrs. Digby had said about Baby Lemon.

"Darn that baby," she muttered.

The page had been torn out and very possibly *eaten,* so if Ruby wanted to discover anything further about this killer actress, then she was going to need to pop to the library.

CHAPTER 16
Look Under V

RUBY WAS JUST PULLING ON HER COAT, having decided to try Penny Books rather than head across town to the city library, when she received a phone call from Red.

"Rube, I'm really sorry to do this, but I've got a bit of an emergency here. . . . You see, my laces were undone and I kinda tripped and sorta sat on my brother's guitar and he needs it tonight, but you know I sorta felt like I should fix the situation before I told him and that's why I wondered, kinda hoped you wouldn't mind if I told him he could borrow yours? It's a lot to ask, I know. . . . Oh, by the way, it's me, Red."

"Hey, Red."

"I feel really bad about asking you; you can say no. I mean, I haven't forgotten what happened to your violin — I mean, I realize I owe you a new one and believe me, I *am* saving."

"Don't give it a second thought," said Ruby. "Who hasn't sat on a violin or a guitar at some point in their life?"

"Thanks, Ruby, you're a lifesaver. I'll come and pick it up," said Red.

It was just at that moment that Ruby was sure she heard a click on the line, like someone was listening to her call — not someone *in* the house; Ruby had her own phone line, so that wasn't possible. No: if she was right, then she was being bugged.

"You know what, I'll bring it over," said Ruby, and two minutes later she was out the door.

Ruby decided, since no one was around to see the color, this would be the perfect opportunity to try out the pink bike. Plus the hyper-speed booster would allow her to stay ahead of any danger she might encounter.

The bike, despite its pinkness, was very impressive. It took little effort to cycle up to Red's place in Silver Hills, and Ruby arrived in no time.

"Boy, you were quick," Red said as she opened the door.

"Yeah, turns out my new bike is kinda speedy," said Ruby. She looked around. "Is your mom not home?"

"She's working late; she has this big movie — lots of costumes to design."

"What kind of movie? Is it fantasy?"

"I'll say," said Red. "It's about these kids who morph into crocodiles. But it's the makeup artist who's got the real headache. I mean, what does a croc-kid look like?"

Ruby shrugged. "My guess would be, Archie Lemon."

It was nice to have the chance to catch up with Red, for despite her proclivity for accidents and her unusual talent for flattening musical instruments, Red was a person who exuded calm. And right now calmness was something Ruby truly appreciated.

Jem, Red's brother, was grateful for the guitar.

"I owe you, Ruby," he said.

"It's not an owing type of a thing," said Ruby. "You're welcome to hang on to it until you get a new one. I don't see myself strumming for the next few weeks."

The three of them hung out for a while, talking about school and the upcoming holidays, who might be having a New Year's party, would Mrs. Drisco ever think of retiring? That type of thing.

"She used to be *my* homeroom teacher," said Jem, "so you have my deepest sympathy — I spent a lot of time in detention."

Finally, they came back to the subject of what on earth a croc-kid would look like.

"My mom told the makeup artist to go talk to Frederick," said Red. "If anyone's going to know how you make a kid look like a crocodile, it's him."

This immediately pinged an idea into Ruby's head. If anyone was going to have the skinny on Marnie Novak, it would be Frederick Lutz.

Frederick Lutz was a Hollywood makeup artist and a nice old man. He had fixed Ruby's face after she'd smashed it up when she and her skateboard had parted company — the resulting black eye had almost ruined her mother's dreams of a picture-perfect photo portrait. Frederick had saved the day with his makeup skills, and no one would ever have guessed that the girl in the picture had collided with a cop car not twenty-four hours earlier.

"Red, do you mind if I make a phone call?"

"Sure," said Red. "Why?"

"I'm thinking I might call in on Frederick Lutz," said Ruby.

Red looked puzzled. "Why? Do *you* need to know what a croc-kid looks like?"

It wasn't much of a detour to get to Frederick Lutz's house. He lived on the edge of Silver Hills, at 119 Derilla Drive, and it was pretty much downhill all the way.

Ruby arrived as evening turned to night.

She rang the bell and when there was no answer she tried the door. It was open.

"Hello?" she called.

"Ruby! Is that you? Come on in."

She found him sitting in his sunroom, looking up through the glass at the stars, his dachshund, Paullie, on his lap.

"I could look at them forever," said Frederick, still gazing up at the twinkling night.

"I don't think much of your security system," said Ruby.

"What does an old guy like me need with a security system? Robbers have got no interest in me," said Frederick. "Besides, I got Paullie here."

He stroked the dog's ears and the dachshund yawned.

Ruby doubted that Paullie was much of a deterrent to

robbers, but then again, she supposed Frederick was probably right; robbers *were* unlikely to give him the time of day.

"Want an old-fashioned lemon soda?" said Frederick, taking a can from his cooler.

"Sure," said Ruby.

He handed it to her.

"So," said Lutz, "what is it I can help you with?"

"I was wondering if you'd ever met an actress named Marnie Novak?" asked Ruby.

"Marnie Novak," mused Frederick. "Now, that's a name I haven't heard in a long while."

"You knew her?" asked Ruby.

"Oh, yes, I knew her," said Frederick. "She was a good actress. On the brink of a glittering career, they said."

"So . . . did she *not* have a glittering career?" asked Ruby.

"Can *you* name five films you've seen her in?" said Lutz.

Ruby shook her head. "Actually, I've only seen *one,* and I didn't even know her name until about two hours ago."

"Which movie was it?" asked Frederick.

"The Shadow's Touch," said Ruby, taking a big gulp of soda.

"Oh, that's a good one," said Lutz. "No one did horror like the Count."

The next thing Ruby felt was soda shooting out of her nose.

"Are you OK, Ruby?" said Lutz.

It took Ruby a few seconds to get any words out.

"It sorta went down the wrong way," she squeaked.

"You're telling me," said Lutz.

Ruby mopped at her face with her sleeve. "This Count, who, I mean . . . you did say Count, right?"

"Yes," said Frederick. "He was the director of *The Shadow's Touch*. Boy, was he a talent."

"*Really?*" said Ruby. "He was good?"

"Better than good; he was an artist," said Lutz. He got to his feet. "Wait there," he said. He came back five minutes later with a large book, a sort of encyclopedia of movie directors. "Here." He passed it to Ruby. "You'll find him in that."

Ruby began flipping through the pages, scanning the Cs.

Clooning . . .

Coburn . . .

Coswell . . .

"He doesn't seem to be here," said Ruby.

"Of course he's there," said Lutz, leaning in. "Well, you're looking under C, that's your problem. What you need to do is look under V."

"V?"

"V for *von Leyden*," said Lutz. "Victor von Leyden."

Pause.

"What? You look like you've seen a ghost."

"Not a ghost exactly," said Ruby. "More of a psycho."

CHAPTER 17
Evil All Around

FREDERICK LUTZ WAS LOOKING AT RUBY with a concerned expression.

"Are you quite all right there?" he asked. "You've gone pale."

"Too many late nights," said Ruby.

"Maybe you should ease up on the horror movies," suggested Frederick. "They're probably giving you nightmares."

"It's real life that gives me the nightmares," said Ruby.

Frederick nodded. "I know what you mean," he said. "There's been a lot of bad things in the news. That poor snake lady, for one—imagine getting poisoned by a bouquet of flowers."

"Yeah, that was creepy," said Ruby. They were both silent for a moment, and then she asked, "So why *didn't* Marnie Novak go on to have a glittering career?"

"She got in the family way," said Lutz. "You know, pregnant."

"So, what, she couldn't work?" asked Ruby.

"Wasn't allowed to work," said Frederick. "You have to remember these were old-fashioned times; people weren't very understanding when it came to unmarried mothers. The father was a big-shot movie producer, and a royal pain in the neck if you were unlucky enough to cross his path."

"Who?" asked Ruby.

"George Katz," said Frederick. "Remember him?"

Ruby certainly did. George Katz had caused an awful lot of grief during his prosperous and happy life, mainly for the women he had dated.

"Why didn't he marry her?" asked Ruby. "Didn't he love her?"

"Oh, love wasn't the problem," said Lutz. "The fact that he was already married was the problem. He didn't want his wife to get wind of what was going on because her daddy was a big-time studio exec, so it was all hushed up. Miss Novak lost her starlet status and never worked again."

"So the baby was nothing to do with Victor von Leyden? I mean, there's no way it was his child?"

"No, that's a certainty," said Frederick. "Lorelei was not his daughter."

"Then why does she have his last name?"

"That was a kindness to Marnie. He was very fond of Miss Novak: she had been his protégée. He tried to help, but it was too late, the cat was out of the bag, the studio didn't want a scandal. George Katz and his wife were a popular couple, so they wanted Marnie out of the limelight and out of the movies."

"So that was the end of her career?"

"As good as," said Frederick. "Victor remained close to Marnie, but no one would offer her work, and so in the end she headed off to Australia in search of a new life."

"With the baby?" asked Ruby.

"She took her along, but it didn't work out," said Frederick. "From what I heard, Marnie became cruel, resentful of her. She told someone I used to work with back in the day that she blamed the child for the ruination of her life, said she couldn't abide to look at the girl."

The story was getting more tragic by the minute, and had one not known the awful deeds, the terrible crimes and cruelties, perpetrated by Marnie Novak and her daughter Lorelei, one might have felt great sympathy for them both.

"So what happened to her, the girl?" asked Ruby.

"Who really knows? My friend Reggie used to say that the only thing *that* little girl was interested in was greasepaint. Victor tried to make an actress of her, but she had zero talent for it."

"But she liked getting herself made up — like a theater star?" asked Ruby.

"More than that. What she was really passionate about was special-effects makeup," said Frederick. "She liked inventing characters and disguising herself, playing tricks on people, pretty mean tricks too." He shook his head. "But she wasn't an actress, more likely to become a con woman than an actress."

"Who taught her to do that? The disguises, I mean."

"Victor, of course," said Lutz. "No one did theatrical disguise like 'Count von Viscount.' He was famous for it. Always had kids hanging around wanting to learn how to transform themselves."

"Where did he get the nickname from?" asked Ruby.

"Oh, *that*, that came from all these gothic horror movies he made — and the fact that he dressed a bit like Dracula, elegant style but creepy, all black with cravat and handkerchiefs, an old-fashioned pocket watch, and if you ever heard him speak, well, he kinda sounded a lot like Dracula too."

Ruby did not need reminding of the quality of the voice that whispered to her from her nightmares.

"I'm telling you," said Frederick, "fit him with a pair of fangs and you'd believe in vampires for sure. So they called him the Count von Leyden, then Count von Victor, and later the Count von Viscount, and finally just the Count — none of it was meant kindly."

"So that was his thing, creating characters?"

"He was one of the best, I have to admit. He pioneered a way of changing faces and voices like I have never seen from that day to this. He kept his secret — never told another person in the industry just how he did it — but everyone suspected it was really down to Homer. It was likely him who came up with it."

"Who was Homer?" asked Ruby.

"A clever fellow Victor worked with in the early days. They were a team: Homer the illusionist and inventor, and Victor the creative — quite a duo."

"So you admired them?"

Frederick's expression turned serious. "I admired Homer — he was always a good man. He became nervous when he saw how a couple of Victor's protégés were using their skill in an ugly way; disguising themselves, conning people — Lorelei was the worst. Anyway, it became nasty. So he ended up breaking their association."

"What about you?" asked Ruby. "What did you think?"

"I admired Victor's talent, but I had no liking for the man he became," said Frederick. "He began his career a reasonable enough fellow, but somewhere down the line things changed. He was shot through with something cruel."

"So he gave up directing?" asked Ruby, though she knew the answer all too well.

"After Marnie, he lost heart, they say, and with his protégée gone, he turned bitter, then he fell out with Homer, and there were rumors he left the country, went abroad somewhere."

If only, thought Ruby.

"Here, take the book," said Frederick. "You can bring it back when you're done."

She thanked him, clipped it onto her bike rack, and rode off into the dark.

Ruby was freewheeling slowly down Derilla Drive when she thought she heard the sound of ringing. Quiet at first, but getting louder. There wasn't a lot of activity on Derilla Drive, not a soul around on this chilly evening, but somewhere a telephone was ringing.

She slowed.

A blue metal pay phone.

She rested her bike against a lamppost and walked over to the phone, waited a second or two before picking up.

"Hello?" she said.

"Been doing your homework, Ms. Redfort?"

A chill spread through Ruby that had nothing to do with the light snow that was falling, or the north wind that was blowing.

It had everything to do with the voice in her ear.

She looked around—she was utterly alone, a girl illuminated by a single streetlamp.

"How did you . . . how do you . . ." she stammered, "how . . ."

"How do I know where you are? Is that what you want to know? I know lots of things you don't know," said the voice, "things you need to know if you are planning on making it past New Year."

"What are you say—" began Ruby.

"You're tangled in a web, Ms. Redfort, and the spider's watching you, waiting . . . ready to wind you in."

"So why don't you just come out and meet me face-to-face?"

"Oh, I don't mean *me*," said the Count. "I'm not the spider; I'm a pussycat compared to this individual." He paused before adding, "A word of advice from one adversary to another—watch your back, Ms. Redfort, there's evil all around."

Ruby felt her legs buckle under her and the receiver slip from her grasp. She lay there watching as it swung back and forth, the sound as it knocked against the phone booth like some dull bell of doom.

**Lenny Rivers
was surprised . . .**

when the hospital called to tell him that the guy he had found lying next to the road, the guy he had thought was just a few breaths away from his last, was now conscious and breathing unassisted.

"He's out of danger?" asked Lenny. It was kind of hard to believe—this man he had seen lying there bleeding on the ground, this man who looked like his final minutes were ticking past, was off the critical list?

"He's actually walking," said the nurse. "A little unsteady, but he's on the move."

"Can I pay him a visit?" asked Lenny. "I'd like to shake the hand of a guy who returned from the dead."

"We'd be glad if you would; no one else has been in to see him and he can't remember a thing before the accident."

Lenny grabbed his coat and hopped into his truck. He was curious to talk to this miracle guy, this Morgan Loveday.

But it wasn't to be. When he arrived at Morgan's room he found the bed empty and no sign of the man who had lain in it.

CHAPTER 18
Location Unknown

RUBY AND CLANCY WERE SITTING in their homeroom, waiting for Mrs. Drisco to return from the principal's office. She had felt it necessary to escort Dillon Flannagon to Principal Levine that morning because she'd had it "up to here" with his "utter disregard for school rules." No one was sure what the misdemeanor was, but it had certainly riled Mrs. Drisco, who was very partial to rules.

"So how come you were visiting Frederick Lutz?" asked Clancy.

"Well, it all has to do with Mrs. Digby. You see, I was watching TV when onto the screen walks someone I know."

"Really? What kinda someone? Someone like a friend? Or someone like an acquaintance?"

"Neither," said Ruby. "It concerns a someone I've met, but not a someone I particularly want to meet again, though knowing my luck, I bet you anything I'm going to run into her at any minute."

"If you're talking about Vapona Begwell, then I can tell you with total certainty you're going to see her today; she's put her name down for the caroling."

Ruby made a face. "Jeepers," she said, "what's *that* gonna sound like?"

"She's trying to get out of litter-picking duty — it's the carol thing or a lot of garbage."

"Oh."

"So I take it it wasn't Bugwart you saw on TV?"

"No, not her."

"So who?"

"You don't want to guess?"

Clancy made a face. "Could you just *tell* me before I fall asleep? I mean, the suspense is just about killing me."

"Well, *there's* a coincidence," said Ruby. "Because this is the sort of lady who might just be able to arrange a killing."

"Who?" asked Clancy.

"The Australian," said Ruby.

The blood instantly drained from Clancy's face. "Why did you have to mention her?" he said.

"You *asked*," said Ruby.

"Yeah, but I didn't think you were going to actually say *her*." He gulped. "I don't like thinking about that evildoer. What was she doing on the news, anyhow?"

"I didn't say she was on the news," said Ruby. "It's a lot more interesting than the *news*."

Ruby filled Clancy in on everything she'd learned about Marnie Novak and her association with the Count.

"The studio fired her when they discovered she was in the family way."

Clancy looked blank.

"Having a b-a-b-y."

"Oh," said Clancy. "What's the deal with that? Why wasn't she allowed to have a child?"

"Wasn't married, but it seems the father was — it could have been quite the scandal if it hadn't been hushed up. These were old-fashioned times, my friend — a baby with a married man was not good for box-office ratings. Plus she wasn't the right shape for the part — a pregnant vampire wasn't what the studio was after."

"Don't tell me, this baby turns out to be Lorelei?"

"Ping! Give that kid a prize."

Mrs. Drisco walked in. "Pop quiz, everyone," she said. "Pens out, please. I'll be handing out a test."

"So I haven't told you the creepiest part," whispered Ruby, her tone anxious as Mrs. Drisco walked around the class giving out papers.

"What creepiest part?" asked Clancy. He looked like he might be on the verge of flapping.

"I don't want any conferring," said Mrs. Drisco, shooting a look at Clancy.

"The phone call," whispered Ruby. "I had a phone call from the Count."

Clancy began to flap. "He called you at home?" he said.

"No, on a pay phone," said Ruby.

"What pay phone?" asked Clancy.

"The one on Derilla," said Ruby. "I was freewheeling down the hill when this pay phone began to ring, and when I picked up, guess who was on the end of the line."

"But that's worse than him calling you at home," said Clancy. "That means he's been watching you."

Ruby shivered. "That's what I thought."

"Ruby Redfort!" said Mrs. Drisco. "I said no conferring! I've got my eyes on you."

You're not the only one, thought Ruby.

When Ruby and Clancy walked up the steps to her house, she noticed that the pastel-pink bike was gone. Had Hal taken it? He hadn't said anything about picking it up. Had someone else come into the Redfort driveway, and made off with it? *Unlikely — who would want a pastel-pink bike?* she thought.

After a brief chat with Mrs. Digby, they went on up to the top of the house, carrying a tray laden with two Digby club sandwiches, a half-dozen cookies, and a carton of banana milk. Mrs. Digby was a big believer in keeping one's strength up.

"You need brain food," she said. Clancy wasn't sure any of the food on the tray was "brain food," but he wasn't complaining.

Clancy was struggling with his French homework, and Ruby was trying to figure out exactly where the Prism Vault might be.

She had a map spread out on the floor and she was peering at it through a large magnifying glass.

"What are you doing?" asked Clancy.

"Looking for water," replied Ruby.

"Excuse me?" said Clancy.

"I'm trying to figure out where the Prism Vault is located."

"Did you say prison vault?"

"Prism," said Ruby, "as in light refractor."

Clancy was still looking confused.

"Look, all you gotta know is that there is this big vault that holds all the archive files relating to Spectrum missions. I want to get in to learn what I can about Bradley Baker and LB. It's called the Prism Vault, I guess, because Spectrum is all about color, which is made of light, and a prism is something that breaks light into its different colors, or bends its path."

"What, like the new telescope?" asked Clancy.

"What did you say?"

"The space telescope," said Clancy. "They had it on the news last night—you didn't catch it?"

"I was all tied up talking to psychopaths on pay phones."

"Oh, yeah," said Clancy, "I forgot. Anyway, this guy was explaining how a telescope is basically like this giant prism made of all these folding mirrors that focus light onto a receiver. It was actually kind of interesting."

Ruby was looking at Clancy with that expression that always made him mad.

"What?" he said.

"So where is this telescope?" she asked.

"Meteor Island," said Clancy. "At the Observatory."

"Oh, yeah, that's right." She remembered now. "The kid at the planetarium mentioned it."

"Do you mind letting me in on whatever it is you have just decided you know?"

She chewed her pencil. She was thinking. What she was thinking was, could that be the place Blacker was talking about?

The Observatory was on a small island, more like a large rock, really, so you'd need flippers and a wet suit to get there. A helicopter was out of the question, and a boat probably not a good idea. Ruby figured Spectrum would be watching the sea and would intercept any vessel coming that way.

Clancy clicked his fingers in front of her face.

"Hey! Earth to Mars, come in Mars."

"Clance, I think you just solved it."

"I did?" said Clancy. He looked pleased.

"I think that's where it could be," she said, thumping him on the arm.

"Oh, great," said Clancy. "What exactly are we talking about?"

"The Prism Vault. I think it could be on Meteor Island, underneath the Observatory."

"Oh," said Clancy. "So now what?"

"I'm going to check it out, of course."

"Of course you are — and do you have clearance to do that?"

She rolled her eyes. "It's the place Spectrum keeps all the most secret of secret documents, the highly restricted files. The ones no one is allowed to see, so that would be no."

"So you're going to break in?"

"That's my plan."

Clancy looked at her. "Now that is a truly bad idea."

"Well," said Ruby, "that's tough, because it's the only one I got."

"What about the codes? There's no point breaking into a restricted file vault if you can't open the files."

"True." She sighed, paused, and said, "I'm pretty sure I know a couple of them; it's the entry code I'm truly stuck on, but I guess I'll just have to figure it out."

Clancy looked at her. "Don't take this the wrong way, but I'm praying you don't."

Some thirty-five years earlier . . .

a kid was eight years old and living in the suburbs of Colwin City, when, while breakfasting on cereal, the kid noticed an unusual ad on the back of the box. It seemed to be a competition with big prize money, but reading between the lines, this was no simple brainteaser.

There was definitely something odd about this particular competition; for one thing, it didn't seem like it was really a competition, and for another, it didn't seem like it was aimed at the average child. You would have to be some kind of genius to see that this was not so much a word search puzzle as it was a code, and an even bigger genius to figure how to crack it. But the Colwin City kid was both of those things.

Once the code was solved, it was plain to see that it was actually an application form for what seemed like a very exciting future. However, there was a problem. Casey was not eligible for a place on this program; that was stated clearly in **bold.** That seemed wrong, unfair and stupid. When were things ever going to change? It was 1938, for goodness' sake!

Then an idea grew: break the rules.

The kid emptied the box, cut out the coupon, and filled in the blanks. A birth certificate was required, so the kid fetched it from the large oak desk that stood in the study. Before sliding this into an envelope along with the coupon, the Colwin City kid made one very simple alteration to the document. That done, the envelope was addressed and mailed.

CHAPTER 19
Minus 10

RUBY LOOKED AT THE CLOCK: it was 2:57 a.m., and she was still wide awake, or at least her brain was. Her body felt like it could do with a whole lot more lying down. But by the time the clock ticked around to 3:33 a.m., Ruby gave up arguing with herself and crawled out of bed. She figured she might as well get dressed, since there was little likelihood of sleep coming her way. Once clothed, she tiptoed downstairs to the kitchen, turning on the low light that hung over the table so it was bathed in a warm orange glow. She took a glass from the cupboard, walked to the refrigerator, and searched around before pulling out a carton of banana milk. She poured herself a glass, took a swig, sat back in one of the kitchen chairs, and stared out at the snow flurry on the other side of the window.

How to get hold of the Prism Vault entry code? She was still sitting there when a slice of toast popped up from the toaster. Sort of surprising, since she hadn't actually dropped any bread into the little silver kitchen appliance.

She retrieved the slice and read it:

Picking you up in 20.
Hitch

Ruby climbed into the silver convertible at precisely 4:00 a.m., and they drove at great speed north out of town.

"Is it really necessary to leave so early?" Ruby yawned.

"Is it early, or is it just very late?" said Hitch.

"It's early," said Ruby. "I know it's early because I was in my pajamas twenty minutes ago, the sun hasn't come up, and the hands on that clock of yours haven't crawled past the six."

"There's breakfast in the glove compartment, if that helps," said Hitch.

Ruby shook her head. "I'm not sure I can eat. My teeth are still asleep."

When Hitch and Ruby arrived at their destination, they were greeted by two familiar faces, Sam Colt and Agent Kekoa. Ruby's heart sank, not because she had anything against these two individuals, in fact she liked them a lot; it was what they represented that was the problem. Sam Colt was a survivalist and survival trainer, and Kekoa was the Spectrum dive instructor. This meant that today was going to be wet and very cold.

"Welcome to extreme-elements survival," said Sam.

"Boy, do I not like the sound of that," said Ruby.

"That's kind of the point; no one does," said Sam. "But with the weather and the storms coming, Hitch here thought it would be a good idea if you took part."

"Gee, thanks, Hitch," said Ruby.

"Don't mention it," said Hitch.

There were seven other trainees there, and Ruby was glad to see Kip Holbrook was one of them. The location was up at Big Sky Lake, which was frozen solid.

"Are you thinking what I'm thinking?" muttered Holbrook.

"Not unless you're thinking about finding the first bus out of here," hissed Ruby.

The first part of the training was easy. Sam Colt taught them some key cold-weather concepts, and none of them involved taking a dip in an icy lake. But quite a lot of what he said involved making sure to keep dry.

"Hypothermia is the number one killer of people in the outdoors," said Colt. "As the old saying goes, 'Stay Dry and Stay Alive.' So seeing as how I'm urging you to keep dry, you're probably wondering where the lake comes in, right?"

Ruby wasn't actually wondering this; she was pretty sure she knew how the lake was going to fit into this scenario.

"Well, let's go take a look," he said, and the eight trainees all followed him out onto the ice.

Two twenty-four-inch holes had been cut in the lake's surface, approximately twelve yards apart.

"First of all, we're going to practice getting a feel for the temperature of the water."

"I don't like where this is going," whispered Kip Holbrook.

"To begin with," said Sam, "you're all going to have a try at swimming from point A to B, under the ice but with a line secured around you so there's no chance of you losing your way."

Ruby was faintly reassured by this news. She might end up frozen to death, but at least they would find her body.

"When you hit cold water, your body's going to do something very unhelpful," continued Colt. "It's called the 'torso reflex.' Basically, the shock of the cold is going to make you breathe in. That's bad. That will get you drowned. So brace, and hold your chest still."

He went through the rest of the principles of surviving a fall through the ice:

"RELAX your body. Conserve energy. Cold shock will set in quicker if you move around too much.

"FOCUS on getting out as quickly as possible without too much splashing around. The longer you stay in the water, the more likely you are to die."

It was as unpleasant as Ruby had feared, but she did it and that was something. The next exercise made the previous one seem easy. This time it was all about finding one's way out of the ice without there being any pre-cut hole.

"OK, so the ideal thing to do if you fall through ice is to look for the hole that landed you in this situation. If you can climb out of the same hole you originally fell in through, you can be reasonably sure that the edges are likely to support your weight while you climb on out. But what I am going to teach you is how to find your way out of an ice-covered lake or river if you *cannot* find your original entry point. LOOK for changes of color in the ice to find a weaker point. These will show up as lighter in color. When you find one, you need to smash through it. If you're lucky, you'll have a suitable tool provided by Spectrum, but if not, you'll need to use your initiative. Once you have broken through the surface, you need to GET HORIZONTAL: slide your arms full length onto the ice, then kick your legs like a seal to propel yourself out. Then you need to ROLL until you get to firmer ice or ground. The key is to get out of the water ASAP."

Ruby was relieved to see both Hitch and Kekoa clad in drysuits and in the water.

"At least there's some chance I might get out of this lake alive," she muttered.

She let her body sink in through the hole.

The cold felt like a punch to the chest.

Relax, she thought.

She swam away from the entry point and began searching for a place to break through.

Focus, she thought.

Around her was all blue and white, and for a moment she had no idea where was up and where was down.

Don't panic, she thought. **RULE 19: PANIC WILL FREEZE YOUR BRAIN.**

Holding her breath, she turned in the water and saw a

rounder, lighter patch to the left and above. Amazed by how hard it was to move with her clothes soaked and the cold in her bones, she made it through and without help from Hitch or Kekoa.

There was a welcome interval where the recruits dried off and warmed up and every single one of them hoped that that would be it as far as cold-water survival was concerned. But as it turned out they were just getting started.

The second half of the training took place at the aptly named Desolate Cove, a windy curve of gray-pebble beach.

Here they were faced with a whole new set of problems.

Survival in the ocean was a very different challenge: a vast expanse of moving water, crashing waves, currents, and riptides.

As the day was coming to a close, Ruby saw a figure picking his way across the beach. It was Froghorn. He didn't look too happy to be there. He was trundling a small cart about the size of a wheelbarrow. He was wrapped up warm against the chill; he had really gone to town on the cold-weather gear.

"What a drip," muttered Ruby.

"Hey, kid," called Hitch. "I have to get back to HQ. So when training's over you can get a lift back with the other trainees. Can I trust you to do the right thing and get home safe?"

"Of course," said Ruby.

"See you later, then," he said. She watched as Hitch walked over to speak to Froghorn. They talked together for a few minutes, all perfectly fine until Hitch appeared to notice something—

perhaps it was to do with Froghorn's attire, it was hard to say from this distance, but Ruby recognized the subtle change in Hitch's body language and knew he was not happy, not happy at all. He walked off to the Spectrum trailer while Kekoa briefed the trainees on the equipment they were about to be issued.

Froghorn's job was to sign out the gear to each of the trainees. Today's items came in a neat little bag, light in weight.

The first was a breathing band, not unlike the breathing buckle Ruby had once acquired from the gadget room, though this device looked a little more up-to-date than that one. It was worn around the wrist, and when one needed air it could be pressed to the mouth so you could draw in oxygen. It was intended for emergencies — the hope was that it would buy you just enough time to get you out of a bad situation.

"Use it only when you really, really have to," warned Kekoa. "Once the five minutes are through, that's it."

The second item got *everyone* talking.

"What's this?" asked Lowe.

"That," said Kekoa, "is a Superskin. It keeps you warm in cold water and aids swimming. You'll find you move significantly faster, particularly under the surface. The suit will keep you totally dry, but the truly remarkable thing about it is that once you step from the water, it will shed every drop within a matter of seconds. You need to take it home with you and practice getting into it — it's not easy."

Ruby looked inside the little bag. "So *that's* a Superskin."

As they trooped back up the beach a quarter-mile on from Desolate Cove, Ruby noticed something written there in the sand. Four words:

L O O K   T O   T H E   S T A R S

The stars were indeed beginning to twinkle, and as she gazed at them, she caught sight of the Observatory, perched as it was on Meteor Island. Stars were so often used to point the way, to navigate. *Could it be,* thought Ruby, *that the stars hold an even bigger secret? Musca,* she thought, *the fly constellation.*

If she looked for *those* stars, then would she find her way?

**Two months after the
letter was mailed . . .**

the kid from Colwin City received a reply in the form of a single line of gibberish. Once deciphered, it told of a location. So, wasting no time, the kid purchased a ticket for the nine-hundred-and-twenty-mile bus ride to reach not an address, but a manhole cover. One thing this kid knew for definite was that even crawling down a drain was preferable to living one more day in the suburbs of Colwin City, and so down the kid went.

The ninety-nine-second test completed, the kid from Colwin City was inducted into the Spectrum 8 JSRP.

No one doubted this kid's brain. "A phenomenal mind," they all agreed. "Aced every one of the junior-agent tests." "The smartest of them all." Well, almost.

They said, "You pass the big one and there's no looking back — make the top eight and your future's Spectrum."

That sounded good. The life of a secret agent made sense like no other life could.

The Colwin City kid felt good, good enough to smile, a rare occurrence indeed.

"You know," said the test agent, "I think one day you might even be up there with Bradley Baker."

The kid from Colwin City felt a sudden jolt, an inexplicable pain.

Who was Bradley Baker?

The training officer continued to drone on about this agent rival.

"Baker was our first junior recruit, joined when he was just seven, but now look at him, thirteen and going places. If you get close to being as good as him, we'll give you a medal."

Mirror, mirror on the wall, who's the smartest of them all?

Not you, not the kid from Colwin City, some other kid's got that badge.

So how to wipe the smile off this Bradley Baker kid's face?

CHAPTER 20
Hold Your Breath

SHE DIDN'T EXACTLY WANT TO HANG AROUND out there once everyone had gone home — she wasn't even sure that she was right about all this; she could have gotten the whole thing back to front and the wrong way up — but the way Ruby saw it, if there was a chance she was right, then it was a chance worth taking.

Getting herself into the Superskin was no small challenge. Neither Blacker nor Kekoa had been exaggerating: it was near impossible to put on and uncomfortable to wear. It sort of stuck to the skin, covering fingers, toes, neck, and head. Only a small oval of the face was visible.

"Weird," said Ruby as she looked down at her feet, "very weird."

To make the vision stranger, the material the Superskin was made from resembled fish scales, and the effect was not unlike a costume from the well-known B movie *Return of the Fish-people*.

She hid her snow parka, boots, and other clothing, concealing them behind a large rock. The water was black and uninviting;

there was no moon tonight, and all in all the cove was living up to its name.

Ruby walked to the water's edge and let the waves lap over her feet, and was surprised when she felt no chill at all. She stepped in farther—no, not cold.

"*Pretty super,*" she said, pulling down her face mask and diving into the slick black water. The Superskin seemed to aid swimming too, and she cut through the water with ease.

When she arrived at Meteor Island, she dived down under the water and searched for a hidden door with her waterproof flashlight. She was looking for a series of marks, or points, that might represent the constellation Musca—the sign of the fly.

It took her a few dives to spot it because she had been looking for something tiny, but the fly constellation was marked on rocks and spanned four feet across.

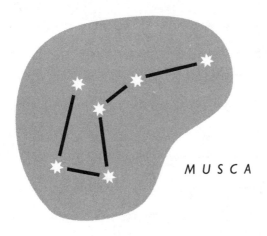

MUSCA

Now it was just a matter of getting in. She felt around, moving her palms along the rock.

At last she found what she was looking for: a panel of glass. When she put her hand on it, a word flashed up: "Capricorn." Ruby pressed in the star points.

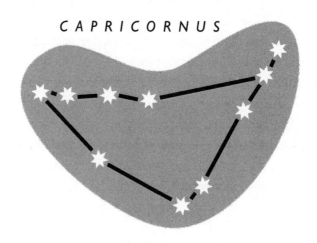

CAPRICORNUS

The screen flashed violet and a new message appeared:

ACCESS APPROVED

The door slid open and in she swam. Now she found herself in a sort of twelve-foot-by-twelve-foot indoor pool, only it wasn't a pool, because pools don't have lids. What this was was a cube full of water, and as she watched the door to the ocean slide shut, she realized she wasn't entirely sure how she was supposed to get out. She swam carefully around and around the cube, searching for a clue that might lead to her release.

Previously, Ruby had only been able to hold her breath for just a second over one minute. Now she was able to do three times that — it wasn't exactly outstanding, but it was enough. She found it just in time — a tiny, tiny image of a fly. Once the fly felt the pressure of her fingertip, the water drained out of the cube and a hatch in the lid slid open, allowing Ruby to climb up a metal ladder and out of the tank into another chamber. By the time she did so, the Superskin had shed every drop of water and she was completely dry.

The space she was now in was not so different from the one she had just emerged from. It was the same shape, same size, same color, but this time the door was *in front* of her, with an entry panel to one side.

HIGHLY SENSITIVE,
RESTRICTED AUTHORITY

There was one violet button next to it. This she pressed and up came a grid. She pictured the books on Froghorn's desk, the ones about error-correcting codes and data transmission.

What she was looking at was an error-correcting code; she could see that. But what kind? Ruby peered more closely at the black and white dots, counting them.

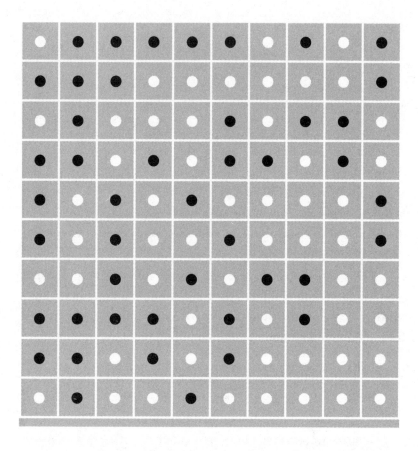

It didn't take her long to realize: it was a parity bit system, and the final row and final column of each grid held the parity bits relating to the black dots, saying whether there was an even or odd number in the row or column.

But how to get a code from that . . . ?

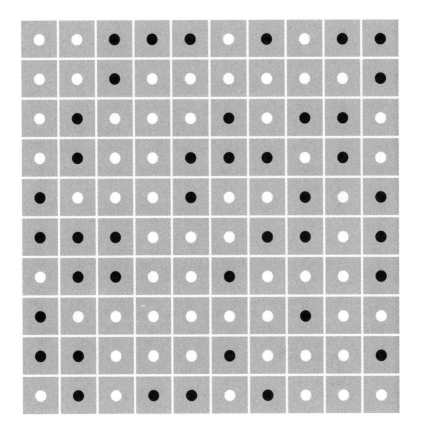

[SEE PAGE 516 FOR AN EXPLANATION OF WHAT RUBY SAW.]

Then she saw it: one row and one column in each grid had the *wrong* parity bit. The fourth row and ninth column in the first, and in the second . . .

She typed four numbers into the keypad:

4 9 1 2

A green light came on. And with a hiss, the door opened . . .

ACCESS APPROVED.
33 MINUTES GRANTED.

The whole room at first glance appeared to be plain white, white floor, white ceiling, white walls; another shiny white cube containing nothing. She ran her hand across the wall and as she did, the wall became color.

Lots of colors, each one a narrow vertical oblong.

She held her hand on one — a dark red. There was a pneumatic hiss and the red oblong slid out from the wall. The file was labeled: THE NEW DELHI AFFAIR. She tried another, an olive green: THE ITALIAN CONUNDRUM.

Ruby looked around the room. *So where to find information on Baker?*

There were no letters, no numbers. She trailed her hand along part of the wall and watched the files turn from shades of green through yellow, through orange, and to red. They glowed for a few seconds before fading back to white wall.

A color code?

On Froghorn's diagram was written FC1 = the spectrum.

File Code One was *the color spectrum.*

So how did this color code work?

Froghorn had said something about Mondays not being good because they were "viridian days." So viridian was a bad thing.

The question was, did Miles Froghorn see everything in terms of color?

Ruby knew that certain people mixed their senses up: the composer Messiaen perceived musical notes as different colors, and the author Nabokov saw letters as colors.

What if Froghorn is one of those people? she thought. *A synesthete? What if he associates colors with ideas? Like days or people?*

It would be another layer of code, and a clever one: anyone wanting to find a particular file would either need to have Froghorn with them or to know what color he had assigned to a file. . . . The trick, Ruby realized, was to figure out which color applied to which mission, or which agent: in this case, Baker. Or LB.

The files on Bradley Baker would be . . . where? What color would be associated with him? First of all, one had to think what he was. Dead, yes, but then no doubt a lot of people in these files had long since slipped away, so looking for colors associated with death or deadness was probably the wrong way to go.

To Ruby his name suggested brown — it was probably something to do with the name Baker conjuring up bread. *Dumb, Redfort, super dumb.* This felt like entirely the wrong avenue to explore — after all, she wasn't the code maker here, was she? Froghorn was. *So think like Froghorn.*

She thought about Baker. Froghorn had said he was like a "sun ray." So it was just possible that to Froghorn, Baker would be represented by gold or sunshine yellow. It took her a few tries to find the right shade, but it seemed she was correct in her thinking — Baker was filed under a golden yellow.

When she opened it, she saw there was a pattern of dots next to his name — a logo, perhaps?

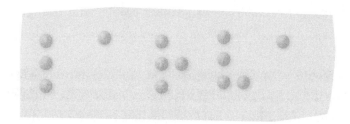

She took out the micro-reader and snapped a picture of it. Then she leafed through the file.

Everything in it seemed to relate to Baker's last flight. It seemed he was in training for some particular mission, though it was unclear exactly what that was. Most of the content was encrypted, and if she wanted to read it she would need to decode it, and that could take hours.

She looked at the clock. *Twenty-nine and counting* . . . No time.

She would have to copy the file so she could come back to this later.

Baker had been returning from ▮▮▮▮▮▮▮▮ when his craft had gotten into "difficulty" — it said nothing about his being shot down by friendly fire.

Come on, thought Ruby, *someone had to know about it.* She read on and saw that the destination Baker was flying to was also blanked.

There were some details about the crash; not a huge amount. It covered the weather conditions that night; it was October, cold but not stormy. It seemed Bradley Baker had been alone when his craft experienced what was thought to be a malfunction. This was the way it was written up, anyway.

```
the pilot died when his craft experienced mechanical
problems resulting in an engine fire and subsequent
explosion. The pilot, though highly experienced, was
unable to save himself due to the speed of the unfolding
calamity. Due to the magnitude of the explosion and force
of the impact, there was little wreckage that could be
retrieved from the crash site. No sign that the ejector
seat had been deployed and no possibility that the pilot
could have survived the consequent inferno.
```

There were several pictures of the crash site, all taken at night. Ruby was not surprised that Baker's body had not been recovered — the craft was just a mangled heap of steel; the fire had consumed everything it could.

It seemed there were layers of truths, or if you looked at it all another way: untruths. There was something cloak-and-dagger about the incident from the outset. On the very last page of the file was typed:

Professor Pinkerton? thought Ruby. Some blurry memory lit up and immediately faded. She shut her eyes to let her mind carry her to it, but all she could see was gray, the color gray.

She closed Baker's file and began to search for Pinkerton's. She hoped that Froghorn would be predictable enough to file it under the color pink. She wasn't far off with this guess. It took her just a few attempts to find the exact shade, a sort of chemistry lab pink, the color of manganese (II).

When she opened the file, her attention was caught by the black-and-white photograph of the man.

Professor Homer Pinkerton.

He looked young in the photograph, though of course there was no knowing when the picture had actually been taken and how long it had been buried deep in the Prism Vault.

Professor Pinkerton, it seemed, was not a full-time employee of Spectrum. He was a consultant and special scientific adviser. There was a whole lot of text detailing some of the projects he had contributed to, both before and after joining Spectrum as a consultant. There was more than she could easily read in a day, let alone six minutes.

She flipped through the pages until something caught her eye. This had to do with a discovery Pinkerton had made regarding what seemed from the unredacted text to be some kind of species of plant life, which appeared to hold amazing life-giving properties, increasing healthy life expectancy by a great number of years. The professor claimed that "the body's aging process is greatly slowed, so that a person of seventy would have the genetic age of a forty-year-old." He also asserted that "the brain's ability to store and process information is also improved by approximately double."

She scanned the following pages in an attempt to discover what this plant was, but she was soon distracted by another interesting thing. Pinkerton had been doing a great deal of research into memory erasure, primarily how it might one day be possible to extract uncomfortable, painful, and harmful memories from the human brain.

Pinkerton's research had been focused on patients who found themselves plagued and tormented by traumatic memories. The patients he'd studied were often the victims of terrible near-death experiences that had resulted in post-traumatic stress. The professor had discovered a way of plucking out and permanently removing memories that tortured the mind. He called this SME, or Specific Memory Extraction.

There was an intriguing line about this:

SME used notably to remove the memories of the participants in but the rest was blacked out. Ruby turned the page, but the majority of what was written here was also blacked out, and stamped across the page in large letters were the words:

RESTRICTED ACCESS:
LEVEL-TWO SECURITY REQUIRED

It was at that exact moment that Ruby caught sight of a clock, the flashing numerals silently counting down toward zero. It was reading 124 seconds now.

Ruby, you bozo!

No matter how interesting this professor's memory research was, she was forgetting her whole reason for being in this forsaken vault, namely to find out if LB was a cold-blooded murderer.

She had broken one of her rules:

RULE 48: DON'T GET DISTRACTED — FOCUS ON WHAT YOU GOTTA FOCUS ON.

She had a little over two minutes to copy as much of the Baker file and the Pinkerton file as she could and hightail it out of there. This she achieved with about 1.4 seconds to spare.

Scrabbling to her feet, she pushed the files back into their slots, slipped out of the vault, and leaned against the heavy door, relieved to hear the loud *thunk* as it sealed itself shut.

Getting *out* of Meteor Island was a lot less complicated than getting in. She climbed back down into the cube, which began to fill with water, and then she searched for the fly, put her finger over it, and the underwater door slid open and she was back in the ocean.

It was during her swim back to shore that her brain flashed up the fragment of memory once more: *the gray clapboard house on Cedarwood Drive.*

She muttered to herself as she heaved herself out of the chilly water.

Why? she wondered.

Ruby by now was about as tired as it seemed possible to get, and her limbs felt very heavy. She wished she still had the stupid pink bike. She wished she had any bike. Here she was, walking alone along the deserted coast road in the dark with a madman on the loose. Correction: a madman, *two* crazy ladies, and a traitorous mole who probably wanted her dead. The worst thing was she had the weirdest feeling someone was watching her.

Watch your back, Ruby, she thought.

CHAPTER 21
C.O.L.D.

UNSURPRISINGLY, RUBY WAS FEELING less than perky the next morning. Her legs ached and so did her arms; in fact, the *whole* of her ached.

She was grateful to have a note from Hitch that stated that Ruby had been battling a cold and had spent the previous day propped up in bed, sipping ginger tea while trying to study. He wrote how Ruby had insisted on coming to class today because she had promised to hand in the work Mrs. Drisco assigned her.

No one, not even Mrs. Drisco, could argue with that.

Ruby spent the day waiting for the school bell to clang so she could hurry home and take a look at what she had managed to glean from her thirty-three minutes inside the Prism Vault.

It was unfortunate, therefore, to find Mrs. Digby in a very chatty mood and quite determined to talk about Cousin Emily, who it seemed had both a bluebottle infestation and a mold problem in her apartment. *You wouldn't believe the smell!* And she was being moved to a new place because *it is just not possible to pay that kind of sky-high rent and live with those low-down creatures, to say nothing of the fungus.*

Ordinarily, Ruby would have been only too happy to discuss the ins and outs of pest control and listen to Mrs. Digby's lurid descriptions of just how bad they smelled—*they would have a skunk holding his nose*—but not tonight. Right now, all Ruby wanted to do was to open up the copied Ghost Files and discover what secret they held.

"Those creatures get everywhere," said Mrs. Digby. "You don't always spot them, but they're tiptoeing about all over the place." She shook her head. "And the damp and the rot." She made a face to show her displeasure. "There's no missing that."

They chatted for around twenty-five minutes, by which time Mrs. Digby insisted it was time for Ruby to eat supper, which Ruby duly did.

At 7:30 p.m. the doorbell sounded, and Mrs. Digby began telling Lou Patchett, who had come to clip Bug's claws, the whole story of the bluebottles and mold right from the beginning, and Ruby was able to excuse herself and slip up to her room. She was careful to lock the door, not that Mrs. Digby ever came in unannounced, but if there was one thing Ruby had learned in recent months, it was that you can't be too careful. She had a rule about it, and these days it seemed more fitting than ever:

RULE 9: THERE IS ALWAYS A CHANCE THAT SOMEONE, SOMEWHERE IS WATCHING YOU.

She took down her posters and cards and bulletin board

and then trained the micro-reader at the expanse of now-blank wall.

But when she pressed the reveal switch on the tiny gadget, what was projected was nothing but blurred text, overlapping letters and numbers in dense lines. The files were scrambled, designed to be copy-proof.

Ruby cursed several times and kicked at a volleyball that happened to be sitting in the middle of the room. It bounced off the door and smacked Ruby in the face, which hurt quite a bit, and she cursed again.

The commotion brought Mrs. Digby upstairs.

"What in tarnation is going on, child?"

"Nothing," said Ruby.

"That's a lot of ugly words coming from your mouth all for the sake of nothing," said Mrs. Digby. "Heaven knows what Lou thought." She peered at Ruby. "What happened to your face?"

"I got hit by a ball," said Ruby.

"I'll keep my thoughts to myself," said the housekeeper.

"I appreciate that, Mrs. Digby."

"Cursing at your age," muttered the housekeeper. "What will people think?"

"That I learned it from you?" said Ruby.

"An old lady's allowed to swear; folks expect it when one gets as aged as I am."

"You know that's not true, don't you?"

Mrs. Digby collected a few dirty plates and cups and walked

toward the door. "By the way," she said, "I'm dropping Bug at the Crews' in the morning because I won't have a minute to walk him tomorrow. You can pick him up on your way home."

"Sure," said Ruby.

"Oh, and you'll be needing your thermals tomorrow. I predict a freeze."

Once the housekeeper was gone, Ruby sat at her desk and wrote down everything she could remember reading in the Ghost Files.

Pinkerton and his life-prolonging plant discovery.

His development of a Specific Memory Extractor.

She knew Baker was on a training mission, but had no idea for what.

But she felt none the wiser about his crash — *had* LB actually been the one to pull the trigger?

And what was the meaning of those dots?

Next time she would be sure to take a notebook.

RULE 11: EXPECT THE UNEXPECTED AND BE READY FOR ANYTHING.

How had she managed to forget that one? Even the Boy Scouts had *that* rule down.

Despite a pretty good night's sleep, Ruby Redfort, aspiring field agent and avid seeker of action, would have much preferred to stay in bed the next morning. Given the choice, she would have chosen to stay in bed the whole day long. She would *even* have chosen to be infected with the Crew family flu rather than endure another day of Spectrum cold-weather survival training. In fact, she was pretty sure the Spectrum cold-weather survival training would lead to her being infected with the Crew family flu.

But, as any spy recruiter will tell you, you do not get to pick and choose your fate when you enroll as a secret agent; you take it on the chin and suffer the consequences.

Ruby had already been plunged into icy water. Today she would be helicoptered up to the mountains in order to be plunged into snow.

"Kid, you're going to love it," said Hitch. "Think of it as a snow day, no school—just eight hours of horsing around."

"Horsing around?" said Ruby. "Since when does Sam Colt let anyone horse around?"

"You have a point," conceded Hitch. "It's going be misery, but just focus on how you'll feel when it's over."

Apparently, it was a *good* thing to know how it would feel to be buried alive in snow. "If it happens, you need to know how you are going to react," said Colt.

Probably by passing out, thought Ruby.

Froghorn was with them again, and Ruby gathered his presence was due to the reduced number of agent personnel at Spectrum 8—it was all hands on deck as far as cover was concerned.

It was clear from his expression that he found being in

charge of handing out equipment rather demeaning. It didn't escape Ruby's notice that he was no longer wearing that dumb pen around his neck. Was that what Hitch had told him at Desolate Cove: take it off—leave it back at HQ? Hitch being Hitch was bound to see it as some kind of safety hazard. *Probably worried the potato head was going to strangle himself,* she thought.

Sam Colt taught the trainees a few of the basics:

C **Keep Clothing Clean.** Clothes encrusted with dirt and grease lose some of their insulating power.

O **Avoid Overheating.** "Might sound crazy when you're hunkering down in a snow shelter, but too much heat can be a problem," said Colt. "When you sweat, you make your clothes damp, which stops them from insulating you properly. And when the sweat evaporates, it drains heat from your body. Try to keep some air circulating."

L **Wear Loose and Wear Layers.** Tight clothing restricts circulation and increases the risk of frostbite. Layers create pockets of air for insulation.

D **Keep Clothing Dry.** Wet clothes can be the death of you—literally. Make sure to brush yourself down before entering a shelter, as any snow left on your clothes will melt and make you wet, which will make you dead.

"One small but vital piece of equipment is a sun visor," said the survival trainer. "If you don't happen to have one with you, you can make your own from a piece of bark." This was apparently the first thing to do if one found oneself suddenly in a snowy cold environment: otherwise, the light bouncing off all the white would quickly blind you.

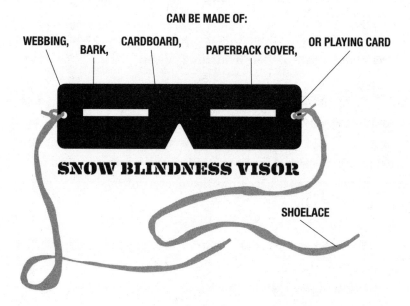

CAN BE MADE OF:

WEBBING, BARK, CARDBOARD, PAPERBACK COVER, OR PLAYING CARD

SNOW BLINDNESS VISOR

SHOELACE

After that, Ruby and the other trainees learned how to make a snow shelter. If you were lucky you might find a cave; if not, you might want to look for a fallen branch and build your shelter against it.

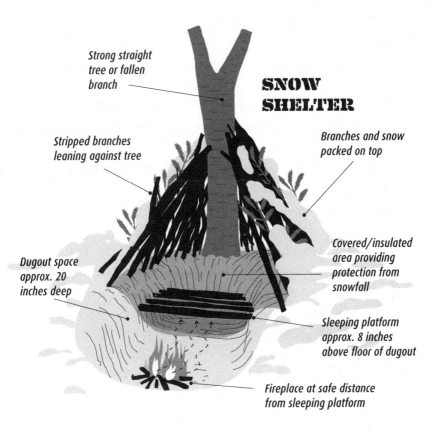

Strong straight tree or fallen branch

SNOW SHELTER

Branches and snow packed on top

Stripped branches leaning against tree

Covered/insulated area providing protection from snowfall

Dugout space approx. 20 inches deep

Sleeping platform approx. 8 inches above floor of dugout

Fireplace at safe distance from sleeping platform

"If you're out in the snow wilderness for a lengthy time," Samuel Colt began, "then you might want to make yourself a fur coat — some of you might find this unpalatable, but you have to keep warm if you want to walk out of there alive. It's just the law of survival."

But the most unpalatable part for Ruby was the whole avalanche thing. She stepped into the hole all right, but as the snow was shoveled in over her head, she began to panic, and there was nothing she could do to control it.

"It's OK, Redfort," said Colt, gripping her hand and lifting her out. "This is just something we're going to have to work on. Mind over matter; you'll get there."

Ruby nodded, but she didn't think there was ever going to be a day when being buried alive was going to be something that she would be able to overcome.

Ruby had asked to be dropped on 72nd Street. Despite the cold and the fact that her brain had almost frozen over, it had not slipped her mind that she needed to pick up her dog from the Crew residence.

She was looking forward to getting home, though. Mrs. Digby would prepare Ruby one of her Mrs. Digby hot-chocolate drinks, and she would once again be able to feel her feet or at least her legs.

Just make it to Clancy's, pick up Bug, and get home, Ruby.

She pictured herself crawling up the front steps, a heartbeat away from hypothermia. Perhaps Hitch would be there to carry her near-lifeless body into the house. . . . No, not Hitch, she didn't want to see *him;* he would probably send her back out again for more of this insane training. What was he trying to do to her, kill her?

She was making her way through the back alley between 72nd Street and Flaubert, mumbling these grumbled thoughts, the alley being the quickest route to Clancy's, and getting to Clancy's was all Ruby could focus on. So lost in thought was she that she almost didn't hear the faint hiss from the shadows.

She stopped — was it something or was it nothing?

Silence.

Nothing, she concluded.

She told herself to get it together, or, as her **RULE 8** had it: **DON'T LET YOUR IMAGINATION RUN AWAY WITH YOU OR YOU MIGHT WELL LOSE THE PLOT.**

She walked on past the trash cans and Dumpsters, keeping her eyes trained on the street ahead; there was nothing to worry about. . . . And then came the sound of a bottle smashing on the cobbles. Her heartbeat quickened.

"Anyone there?" she called.

A cat ran out of the darkness and leaped onto the wall.

She closed her eyes. *Get a grip, Redfort.* She really shouldn't be walking down dark alleys if it was going to get her freaking out like this. But then came that whispered sound again. It definitely seemed human.

She tapped the Escape Watch, which triggered a bright beam of light to shine from it. She directed it into the shadows and over the stacked-up crates and piles of garbage. She heard a noise behind her and turned to see a figure trundling a shopping cart across the top of the alley. *Mrs. Beesman?* she wondered. But in the dark, one old lady pushing a shopping cart looked very much like another.

She was about to move on, using her watch flashlight to make one more sweep of the alley, when she saw it. It was chalked on the ground, freshly written, she guessed, because the chalk was only just beginning to bleed into the damp surface of the alleyway. It was hard to make it out in the dark, but when she did, she saw it was a message and she could be in no doubt that the message was for her and her alone:

Beware the child who yearned to be Larva, disguised as a fly, but emerged a spider.

Ruby had no intention of hanging around, but her legs had become sort of rubbery, and she tripped and went sprawling forward, her coat now tangled in a section of chain-link fence that ran down one side of the alleyway.

She tried to yank herself free but couldn't.

She pulled at the zip, slid herself out of the parka, and left it where it lay ensnared.

Then she ran and ran and she didn't look back.

CHAPTER 22
Something Remembered

RUBY ARRIVED AT THE CREWS' PLACE, teeth chattering and unable to feel her feet.

The door was opened by eleven-year-old Nancy.

"Hey, Ruby, I guess you've come to pick up Bug?"

Ruby nodded, almost too cold to speak.

"Clance!" Nancy yelled. "Ruby's here. By the way, where's your coat? It's cold out, you know."

"Yeah, Nancy, I noticed that too."

Clancy appeared, followed by Bug and the Crews' own little dog, Dolly, who trotted along behind. Ruby reached out to pat the husky, but her hands were so numb she could not feel the dog's fur.

"Are you OK? You've gone sorta blue," said Clancy.

"Where's your coat?" said Olive, skipping across the hall.

"*Oh*, am I *not* wearing one?" said Ruby, her tone sarcastic, though Olive seemed unaware of this.

"No," said Olive. "My mom says it's stupid to go outside in winter without a coat."

"*You* should talk," said Nancy. "You are always doing stupid things."

"Get inside, Rube," said Clancy, pulling her into the house and slamming the door shut.

"My fingers are actual icicles," said Ruby.

"You want a ginger tea?" asked Clancy. "It might thaw you out."

"Sure," said Ruby. "Right now I'll take anything."

"Did something happen?" asked Clancy.

"You could say that," said Ruby. "Though where to start?"

They sat up in Clancy's room drinking tea. With a woolen blanket wrapped around her and two hot-water bottles under her feet, Ruby was slowly beginning to thaw.

She told Clancy about the survival training and her failure to complete the avalanche task.

"Give yourself a break, Ruby. I mean, it is actually your deepest, most profoundest fear," said Clancy.

"The point is, that doesn't matter an iota; fear—whether deep, profound, or just regular—has to be handled. What if I end up buried alive somewhere and I find I just can't cope?" She looked at him, her expression deadly serious. "I mean, I'd be a goner, right?"

"You'd handle it, Rube. I know you would."

"Thanks," she said, "but I think I'd rather come face-to-face with a bear than be buried alive."

"Did they teach you that?" asked Clancy.

"What's to teach?" said Ruby.

This was a running thing between the two of them. Ruby had compiled a lot of rules, 80 in all, and **RULE 79** was the rule for bears. It was more of a joke than a rule, really, one that she and Clancy shared: **WHAT TO DO IF YOU MEET A BEAR — WISH YOU HADN'T!** The reason being that if you met a bear, there were a number of ways you might persuade it to back off, but only the bear knew which of these approaches was going to work.

"I've been thinking about that whole bear problem, actually," said Clancy.

"Oh, yeah?"

"Yeah," said Clancy. "What you have to do is go on instinct; you have to use your sixth sense — if you don't, you're dead."

"And what if you don't have a sixth sense?" asked Ruby. "What then?"

"Everyone has a sixth sense," said Clancy. "It's just most people have forgotten how to tune in to it."

"OK, so suppose I tune in and I go with my gut and I'm wrong because I just feel it wrong."

Clancy shrugged. "Then I guess you're dead, but at least you can die reassured that you'd be dead anyway. Tuning in to your sixth sense just gives you a better chance; I can't promise you that it will save your life."

"Great," said Ruby, "truly terrific. Personally, I think what you gotta do is read the signs."

"*The signs?*" spluttered Clancy.

"Check out the bear's behavior, what signals he's giving you."

"You read bear signals now?" said Clancy.

Ruby ignored the ridicule in his question. "You just gotta react to what he's giving you. Is it curiosity? Is it fear? Or is it simply that there might be something on your person that he wants to eat?"

"What, like your head?" suggested Clancy.

What they did both agree on is who would be the person most likely to save you if you were unfortunate enough to find yourself in this bear clinch situation.

"Mrs. Digby," said Clancy.

"Without a doubt," said Ruby.

The bear problem didn't apply only to bears. It applied to all people or problems that were unpredictable. *It's something of a bear problem,* Ruby would say when she just couldn't figure out how things might go.

Some problems started off as bears, and then, given time, one could see how they might be tackled, but others remained unpredictable and unsolvable. The Count was perhaps the biggest bear problem of them all.

"If there are bears around, maybe you should be wearing that barrette of yours," suggested Clancy. "You might need rescuing."

"What do you mean?" said Ruby. "I always wear the fly barrette—see?" She went to pat it with her hand, but it wasn't there.

"Oh, jeepers, I lost it!"

"No, no, it's there," said Clancy. "It's caught in your sweater."

"Boy, that's a relief," said Ruby. "I thought maybe it had fallen out when I tripped and got tangled in that fence."

"You got tangled in a fence?" said Clancy.

"Actually, yeah," said Ruby. "My coat got caught up in it, and I just sorta left it there."

"Why?" said Clancy. "Why would you just leave your coat?"

"I got spooked by something," said Ruby.

"What kinda something?" said Clancy.

"Something a bit like a bear," said Ruby.

Clancy looked at her, his eyes round as saucers.

"He left a message for me," said Ruby.

"He? You mean the Count?" said Clancy.

Ruby nodded. "Uh-huh."

"You're sure?" asked Clancy

"I smelled his cologne."

"So what was the message?"

"It said: *Beware the child who yearned to be Larva, disguised as a fly, but emerged a spider.*"

"Creepy." Clancy shivered. "What does it mean?"

"I have no idea, except for the fly part, which stands for agent, and I guess spider could be fly killer."

"Where was it, the message?" said Clancy.

"In that back alley that joins Flaubert."

"You walked down that alley at *night*? When it's *dark*?" said Clancy. "What are you, on some mission to be murdered?"

"It's not that bad," said Ruby. "It's just a back alley full of trash cans and garbage."

"And, it would seem, murderers," added Clancy.

"OK," said Ruby. "Maybe it was a little dumb."

"What you have got to ask him," said Clancy, "if you ever get the chance to speak to him, that is, is: Who *is* this boss of his?"

"I'll be sure to ask him next time I run into him."

"I'm not kidding," said Clancy. "You need to know."

"Seriously?" said Ruby. "Shouldn't you be saying, *Whatever you do, don't run into this guy again?*"

"Ordinarily yes, but I have a feeling that's no longer an option. I have a hunch you have to face facts here — you figure this out or you move to a secret bunker somewhere."

"I hate to say it, Clance, but I know you're right."

It was as she was walking home, hands pushed deep into the pockets of Clancy's snow jacket, that she felt something dig into her palm.

"Ow," she squealed.

The dog looked alarmed, alert for danger.

"It's OK, Bug."

Ruby pulled out her hand; a tiny bead of blood was there in her palm.

What?

She fumbled in the pocket and out fell the pin.

A small circle of white, barely visible against the snow that had recently fallen.

Her pin.

Looking at it lying there next to the curb shook up another memory from the depths of her brain. This time she saw a yellow leaf flutter through the air. She stood stock-still, trying hard to join the image of the yellow leaf to something else and anchor it to something real. She had found the pin a long time ago on the street near her house. She used to keep it pinned to the inside of her coat.

It had begun, this habit of secrecy, because she had not wanted her parents to take away this "found thing." She, being an intelligent child although not yet three, knew that once her parents saw its sharp spike of a pin they would most certainly confiscate it and no doubt bury it deep in the trash bin.

Later on, as Ruby got older, the pin had become a sort of charm, something she liked to have with her. And then in June, she had lent it to Clancy when he'd had to take part in the spring swimathon. She had persuaded him that it was some kind of talisman and would protect him from sharks and sea monsters, and generally ward off nibblers. He had believed her. It worked.

She had all but forgotten it, the pin, replaced now by *actual* lucky charms in the form of high-tech Spectrum gadgets: the voice thrower, the Escape Watch, the fly barrette, and a whole lot more.

Now she looked at the metal pin with renewed interest, a white circle embossed with random bumps. Her dog was still looking at her, waiting to know what was next.

Something lost, something found.

"Come on, Bug," she said. "Let's go."

When she reached Cedarwood Drive, Ruby did not make straight for Green-Wood House. Instead she walked the whole length of the street, up one side and then down the other. She concentrated hard, trying to remember the place she had found this circle of tin. She walked up the road and down the sidewalk until she arrived just outside the gray clapboard house with its white picket fence, and flash went that memory.

Gray house, yellow leaf, white circular pin.

Slowly, she turned and crossed to her house and began walking up the steps. Bug began to bark, and Ruby slowed as she saw something lying by the front door. She could not make out what the thing was. She got closer. Not a living creature. Stranger than that. A shiver went down her spine as she realized that it was in fact her *coat.*

CHAPTER 23
A Man's Best Friend

MRS. DIGBY'S VOICE GREETED RUBY as she stepped into the hall. "Child? Is that you?"

"Uh-huh, yeah," called Ruby.

She hung Clancy's coat on the peg and went upstairs to the kitchen, where she found Mrs. Digby dicing apples.

"Did you happen to notice anyone outside?" asked Ruby. "Earlier, I mean — like an hour ago?"

Mrs. Digby shook her head. "I don't spend my time standing on the stoop looking out into the darkness," she said. "I keep the door shut in winter and the lights lit. Best not ponder on what lurks out in the gloom."

Ruby went to the window and peered into the dark. A few houses were lit up brightly, but most people had their curtains drawn against the chill. From here she could see the little gray clapboard house.

"Who used to live there?" she asked.

"Where?" said Mrs. Digby

"In the gray house just down the street, where the Joneses were living until about a week ago."

"Why, the Hendons," said Mrs. Digby. "Remember they had that awful parrot? Mr. Parker threatened to strangle it, and plenty would have been grateful to him."

"No, before the Hendons; I mean a long time ago."

The housekeeper gave her a suspicious look. "What's got you asking that?" she said.

Ruby shrugged. "I don't know, just wondered is all. Maybe because I was thinking about the tornado and how that little house was lucky not to be whirled away."

Mrs. Digby nodded. "That house is lucky, all right: survived earthquake *and* tornado."

"Have you ever been inside?" asked Ruby.

"Oh, yes," said Mrs. Digby. "Oftentimes back when it belonged to the old gentleman — I spent many a sweltering day sitting on that porch, getting a little shade."

"Who was he, the old gentleman?"

"His name was Mr. Pinkerton," said Mrs. Digby.

"P i n k e r t o n?" said Ruby slowly, letting the name tumble around her brain.

"Pinkerton, that's right. He was a nice old fellow. We saw eye to eye on things."

"Was he a professor?" asked Ruby.

"Why would you ask me that?" she said. "No, he was just plain old regular Mr. Pinkerton, though I'll admit he was as *smart* as any professor I ever met — not that I'm sure I've met a whole clutch of them. Educated is what you'd call him, traveled the world, so he told me. He seemed to know everything, memory like an elephant."

"How come *I* don't remember him?" asked Ruby.

"I don't see how you could," said the housekeeper. "You weren't much more than the size of a turnip when you first met him. It was the day the old Fairbank house was turned into matchsticks during the earthquake of 1960. Mr. Pinkerton took us in for a few nights. We became firm friends after that." She shook her head. "It's a real shame he left, quite sudden it was, a few days before your first chess tournament: you were not even three. He'd promised he'd come along because he'd been coaching you."

"He had?"

"Yes." She nodded. "He said you had an aptitude for it; he said you had brains. Said you were the most interesting infant he had ever studied — *met,* I think is what he meant; he always talked peculiar."

"So where did he go?" asked Ruby.

Mrs. Digby stood, hands on hips, gazing out the window at the moonless sky. "Now, you got me there," she said. "I really don't know — all I heard was he was dead."

"Who told you that?"

"The sheriff," said Mrs. Digby. "The police investigated his disappearance, and one day they turned up evidence that suggested poor old Mr. Pinkerton was no more. I wasn't so surprised."

"Why not?" asked Ruby.

"He was a broken man," said Mrs. Digby. "After . . . what was it called . . . what was its name?"

"What was whose name?" asked Ruby.

"That dog of his, name something like *Nemosign;* I never could say it right. . . ."

"Mnemosyne?" asked Ruby.

"That was it!" said Mrs. Digby. "How did you know?"

"I sort of guessed," said Ruby.

Mrs. Digby tutted. "Why people insist on calling animals stupid names is beyond me."

"She was the Greek goddess of memory," said Ruby.

"Who was?" asked Mrs. Digby.

"Mnemosyne," said Ruby.

"If you say so," said the old lady. "But all I know is, when that mutt disappeared, that was that." She sighed. "The heart and soul went out of him — never saw a person more chewed up about an animal, a small one at that."

"It ran off? Was lost?"

"That dog was too loyal to leave and too smart to get itself lost; smartest dog I ever met. My old pa used to say, the only dog worth its keep is a smart dog."

"Like Bug," said Ruby.

"Smarter," said Mrs. Digby. "You know, I taught it that trick, the one my pa taught my hound and I taught Bug."

"The go find trick?" said Ruby.

"Yes," said Mrs. Digby. "I'll tell you what, that mutt learned it in one day flat."

"What type of dog was it?"

"The small and pointless kind, looked funny, like a cat—fluffy thing, big bulgy eyes, black nose." Mrs. Digby made a face.

"Pekingese?" guessed Ruby.

"Pekingese." Mrs. Digby tutted. "He always did keep that breed—photographs everywhere of Pinkerton and those darned Pekingeses, decades' worth of them, and each one looked the spit of the one before. If an uglier breed of dog exists, then I've not seen it and nor would I want to."

"So what do you think happened to Mnemosyne?"

The housekeeper sighed. "Well, the reason it hit the old fellow so hard was because the dog wasn't *lost*, she was stolen, dognapped while Mr. Pinkerton was helping some truck driver with directions."

In the far reaches of Ruby's mind, a memory was stirring.

She saw again the yellow leaf whirling through a cold blue sky. "When was this?" asked Ruby. "What time of year?"

Mrs. Digby looked up and tapped her head. "There you got me." The old lady thought for a moment. "November, I think—no, it was October; I know that because I was preparing pumpkins for Halloween."

"Was it windy that day?" Ruby asked.

"How should I ever remember that?" said the housekeeper, looking at the girl like she was an egg short of a dozen. "But what

I do know is that it wasn't any wind that stole that dog away, it was a moving truck."

"That's kinda *weird,* isn't it?" said Ruby. "Stealing a dog, I mean, unless it was some sort of pedigree pooch."

"The only reason to steal it," said Mrs. Digby, "was to make that poor man suffer."

"Suffer how?" asked Ruby.

"By taking what was most precious to him. It was all he had."

"No family?" asked Ruby.

"Not a one, but he was a good, kind soul, that man, the only person who ever managed to befriend Mrs. Beesman."

"Mrs. Beesman?" spluttered Ruby. "How did he manage that?" Ruby had never gotten much more than a grunt out of the woman.

"Charm," said Mrs. Digby. "He had a lot of charm. And I'm not talking about a superficial, meaningless sort of charm — I'm saying he was through and through a good sort."

Ruby thought about Mr. Pinkerton and imagined the grief he must have suffered at the loss of Mnemosyne — how *she* would cope if she ever lost Bug. Bug, who was more than just the family pet. A more loyal soul would be hard to find, a hound who would risk his life for hers, *had* risked his life for hers.

Mrs. Digby, once again picking up her chopping knife: "I can't say I don't miss him. He was *the* most interesting fellow, smart as anything and twice as amiable, that Homer Pinkerton."

"Did you say Homer?" said Ruby.

"Well, that was his name," said Mrs. Digby. "Homer Pinkerton — unusual name, I'll grant you."

Mrs. Digby was still talking when Ruby was halfway up the stairs.

There was the connection. The chances of this Homer Pinkerton not being the Spectrum Homer Pinkerton she'd read about in the Ghost Files seemed very remote.

Ruby sat at her desk at the top of the house, took out her notebook, and added Homer Pinkerton and his dog Mnemosyne to her map of names.

```
Homer Pinkerton: discovered a plant that
enhances the memory and prolongs healthy
life.

While working at Spectrum he developed a
device that allows single memories to be
extracted from the brain without harm to
the patient.

Question:
Who had sought to make this man suffer?
```

She pondered this before writing:

```
Could the Count somehow be part of this?
```

As she stared at her notes, her mind cast back to her conversation with Frederick Lutz. Hadn't he mentioned a man called Homer? An inventor who had worked alongside the Count back in the early days, when Count von Leyden had sought only to thrill with horror rather than kill.

She found the movie encyclopedia that Frederick had lent her and, lifting it onto her desk, she thumbed through it until she reached the index. Then she searched the names, "N, O, P . . . P . . . P!"

And there it was:

Homer Pinkerton, *props and special effects. Worked on a number of films alongside Victor von Leyden.*

Everything was connected.

It wasn't that Junior Agent
Baker wasn't friendly.
He was, he was more than nice,
he was super nice. . . .

It wasn't that he wasn't generous or helpful or skilled at working as part of a team, because he was all these things. In fact, he seemed to have no flaws, not one. He was perfect, horribly perfect, and the kid from Colwin City found it was impossible not to be eaten up with a desire to see him fail, and the nicer Junior Agent Baker was, the more the kid hated him.

It was during the final field test that the kid had a vision of how things could be, would be, if only the boy, Bradley Baker, were out of the picture; if only Bradley Baker was wiped out, and wiped out permanently.

An accident, a stupid mistake, dumb luck, a regrettable but very fatal incident.

CHAPTER 24
Hypocrea Asteroidi

THE VERY LAST THING RUBY WANTED TO DO at 4:00 a.m. that Saturday morning, aside from run into the Count again and perhaps be buried alive, was to get back into the freezing-cold ocean and swim across to the Observatory on Meteor Island. However, if she was going to find out more about LB and Baker, and what the link was between them and whatever was going down between Pinkerton, Spectrum, and the Count, then she didn't have a whole lot of choice.

This time she had brought with her a pencil and a notebook, which she zipped inside her Superskin.

She took the bus to Desolate Cove, swam the short distance to the rock, dived down to the underwater door, and held her breath while she waited for the question to pop up on the code panel.

CASSIOPEIA

She tapped in the constellation and the door slid open.

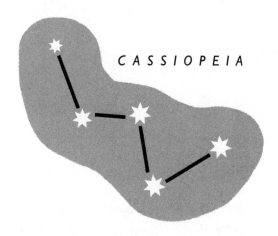

CASSIOPEIA

Once she was in the water chamber, she set about searching for the tiny fly image. When she found it, the chamber emptied and Ruby climbed the ladder to the vault room.

Ruby was faced with another error-correcting code — she wasted no time in figuring out which rows and columns had the wrong parity bits, and punched in the resulting four-digit number. The door swung open and she was in.

Ruby decided to return to the Pinkerton file first. She wanted to read the information she had failed to copy on her last visit. She thought perhaps if she read this, she might discover the connection between the professor and Baker. *Actually,* what she discovered was the name of the life-prolonging plant Homer Pinkerton had discovered. It was a fungus called *Hypocrea asteroidi,* something he had dubbed the Mars Mushroom, or the memory mushroom.

She took out her book, ready to make some notes, but when she pressed the pencil to the paper, nothing happened. Somehow the pencil had become useless, unable to make even a mark. *Not an accident*, thought Ruby — this was by design.

OK, don't get sidetracked, just get on with it, she told herself.

Ruby set down the pencil and notepad and instead drew on her memory skills.

She would have to absorb as much information as she possibly could and get out of there in the thirty-three minutes the clock had allowed her.

Why? thought Ruby. *Why the Mars Mushroom? Did Pinkerton believe this plant had actually arrived on Earth from Mars?* She read on and it seemed, *yes, he did.* She considered this for a moment. It wasn't so far-fetched; a lot of scientists believed that Earth was seeded by organic matter from outer space. Pinkerton was convinced that the fungus had arrived stored in an ancient meteorite that had hit Earth many hundreds of thousands or even hundreds of millions of years ago.

If Ruby allowed herself to think like Clancy, or rather to feel for answers like Clancy, then she would have to say there was something about Pinkerton's file that made her uneasy.

Was *he* troubled by Spectrum, or was it the other way around? Either way, there was something about the tone and wording that suggested there might have been some kind of rift or perhaps even a fervent disagreement between them.

But about what? Ruby wondered. She read on, and as she

digested what the file contained, it became apparent that part of the falling-out seemed to have to do with the lack of information on where this Mars Mushroom grew. Spectrum wanted to know; Pinkerton wouldn't say.

Why? thought Ruby. Why would this professor not want to share such a valuable discovery? A plant that could not only halve one's seeming biological age but also double the amount of memory and information one's brain could hold . . .

Could it be that Pinkerton wanted to protect humanity from this miraculous plant? Had he perhaps agonized about what might happen if the privileged few were able to purchase long life and heightened intelligence in exchange for thousands of dollars, perhaps even hundreds of thousands of dollars, so allowing society's luckiest to reap the benefits?

And what about his other breakthrough, his pioneering research into the erasure of traumatic memory? A power for good, or in the wrong hands, a power for evil. Did he wonder what might happen should either of these discoveries — the life-giver and the memory-taker — leak out into the wider world?

Or was it he who was the dark force here, seeking to wield power by holding on to his secrets and selling to the highest bidder?

Ruby considered this version, but it just didn't fit with Mrs. Digby's description of the nice old gentleman sitting on the porch, the charming fellow who was kind to everyone.

Mrs. Digby had rated him highly, and Mrs. Digby was a good judge of character.

This was as much as this file was going to tell her. . . . Except no, there was one other piece of information. That logo again, the same as the one stamped in Baker's file, and some letters this time too: JSRP, printed in sky blue and black.

JSRP

Underneath, it said:

PARTICIPATED IN THE JSRP CLEANUP OPERATION.

She ran her hands along the file wall until she found a blue file of the exact same color, but when she tried to pull it from the wall, a message flashed up on the control panel to the left of the door, declaring it was level-two access. She pressed the violet button and the panel revealed a keyboard.

File Code Two—Chromatic.

The keys for one chromatic scale were numbered.

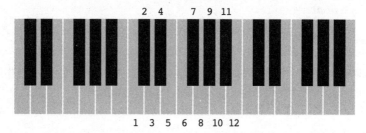

Below this was a button simply saying: ACCESS.

So Ruby pressed it.

A tune played. Then a robotic voice said, "Enter code now."

Ruby frowned. *Some kind of missing-note sequence?*

She pressed ACCESS again.

Another tune played. "Enter code now," said the voice. "One attempt remaining."

Ruby didn't need another attempt — she'd been listening carefully. Not for the first time, she was grateful to have perfect pitch, and she knew both the notes she had heard and the sequence they were following: the Mongian shuffle.*

Quickly, she pressed the keys for the notes she *hadn't* heard, the final four notes in the sequence: 2, 11, 1, 12.

A beep, a hiss, and the file was released. She pulled it from the wall.

JSRP was printed on the cover, and underneath the letters was that pattern of dots again, this time embossed on the paper. *Not a logo,* thought Ruby, *a language. Braille.*

*FOR AN EXPLANATION OF WHAT RUBY WORKED OUT HERE, SEE PAGE 520.

She read each letter: together they spelled LARVAE.

Larvae were undeveloped flies. Spectrum used the fly as its symbol for active agents. So was the word "larvae" being used here as the collective term for junior spies?

Could this be what the "JS" in "JSRP" stood for? And what was the "RP"—a recruitment program, perhaps?

Then she thought back to the chalk message: *Beware the child who yearned to be Larva.* Did something go wrong with one of these junior spies?

Though much of the file was encrypted, it *was* possible to conclude that Spectrum had indeed once upon a time recruited children, intending to train them up as agents, she supposed. The only other child agent Ruby had *ever* heard anyone talk about was Bradley Baker. She had not been aware that there was a whole troop of these spy kids—why had no one ever told her? But it seemed that Bradley's successful transition from tiny recruit to teenage fully fledged agent had made an impression. And so six years after Baker's recruitment, Spectrum had decided to roll out the program. They had found their recruits by printing what appeared to be kids' quizzes and puzzles on cereal boxes and milk cartons. However, to the genius child it was only too obvious what they were looking at. These were no ordinary puzzles but in fact highly sophisticated, highly secret application forms.

The next surprise was that this exciting-sounding program was abandoned only months after it had been set up. This was due to a near-tragic incident that had taken place during an overseas training exercise. There was a report on this drama that had led to the dissolving of the JSRP.

It detailed a story of attempted murder, of how one agent had tried to murder another. It would have been an unpleasant enough tale had these agents been beyond school age, but the fact that they were both still children added an extra twist to the gruesome story.

It had happened in the northern territories of Australia, crocodile country. It had been set up to look like an accident. The recruits were striking camp and planning to paddle upriver. The victim had been busy loading his raft with his camping gear when somehow the rope that moored it became untied. When he reached for his paddle, he found it wasn't there. Not only was he now heading for the rapids, but his raft was taking on water—someone had scuttled it. Had he not been rescued, his raft would have sailed him over the waterfall, where he would surely have drowned or, perhaps worse still, his sinking raft would have landed him in the river where the crocodiles swam.

While this drama was unfolding, another was taking place—the screams of a boy who had apparently fallen into the shallows but managed somehow to scrabble onto one of the rafts. He had incurred a life-threatening injury from a fifteen-foot crocodile, but he was lucky—his cries had alerted rescue, and he was dragged from the river before he could be taken by the reptile. The boy suffered severe shock and could not be questioned about the incident.

One of the strange things about this report was the lack of information when it came to the individuals involved.

Only two of the junior agents were named.

The first was the victim of the sabotage, thirteen-year-old Bradley Baker. The second, the boy who was almost swallowed by the crocodile, was named as Art Hitchen Zachery.

Ruby paused when she read this. *Could it be . . . ?* she wondered. It seemed unlikely, but it could be, couldn't it? The name was so similar. *It* could *be Hitch.* But then why wouldn't he have told her? What was really interesting about the report was how Bradley Baker had been saved. It was not due to his skill or experience as a field agent, or to some lucky river current carrying him to shore. It had been an incredible fluke.

A local kid had been camping out on the riverbank, fishing or some such. This kid had seen it all and raised the alarm; not only that, but had bravely climbed across the rocks and dragged the unconscious boy up and out of the water.

Question: Who *were* these kids?

Who had sought to kill, and who to save?

Beware the child who yearned to be Larva,
disguised as a fly, but emerged a spider.

Ruby searched the rest of the JSRP files, hoping to find a name, a clue to who might be responsible for the attempted murder of Bradley Baker.

By the time she was two-thirds through, it occurred to her that she had yet to see the face of a girl staring back from one of those inch-sized squares of photographic paper. Had yet to read a name that clearly belonged to someone who was not male.

All these Larvae recruits had been taken on twenty years before Ruby was born. *A sign of the times,* she thought. Not such a great time to be a girl if you were the sort of girl who liked action, adventure, or even the chance of a challenging job.

Ruby's eye caught sight of the clock on the wall.

:10

Geez, gotta fly.

:09

She grabbed the file.

:08

Pushed it into the slot.

:07

Snatched up her notebook from the floor.

:06

Where is the door's release switch??

:05

Don't panic.

:04

Switch found, door opening triggered . . .

:03

Tripping, almost falling . . .

:02

Pushing through the vault door, door closure triggered . . .

:01

Thunk.

Sinking to floor, breathing heavily.

"I'm outta here."

CHAPTER 25
Mushrooms from Mars

IT WAS APPROXIMATELY SIX A.M. when Ruby returned home. She fixed the DO NOT DISTURB sign to her door and had barely crawled into bed when the lobster phone began to ring.

"Rube, it's us, your *mère* and *père*."

"*Bonjour, c'est moi, vôtre fille, Ruby.*"

"Hello?"

"Howdy."

"We're coming home!"

"*Quand?*"

"Bless you."

"No, when are you coming home?"

"*Mardi.*"

"Tuesday?"

"No, Sunday."

"You mean *Dimanche*?"

"I thought that meant dinner."

"No, it means Sunday."

"Oh."

"*C'est merveilleux nouvelles.*"

Silence.

"This is wonderful news!"

"*Oui*, we agree! Can't wait to see you, bye, bye, bye."

"*Au revoir, au revoir, au revoir.*"

Ruby found herself unable to drift back to sleep because she was going over and over what she knew about Bradley Baker. It seemed to her that the two most significant things that had happened during his life were the way he had died and the way he had almost died. Of course, he had also had that nasty near-death encounter with the Count, but this, though traumatic and certainly terrifying, was not nearly as sinister as being killed by one of your own. So if LB had been the woman responsible for ending his days by destroying his aircraft, then who was responsible for *attempting* to end his days at the crocodile rapids? Why would a kid want another kid dead? Jealousy, envy, ambition? Could it be that simple?

And why might LB have decided to terminate Baker's life? She shuddered; the phrase "terminate his life" gave her the chills. How much easier, how much more palatable, to consider this agent's life being *terminated*, like a machine being switched off; *much more* palatable, say, than issuing orders to have him killed in cold blood. Either way, the question still remained: Why?

And then there was the question of what linked Baker to Pinkerton. And what Pinkerton's involvement had been in this "JSRP cleanup operation." If she wanted to know, then she was going to have to go back.

Oh, geez! she thought.

The one thing she *could* do without having to swim back to Meteor Island was to see if she could find something out on these memory mushrooms from Mars, and she knew just who to ask. She decided it could wait a day: the rest of Saturday she would devote to sleeping.

When she arrived at Little Mountain Side the following morning, there was something of a commotion just up the hill from the grocer's store. A whole crowd of people had gathered there, and they were all looking up as if searching the sky. Curious, Ruby wandered along to see what the attraction was. What she saw was a man climbing what looked to be a pretty unclimbable tree. He was perhaps seventy or eighty feet off the ground.

"He's got it!" shouted a man.

Got what? thought Ruby.

It was only when the climber got a whole lot closer to the ground that Ruby saw he was clutching some kind of animal.

"Is that a cat?" said Ruby.

"Uh-huh," said the woman next to her, "that's Ginger, all right."

"Who's that with it?" asked Ruby.

"Why, that's Mo from Daily's," said the woman. "Isn't he magnificent?"

"That's one word for it, I guess," said Ruby.

Applause broke out as Mo reached earth, and people walked

over to shake his hand and slap him on the back. Ruby waited until the fuss had died down and then followed him back to the store.

"Quite the action hero, aren't we?" said Ruby.

"It's been mewing all night," said Mo. "Someone had to get that fur-ball down."

He passed the cat to Ruby. "Here, take it, would you? I'm not a cat person. Too much hair, too many claws."

"Yet you can climb seventy feet up a two-hundred-foot sequoia," said Ruby, setting the cat on the ground.

"Trees never bothered me," said Mo, plucking the orange cat hairs from his jacket.

"So, what, you used to be a construction worker, a lumberjack, a high-wire walker?" said Ruby.

Mo shrugged. "In a past life, maybe."

"With skills like that you might want to join the circus or the fire department," said Ruby.

"Nah," said Mo, "I like an uneventful life."

"Uneventful? Are you kidding?" said Ruby. "You think grabbing cats from crazily tall trees is uneventful?"

"So what are you doing up here, anyway?" asked Mo. "I told you, the maitake won't be in for a couple of days."

"I know, but I wanted to ask you about *another* kind of mushroom," said Ruby, "seeing as how you're such a mushroom expert and everything."

"Mycologist," said Mo.

"Exactly," said Ruby.

"So try me," he said.

"Have you heard of a Mars Mushroom?"

"Sounds like a question for Walt," said Mo.

"I'm serious," said Ruby.

"Are we talking mushrooms from Mars or mushrooms that look like alien things?"

"Don't all mushrooms look like alien things?"

Mo shrugged. "Does it have a proper name, this Mars Mushroom?"

"*Hypocrea asteroidi,*" said Ruby.

"That sounds kinda familiar," said Mo. "I feel like I must have read about that somewhere. I can have a look through some of my journals and specialist books if you'd like me to."

"I'd appreciate that," said Ruby, although she didn't hold out much hope that he would find anything. If Pinkerton was trying to keep it secret, then it seemed unlikely that there was going to be anything in print.

As soon as Ruby stepped out of the store, it dawned on her just how hungry she was; she hadn't eaten a bite all morning.

She crossed the road to the diner and ordered herself the Pluto Plate, which was basically pancakes with all the extras.

Walter and Duke were sitting at the counter in the same seats, eating the same food they had been eating when she'd first met them that previous Sunday.

They were talking about UFOs, and it made entertaining

listening. She looked up when the bell on the door jangled, and in came another familiar character. It was the cryptic-crossword guy, Sven. She watched him lift Spike from the baby chair thing he had on his back. He looked around, trying to figure out where to perch the baby, then he saw Ruby.

"Would you mind grabbing him a second while I get my coat off?" he asked.

Ruby grudgingly obliged. "Boy, this kid weighs a ton," she said. "He's like some thirty-pound sausage."

Sven smiled like he was pleased with that assessment of his kid. "Spike's a big eater," he said.

He unwound his scarf and shrugged off his coat and hung it on one of the hooks by the door. It was as he turned back toward her that Ruby saw the image printed on his sweatshirt: a sequence of interlocking triangles.

"Cool sweatshirt," said Ruby. "Where'd you get it?"

"This?" he said, pointing at it. "From my old man. He used to work at the power plant over the mountain."

"So it definitely wasn't a space base?" said Ruby. "I heard those guys say it was."

"No," said Sven. "I can tell you that for nothing — Walter and Duke would like to believe it is, but it ain't."

"No Mars missions, no alien communications," said Ruby.

"Just good old electricity," said Sven.

She shrugged. "That's a shame," she said.

When she had finished eating, she caught the bus back down the mountain. She was pretty tired, and it didn't take more than a few minutes before she had fallen asleep.

What woke her was a sudden jolt as the driver swerved across the road. He cursed loudly before calling out, "Boy, that was close!"

"What happened?" asked Ruby.

"Bambi just got lucky," said the driver.

"Huh?"

"We nearly hit a deer," explained the woman sitting in the seat across from hers.

Ruby's backpack had catapulted off the seat, and some of her things were now rolling around on the floor. She reached to gather them up, but when she checked to make sure everything was now back in the bag, she realized her pencil was missing. It wasn't under the seat; it wasn't anywhere.

So where was it?

Where it was, was safely locked away in the most secure vault in Twinford.

Redfort, you're a duh brain, she cursed, *and you're probably gonna be fired from Spectrum, but not before you're murdered by your boss, who probably is a bona fide agent-killer and knows that you know it!*

CHAPTER 26
The Trolley Problem

WHEN RUBY GOT BACK TO TWINFORD, she felt her watch vibrate as a message came in.

It was from Hal in Gadgets.

```
>> IF YOU GO TO THE PARKING LOT UNDER THE ICE RINK,
        YOU'LL FIND A BIG SURPRISE.
```

The parking lot under the ice rink was also the parking lot above Spectrum. *So why does he need to leave whatever he is leaving me in the parking lot?* she wondered. *Why not just tell me to pick it up from the gadget room?* For some reason the whole mystery of it irritated her. There were too many mysteries, and she was beginning to crave clarity; clarity on anything would be nice.

She messaged him back.

```
>> WHY CAN'T I JUST COME DOWN AND PICK IT UP?
```
she asked.

>> BETTER THIS WAY, he wrote. BAY D 57

"Have it your way," she muttered.

Ruby made her way to Bowery Street and on toward the ice
rink. She had never actually been in the underground parking
lot before; she had never needed to—the elevator took her to
Spectrum directly. She walked down the stairwell into the lot
and felt glad that this was not a regular thing. The place was
creepy; it also smelled bad. She looked around her, searching
for the D zone.

Bay 57 was almost at the end, but she didn't need to get close
to make out what it was.

"You gotta be kidding me—red?" she muttered. "I wouldn't
be caught dead on a *red* bike."

She was going to have to do something about this. Red was
worse than pink—well, almost. It was so "jolly"; so "my first
bike." Why didn't Hal just go the whole mile and stick a basket
on front and attach one of those little colorful whirling pinwheels
to the handlebars?

She didn't register the footsteps behind her—maybe because
the woman moved almost without sound.

Ruby kicked at the wheel. There was no way she was taking
that thing home with her. *He's torturing me.*

There was a cough and then a gravelly voice spoke. "A little
ungrateful, aren't we?"

Ruby spun around to see a woman dressed entirely in white, her face without expression. Ruby had never once seen her boss outside the confines of Spectrum. If LB had a life beyond the agency, then Ruby couldn't imagine it.

"Is this how you treat state-of-the-art Spectrum technology?"

Ruby began to speak but found herself stammering; no words were forming.

"You seem . . . what's the word . . ." LB paused as she searched for the precise adjective. *"Edgy."* She stared hard at Ruby, and Ruby looked away. It wasn't a comfortable experience to be trapped in this place with an agent-killer.

"I'm concerned, Redfort, I really am. Your behavior has been a little"—again, she seemed to be groping for the word—". . . off."

"I'm just tired," said Ruby.

"Tired? And what exactly is making you tired?"

"Oh, I don't know, maybe it's"— her mind had gone blank—"school . . ."

"School?" repeated LB. "School is making you tired?"

Ruby bit her lip. "No, I guess it's more likely to be the training—not that I'm complaining or anything; it's nothing I can't handle."

LB just stared at her, an unblinking stare. "Maybe I can drive you somewhere?"

"Well, I should probably, you know, unlock my bike and, you know, *ride* it home, I mean, since Spectrum went to all the trouble of getting me this machine and . . ."

"Except you can't possibly do that, Redfort."

To Ruby's ears that sounded like a threat. And what LB said next sounded a whole lot worse.

"I mean, who *would* be caught dead on a *red* bike? Certainly not *you*. So on what color bike would you be prepared to be caught *dead*?" She put such emphasis on the word "dead" that a shiver ran right down Ruby's spine.

LB was beginning to remind her of someone, the someone who wore the Italian shoes and the old-fashioned suit.

"I don't mind the color, not at all, actually, I mean, red's so jolly, so like . . ." What was it like? She couldn't think of a thing other than, well, blood.

"Santa? Is that the word you're searching for?"

"Yes, that's it exactly, so I might just jump right on and get back, get back home or not home, but somewhere . . . somewhere else."

"You're acting peculiar, Redfort. Something on your mind?"

The way she said it, the words almost sounded like a challenge.

"I'm cold," said Ruby. "Just need to warm up; it's hard to think straight."

"So your survival training has been a waste of Spectrum resources — is that what you're saying?"

"No, not at all, I'm just . . ."

"Just what?"

The light overhead went out, and Ruby jumped.

"Relax," said LB. "They do that." She waved her hand, and they came back on. "They're motion sensitive."

Ruby was looking around her now. Which way should she sprint? She must be able to outrun LB. She knew she couldn't out-fight her, but outrun her, surely.

"You found something out, didn't you?" LB didn't step closer, didn't move an inch, but it felt like she had. "Why don't you just spit it out, Redfort? There's something you know that you don't want to tell me."

This was it, this was the moment when the Spectrum 8 boss would pull out some agent-terminator weapon and that would be that.

She might just as well say her piece.

"You killed Bradley Baker." The words echoed around them. Silence.

LB paused before saying, "The Count told you?"

"So you're not denying it?"

"No."

"You murdered him."

"In a manner of speaking."

"How could you do that? He was your friend, more than that, he was . . ."

"It sounds to me like you're passing judgment here." LB stared hard at Ruby, her eyes unblinking. "Yet what do you really know? You have a few facts and the word of a psychopath, and yet you feel equipped to condemn me?"

Silence.

"Imagine this, Ruby Redfort. Imagine you have just seconds to make the biggest decision you will *ever* make; imagine that whatever you decide will be wrong. There is no right in this — don't fool yourself into thinking that."

Silence.

"There's a thought experiment in ethics," said LB. "It's called the Trolley Problem. You may have heard of it?"

Ruby shook her head.

"No? Well, lucky you. You see, it's a question of life and death. When I joined Spectrum, part of the training was to consider what you might do if faced with the gritty question: In whose direction do you point the Grim Reaper's scythe?" She smiled a cold smile. "No, it's worse than that. You *become* the Grim Reaper, *you* decide: Is one life worth more than five? Is the life of someone you *value* worth *more* than two that you don't? Is the life of a child worth more than that of an adult? These are the unpleasant issues you have to consider when you become a person who deals in life and death for a living — you become the man with the scythe."

Ruby said nothing.

"So imagine a trolley car is hurtling down a rail track and it's going to hit five innocent people. You can save them *if* you pull the points lever, so diverting the trolley car onto the parallel track. On this track there is just one person who will die. One life for five? What do you do?"

Ruby said nothing.

"In my case, the situation was a little more dramatic. A package was delivered anonymously to me at home, and when I opened it, I found a detonator and instructions to turn on my TV set. Every channel was tuned to the same broadcast, a live countdown, a ticking bomb counting inevitably toward zero.

"A scrambled voice told me what I already knew: a whole site would be destroyed and along with it every one of its one thousand and twenty-seven staff. However, I was offered an alternative outcome: I could save them, every one of them. All I had to do was to press the yellow button there on the detonator. There was a catch, though — there always is in situations like this, always a price to pay.

"'We can trade.' That's what the voice said. 'One thousand and twenty-seven lives for one.' And then the TV flashed up another image: a tiny silver-white craft moving across a blue sky. And it looked so safe, somehow, so small in this enormous ocean of sky, and I let my eyes follow it and I knew it was Baker."

She turned to look at Ruby, eyes unblinking. "And that was my choice."

"I . . ." said Ruby. But she could think of nothing to say. She could see the truth in LB's eyes.

"So do I do nothing?" continued LB. "In which case, Baker, the person I regard more highly than any other being on this planet, goes merrily on his way, or do I choose to save one thousand and twenty-seven people that I have never met, probably *will never* meet, and until now have never thought about."

She paused, staring Ruby hard in the eye. "But are they not equally deserving of my protection? Would it not be monstrous to sign the death warrant of so many?" She pondered the question, and then said in a distant voice, "I will never forget the final question he hissed into my ear. 'The clock is ticking, dear LB, what price love, what price life; are the heartbeats of many worth more than your heart's one true desire?'" Her voice was almost inaudible now. "Ninety-nine seconds is all it took to drain all color from my life."

Ruby still could find no words.

"So before you judge me, think about what you would do," said LB. "One thousand and twenty-seven people who mean nothing to you, or Clancy Crew?"

"I . . ." began Ruby, "I mean, it's not possible . . . to make the right decision; how could one, how could *I* . . ."

"As I said, there *is* no right decision," said LB. "It's all about your gut instinct. I chose to *save* one thousand and twenty-seven people, but no matter how one tries to square it, it doesn't change the fact that I killed *someone, my friend, my* choice, no one made me pick *him. I* pushed a button that caused the death of the person I happened to like"—her voice cracked—"to love more than any other living soul on this sad planet."

LB turned, strode to her car, climbed in, and drove off.

**Casey Morgan
heard the shouting. . . .**

People were running to the river's edge. Casey saw the boy get pulled out of the rapids: he wasn't moving. There was more shouting, more attempts to resuscitate.

"I think he's dead," cried a voice. Silence fell.

Samuel Colt didn't give up, wouldn't give up. "Come on, kid, you need to breathe."

A cry: "He's alive, the kid's alive!"

Casey turned and ran, and never looked back.

CHAPTER 27
À la Mode

RUBY HAD ONLY JUST MADE IT HOME from midtown when she heard the sound of a key in the front door.

"Bonsoir!" called Sabina. "There's something wrong with my key, could someone let us in?"

Mrs. Digby went down to open the door. "Well, howdy there, travelers," she said, wiping her hands on her apron.

"I thought perhaps we'd been away so long you had decided to change the locks." Sabina laughed.

"We have," said Mrs. Digby.

"You did?" Sabina said.

"Only because Hitch mislaid his keys," explained the housekeeper. "It wasn't personal."

"Well, that's a relief!" said Brant. "When a man isn't welcome in his own home, where is he to go?"

"Hey, Mom, hey, Dad, you actually made it home," called Ruby as she ran down to greet them.

"Je suis désolée," said Ruby's mother, giving her daughter a dozen kisses. "We just got utterly stuck in Paris."

This was followed by more apologies and a twirling embrace from her father.

"I'm glad you're home," said Ruby in a strangled voice.

"Good to see you back where you belong," said the house-keeper.

"Good to see you too, Mrs. Digby," said Brant Redfort, giving the old lady a hearty hug.

"Darling Mrs. Digby," said Sabina Redfort, kissing her on each cheek (a new habit she'd picked up), "it's so *très bien* to be back, I can't tell you the ways we've missed you."

"I can believe it," said Mrs. Digby. "Starting with the need for a decent home-cooked meal, no doubt."

Brant Redfort smiled, remembering the many *more* than decent home-cooked meals he and his wife had devoured during their stay with the Minister for Culture, whose kitchen was under the command of celebrated chef Antoine Moreau. However, not wanting to disappoint, he nodded and said, "You can say that again, Mrs. D."

"Boy, am I tuckered out," said Sabina Redfort.

"I'll get you a nice cup of English tea," said Mrs. Digby, reaching for the kettle. "You put your feet up."

"Oh, make mine a large café au lait, *s'il vous plaît*."

"Coffee? At this time of day? I thought that bad habit belonged to Hitch alone."

"It's morning in Paris," said Sabina, yawning.

"Well, I never," said Mrs. Digby, turning to Mr. Redfort. "So will you be wanting coffee too?"

"Sure, why not," said Brant. "When in Paris."

"We're *not* in Paris," said Mrs. Digby.

"I'll take mine in a bowl," said Sabina.

The housekeeper looked at her like she hadn't heard right. "Why ever would you drink coffee from a bowl?"

"It's à la mode," said Sabina.

"Pardon me?" said Mrs. Digby.

"It's what the French do," said Brant.

"I'm sure there are plenty of bizarre things the French do, but it doesn't mean we should get in on the act."

"You should try it, Mrs. D. There's nothing like drinking coffee from a bowl."

Mrs. Digby sniffed. "I'll stick with my cup, if you don't mind. I've always felt handles were there for a reason."

"I'll take *my* coffee any way it's going," said Hitch, walking into the room.

Sabina clapped her hands. "How *merveilleux* to see you! We've missed you to distraction."

There followed a whole lot more kissing on two cheeks and general fussing and then coffee. Beautifully wrapped gifts were distributed to all, and everyone was very pleased.

"Eiffel Tower cuff links!" said Hitch. "Just what I need. I mislaid a cuff link a few weeks back, and there's not a chance I'll find it."

"Ironically, I lost one of mine at the top of the Eiffel Tower," said Brant. "They're such fiddly things—a total liability."

"Well, I'll do my best to hang on to these," said Hitch.

"You must join us for supper," said Brant.

"I'm afraid I'm expected elsewhere," said Hitch, glancing anxiously at his watch.

"Oh, no, *really*?" exclaimed Sabina.

She looked so forlorn that Hitch found himself saying, "You know what? How about I stay for the starter — it really looks too good to miss."

But unfortunately, just as he raised his fork to his mouth, an urgent message flashed up on his watch. No one saw it, no one noticed him read it — no one but Ruby. Hitch made his excuses — an elegant lie — and he promised to make it up to them, and left.

It was a shame, because it was a sumptuous meal Mrs. Digby served that night, and although there was some disappointment on the old lady's part that she had not been able to rustle up the hen of the woods stew, no one else minded a bit.

Ruby was relieved to have her parents back, relieved to discover her boss was not a ruthless killer, and happy to have everyone together again under this one safe roof. So merry was the mood that the four of them all stayed up late into the evening playing cards and chatting, and Ruby only went upstairs when she saw that both her mother and her father had fallen asleep right there on the couch in front of her — Mrs. Digby having already crept away to her bed an hour earlier.

The first voice Ruby heard the next morning was on the phone. The call came through as she was about to leave the house.

"Twinford complaints and moans, what's your grumble?"

"Kid?"

"Go ahead, caller."

"You want me to list my grumbles?" said Hitch. "Well, one of them would be that the coffee where I am stinks and the cooking is pretty despicable too. You can tell your folks that I can't wait to make it home tonight."

"Is that why you're calling?" asked Ruby.

"Just checking in. Is everything A-OK?" he asked.

"I guess," said Ruby. She couldn't exactly discuss the chalk message over the phone. She couldn't discuss *anything* important. He knew that, didn't he?

"How's the bike working out for you?" he asked.

"It's red," she said.

"That's a problem?"

"Would you ride a red bike?" she asked.

"Depends on the circumstances — now, could you pass me on to that wonderful woman who attends to your every need?"

Ruby put Hitch through to the housekeeper's apartment and then set off for Twinford Junior High.

The first voice Ruby heard when she biked through the school gates was Del Lasco's.

"Redfort, why are you riding that red bike?" she shouted.

"'Cause it's the only one I got," said Ruby.

"I saw you on a pink one the other day," said Mouse.

"It wasn't jolly enough," said Ruby.

"It doesn't look right," said Del. "*You* don't look right."

"Yeah, well, too bad, 'cause it's either this bike or no bike."

"Yeah, but . . . *red*?" said Del.

"I'm getting it resprayed, OK?" said Ruby. Until that moment she hadn't considered that option, but now that she thought about it, it seemed like a very good idea. Maybe she could do it herself.

Ruby was disappointed to find no Clancy in her homeroom. She could really do with talking to him.

"Where is he?" she asked Elliot.

"Out sick, I heard," said Elliot. "That's what Nancy told Red."

"He's probably come down with Crew flu," said Mouse.

"That or French flu," said Ruby, who was well aware of the upcoming French exam.

"I wouldn't mind catching it myself," said Mouse.

"Catching what?" asked Ruby.

"Crew flu, *any* flu."

"Why d'ya wanna catch the flu?" asked Ruby.

"To get out of this table tennis tournament," said Mouse. "I know I'm gonna get destroyed. It's gonna be awful."

"You're crazy to say that, Mouse. You're the best player we have; you're gonna win, I know it," said Ruby.

"How? Just thinking about it makes me drop my paddle."

CHAPTER 28
Nothing but Glamour

AFTER SCHOOL, Ruby rode over to Ambassador Row. The door was opened by a perfectly healthy-looking Clancy.

"I thought you were supposed to be sick," said Ruby.

"I am," said Clancy. "Come on in."

"Are you contagious?" asked Ruby.

"Only if my mom gets home early, then you better make a swift exit."

"I knew you were faking it."

They went and sat in the den with some popcorn and a couple of sodas. The house was quiet; all the other Crews were out.

"You know, you look a bit shaken up," said Clancy, "not quite your usual self."

"Why do you say that?" said Ruby.

Clancy shrugged. "I don't know — something about your eyes. They seem twitchy."

"They do?" she said.

"Yeah, it's either something to do with that new red bike or maybe your contact lenses are bothering you or . . . it's something else," said Clancy.

"That's very perceptive of you, and as it happens I *am* a little freaked," said Ruby. "It's because . . ." She paused. "It's because I ran into LB last night."

Clancy's eyes immediately became wide. "Were you alone?"

"You could say that. I was in the underground parking lot."

"No way," said Clancy, who was beginning to flap his arms. "How did you get outta there? I mean, did she try to kill you?"

"No," replied Ruby.

"Well, that's something," said Clancy.

"Yeah, I was kinda relieved," said Ruby. "I thought my number was up for sure. I mean, there I am in a deserted parking lot with the woman who killed Bradley Baker."

"So it's true!" said Clancy, his voice a sort of whispered shriek. "She really did murder him."

"It's more complicated than that," said Ruby.

"More complicated than her murdering her best friend?"

Ruby nodded and then she gave him a word-for-word account of what had happened.

"Jeepers," said Clancy, "that's one of the most tragic stories I ever heard."

"It's beyond tragic," said Ruby. "I don't know how she can handle the guilt. She basically had to kill her best friend to save a thousand strangers."

"Makes you think," said Clancy. "I mean, you gotta say, she is quite an agent. She sacrificed him and her happiness, *everything,* because it was the lesser of two evils."

"She's brave, that's for sure," said Ruby. They sat for a while not talking, just contemplating the magnitude of what LB had done.

After a minute or more, Ruby said, "The thing that gets me is now I'm feeling sorry for the guy."

"Who?" asked Clancy.

"Bradley Baker," said Ruby. "He's always been this massive pain in the butt, and now I'm having a hard time hating him, and I wanna hate him."

"Why?" asked Clancy.

"Because . . . I'm fed up with being told how great he is. You should hear that potato head Froghorn — he literally thinks Baker *is* the sun."

"He probably *was* a really nice guy," said Clancy. "I mean, you don't get that many people saying how *nice* you are if you're *not nice*."

"Well . . . I mean, it *does* happen," said Ruby. "Sometimes people feel they should speak well of the dead. It's a kind of an unwritten law."

"You don't want to like him because he was smarter — because some people *say* he was . . . more . . . you know, more experienced than you," said Clancy.

"You were probably right the first time; he probably was smarter than me," said Ruby. "It's just, do you know how hard it is to be continually compared to someone who happens to be a lot smarter than you?"

Clancy looked at her like she had said something really dumb. "Yeah, Rube, as a matter of fact I do."

"OK, sorry, I just mean, working in Spectrum, I get it all the time. They're crazy about this guy."

"You're just not used to it," said Clancy. "I have a lot of practice in this area, so I have learned the art of humility."

"What?"

"I'm not so full of myself."

"Do you want me to help you with your French or *not*?" said Ruby.

Clancy gave her a panicked look, and she punched him lightly on the arm. "You do know my homework assistance is unconditional?"

"I appreciate that," said Clancy. "So," he said, changing the subject, "at least you're done with the Prism Vault. I mean, now that you know the truth about LB, you never have to go back *there* again."

"Are you kidding?" said Ruby. "Now I absolutely *have* to go back."

"Why?" spluttered Clancy. "Why do you have to go back?" He was flapping his arms again.

"Because I need to get into the file that tells me who tried to kill Baker the first time around."

"What?" said Clancy.

"There was this kid who tried to kill him a long time ago, a kid who ran from the scene. I discovered this when I read a file on this junior spy program Spectrum used to run, and the thing is, if I were you, which I'm sorta trying to be — you know, go with my gut and all — then I would say I have a *hunch* that there's something weird about the way a lot of the important information isn't there anymore."

"You mean you have a hunch someone's tampered with the file?" said Clancy.

"That's exactly what I mean," said Ruby. "Blacker told me it's impossible to erase or remove the Ghost Files, but I guess it *is* possible to *move* something from one file to another and hide it — so I have to go back and try to find it."

"Tonight?" said Clancy. He looked alarmed.

"No," said Ruby. "First I have to figure out the final file code. Froghorn had it written up as a question mark, which I guess leaves me guessing."

"Not a clue?" asked Clancy.

"Not a clue," said Ruby.

Ruby was careful to ride home along the most brightly lit streets, with the most traffic and most restaurant-goers, but still she felt an uneasiness, as if someone was watching. Though she was tempted, she did not activate the hyper-speed booster — she was trying to keep a low profile, and a kid riding a bicycle along Amster at an implausible speed was likely to raise a few eyebrows.

It was as Ruby passed Lime Street that she noticed a parked car pull slowly away from the curb. Rather than overtake her, it began to crawl behind her. She sped up, and though she couldn't be sure, it seemed as if the car began to move faster. When she reached Oakwood she turned right, expecting the car to drive on, but it didn't—it followed. Now she *was* spooked. She swept on past her turn and then suddenly squeezed hard on the brakes, causing the bike to skid around so she was pointing in the direction of Cedar Street; she pedaled hard, turned into Cedarwood Drive, and ten seconds later was home. The car did not follow.

She ran up the front steps, fumbled for her key, dropped it, picked it up, found the keyhole, opened the door, and was in. She made sure to slam it behind her, listening for the reassuring clunk of the lock.

"Ruby, is that you?" called her mother.

"Uh-huh," replied Ruby, panting as she climbed the stairs. She walked into the living room, where she found her mother at her desk.

"Are you all right, honey?" Sabina asked. "You look a bit flushed."

"I've been biking," said Ruby.

Her mother looked at her sternly. "You be careful out there in the dark, Ruby. Always remember to keep your lights on and your wits about you."

"I'll remember that," said Ruby; it actually sounded like good advice.

"Your father won't be home until late, as Mr. Cleethorps is having a company dinner. I managed to wriggle out of it;

it sounded rather tedious," said her mother. She held something up, a square of card. "Good news, though! We received our invitation to the Eye Ball."

"The Eye Ball?" repeated Ruby.

"You haven't heard about it?" asked Sabina. "*We* heard about it and we were in Paris. The New Year's Eve party at the old Eye Hospital. It's been renovated up to the eyeball — literally."

What Ruby's mother meant was that every floor of the old thirty-four-story building had been renovated apart from the top story, where the giant neon blinking eye was fixed to the outside of the building.

"They've even got that big old eye sign blinking again," said Sabina. "Actually, they still have work to do on the east wing of the thirty-third floor, so unless the construction team get a move on, the grand dining room won't be ready."

"That's very disappointing," said Ruby, who was eager to cut this conversation short.

"I know." Sabina sighed. "It means no second buffet area."

"Tragic," said Ruby.

"And there was going to be a catering elevator too, you know, like a dumbwaiter, carrying food up and down from the kitchen — goodness knows what Consuela will do without it. She's catering the event, of course."

"Cool," said Ruby, who was by now on autopilot.

Even Sabina could sense her daughter's lack of interest in the behind-the-scenes details of the Eye Ball, and changed tack.

"The party is space themed, you know," she announced. "Space is so hot at the moment, with the new observatory and the launch of the space station."

"Sounds out of this world," said Ruby.

Her mother did not pick up on her tone.

"It's the must-have ticket this season. It's going to be nothing but glamour," said Sabina, enthusiasm bubbling out of her. "And you're coming too, so get excited."

"I feared as much," muttered Ruby.

"Pardon?" said her mother.

"I can hardly wait," said Ruby.

"That's the spirit, honey — talking like a Redfort!" said her mother proudly. "So, what will you wear?"

"I need to decide *now*?" said Ruby, who was hoping to concentrate on more important matters, like how to get a hold of her lost pencil.

"Well, you can't wear just *anything*," said Sabina. "No jeans and no T-shirts."

Ruby looked down at her T-shirt. "Actually, this one *is* space themed."

It read: *space cadet.*

"I hope you're kidding," said her mother.

"I think it would be perfect," said Ruby.

"So long as you don't wear that black jumpsuit," said Sabina.

"It's very fashionable," said Ruby.

"But it's not *right* for a party like this," said her mother.

"I mean, I doubt if you would team it with heels, am I right or am I right?"

"Sneakers," said Ruby.

"Give me strength," said Sabina. "Or better still, a martini. Hitch!"

"He's out for the night," called Mrs. Digby.

"Why?" called Sabina.

"How should I know?" came Mrs. Digby's reply. "Perhaps he's meeting up with an old friend."

"I didn't know he had any," said Ruby.

"Of course he has friends," said her mother. "Look at him—he's everything a friend could want."

"Well, he's out," said Mrs. Digby, "and that's a fact."

"He called this morning," said Ruby. "Said he was coming home."

"This entire household is falling apart," said Sabina.

"You can't rely on anyone these days," said Ruby.

Mrs. Digby appeared, carrying a martini on a tray.

"Mrs. D," sighed Sabina, "you spoil me to pieces."

"Tell me something I *don't* know," said the housekeeper. She walked over to the window and glanced into the darkness.

"I wouldn't be knocked down with surprise if we got some snow tonight," she said.

"Do you think?" said Sabina. "It would be better for me if it happened next week. My good warm coat is still at the dry cleaner, and I really don't have a nice alternative."

"What about that one hanging in your closet?" said Mrs. Digby.

"The pink one? I never think of pink as a winter color, do you?"

"What does pink have to do with it? It's fur lined," said Mrs. Digby. "If it's warm, it's warm." She remembered being caught in a freak blizzard when she was barely five and she would have been glad of a pink coat, any coat—she often told the story. *"If my pa hadn't heard the wolves howling and come out looking for me, I would have died of cold as sure as toadstools attract flies."*

CHAPTER 29
Yellow Notebooks

RUBY WENT UPSTAIRS. She stood gazing out the window, watching to see if Mrs. Digby's snow premonition was right, but there was not a single snowflake, not yet anyway. What she could see was the gray clapboard house, silent and empty, the new occupants still not moved in. Her mind wandered back to Homer Pinkerton.

If Pinkerton's death is connected to Bradley Baker's, she thought, *then this all began many years ago, long before you stepped a tiny toe on the planet.*

So what important thing connected Pinkerton to Bradley Baker? What had happened to his dog? Where had he disappeared to? This thought set her wondering what answers she might have, what everyday observations might hold a truth.

Start at the beginning, Rube. You saw Mr. Pinkerton's dog kidnapped, though you don't remember it. What else might you have observed?

She got down on her knees and began rolling back the small geometric-patterned rug that covered one portion of the wooden floor. Then she took a screwdriver from her drawer, pushed it between two of the boards, and neatly lifted up a single short plank. In the cavity between the joists were her 624 yellow notebooks.

Ruby had spent more than a lot of hours making notes in these little books, recording the everyday goings-on, to-ings and fro-ings, snippets of conversation, strange occurrences, blandly dull incidents. Because, as Ruby would say, **EVEN THE MUNDANE CAN TELL A STORY.** It was her **RULE 16.** And though each notebook was not many pages long, and though Ruby was an exceptionally fast reader, there was still no way she was going to manage to read each one cover to cover that evening. It was hard to know where to start, so she began at the beginning.

It was when she was halfway through notebook **46** that she realized one of the occurrences she had noted down was very similar to something that had taken place one previous July in notebook **22.**

NOTEBOOK 22

```
My grandmother almost swallowed my mother's
diamond earrings. She found them at the
bottom of her teacup.
    She said, "Is this expensive tea or what?"
```

NOTEBOOK 46

```
My grandmother swallowed a pair of my
```

mother's emerald earrings and we spent most
of Saturday sitting in the emergency room.
The doc said, "It shouldn't prove fatal
and probably will cause you very little
discomfort."

My grandmother wanted to know how the doc
proposed she get them out of her system.

And the doc said, "In the usual way."

My grandmother said the experience had
really put her off tea, even if she was
thirty thousand dollars more valuable than
she had been eight hours earlier.

My mom said she would never be able
to look at those emerald earrings without
imagining the journey they had been on. She
has given them to my grandmother.

My grandmother said it wasn't
compensation enough for what she was about
to endure.

Both these jewelry mishaps reminded Ruby of something she
had written down in her more recent list titled:

WHAT I DON'T KNOW
Where my mom's snake earrings are.

And now she was pretty sure she did. They would no doubt be in a teacup somewhere in her grandmother's New York apartment. She hoped the old lady was sticking to coffee as she had vowed.

Ruby made a note to telephone her grandmother. Not now, though. Suddenly overwhelmed with tiredness, she put back the notebooks, slotted the floorboard into its gap, and replaced the rug. Then she got changed and climbed into bed.

School was pretty dull the next day. The only thing that happened that might be considered of interest was due to Del Lasco. Mrs. Drisco had caught her roller-skating down the main corridor. It was a long passage, and the floors, being freshly waxed, made for excellent skating.

Mrs. Drisco had given Del three hours litter-picking and confiscated the skates. Del had not taken this lying down; she had argued that there was nothing in the school rules that said one couldn't roller-skate down the hallway.

Mrs. Drisco argued that "since running was not allowed, it was hardly appropriate to skate."

Del said this was "not the point," since skating was *not mentioned* in the "long list of activities" one was "not allowed" to perform in the corridor. And had she known this was a rule, then "of course" she "would *never* have done it."

Mrs. Drisco said she "found this very hard to believe."

Del said she felt "very undermined by that statement."

Mrs. Drisco said "rules were rules."

Del said she "didn't have a problem with the rules," she said she "only had a problem with the things that weren't rules but were being bandied around as if they were rules in order to get innocent parties onto litter-picking duty."

Del spent the rest of the morning in Principal Levine's office.

When she came out, she said she was going to take this "all the way."

Knowing Del, Ruby felt it was likely she would win; either that or get expelled.

When school was out, Ruby rode the bus to the Cherry Cup and on the way she pondered the File Code Three conundrum. How to figure out a code when you didn't even know what type of code you were trying to figure out?

Ruby had arranged to meet Mouse after her dental checkup. Mouse was feeling increasingly nervous about the Twinford Table Tennis Championships, and the prospect of fillings had only served to make her more jumpy still.

As Ruby walked into the Cherry Cup, a young woman attempted to hand her a flyer advertising the upcoming Ice Capades.

"I'm not interested," said Ruby.

"It's going to be space themed," said the woman.

"Isn't everything?" said Ruby. She took the flyer without enthusiasm and pushed open the door to Cherry's.

Ruby found her friend doing a word search puzzle.

"Hey, Mouse. That looks boring."

Mouse made a face. "It is," she said. "I was just trying to keep focused."

"Focused on what?" asked Ruby.

"Focused on not thinking about the match," said Mouse.

"What's the deal with the match?" asked Ruby.

"I'm going to have to beat Penelope Fingelhorn."

"So?" said Ruby. "You can smash her, no problem."

"I know," said Mouse. "And then I'm going have to beat Kitty Kuramara."

"So you'll smash her too," said Ruby.

"I just don't know, Rube. I sorta think this girl's got me beat, you know what I'm saying?"

"It's all in your mind, Mouse," assured Ruby. "You can do it, you know you can, you've won a zillion games more difficult than this one. Kitty Kuramara isn't such a big deal." As she talked, Ruby noticed every time the name Kitty Kuramara was mentioned, Mouse would start winding the Ice Capades flyer around and around a drinking straw. It was as Ruby watched her do this for the fourth time that two thoughts dawned.

The pen on the cord, the one Froghorn had looped around his neck like he really, really didn't want to let it out of his sight, that was the first thing that came to mind. The pen was a new addition: until this last week, Ruby had never seen it before. Then there was Froghorn's new assignment — as coder of the Prism Vault. He was pleased about that, eager to let Ruby know that he was the coding agent tasked with creating all the code levels.

She had noticed without really being conscious of it that when she brought up the subject of the Ghost File codes he had begun twisting the pen in his hand, and later when he was really flustered he had begun rolling it into his tie, just as Mouse was doing with the straw and the flyer.

Ruby was so preoccupied with this thought that she almost lost the thread of her Mouse pep talk.

"So what would *you* do, Ruby, if *you* were faced with Kitty Kuramara?"

"Um . . . you know what I'd do? I'd just forget it's Kitty Kuramara. I mean, pretend she's Elliot or some other kid you know you can slam. You gotta adjust your thinking, Mouse; it's all in your mind," assured Ruby. "The thing is you're thinking defeat and you should go in there meaning to win." It was Ruby's **RULE 12: ADJUST YOUR THINKING AND YOUR CHANCES IMPROVE.**

"That's easy for you to say, Ruby," said Mouse. "You're not easily intimidated."

Ruby thought for a moment and then said, "So I heard this woman talking on the TV, about how if you adopt a strong pose, like, say, Wonder Woman — you know how she stands: feet apart, hands on hips, defiant expression? Well, she thinks it does something to your brain's chemistry — it has an actual physical effect; in an interview situation it makes people want to offer you the job, listen to your point of view, so in a tournament situation it's gonna have the same result; it's gonna make you a winner."

"Are you sure about that?" said Mouse.

"Sure, I'm sure," said Ruby. "All you have to do is take a few minutes in the restroom, adopt the Wonder Woman pose, and when you face Kuramara, you're gonna smash her game."

"I just hope no one comes into the bathroom while I'm doing it," said Mouse.

By the time Ruby left, Mouse was looking a lot happier, and Ruby was feeling like she might be onto something.

When she arrived home she went straight to her room and scanned the bookshelves until she found the little indigo codebook, author unknown.

She leafed quickly through it, stopping when she reached page 101: transposition ciphers. There were a number of these, but the one she was interested in was the scytale, used in particular by the Ancient Greeks and Spartans to communicate orders in military campaigns. Random-seeming letters or numbers were written on a strip of leather. To form the plain text, the leather was wrapped around a cylinder of a specific size and shape, and then the correct symbols would line up.

The cylinder could be a pen, couldn't it? Or something that looked like a pen. *A pen on a cord?*

The strip of cipher text, she figured, would be at the vault location. The cylinder would have to be *brought* there by whoever wanted to gain access to one of the level-three security files.

OK, thought Ruby. *All you gotta do is get hold of Froghorn's pen — how difficult can it be?*

CHAPTER 30
A Stroke of Luck

RUBY SLEPT SOUNDLY FOR ALL OF THIRTY MINUTES until she was woken by a buzzing. Her watch flashed, and there was a message:

>> HQ ASAP.

Ruby reported to reception, but before she could open her mouth, Buzz raised a hand to say, *Wait there*.

Ruby sat and waited.

And waited.

After ten minutes she began to get restless.

After twenty minutes she started to get annoyed.

"So why am I here?" asked Ruby. "I'm guessing you didn't drag me all the way into HQ just to have me sit on a bench, though then again . . ."

"I didn't drag you in anywhere, I just sent a message as instructed." Buzz was nothing if not literal.

"So, Buzz, do you ever feel like a mushroom sitting there in the middle of that desk?"

"Why would I feel like a mushroom?" she asked.

"It's just something about the way you're sticking up through that hole in the table like you're growing out of it," said Ruby. "And, you know, mushrooms grow in the dark, and this place is underground."

"But it's *not* dark," said Buzz, blinking up at her. "Spectrum is very well lit."

"Buzz, do you ever see the funny side of anything?"

"Were you being humorous?" said Buzz.

"I guess not," said Ruby.

There was zero point trying to engage the administrator in any further conversation, so Ruby sat back down, took out her indigo codebook, and began reading. She might just as well use her time and learn a little. Finally Buzz beckoned her over. Ruby picked up her coat and went to find out where she was meant to be and who she was meant to see. But a strange thing happened as she approached the desk. The administrator seemed to change color, from pale to even paler.

"What?" said Ruby. "What happened? You kinda look like you just saw a ghost."

But Buzz seemed unable to speak. Ruby followed her gaze and saw what she was looking at — it was the little white pin attached to the inside of her parka.

"Is it this?" said Ruby, but Buzz did not answer; instead, she said, "LB is expecting you," then she picked up the green telephone that had begun to ring and said, "Spectrum 8, *declarar sua divisão*."

The atmosphere was chilly when she walked into LB's starkly white office. This time when Ruby looked around at the color-free space she saw meaning in its whiteness. This interior was not *colored* white; it was white because it was *without* color. And in Ruby's head she heard her boss's words: *"Ninety-nine seconds is all it took to drain all color from my life."*

"Sit," ordered LB.

Ruby sat.

"What we discussed the other night," said LB. "I trust it will not go any further: the last thing I want is rumors and half-truths spreading through Spectrum 8."

"Of course," said Ruby.

"It was decided to keep what happened confidential because it was thought it would harm morale if the truth got out."

"I understand," said Ruby, "and I'm sorry."

"Sorry?" said LB.

"Sorry for what happened," said Ruby, "sorry for my lack of judgment. I wasn't thinking. It's this whole business with the Spectrum mole."

"Double agent," corrected LB. "Never underestimate the power of paranoia." She looked down at the stack of files in front of her and then looked up at Ruby. "When we are aware that *one* of us cannot be trusted, it means *none* of us can be trusted."

Ruby shifted in her seat: the statement made her uneasy.

"So we are clear on this?" asked LB.

"Yes," said Ruby.

"So keep it zipped," said LB.

"You can count on it," said Ruby.

There was a knock at the door, and Hitch entered the room. "You need to get going — the helicopter's waiting for you," he said to LB.

The Spectrum 8 boss was about to dismiss Ruby with a wave of her hand, when Ruby found herself saying, without really meaning to . . .

"Buzz looked at me funny just now when I came in."

"Excuse me?" said LB.

"I wouldn't mention it ordinarily, but she's never done that before," said Ruby.

"I'm not following," said LB. "Is this a complaint or an observation? Has she offended you in some way? Because if she has, then could you take it up with the human resources team or just, better still, get over it."

"It was when she saw *this*," said Ruby, holding up her coat and the little white circle that could be seen pinned to its lining.

The atmosphere changed quite suddenly. It was like a specter had just entered the room.

"Where did you get that?" said LB.

Hitch reached for the coat. "Kid, did you find this or was it given to you?"

"I found it," said Ruby, her voice uncertain, "a long time ago. I found it not far from my house on Cedarwood Drive."

Hitch was inspecting the pin.

"Is it . . . ?" asked LB.

He nodded. "Yes," he said, "it has the mark."

"What mark?" asked Ruby.

"The Larva mark," said Hitch, running his fingers over the Braille bumps.

"How did it get to be *there*?" said LB. "It went missing more than thirty years back."

"What is it?" asked Ruby. "Who did it belong to?"

Without another word, LB opened the door to the hidden room that adjoined her office, a room Ruby had been in only once before and much to the fury of her Spectrum 8 boss. It was a room lined with photographs, pictures of locations, pictures of agents, some formal photographs, some casual. Some showed dramatic scenes of agents leaping across gullies or climbing up cliff faces; others were off-duty pictures like the one of Hitch eyeballing a huge crocodile, Hitch making a stupid face, his eyes crossed. But the photograph LB was pointing to was in black and white and of a smiling boy sitting in the cockpit of a plane. Hitch reached up, took it from the wall, and handed it to Ruby.

She recognized the photograph; she had noticed it just minutes before LB had discovered her snooping in her private gallery. Back then Ruby had believed she was looking at some agent's son who had been allowed to sit in the pilot's seat and pretend to be flying the plane. Now she knew she was looking at the pilot.

"Is that who I think it is?" asked Ruby.

"I don't know," said LB. "Are you thinking, Is that Bradley Baker?"

"That's what I'm thinking," said Ruby.

"Then yes, that's Bradley Baker."

The boy was eight, perhaps nine, but that wasn't the interesting thing about the picture. What was catching Ruby's attention was the little circle of white pinned to his T-shirt.

"This was his pin?" asked Ruby.

"He was given it when he made it through the JSRP training. He was the only one to graduate — the whole 'kid recruitment' was given up as a bad idea."

Ruby kept her expression closed, giving no sign that might betray her knowledge of all this.

"This was the only Larva pin issued?" she asked.

"The only one ever made," said LB.

"So it is *definitely* his?" said Ruby.

"Without a doubt," said Hitch.

"So how did it end up a few yards from my house?" pondered Ruby.

"How indeed," said Hitch.

LB's watch beeped loudly and she strode toward the door.

"Lock up here, would you, Hitch?" She left the room, taking the Larva pin with her, and the little circle of tin, so long a part of Ruby's psychological armor, would now be locked away in some drawer, and she wondered if she would ever lay eyes on it again. She supposed not.

As they turned to leave, Ruby caught sight of a series of photographs capturing a young woman falling through the air. She looked dazzling because she was clad in a skin of gold that flashed and gleamed as the sun hit it. Around her shoulders was a little white fur-hooded cape, and in the final three pictures one could see her hand reach across her chest as she deployed a parachute, the next showed the chute emerging like a puff of gold, and in the final frame the woman sailed down to earth, a perfect golden canopy floating high above her head.

"Who is that?" asked Ruby.

"That's your boss," said Hitch.

"You have to be kidding," said Ruby. "You're telling me LB did stuff like that?"

"Sure she did; she was Spectrum's first female field agent, and she was one of the best too."

"That's some suit," said Ruby.

"Yeah," said Hitch, "it's a cold-climate skydive suit; it will keep you alive in pretty extreme temperatures."

"Any chance Spectrum might issue me with that parachute cape?" said Ruby, her gaze trained on the cloud of gold. "It's the coolest outfit I've ever seen."

"I think you'd have to do something pretty remarkable before LB let you get your hands on her parachute cape."

"Remarkable like keep my mouth shut? 'Cause I can do that."

"No, I think it would have to be remarkable like finding lost gold."

"I'll do my best," said Ruby.

"No one can stop you from dreaming, kid."

Hitch and Ruby stepped out into the atrium.

"So I was wondering," she said. "Were you ever in the JSRP, you know, alongside Bradley Baker?"

"What?" said Hitch.

"Did you train with him, you know, back when you were a boy?"

"Just how old do you think I am?"

"I don't know," said Ruby, "fifty-five . . . fifty-seven."

"Kid, I'm forty-two." He shook his head. "Boy, never ask a child to guess your age; they'll always have you pegged at just shy of decrepit."

"Didn't mean to offend," said Ruby.

"Don't mind me, I got skin thicker than a crocodile's," said Hitch. "But no, I wasn't in the JSRP."

She looked at him — if he was lying, then he was the best in the business. *He's telling the truth,* she thought.

"Speaking of crocodiles," she said, "what's with that photograph?"

"What photograph?" asked Hitch.

"The one of you looking into the eyes of that old croc."

"Oh, so you spotted that? I look good, don't you think?"

"It made me wonder."

"Made you wonder what?"

"How you, with your big fear of crocodiles, could get up close and personal with such a huge reptile."

"Are you kidding?" He began to laugh, really laugh. In fact, he laughed so hard that he didn't look like he was ever going to stop.

"*What?*" she asked, annoyed that she wasn't in on the joke.

"That picture was taken at *Disneyland.*" He wheezed. "He was made of rubber. Kid, you might want to get a new pair of glasses." He stepped into the elevator.

"Where are you off to? I thought maybe we could get a donut or something," said Ruby.

"I'd love to, kid, but I've just got places to be." As the doors closed, he called, "See you later, alligator!"

"Funny," muttered Ruby, "real funny."

She pulled on her parka, zipping it up ready for the cold she was about to step into, but just as she reached the door, she bumped into Hal coming the other way.

"Thanks for the red bike," she said.

HAL: *I thought it was green.*
RUBY: *It's red.*
HAL: *Ah.*

Pause.

RUBY: *You're color-blind?*
HAL: *Yep.*
RUBY: *Priceless.*
HAL: *So, you happy?*
RUBY: *Do I look happy?*
HAL: *I don't know, do you? We're not that well acquainted. Happy for you might be a whole different deal than for most kids.*
RUBY: *I'm not most kids, and I'm not looking happy.*
HAL: *Why not?*
RUBY: *Why would I want a red bike?*
HAL: *Because it's jolly?*
RUBY: *I'm not a jolly type of person.*
HAL: *Then . . . because your name's Ruby?*
RUBY: *Man, that's lame. I would like the bike to be green.*

My bikes are always green.

HAL: *You do realize the color of the bike doesn't affect your ability to ride it?*

RUBY: *In my case it does; in my case it has a pretty big effect on my ability to ride it.*

"Leave it with me," said Hal. "I'll have it resprayed."

"You know what, I think I'll just do it myself," said Ruby. "I got a feeling if I leave it with you it might just end up purple, and then I really will be distressed."

"You not a fan of purple?"

"What do you think?" she said.

Ruby's worry ran deeper than purple, of course. The real reason she wasn't about to hand over her new and improved bicycle was because if one was in the business of needing some kind of getaway vehicle, then a Spectrum bike fitted with hyperspeed booster was a pretty good option.

"Come with me." Hal sighed. "I'll get you a can of green paint."

She followed him down to the gadget room and waited while he got someone to fetch her exactly the right shade of green.

"You'll find it goes on really easily, no drips, dries instantly."

Ruby thanked him a little grudgingly and turned to leave.

"I'm supposed to walk you to the exit," said Hal.

"Oh, come on, man, I can see myself out and you've got a ton of work to do, right?"

"I got plenty," agreed Hal.

"So I'll skip along outta here and save you the trouble."

"OK," he said, "but no funny business."

"I can assure you of that," said Ruby, her expression angelic.

And off she went down the corridor, just like she should—only once she rounded the corner, she doubled back, turned left instead of right, and sprinted along until she reached the violet door of room 324, the "Frog Pod," as Blacker liked to call it—Froghorn's office. She knocked, but there was no reply. She tried the door. It was locked, hardly a surprise, but Ruby had no difficulty getting past that little problem. She knew Miles Froghorn's code because she'd had to figure it out not so long ago: it was pretty straightforward.

What she was looking for would surely not be on his desk. It would be locked away in his little safe underneath. She walked quickly around to the other side, but her bag caught the pen holder on top of the desk, and its contents scattered across the surface and one by one each pen rolled off the desk and onto the floor.

"Darn it!" cursed Ruby, grabbing up the pens as they fell.

And there it was in her hand: the scytale cylinder pen. Froghorn had hidden it in plain sight right there in his neat little pen pot. Ruby hesitated for only a second before snatching it up and slipping it into her pocket. Then she got out of there fast, aware that she needed to make it to the Prism Vault before Froghorn discovered that the decoder was gone.

**The man looked down
at the bedraggled child and
wondered how the creature
had found him. . . .**

"So what do you imagine I can do for you?" he asked. "Other than have you rounded up by the child-catcher . . . if only."

"I want to become your apprentice."

He laughed at that. "I don't take on worker bees."

"You should; I'm smart."

"I'm smarter than you and me put together," said the tall thin man. "Besides, I like to keep my own company. I have no trouble recruiting helpers when I require help. You'd be surprised how many upstanding citizens are prepared to sully their souls for the promise of a little money."

"I don't want money."

"Everyone wants money."

"Not me."

"I'm intrigued by your naïveté," said the Count. "Don't tell me you are prepared to become my drudge and yet want nothing for your trouble."

"I don't want nothing."

"I thought not. We all have our price — what's yours?"

"I want to know what you know."

"You want me to teach you the ways of the underworld? And what can you possibly give me in return?"

"I know things you want to know."

"A wretch like you? I doubt that. Name a subject you might possibly know more about than I."

"Spectrum."

He was silent for a moment.

Then:

"So tell me; what's your name?"

"I have no name. I'm going to shed my past like a snake sheds its skin."

"How very poetic," said the Count.

CHAPTER 31
Place of Death

THIRTY-TWO MINUTES LATER, Ruby was standing inside the Prism Vault. She had expected to see her pencil lying there on the floor, but it was gone. Clearly someone had found it.

Question: If some other Spectrum agent authorized to visit the Prism Vault had found her pencil, then why had they not notified security? Why had they not at the very least checked to see who had Ghost File clearance?

Don't think about that now; just find what you need and get out of here.

She tapped in the level-two security code and wasted no time finding the Larvae files. What she hoped to find was the name of Bradley Baker's would-be assassin. She wanted to know if it was possible that this young recruit had not let go of his murderous intention to rid the world of Spectrum's brightest young hire.

The writing in the alley had implied this could be so.

Beware the child who yearned to be Larva,
disguised as a fly, but emerged a spider.

Perhaps this kid had bided his time and waited patiently for the perfect moment to bring his plan to fruition.

She read through the pages quickly, searching for information about the rapids incident and for the names of those there that day, but still she found nothing useful—only pages of encrypted text and blanked-out words with meaningless sections in between. She shook the file in frustration and then slammed it shut, and it was this action that seemed to dislodge a loose paper that had been tucked under the file sleeve.

It was a report of what had occurred that day at the rapids, and in it appeared two names that until then had been missing.

The first was the name of the child thought to be responsible for the attempted murder of Bradley Baker. A kid named Casey Morgan. Nothing could be proved—there seemed to be no witness to the incident, and if Art Hitchen Zachery had observed anything, he was possibly too traumatized to recall it. As for Morgan, he had run from the scene and had never been found, so his guilt was naturally assumed.

The second name in the report was of the child who had pulled Baker from the rapids, a kid named Loveday. That was it, nothing more.

Ruby had spent so long looking for this information that she was fast running out of time to search for the other thing she needed to know: Why had Baker's last radio contact been with Pinkerton? Pinkerton, an old man, retired and living quietly in leafy West Twinford? She had not a clue where to look for this information, and in any case she doubted that what she hoped to find would be written in one of these files. She suspected that Baker and Pinkerton had communicated in secret. Perhaps they were aware of the presence of a mole even back then? As a last resort she decided to try the black files. *Might they represent the dead?* Was there some minuscule chance that one of these black files might contain information about Baker and Pinkerton, two Spectrum employees whose deaths were somehow intertwined?

It was a long shot, but long shots were all she had.

The black file was level-three security, and it directed her to the panel on the right-hand side of the door. She clicked it open and there found a narrow strip of paper that was printed with a long series of seemingly random letters. Next she took the cylinder pen from where it was tucked into her Superskin and wrapped the paper so the letters lined up. It said: cjk6xAsihX.

"That can't be right," she muttered.

She tried again, the letters made a word: "Archilocus." The Greek poet who first mentioned scytales.

Totally Froghorn, she thought.

She tapped the letters into the keypad, and this time when she went to withdraw the file, it was released without problem.

What she found there nearly knocked her off her feet.

Black stood for space, not death, and what she read in this file filled in a lot of gaps.

Baker was part of the Spectrum Space Encounter program.

Space Encounter had top-secret status, it said so all over the file, and the main body of the document was still encrypted. She had heard not so much as a rumor about it within Spectrum's walls; it was obviously a very well-kept secret.

The Spectrum Space Encounter program had officially begun in 1961, the year President Kennedy had authorized the US space program and its ambition to get to the moon.

She thought of Froghorn's strange line about Baker jumping from 14,000 feet: *"It wasn't a regular plane."*

Had it been a spacecraft of some kind? A shuttle?

She glanced at the clock.

Three minutes and counting.

From what Ruby could read around the encrypted content, it seemed this ambition to conquer space had been in the planning for a number of years, dozens of years, in fact.

2:00

Spectrum had been selecting recruits for years, young recruits, very young . . . kids.

She turned the page: JSRP, the J, the R, and the P all pale blue; the S was black.

What does this mean? It means something, but what? Ticktock, ticktock. *Think, Ruby, think.*

Pale blue was Froghorn's code for kid, black was his code for space.

1:00

Got it!

JSRP did not stand for Junior Spy Recruitment Program; it stood for Junior *Space* Recruitment Program.

So where was this Spectrum space base?

She leafed through the pages as quickly as she could; the minutes were already gone — now it was the seconds that were ticking by.

:51

:50

:49

:48

Place of death:

en route in Delta V DSO

to base at

No kidding.

:44

:43

:42

Instead of a name, there was just that symbol. Three triangles interlocking. A skyline of mountains, the moon above.

Just like on Sven's sweatshirt.

Bradley Baker had been flying somewhere in the Sequoia Mountains when someone had forced LB to choose between shooting down his craft or destroying not a power plant . . . but the Spectrum space base.

:10

:09

:08

:07

:06

:05

:04

She had left it too late. There was a beeping and then the door began to close.

:03

She scrabbled to her feet, pushing the file into place . . .

:02

she ran for the exit,

:01

threw herself through the gap, and

:00

the door *thunked* shut.

She lay there for a minute, her heart racing, grateful to have made it out of the vault in time. She got to her feet and pressed the exit button, the door in the floor slid open, and she climbed down into the tank. This time it was already full of water. That didn't seem right.

The opening closed overhead and she began searching for the fly on the wall. She saw it and swam toward it, but as she reached out her hand to touch it, it moved. She tried again, but again it got away from her, over and over she attempted to catch it but found it impossible. She was running out of air; she could hold her breath no longer.

Don't panic. Think!

She felt for the breathing band. Five minutes of air, five precious minutes to figure this out.

She watched the fly as it moved from wall to wall, ceiling to floor, and figured there was a pattern to it. If she predicted its move before it landed, swatted it before it had settled, she would get it.

On the third attempt she did it — her hand slapped at the wall and the exit slid open, and Ruby kicked out into the ocean and up to where she could breathe. She swam slowly to shore and emerged from the black, dragging herself out of the water like some strange and half-dead sea creature. She lay there for a minute or two, and when she looked up she spied a figure sitting on the rocks.

Her pulse quickened.

Not him, she thought. *Please not him.*

She froze, wondering if it might not be best to head back out to Meteor Island. She was so exhausted she wasn't sure she could make it that far, but she would prefer to drown than face whatever the Count might have in store for her.

The figure stood up, and the silhouette alone told her it was not him. The Count would not be dressed in a modern down jacket and ear-flapped hat.

Darn it, Froghorn! Does it have to be you?

She had thought she might just be in the clear, that perhaps she had escaped undetected.

There was no point running, certainly not while she was wearing the Superskin—so perfect for swimming but useless for sprinting. So she got to her feet and trudged up the beach to face what was no doubt going to be a very uncomfortable barrage of righteousness.

But as she got closer she saw she was mistaken: not Froghorn but . . .

"Clancy?" she said.

CHAPTER 32
Hit-and-Run

HEY RUBE," SAID CLANCY. He sounded cold, his teeth chattering.

"What are you doing here?" she asked.

"Waiting for you." He shivered.

"But how did you know I would be here?"

He shrugged. "A hunch, I guess. You *did* say you would be coming back, and I tried to call you a few times earlier, and when you didn't pick up I sort of supposed you would be swimming out to Meteor Island. I mean, what else would you be doing at five a.m.?"

They rode their bikes back along the coast road and stopped in at Green-Wood House so Ruby could change and pick up her schoolbooks. It was still early and the household was not yet awake, so the two of them slipped back out and made their way to the diner on Amster. Ruby ordered a double breakfast, and Clancy listened while she described all that had happened.

And finally she told him of her mistake at having imagined Hitch could have been a junior recruit.

"I think I might have offended him," said Ruby.

"How?" asked Clancy.

"He asked me how old I thought he was."

"What did you say?"

"Fifty-five."

"If you said that to my mom," said Clancy, "she would have you on double chores for the rest of the decade."

School dragged a bit, but it couldn't be helped. Had she skipped another day of school, Mrs. Drisco would be well and truly on the warpath—it was becoming a challenge to think up reasonable excuses.

When the bell clanged, Ruby knew exactly where she was headed.

The city library was busy, but Ruby found a place at one of the smaller tables toward the back. Dumping her coat, she walked up the steps to the archive room and started to go through the store of newspaper microfiche.

What she knew now was that Walter and Duke were right: there *was* a secret space base somewhere in the Sequoia Mountains and not so far from Little Mountain Side. She *also* knew that Bradley Baker had been flying there in some kind of spacecraft when he got shot down.

What she wanted to know was: Had his crash been reported in the local news?

She had a pretty good idea of what she was looking for and a pretty good idea of what she was expecting to find.

However, after a few hours of peering through the microfiche viewer at archived newspapers, Ruby had come up with absolutely nothing regarding a western-mountain plane crash in the fall of 1962.

There was no mention of it in the national papers, but perhaps she shouldn't be surprised — a small aircraft crashing would hardly be of great interest to the nation at large, especially since the guy piloting the plane was no one of note. To the wider world, Bradley Baker was a nobody.

Ruby didn't give up there; instead she began working her way through the *local* papers, the *West Mountain Tribune* and the *Ridgepoint Gazette*. In this second paper she found a report of a bright light followed by a thunderous noise somewhere just off the mountain road known as the Pine Forest Pass. A small area of woodland had been destroyed and a crater formed, but nothing else: no debris, no human remains. There was speculation as to whether the cause was a meteorite entering Earth's atmosphere.

Only one newspaper, the *Sequoia Herald*, raised the possibility of a plane or other aircraft exploding midair, though this idea was quickly rejected by one witness:

"If it was a plane, then it must have vaporized, as there was no sign of any wreckage whatsoever."

The witness was a member of the Sequoia Mountain forestry

team, and though he had not been present on the night of the explosion, he *did* visit the site the following day and found nothing to lead him to believe that the cause of the explosion could have been an aircraft. All the local articles reported pretty much the same inconclusive findings, with no explanation or useful detail.

However, things got a little more interesting and a little weirder when Ruby picked up Little Mountain Side's UFO quarterly journal, titled *Unidentified*. It was an amateur publication, put together by enthusiastic UFO watchers.

Most of the magazine was taken up with blurry photographs of bright lights in the sky, which, due to the poor quality of the images, could have been anything from helicopters to streetlights. There were also articles about little green men, things that went bump in the night, and alien encounters, but it was when Ruby turned to page seventeen and found the interview with local man Lenny Rivers that her interest was piqued.

Lenny had been driving back home along Pine Forest Pass in the direction of Ridgepoint when he had spotted an injured man lying on the road.

"A hit-and-run, probably a logging truck, I reckon; poor soul had been left for dead. I half-lifted, half-dragged the fella, and eventually got him into my truck with the intention of driving him on to Ridgepoint Hospital—they got a pretty well-equipped emergency unit there. I hadn't gone more than a quarter mile when I find the road cordoned off, detour, it says, maybe a fallen tree, I'm thinking, but I'm in my truck, got my chainsaw with me, and I figure I can deal with that, and heck, I don't have much choice here—the guy's dying; I gotta get him some medical attention and quick. I don't have the time to drive fifty miles in the other direction."

It was en route to Ridgepoint that Mr. Rivers witnessed his second dramatic happening of the night:

"It was 1 a.m. or thereabouts and pitch-dark and then all of a sudden I start to see lights in the trees, all these flashlights and something glowing. Then I begin to make out figures; as I got nearer, it was possible to see that these figures were official-looking fellows, black suits, that kind of caper, and all talking on walkie-talkie devices—like FBI agents, maybe. I slowed down to ask if they might be able to give my passenger some medical help, but I was waved back, quicker than you can spit, told me the road was closed, like they couldn't get me outta there fast enough. Had to find another route to the hospital, which lord knows wasn't easy." Mr. Rivers drove out there the next morning but found "there wasn't a darned thing to see other than a pretty big dent in the ground."

When *Unidentified* asked Mr. Rivers what he believed was the cause of all this "official" attention, he said:

> "Folks in town were talking about a meteorite, but if you want to know what I think, it was a UFO, some kinda spaceship had come down."

Ruby sat back in her chair. Lenny Rivers wasn't wrong. A meteorite wouldn't have FBI types closing off roads. If it had been a plane that had crashed, a regular plane, there would have been no reason to keep it hush-hush.

A spaceship full of Martians? Hard to believe.

A spacecraft, not alien but part of the Spectrum Space Program? Possibly.

When Ruby had finished reading every single article, paragraph, and sentence relating to the Pine Forest Pass incident, she sat back in her chair and wondered what might be her next move.

Go find Lenny Rivers, she thought.

Finding Lenny Rivers's address was the easy part; he was in the phone book.

No time like right now, she thought. She went downstairs, grabbed her coat, and headed off toward the bus depot.

When Ruby arrived at Lenny Rivers's house, the door was answered by an elderly woman.

"I'm sorry to bother you," said Ruby, "but I was wondering if I could speak to Mr. Lenny Rivers?"

The woman looked puzzled. "My husband passed on eight years ago now."

"Oh," said Ruby. "I didn't know, I mean, I wasn't thinking. . . . Geez, I'm sorry."

"Quite all right, dear," said the woman. "Is there something *I* can help you with?"

"Maybe," said Ruby. "That is, if you don't mind."

Once Ruby had properly introduced herself and explained what had brought her to Ridgepoint, and more specifically, why she was standing there on the stoop, they went inside.

"If it's unidentified flying objects you're looking to discuss, then I'll be needing tea—you want a cup?"

Dora Rivers was a nice woman—in her eighties now, but still what Mrs. Digby would describe as "with it" in the brain department.

"Oh, Lenny was pretty convinced about those UFOs. Every once in a while he would spot one—or at least imagine he had."

"You don't believe in them?" asked Ruby.

"I've seen some weird things, believe me," said Dora, "but my view is, there's always a reasonable explanation for everything. A bright light in the sky doesn't make it a flying saucer."

"What about the weird activity Lenny saw in the fall of 1962? Do you know anything about that?"

Dora scratched her head. "As I recall it, Lenny was always seeing weird things."

"This was probably weirder than most," said Ruby. She opened her satchel and took out the copy she had made of the *Unidentified* article. "It was out at Pine Forest Pass," she said. She handed the piece to Dora, who reached for her glasses and looked at it a while.

"Oh, yes," she said. "I *do* remember this one; I remember it *very well,* because Lenny came home all animated. It was late, maybe three a.m."

"So what did he tell you?" asked Ruby.

"He told me he had found a fella on the road, knocked down by a truck and left for dead."

"Yeah, but what did he say about the *UFO*?" asked Ruby.

"Oh, he was very excited about that, all these men in black suits, he said, all on walkie-talkies. He was very suspicious, thought they were the FBI."

"Was he right?" asked Ruby.

Dora shrugged. "How to know? No one was interested in Lenny's theories, I'm afraid me included. I was much more concerned about the poor soul he took to Ridgepoint Hospital. Lenny didn't expect him to see the night through."

"But he did?" asked Ruby.

"Yes," said Mrs. Rivers. "Confounded all the doctors." She paused, musing on the memory. "Then the fellow disappeared into thin air. According to what the nurse said, he was there one minute and gone the next, never seen again. Of course, that made Lenny think that perhaps the fella was actually some sort of Martian and he'd been beamed back up into his spaceship." She began to laugh at that.

Ruby smiled. "But the FBI guys, or at least the men Lenny took for FBI guys, did they ever come *back*?" she asked.

"No," said Mrs. Rivers.

"And the explosion," asked Ruby, "I mean, did your husband ever change his mind about that, ever think that maybe it was something other than a UFO?"

Mrs. Rivers shook her head. "He was sure as eggs that something fishy was going on. He said if it was a meteorite, then why the fuss? If it was a plane crash, then it was some special sort of plane, because they cleared that crash site pretty good and quick."

Ruby sighed. It was all interesting stuff, but this conversation wasn't taking her anywhere she hadn't already been.

"Say," said Dora, getting to her feet, "why don't you take this with you?" She went over to the desk by the fireplace and opened a drawer — out of it she pulled a little beige notebook.

"It's Lenny's UFO sightings diary. He wrote up every weird and peculiar happening in that book, a kinda hobby of his." She handed it to Ruby. "You've got more use for it than I have," she said. "That I can promise you."

❋ ❋ ❋

Ruby began reading as soon as she got on the bus back to Twinford.

Lenny's account was pretty detailed. There was a good description of the lights in the forest, the men standing around as if guarding the site. He had also made a note of everything the dying man had said to him; he had wanted to remember in case he could be of help when the family came to find him or, more likely, to claim his body. Lenny had written:

The fella was talking about himself as if he had already passed, like he knew he was going to die. It was the way he answered when I asked him his name, he said:

"Loveday. It was Morgan . . . Loveday."

Ruby stared intently at those five words.

Could it be a coincidence that both these names were echoed in the Ghost Files?

That would be a pretty *big* coincidence: a kid named Casey Morgan, a kid named Loveday, and a disappearing man named Morgan Loveday — all three connected to strange events. The name of the suspected would-be assassin merged with the name of the rescuer, making another name for a man who appeared from nowhere and disappeared to nowhere.

What if the injured man had not been the victim of a hit-and-run? What if the injured guy had fallen from the sky and crawled from the wreckage of his *aircraft*? What if his aircraft had been no ordinary plane or helicopter but some kind of spacecraft connected to the Spectrum Space Program?

What if the whole thing about the meteorite had been made up and fed to the local newspapers, a cover-up? What if the men in black suits were cleaning up the site so no one would be any the wiser about this space activity?

Ruby mumbled the words the injured guy had spoken to Lenny Rivers:

"Loveday. It was Morgan Loveday."

She repeated them over and over, altering the stress so that the words became a message. Loveday, it was *Morgan*. Loveday?

What if this guy had not been telling Lenny Rivers his *name* but actually had been trying to tell him something else like, *Tell Loveday it was Morgan*?

Loveday, the kid on the riverbank, the kid who had saved Baker's life when he was a boy recruit.

Morgan, the kid who had tried to *take* his life.

What if the man on the road was telling this kid from way back that *Morgan* was responsible for his near-drowning, a throwback memory, all confused from a blow to the head.

Or . . .

What if he had kept in touch with Loveday, and he was telling the only person left on this planet who actually remembered what had happened all those years before that Morgan had come back and he was the one responsible for the explosion?

If that was true, then there was only one reasonable conclusion. It seemed more than unlikely, it seemed verging on crazy, but not impossible and, as Sherlock Holmes once said: *"When you have eliminated the impossible, whatever remains, however improbable, must be the truth."*

Everything seemed to be pointing to the fact that the pilot of this craft, the man Lenny Rivers had rescued, must be Bradley Baker.

"I want somebody dead,"
said Casey Morgan. . . .

The Count shrugged. "Don't we all."

"This is different, this boy —"

"A boy!"

"You're not listening. . . ."

The man flashed back a look of steel-cold loathing, pointing his finger so close to Casey Morgan's face that the child stepped back. "What reason would I have for helping a wretch like you?"

Casey Morgan took a breath and said, "Because this is no ordinary boy; this boy is Bradley Baker. Take him down and take down Spectrum."

CHAPTER 33
One and the Same

HER PARENTS WERE SITTING WATCHING TV when she came home.

"Hey, honey, you're back late," said her father.

"Have you been at Clancy's?" asked Sabina.

"The library," replied Ruby.

"Rube, you study too hard," said her father.

"Your father's right," said her mother. "You got to start letting your hair down."

"You know what they say," said her father. "All work and no play makes Jack a dull boy."

"Ruby a dull boy," corrected her mother.

"Right," said Ruby. "I'll bear that in mind."

She went into the kitchen to fix herself a snack. Bug was asleep under the table but stirred from his slumbers when she came in. She scratched the dog behind his ears and pondered what she knew or thought she knew.

The question was, if Bradley Baker *was* alive, then why had he not returned to Spectrum?

Because he thinks someone is trying to kill him?

No, this couldn't be the reason. Baker might spend a few months lying low, trying to figure out who he could trust, but not a whole decade.

She needed someone to speak to about this. Not LB—that didn't seem wise.

Blacker? She considered it and then dismissed the idea.

Hitch? Had to be.

She tapped a message into her Spectrum watch:

>> NEED TO SPEAK TO YOU ASAP.

and waited for the message to be received.

It didn't take more than seven seconds.

>> MONITORING A 678. UNLESS YOU'RE DANGLING BY
A FINGER FROM THE SKYLARK BUILDING, I'LL HAVE TO
CATCH UP WITH YOU LATER, KID.

"What's a 678 called when it's happening at home?" muttered Ruby.

She reread the notes Rivers had made regarding this Morgan Loveday.

The doctors told me that apart from his name, he can't seem to remember a darned thing about himself.

So what if his memory had never come back?

Ruby thought for a moment. *Then why wouldn't he seek help?*

What would Clancy say? she wondered. She could almost hear her friend's voice in her ear; he was saying:

Because Bradley Baker's sixth sense is talking to him.

Because he has a hunch that it's not safe to come back.

Because Casey Morgan is still out there.

When Ruby returned to her room, she found the message light on her answering machine was blinking. She flicked the playback button and listened.

Beep: "Hey, Ruby, this is Red. I'm really sorry, but something's happened and well, kinda slightly, actually totally destroyed your guitar; you might not believe this, but for once it wasn't my fault, this time the ceiling collapsed in the kitchen — squashed it flat. Anyway, that's not the point. I'm gonna replace it, but I'm gonna be saving for a while, you know, but hang in there, I got a Saturday job now. Sorry, call me, OK, don't be mad, I mean *do* be mad, but I'm super sorry, so keep that in mind."

Beep: "Hi, Ruby, it's Quent. I have this invitation, it's for a bring your dog party and I'm going to take my dog and I'm allowed to bring one person with me and *their* dog and I wondered if" — *oh, brother,* thought Ruby, *here it comes* — "you and Bug would be my plus twos!"

Beep: "A message for Ruby Redfort. This is Daily Supplies up in Little Mountain Side; those hen of the woods mushrooms you were after have finally come in. If you can get in early tomorrow, I'll be there, but later than noon I'm shutting up the store. I got an appointment I can't miss. But don't worry, I'll leave them with Clara in the bookshop; can't risk leaving them at the Little Green Diner — they might eat 'em. So just say Mo Loveday left you a box behind the counter."

Bang.

Mo Loveday.

Morgan Loveday.

One and the same.

CHAPTER 34
I Remember Nothing

RUBY LEFT EARLY IN THE MORNING on the first bus out of Twinford, the dawn bus. She changed at the city terminal, then took the mountain road bus to Maple Falls and the mountain pass bus up through the Sequoias to Little Mountain Side.

She was there waiting for him when he arrived at 7:00 a.m. to unlock the store, sitting on the little wooden bench, bundled up against the cold.

He smiled in a puzzled sort of way.

"Ruby?"

She peeped out from the hood of her snow parka.

"Boy, you must want these mushrooms a lot."

She didn't reply.

He took his key from his pocket and turned the lock. "I'm telling you, you're not the only one; I've had a lot of orders."

Silence.

"Are *you* going to be cooking them up or are you going to leave that to somebody else?"

Still she said nothing.

"Hey, kid, I gotta be honest here; you're spooking me a little."

She took a deep breath. "There's something I need to tell you."

He stood on the threshold, looking at her, and then, "Sounds serious. I guess you might want to come inside." He switched on the lights.

"You look near frozen. You want tea, cocoa, coffee?" he asked.

Ruby nodded. She didn't much mind what the beverage was, so long as it was piping hot.

He lit the wood burner and went into the back room to boil the kettle. Ruby thawed her hands and waited to deliver the news that would erase Morgan Loveday quicker than you could blink.

He returned with tea and a couple of muffins, which she was grateful for, having left the house with nothing but a pack of bubble gum — chewing on that only made the hunger grow.

He sat down opposite her and said, "So what's the big deal, why the early visit?"

"I figured something out," she said.

"Must be pretty important to have you on the dawn bus from Twinford."

"It's big," she said. "Important."

"Important to me or important to you?" he asked.

"Important to everyone," she said.

He nodded. "OK, so what is it?"

Ruby looked him hard in the eye and said, "You're not Morgan Loveday."

The guy smiled. "I'm not?"

"No," said Ruby.

He shrugged. "I'd argue with you, but I don't have much of a memory."

"And why is that?" asked Ruby.

"I was hit by a truck, got a nasty bang to the head."

"You *think* you were hit by a truck, but there were no witnesses," said Ruby.

"OK, there's no proof, but I do have the scars, pretty good ones too." He rolled up his sleeve. "Plus there's my leg injury, and let's not forget a punctured lung — they had to be caused by something pretty dramatic, right?"

RUBY: *I agree, but what were you doing walking along that stretch of mountain road?*

MO: *Hiking?*

RUBY: *Doesn't it strike you as odd that you were out there alone, no backpack, no flashlight, no hat, no gloves in, what was it, October?*

MO: *So maybe I was driving; maybe I crashed my car and it rolled down into the gully?*

RUBY: *Lenny Rivers, the man who found you, went back and he searched, but he didn't find any wrecked vehicle, nor was there any sign of tire marks — I read his whole account.*

MO: *Sounds like you've been doing your homework. So what's your take on it? What hit me?*

RUBY: *I think there was an aircraft.*

He furrowed his brow.

MO: *You're suggesting a plane hit me?*
RUBY: *Not* hit *you, of course not hit you. I'm saying you were in an aircraft, and that craft crashed.*
MO: *But then wouldn't every TV station in the state have reported it? They would have known who died, who survived.*
RUBY: *But you weren't flying a passenger plane.*
MO: *Wait a minute, you're saying I was* flying *the plane?*

Ruby nodded.

MO: *I can fly planes?*
RUBY: *You can.* Pause. *Well, you* could; *you're probably a little rusty now. I mean, don't go climbing into a cockpit anytime soon.*
MO: *So what kind of plane was I flying — a freight plane, a light aircraft?*
RUBY: *A Delta V DSO.*
MO: *I don't even know what that is.*
RUBY: *Well, no one does, at least no one who isn't part of Spectrum's space program.*
MO: *I have no idea what that is either — Spectrum? You've gone all sci-fi on me.*

RUBY: *Well, I guess it is a little sci-fi.*

He cocked his head, trying to understand what she was saying.

RUBY: *Listen, it's probably gonna blow your mind, but stay with me because it gets weirder.*

He nodded the way someone who was under hypnosis might nod.

RUBY: *Spectrum is a secret agency.*
MO: *And you work for Spectrum?*
RUBY: *Yes.*
MO: *And you're saying I did too?*
RUBY: *Uh-huh.*
MO: *So, are we the good guys or the bad guys?*
RUBY: *Excuse me?*
MO: *Spectrum.* Pause. *Are we the good guys or the bad guys?*
RUBY: *Oh, we're the good guys.*
MO: *Everyone always thinks they're the good guys.*

Ruby smiled, remembering how she had uttered the exact same words when she had first learned about Spectrum.

RUBY: *Actually, you have a point. To be totally honest, I'm no longer sure.*

MO: *That doesn't sound good.*

RUBY: *No, but I think it's all connected to what happened to you.* Pause. *Someone infiltrated Spectrum. It wasn't an accident, the order to vaporize your aircraft; it came from someone inside the agency . . . well, the boss, actually.*

MO: *My boss tried to kill me. We not get along or something?*

RUBY: *You got along pretty well.* Pause. *Actually, better than well. To be clear — your boss was your most trusted ally.*

MO: *I guess I'm a pretty bad judge of character.*

RUBY: *Actually, I think you are a good judge of character.*

MO: *So you mean maybe I deserved it?*

RUBY: *No, I don't think that's right either. Nothing I read in the files or anything anyone has ever said about you leads me to believe that you were anything but on the level.*

MO: *So . . . ?*

RUBY: *So, I got it from the horse's mouth, meaning the boss, and it all made sense.*

MO: *How so?*

RUBY: *You ever heard of the Trolley Problem?*

MO: *Maybe, maybe not.*

RUBY: *So, your boss was given an impossible decision. One life or one thousand and twenty-seven lives. −1 = + 1,027.*

MO: *So my boss chose to minus one.*

RUBY: *You.*

MO: *So he made the right decision.*

RUBY: She — *she made the right decision, if there is a right decision here.*

MO: *OK,* she *made the right decision.* Pause. *So, what's her name? This boss of mine who likes me so much she decided to kill me.*

Ruby looked at him.

RUBY: *LB.*

He blinked several times, like he was trying to conjure some long-dead memory.

RUBY: *You remember her?*

MO: *No.*

RUBY: *Do you believe me?*

MO: *About what?*

RUBY: *Everything.*

He looked at her then and nodded. He was sure. It was something to do with the way the girl was staring at him that made him believe; something to do with her green eyes made him trust that what she said was true.

RUBY: *You see, if you are him, it explains why a guy with a not-so-great leg is able to virtually run up a giant redwood and solve cryptic crossword clues without a second thought.*

He was looking at her, really looking at her. This thirteen-year-old girl had his past, and *understood* what he had struggled for more than a decade to know. This kid held the answer to the most important question he had ever asked himself: Who am I?

RUBY: *All along I just thought, boy, this guy is unusual for a grocer, but I really had no idea who you really were. How could I?*

"So who am I?" he asked.
Ruby looked him hard in the eye and said:
"You're Bradley Baker."

CHAPTER 35
Who to Tell?

RUBY WAS TRYING TO FIGURE OUT what she should do next. It was one thing locating a dead man only to find him alive and in pretty good shape (if you ignored the slight limp and the long-term amnesia), but now she had the problem of who to tell and how to break it to them.

Hitch? Well, of course she should tell Hitch, but he'd said "Unless you're dangling by a finger from the Skylark Building, I'll have to catch up with you later, kid."

LB?

Ruby wasn't sure how her boss was going to take this news. How do you tell a person that the man she had shot out of the sky more than a decade ago was actually alive and well and eating a blueberry muffin in the grocery store he now ran in a one-horse town in the Sequoia Mountains? *Oh, and by the way, LB, he has no idea who you are.*

Yes, if anyone was going to deliver this news, then it sure as eggs wasn't going to be her.

Of course there *were* other agents of senior rank, but there was no one she felt comfortable broadcasting this news to. For a start, she had a feeling she would spend a whole lot of time trying to convince them that it wasn't some prank.

The other question was, who to trust? Blacker? Of course, she could trust him with her life, but this was bigger than Blacker.

Agent Delaware? She couldn't contact him without going via Hitch or LB. Agent Trent-Kobie, same problem.

In the end, it was Hitch she told. Although she didn't actually *tell* him anything, she just contacted him via the fly barrette emergency locator and left it at that. Let him figure out where she was.

She left the barrette in the coffee shop with a note attached that simply said:

```
wait here
```

because she knew Hitch would need several good cups of coffee when he came face-to-face with this news and his old colleague Agent Bradley Baker.

When Ruby and Baker walked into the Morning Star coffee shop half an hour later, Hitch was already sitting at a table in the back. He was pouring a heavy dose of sugar into a mug of coffee and stirring it slowly around and around with a teaspoon. While he stirred, he gazed out the window at the view. He was twitchy, but he wasn't showing it—only the tiny movement of his jaw muscles betrayed him. He didn't catch sight of Ruby until they were almost at his table, and by the look in his eye he was pretty mad.

"You know, you don't look like you're hanging by one finger from the Skylark Building."

"No," agreed Ruby, "but what I have to tell you is a thousand times more dramatic, and if by the time I finish telling you you don't agree, then I promise to go directly to the Skylark Building and get climbing."

"All right, kid," said Hitch, "you've got my attention. Why the big mystery? How come you've got me helicoptering out to the back of beyond at . . ."

He didn't finish his sentence — something to do with the man standing just behind Ruby.

He squinted as if the strangest thought was occurring to him. He dropped the spoon, which fell into the coffee, which splashed onto his suit. He stood up, knocking the cup onto the floor, but he didn't seem to register any of this. All he could see was that the man standing there in the Morning Star might just as well be the man from Mars.

"Bradley?" he said. "Bradley Baker, is that you?"

"Actually, I have no idea," said Mo.

"You're not dead?" said Hitch.

"So I'm told," said Mo.

"So how . . . why . . . who . . ." Hitch wasn't getting his words out.

"I'll let your friend here field the questions," said Baker.

"I still feel a lot like the guy who runs Daily's grocery store in Little Mountain Side."

Ruby explained as much as she could, as much as she had managed to put together, that is.

RUBY: *I wasn't even trying to find him; I mean, why would I? As far as I was concerned he was dead. So the fact that I had actually met him never occurred to me.*

HITCH: *I can see that.*

RUBY: *I've only seen two pictures of Baker, and in neither one did he have this whole wild-man-of-the-woods deal going on.*

HITCH: *You mean the facial hair?*

BAKER: *It's just a* beard, *for crying out loud.*

HITCH: *How are you not dead? No one thought it was possible you could have survived.*

BAKER: *Did anyone look?*

HITCH: *Sure, they looked, but when you weren't found, the area was cleared because the mission you were on was top secret, and the explosion and subsequent fire and crater in the mountainside . . . well, that was all left to the public imagination.*

RUBY: *Most people concluded it was a meteor.*

HITCH: *So how did you make it out alive? Did you deploy the ejector?*

BAKER: *I remember nothing — remember?*

HITCH: *I forgot, sorry.*

RUBY: *The knock on the noggin erased his past.*

HITCH: *All of it?*

RUBY: *He retained all the stuff about rescuing cats up two-hundred-foot trees, but he can't remember the name of a single person he once called friend.*

HITCH: *Really?*

BAKER: *Try me.*

HITCH: *Did you know me?*

BAKER: *I have no idea.*

HITCH: *We worked in the same department for about seven years straight.*

Baker shrugged as if to say, *You see?*

HITCH: *So where does the name Morgan Loveday come from?*

RUBY: *It's what he mumbled to Lenny Rivers, the old guy who found him dying on the road.*

HITCH: *So who is the real Morgan Loveday?*

RUBY: *There isn't one. I mean, of course there is likely to be a Morgan Loveday somewhere in the world, probability and all that, but Bradley didn't acquire the name from an actual person.*

BAKER: *You're suggesting they are random names I came up with?*

RUBY: *Oh, no, not random, not random at all. Just . . . two people's names, squished together.*
BAKER: *So, people I know? People I like?*
RUBY: *Yes and no.*
BAKER: *OK. So who was Morgan?*

Ruby took a deep breath.

RUBY: *A kid who tried to kill you.*
BAKER: *A kid?*
RUBY: *Yeah, a kid.*
BAKER: *This kid, did he catch me by surprise or something?*
RUBY: *Yeah, but if it makes you feel better, it happened more than thirty years ago, and you were a kid too.*
BAKER: *And Loveday?*
RUBY: *The kid who saved you.*
BAKER: *Where did this happen?*
RUBY: *Australia.*
BAKER: *How did I come to be in Australia?*

Ruby looked across at Hitch, expecting him to at least question how she had come by all this confidential information, but he said nothing, so she continued.

RUBY: *You were part of the Junior Space Recruitment*

Program, also known as Larvae. In fact, you were the first kid ever recruited, therefore older than the others. Larvae got shut down when Casey Morgan, the one who tried to kill you, went rogue.

BAKER: *What did I do to make this kid Morgan so mad?*

RUBY: *You made it to Larva level, meaning you became a recruit for the Spectrum Space Program. Morgan's ambition was to be part of the Space Encounter team, but from what I read, he couldn't even graduate to Larva recruit — he had too much self-interested ego to make it to agent or astronaut.*

BAKER: *And this kid who saved me was also from the program?*

RUBY: *No.*

BAKER: *No?*

RUBY: *This was a kid who just happened to be there, a kid who was fishing or camping out or something and observed the whole thing.*

BAKER: *So do we know if Loveday is a first name or a last name?*

RUBY: *Only thing I know is that Loveday is Australian and was around the same age as you.*

HITCH: *As I understood it, you were almost dead when they fished you out of that river, so who says you even got to meet Loveday? Why would this name come to mind when you were found half dead on the road?*

RUBY: *So perhaps they did meet; perhaps Loveday became someone Baker trusted.*

HITCH: *I don't see how we can ever know the truth if we don't know who the kid is.*

BAKER: *So the million-dollar question is: Who is this Loveday?*

It was only then that they became aware of the woman standing not far from the table.

"Me," said LB.

CHAPTER 36
Loveday

NO ONE HAD NOTICED the Spectrum 8 boss enter the Morning Star coffee shop. She had picked up the distress call to Hitch and, wary of recent events, had made the decision to follow up.

She'd stepped quietly in through the door, without a sound, and had been watching them unobserved.

When LB spoke, her voice was steady, not a hint of shock, surprise, or emotion, but Ruby couldn't help wondering on what kind of inner reserves she must be drawing, what it was costing her to hold it together instead of collapsing clean to the floor.

Several seconds passed before anyone said anything, and when they did, it was Ruby who said it.

"You are Loveday?"

"I am," said her boss, her eyes trained on the man sitting opposite Hitch.

"L for Loveday, so B for . . ."

"Byrd," said LB.

Baker stared back at LB as if he was struggling to pluck some memory.

"Loveday Byrd?" mused Ruby.

"My parents had questionable taste," said LB.

"It's very . . . sorta . . ." Ruby began.

"Romantic . . ." suggested Baker.

"Loveday Byrd . . ." She switched to a whisper, "*Uggerlimb.*"

"Ah," said Baker.

"Which is why I went with the initials."

"I can see why you dropped the U," said Ruby. "What I don't get is how can no one know your real name?"

"I changed it a long time ago. The only person to know me as Loveday was Baker . . . and I thought he was dead."

She sat down. Her face was hard to read.

LB was looking directly at Baker when she said, "We never found your body; we thought it had been consumed by the flames. There was no sign of you, no sign that you had managed to struggle from the wreck or eject from the craft, no time to go over the area with a fine-tooth comb. We had to erase the evidence before the TV crews and newspapers showed." She paused, turning to Hitch. "And by the way, it wasn't an accident."

"What wasn't an accident?" asked Hitch.

"The crash."

"The crash was planned?" said Hitch. "Someone shot down Baker's spacecraft — who?"

"Her," said Baker, pointing his thumb in LB's direction.

"How do *you* know? I thought you had amnesia," said LB.

"*She* told me," said Baker, now pointing his thumb at Ruby.

"You read *that* in the Ghost Files?" said Hitch, looking at Ruby.

"Run that by me again?" said LB.

"The kid broke into the Ghost Files," said Hitch.

"She *what*?" said LB.

"How do you know I broke into the Ghost Files?" asked Ruby.

"Someone found your pencil," said Hitch, producing it from his pocket.

"So why didn't you say?" asked Ruby.

"I had my reasons," said Hitch.

"I'd love to hear them," said LB.

"And I'm sort of dying to know why you decided to kill Baker," said Hitch.

"Reading the Ghost Files won't tell you," said LB.

"No, that's right," said Ruby. "It was the Count who told me."

"Told you what?" asked Hitch.

"Told me that it was LB who killed Bradley Baker."

"As everybody is beginning to figure out, I'm not actually dead," said Baker.

"Which is a miracle," said Hitch.

LB turned to Baker. "I had to make a choice between one life and more than a thousand. I chose to save the thousand and twenty-seven — I chose to kill you."

Baker smiled. "How could you not? It had to be that way."

And she flashed him a look that told of pain and grief.

There followed a debriefing of sorts, where Ruby explained again what had led her to Baker and how she had discovered all she had discovered.

LB was unusually calm about the three break-ins to the Prism Vault. But then again, how could she possibly be angry? Without Ruby's total inability to abide by Spectrum rules, Bradley Baker would still be up in Little Mountain Side, standing behind a counter in a grocery store, chatting with customers and filling in the squares in the cryptic crossword. Grateful though she was, LB did make an emergency call to Froghorn and tell him to reconfigure the Prism Vault code.

"And Froghorn," her voice was stern, "do better this time."

Hitch looked at his watch: the weather forecast predicted snow flurries.

"Kid, we should go if we want to get that helicopter back to base."

They left the Spectrum 8 boss and former agent Baker sitting at the little table in the Morning Star coffee shop, deep in conversation and barely seeming to register their colleagues' departure.

Once outside, Ruby turned and, looking back through the window, what she saw was a couple lit up by the cozy glow of the cafe, snowflakes beginning to drift across the scene. It looked for all the world like a Christmas card.

CHAPTER 37
A Safe House

BRADLEY BAKER LEFT LITTLE MOUNTAIN SIDE the very next day. It was decided that it would be impractical for him to stay on there. He was reluctant to leave, but he understood that the debriefing would take time — there were a lot of missing memories, and no one was sure if they could be recovered. It was LB's feeling that while security was compromised at HQ, Spectrum would not be a safe place for Baker to be. Furthermore, information regarding Baker's survival should be restricted to those agents LB had faith in and could trust with her life; these individuals would have to work outside Spectrum headquarters.

So after much discussion and deliberation, it was decided that the safest place for Bradley Baker was Green-Wood House. Baker would be well protected: on the one hand, there was the new state-of-the-art security system, and on the other, living with the Redfort family would provide perfect cover. Since no one was aware Baker was alive, no one was going to come looking for him.

"Not a word of this gets discussed over the airways, are we clear?" said LB. "Baker's name should not be mentioned in company, nor anywhere in the Spectrum building, and no one but those *authorized* to know should be made aware of his existence."

So just like that, Bradley Baker became a guest of Sabina and Brant, only he would be known as Mo Loveday. Hitch made the call, which went something like this . . .

"I hope you will understand, Sabina" (Sabina Redfort had always insisted on informality) "if there were any alternative I would certainly take it."

"Why yes, of course, Hitch, but what are you asking, exactly?"

"My cousin from out of town?"

"A cousin, how wonderful!" Pause. "What about him?"

"You didn't get my message?" said Hitch, who hadn't actually left her a message.

"No," said Sabina. "I've been so busy with the Christmas shopping I just haven't had time to do another thing; I'm so sorry."

"Well, I left a note to say my cousin Mo has just had a spell in the county hospital, and I want to keep an eye on him."

"Oh, dear, what happened to him?"

"He had an accident of sorts. . . ."

"Oh, my, how awful. What sort of accident?"

"It involved a chicken of the woods."

"He was attacked by a wood chicken?"

"No, it's an edible mushroom, not to be confused with the hen of the woods, a different fungus altogether. Anyway, he ate a chicken of the woods and suffered a bad reaction. It happens from time to time."

"How dreadful," said Sabina; she paused and then said, "and oh, dear!"

"What is it?" said Hitch.

"Oh, dear, oh, dear, I believe Mrs. Digby is preparing a maitake, that's hen of the woods, mushroom stew for this evening's supper, and your poor cousin really won't want to look a mushroom in the face after what he's been through! I mean, I should know after that terrible bout of oyster poisoning I contracted."

"He'll be fine," said Hitch. "He's a bit disoriented is all; just don't ask him too many questions. Questions tend to throw him."

"Oh," said Sabina, "I'll be sure to tell Brant, *no* questions."

"Anyway, the thing is, I don't like the idea of Mo being alone, what with his . . ."

"Confusion?" said Sabina.

"Exactly," said Hitch.

"Right," said Sabina, herself confused. "Of course you don't, Hitch — neither do I. He must come and stay; we have the guest room and he's welcome to use it."

The Green-Wood guest room was actually more like a guest *apartment*, which meant if the guest so wished, there was no need for him to venture into any other part of the house. But this was not how the Redforts liked things: they enjoyed company, and they prided themselves on being good hosts.

"I can't wait to meet him," said Sabina, clasping her hands excitedly. "I will make such a fuss of him."

"No fussing," said Hitch. "He's not good with fussing."

"No fussing," promised Sabina, "but I really will have to change the menu."

When Baker arrived that Saturday, it was by the city bus — no fanfare, no big welcome party, everything was deliberately low-key. Ruby and Bug met him at the corner of Cedarwood Drive, and they walked casually on toward Green-Wood House.

"Nice to see you out and about. I hear you suffered some kinda toadstool poisoning?"

"I think that's unlikely," said Baker. "I kinda know my mushrooms from my toadstools by now, but I'll play along."

Ruby filled him in on the occupants of Green-Wood House.

"Mrs. Digby you'll like; she's a straight talker, and so long as you appreciate her cooking and never interrupt her when she's playing TV bingo, you'll get along just fine. Though she's furious with you."

"What, already?" said Baker.

"You're the reason her hen-of-the-woods stew had to be abandoned."

"But I love hen-of-the-woods stew," argued Baker.

"Yeah, but you've just suffered a bad case of mushroom poisoning," explained Ruby.

"This is a very inconvenient lie," said Baker.

They crossed the road, and once on the other side, Baker stopped and looked around.

"What is it?" asked Ruby.

"I don't know, just a feeling," said Baker.

"Like you've been here before?"

He shook his head. "Something else," he said.

They walked on up the steps, and before Ruby could reach for her key, the door was flung open and there was Sabina Redfort, smiling her biggest Sabina Redfort smile.

"Hey, Mo!" she said. "Come in, come in, how lovely to see you, you must make yourself comfortable, how was your journey? Are you tired? Do you want a tea? A coffee? Oh"—she remembered what Hitch had said about questions, *no questions*—"just come in, let me help you with your bag, do *whatever* you want, take your boots off, keep them on, if you're cold turn up the heat, if you're hot open the windows, anything goes. . . . Oh"—*no fussing,* she remembered, and quickly corrected herself—"I mean, just go right ahead and help yourself and I'll leave you to it." She walked quickly upstairs and disappeared into the den.

Bradley Baker looked confused, but Ruby shrugged. "My mom's a little strange," she whispered. "Just go along with it."

Mrs. Digby sniffed when she saw him; it was a disapproving sniff, and he picked up on it right away.

"I am all apologies, Mrs. Digby. I don't know what to say; all the efforts you've gone to producing a wonderful supper and I've ruined it by almost dying of mushroom poisoning—some houseguest," said Bradley.

This did the trick, and two minutes later Mrs. Digby and

"Mo Loveday" were chatting away while he sliced onions and she boiled potatoes. They talked of foraging and survival, and Mrs. Digby explained how her old pa had taught her to move without sound when stalking prey.

"I don't often get the chance to use this talent," she said, "but I tell you, once in a blue moon it comes in very handy indeed."

By the time Ruby decided to turn in for bed, Sabina, Hitch, Bradley, Brant, and Mrs. Digby were settled in for a long night of poker.

CHAPTER 38
Lost and Found

HITCH HAD ARRANGED THINGS WELL: it was Sunday, and Brant and Sabina had suddenly found themselves invited to an exciting auction of rare and hitherto unseen works by the artist Pietro Tomassini. This exclusive event was celebrated with a grand lunch hosted by Miersons Auction House and held at the Circus Grande. This was to be immediately followed by the opera — Hitch had somehow managed to get his hands on a pair of tickets for *L'Amitié est Aveugle*.

"He must have connections," said Sabina. "Tickets to see Flora Steffanelli sing are just about gold dust."

"He's some butler," remarked Brant.

"Honey, Hitch is a house manager," corrected Sabina. "He doesn't like to be called a butler; he's very particular about that."

"Well, he's some house manager," said Brant.

The point of all this was to get the Redforts out of the house. Hitch had dispatched Mrs. Digby to an all-day, all-night poker session. He'd been tipped off about the game by an acquaintance known as Bunny All Thumbs, and Mrs. Digby, needless to say, couldn't get down there fast enough.

Once the coast was clear, it was easy enough for Spectrum to come and go without arousing suspicion.

Dr. Harper arrived first. She was there to check Baker's blood pressure, shine a light into his eyes, tap a little hammer on his knee, that sort of thing.

"So you're the great Bradley Baker?" said Dr. Harper. "Everyone does talk a lot about *you*, don't they?"

"I'm afraid I wouldn't know. You gotta remember, I've been dead for eleven years."

"How could I forget? Someone brings that fact up at least once a week," said Harper.

"Sounds tedious," said Baker.

"You get used to it," said Harper. "I'm just happy I finally got to meet what all the fuss was about."

The examination didn't take a great deal of time, but when it was done, and doctor and patient walked back into the kitchen, Ruby saw something different in Harper's expression, though she could not pinpoint what it was.

"So, Doc, can you do anything about the missing pieces?" said Bradley, tapping his finger to his head.

"That's a question for SJ. She's our memory expert."

"SJ?" said Baker.

"That's me," said SJ. "Good to see you again, sir." She stepped forward.

"Glad to see you too, SJ," said Baker, shaking her hand.

"Forgive me for not remembering you; let's hope you can put that right."

"I'll do my best, Agent Baker—you can count on it," said SJ.

Dr. Harper handed SJ a file before pulling on her coat. "A real privilege to meet you, Agent Baker," she said, picking up her doctor's bag.

"Likewise," said Baker.

Harper disappeared, LB arrived. It was the weirdest day, seeing the great and good of Spectrum walk in and out of the Green-Wood House front door.

"So what are we thinking?" said LB, sitting down at the Redforts' kitchen table. "Any chance of restoring the memory?"

"Is it even possible?" asked Baker.

"I think we might be able to gradually restore your memory, piece by piece, but to try and bring it back too swiftly could be damaging," said SJ. "I can't say we have ever done anything as radical as restore biographical memories. We have had great success restoring partial memories: how to tie shoelaces, things like that . . . But what Baker here has is more difficult than that. He remembers how to do things, how to speak . . . He just doesn't remember his life. When Pinkerton was alive, we spent a lot of hours trying to understand how memories are laid down and recovered, but—"

"You *knew* Pinkerton?" said Ruby. "Homer Pinkerton?"

"Of course," said SJ. "When I first started at Spectrum, I was

Professor Pinkerton's lab technician. He taught me everything I know about memory."

SJ picked up Baker's file and went to set up whatever it was she needed to set up downstairs in the guest apartment. Not quite forty minutes later, she returned.

"So, we're ready," she said. She glanced at LB. "I'll push the treatment as far as I can, but Baker has to take it easy." She glanced down at the file Harper had given her. "Anything too stressful, any physical overexertion could be very dangerous"—again she looked at LB, her expression suddenly very serious—"fatal, even."

LB just nodded. "Baker, are you willing to do this?" She reached out and touched his arm, and Baker smiled at her. "Of course," he said. "Without memories, what are we?"

Ruby had never seen LB make any kind of gesture that might suggest actual affection, but with this one small movement Ruby saw the tiniest hint of what Bradley Baker meant to her.

"OK," LB said, "so go easy on him. Time's not on our side, but let's not go killing him in the process."

While Baker was having his memory worked on, Ruby went up to her room to continue her trawl through the yellow notebooks.

What she found was not particularly enlightening.

Much of it involved watching the Lemons trying to collapse Archie Lemon's stroller, or get their dog, Dudley, to fetch a ball.

Dudley seemed to spend most of his waking hours howling at squirrels.

A few hours later she came back downstairs to the kitchen to find SJ writing up notes in her file.

"Where's LB?" she asked.

"Back at HQ," said SJ.

"Where's Baker?" asked Ruby.

"Resting," said SJ. "Probably fast asleep; this recall treatment really takes its toll."

"Want a snack?" asked Ruby.

"What you got?" asked SJ.

"Cookies or crackers," said Ruby.

"Cookies," said SJ.

But before they could open the jar, Blacker walked in with five bags of takeout.

"Hitch sent me," he explained.

"Where is he?" asked Ruby.

"Back at HQ," said Blacker. "He's got a lot on his plate. So who's for lunch? I got Chinese, Lebanese, Japanese," he announced. "I wasn't sure what you'd prefer, so I kinda ordered everything."

While they were eating they talked about Baker, his work, his recruitment, and how he had been the only kid to actually make the grade, the only one to become a fully qualified Larva junior agent.

"As I guess you already know," said SJ, turning to Ruby,

"Baker was taken on a few years before the JSRP was set up. He was such a bright kid, and a *good kid* — by which I mean he had a sense of responsibility, strong moral compass, that sort of thing — basically an all-around nice person."

"Yep, he was one in a million, you might say," agreed Blacker, reaching for a napkin and dabbing at a splash of soy sauce that was never going to come off his shirt. "But I think his brilliance sorta clouded Spectrum's judgment, made them think it would be easy enough to find a whole troupe of children who could do just what he did."

"But they only abandoned the Larvae Program when Casey Morgan went rogue?" said Ruby. "Morgan was just *one* rotten apple, right?"

"As I understand it, the cracks were beginning to show before that," said Blacker, reaching for the Singapore noodles. "I read that there were a lot of senior Spectrum staff who thought bringing kids into this business was a crazy idea, and when LB joined a few years on, she absolutely refused to even consider hiring junior recruits."

Yet I'm here, thought Ruby, but what she said was "OK, so what I don't get is, what happened to these junior recruits once they stopped *being* junior recruits? I mean, they were training to be agents and space recruits and then they were returned to normal life. Wasn't Spectrum worried they might blab?"

SJ put down her chopsticks and took a gulp of water. "OK, so after the Casey Morgan incident, Spectrum realized the whole thing was a very bad idea. They disbanded the program immediately, but before they sent the kids home, all memories relating to the JSRP were extracted and replaced with benign childhood memories; only then were the boys sent home to Mommy and Daddy, no harm done."

"Specific Memory Extraction?" said Ruby.

"That's right," said SJ, "SME."

"But *Baker* didn't undergo the SME?" said Ruby.

"No," said SJ, "because there was no need — Bradley was the only child recruit Spectrum retained from the training program. He was older than the other boys and had been Larva for a number of years."

"And Morgan?" asked Ruby.

"Now, here's the thing: Casey Morgan ran," said SJ.

"And Spectrum never caught up with him?" asked Ruby. "I mean, never?"

"According to records, he just seemed to disappear without a trace," said Blacker.

"But how is that possible?" asked Ruby.

"Pinkerton had a theory on that," said SJ. "Most in HQ thought it was a little far-fetched, a little paranoid."

"Why?" asked Ruby.

"He was sure Morgan had sought out the Count, had become one of his apprentices," said SJ. "He was sure Morgan had completely reinvented himself — if this were true, it would mean his own mother wouldn't recognize him, not even if she shook his hand."

"And what do you think?" asked Ruby.

SJ looked first at Blacker and then back at Ruby. "I'm beginning to come around to his point of view," she said.

"So why did the professor quit working for Spectrum?" asked Ruby.

"There was a falling-out," explained SJ. "Pinkerton wanted SME used as a cure — that was the point for him. His vision was to research how harmful memories might be isolated and removed, so freeing victims of the trauma of crippling memories. He disagreed with Spectrum using SME on the kids — the youngest ones were ten — and he began to be troubled by the idea his pioneering work might be used unethically. Pinkerton thought this was like dipping a toe into something dangerous — he began to wonder what might happen if SME got into the wrong hands."

"So did he destroy his work?" asked Ruby.

"He told me that he hid it," said SJ. "He split the formula into two parts; one piece he gave to Baker and the other"— she shrugged —"he never told me."

"Effectively, he stole the SME code," said Blacker.

"Stole it?" said Ruby. "But how could he steal it? He developed it, after all."

"Technically, he developed it with Spectrum resources when

he was on the Spectrum payroll, so it belonged to Spectrum," said SJ.

"So you thought what Pinkerton did was wrong?" asked Ruby.

"*Morally* I am in agreement with him. I think Spectrum's use of SME was questionable," said SJ. "But, however you want to look at it, Pinkerton *did* remove something that did not belong to him."

This discussion over, Ruby and Blacker cleared the table, and SJ went down to check on Baker.

"One thing I noticed from the files," said Ruby. "There were no girls recruited as Larvae candidates, not a one."

"Old-fashioned times," said Blacker. "There were no female field agents in the whole of HQ, not until LB arrived and shook things up."

CHAPTER 39
Cousin Mo

THE NEXT MORNING Ruby had breakfast with Bradley Baker, chatted about basketball, dogs, record collections, movies, hen of the woods, chicken of the woods, snow sports, and breakfast preferences.

"Of course you gotta have maple syrup; what's a pancake without it?" said Bradley.

"That's what I spend my life explaining to my mother," said Ruby.

"I'll have a word with her," said Bradley.

It was like a miracle: one week ago Bradley Baker, legendary agent and onetime hero, had been dead; today he was alive and well and discussing pancakes in the Redfort family kitchen.

"So who's that guy?" asked Del before Ruby had even had a chance to take her seat on the bus.

"What guy?" said Ruby.

"That guy," said Mouse, pointing to the man on the sidewalk outside the Redfort house.

"Oh, that guy," said Ruby.

They watched as Bradley Baker and Bug crossed the road.

"Is he the new dog-walker?" asked Mouse.

"No," said Ruby, "that's Hitch's cousin Mo; he's staying with us for a couple of weeks."

Ruby watched him from the window, turning her head as the bus passed by. He stopped when he reached Mrs. Beesman, and she saw him help the old lady maneuver her heavily laden shopping cart onto the sidewalk. Ruby wasn't sure, but they actually seemed to be exchanging words. Now, that was unusual, super unusual.

"You have Bradley Baker living in your *house*?" whispered Clancy in class. "Your actual house?"

"Yeah," said Ruby, her voice hushed, "and no one's to know — at least, no one's to know his real name. He's called Mo, not Bradley, OK?"

"OK, but he's alive? Bradley Baker's alive?" Clancy was flapping excitedly.

"Would you quit flapping, Clance? He's supposed to be just some old cousin of Hitch's."

"But really?" said Clancy again. "He's a-l-i-v-e?"

"Well, yeah, Clance," hissed Ruby, "he's not some sorta specter, if that's what you're wondering."

"But how?" said Clancy.

"I'll tell you later, but all you gotta know right now is that he's called Mo Loveday and he's Hitch's cousin from Little Mountain Side."

"OK," said Clancy, "got it." Pause. "So why's he staying with you?"

"On account of the fungus poisoning," said Ruby.

"He ate a toadstool? I thought he was some kind of fungus expert."

"No, not really!" said Ruby.

"He isn't a fungus expert?" said Clancy.

"No, I mean *yes*! He *is* a fungus expert, but he *didn't* eat a toadstool — it's just something Hitch told my mom to account for him needing to recuperate at our place."

"So what kind of toadstool did he not eat?" asked Clancy.

"A chicken of the woods," said Ruby.

"But that's a mushroom," said Clancy.

"When did you get to be such an expert?" asked Ruby.

"I've been reading up on them," said Clancy.

"Well, my mom has decided they are toadstools," said Ruby.

"Oh," said Clancy, "I got it. . . . I think."

"Good, so long as you don't go around blabbing about Bradley Baker, everything should be fine."

"What do you mean, blab? When do I ever blab?"

"Never, OK? Don't get your underwear in a bunch."

"So what happens next?" asked Clancy.

"There's this whole debriefing thing, you know, to find out what Baker knows or remembers he knows."

"Has he lost his memory?" asked Clancy.

"Yeah, but LB thinks there might be a way of restoring it, or at least part of it."

"Like with hypnosis?" asked Clancy.

"No . . . I mean, well . . . I don't actually know," said Ruby.

"Do you think they have this kinda time-machine chair like in that movie, you know, where the guy gets transported back into all his different memories?" suggested Clancy.

"No, Clance, I don't," said Ruby. "Like I said, I don't know how it works, but I'm pretty sure there won't be some special chair."

"So who administers the memory serum?"

"What memory serum?" said Ruby. "Actually, forget I asked. I have no idea how any of this works, but that doesn't matter, because SJ does."

"She's the scientific one?" asked Clancy.

"Well, if you're getting technical, then yeah, she's the scientific one."

It was after school and Ruby was sitting up in her room reading through notebooks 400–450. She had discovered a lot of interesting things, but nothing that could be considered useful to this case.

There was a knock at the door. "Who is it?" called Ruby.

"It's me," said Baker.

"Come in," she said. She forgot about the notebooks spread out across the desk.

"What are *they*?" he asked.

She hesitated a second. "I make notes," she replied. "Jot down things that I see—anything, really."

He nodded. "Good idea," he said. "I mean, even the mundane can tell a story, right?"

"Right . . ." said Ruby slowly.

He looked at her. "Look, Ruby, I know I don't have much in the memory bank, but why don't you try and bring me up to speed on things; who knows?" he said, tapping his head. "Something might flicker on in there—worth a try, you think?"

"Uh-huh," said Ruby. "Anything's worth a try."

"So start at the start," said Baker. "How did this all begin?"

"With the Jade Buddha of Khotan," said Ruby. "It was missing for a long time, around a thousand years, to be approximate, until it was recently rediscovered encased in a block of ice somewhere north of Alaska."

"I read about that," said Baker. "So who found it?"

"Enrico Gonzales, the curator of the City Museum," said Ruby.

"He found it by accident or was he looking for it?"

"An anonymous donor sponsored the search. It took years to find it."

"I heard it was quite the artifact—most beautiful thing since sliced bread."

"You could say that," said Ruby.

"People do seem to rave about its eyes; gems, aren't they?"

"Rubies," said Ruby.

"Almost made me want to drive into the city so I could take a look, and I'm telling you, I *never* come to the city, not unless I absolutely have to."

"Well, you certainly missed something," said Ruby. "Not just the Buddha; you missed the explosion at the bank and the museum break-in and quite a few wannabe murderers too."

"That's exactly why I avoid coming into Twinford," said Baker.

"Yeah, well, most of the time that doesn't happen," said Ruby.

"So who was responsible for all this mayhem?" asked Baker.

"They call him the Count," said Ruby. "Real name, Victor von Leyden."

She went to her desk and took out the movie encyclopedia Frederick Lutz had loaned her.

"Here," she said, "this is him."

Bradley Baker leaned forward in his chair. He looked at the picture for three long minutes before announcing, "I *know* this man. I *remember* him."

"Of all the people to remember," said Ruby, "you remember *him*?"

Baker frowned. "Yeah, I'm getting that." He looked at Ruby. "He's a killer, right?"

"Killer is a nice word for what he is," said Ruby. "I believe he tried to murder you one time."

"Did he?"

"He tried," said Ruby, "but you got away. He's just not a nice guy. I mean, he attempted to bury me in sand once, and paralyzed me with jellyfish venom another, and I'll never forget the giant-octopus incident. . . ."

"I'll bet not," said Baker.

"What I now know for sure," said Ruby, "is that that night back at the City Museum wasn't about stealing the Buddha. I'm not saying that wasn't a part of it, but there was a bigger prize."

"How do you mean?" said Baker.

"Well, if it was all about acquiring the Buddha, then why would the Count waste time looking into its eyes?"

"He got distracted, maybe?" suggested Baker. "The myth of the Buddha is something that has perplexed a lot of people through the centuries. What is it they say about that Buddha? Look into its eyes at midnight and double your wisdom and halve your age."

"But the thing is, he wasn't just looking into its eyes," said Ruby, "he was *really* looking into its eyes, with a little infrared light thing, and he didn't just *happen* to have a little infrared light tool *with* him — he knew what he was doing here."

"OK, so what was he doing?" asked Baker.

Ruby took a deep breath. "OK," she said, "I think he had been hired, commissioned, instructed, whatever, to find something and he was insuring himself against the worst-case scenario that his plan to steal the artifact failed."

"In other words, the objective of the whole operation was to *read* the eyes," said Baker. "That was the prize?"

"Yeah," said Ruby. "The icing on the cake would have been to walk away with the Buddha itself."

"So you concluded the Count is working for someone else?" asked Baker.

"I know that now, but I didn't know it at the time," said Ruby.

"What does Hitch think about that?" asked Baker.

"That it's perplexing because the Count has always been independent."

"Not an evil genius for hire, you mean?" said Baker.

"No," said Ruby. "Hitch says the Count has always committed crimes purely for the pleasure of it." She paused. "Well, that and his weakness for souvenirs."

"What kind of souvenirs?"

"You know, priceless treasures like eighth-century Buddhas, eighteenth-century ruby necklaces, twentieth-century invisibility skins," explained Ruby. "So what I'm thinking is: Why is this master villain spending his precious time helping some other villain do their dirty work? He doesn't need money."

"Sounds like someone has something over him," said Baker. "Either this person is blackmailing him—unlikely under the circumstances—or, a lot more likely, they have something *he* wants and the only way to get it is by doing as he's told."

"That's the conclusion I came to," said Ruby. "Oh, and there's one other thing: Homer Pinkerton used to work with the Count, a long time ago when the Count was in the movie business."

"Is that so . . ." pondered Baker. He was quiet for minute before he looked up and said, "So what else you got?"

And so one by one they went through each and every crime, examining every little piece of evidence. Until they had it all written up and spread out on the floor.

CHAPTER 40
On the Cards

THREE HOURS LATER, Ruby was vaguely aware of the ring of the doorbell and the footsteps on the stairs, but her mind was focused on the task in front of her and she only really came to when she heard Clancy's voice.

"Rube, it's me." He stuck his head around the door. "Can I come in?"

"Of course."

He stepped into the room, being careful not to stand on the arrangement of colored cards spread out across the floor.

"I called you about ten million times."

"I unplugged the phone."

He looked around her room at the many telephones.

"What, all of them?"

"Yeah, I needed to concentrate."

"What are you doing?" asked Clancy. He was staring down at all the cards, which he now saw were covered in notes. As he stood looking, Ruby continued to move them as if trying to find an order to a puzzle that she did not understand.

"Bradley and I are trying to figure how they connect," said Ruby. "I've been talking him through the events of the past ten months. Boy, is he a quick learner."

"I guess he would be," said Clancy. "So are you getting anywhere?" he asked.

"Yes and no," said Ruby. "You see, there has to be a connection between the Jade Buddha and the truth serum and the cyan scent and the key tag and the snake lady, but so far we can't see what it might be."

"So what did Bradley say about the key tag?"

"That's one of the many memories that hasn't drifted back yet," said Ruby. "But I asked LB about it, and she told me the reason she held on to that tag all these years is because it was found not far from the crash site by one of the clearance crew. Baker's fingerprints were all over it."

"Had she ever seen it before?" he asked.

"Uh-uh; turns out you were right about that — it wasn't that she was sentimental about it because it had belonged to Baker. It was important because it was the last thing he'd touched."

"But no one knows what it is?" asked Clancy.

"No," said Ruby. "No one knows."

Clancy looked around. "So where *is* Bradley?"

"He's gone to Penny's Books," said Ruby. She was still looking down at the cards. "The truth serum, I understand. It's like we discussed. It's useful: You can get a very unblabby person to talk with a truth serum."

1 SHOWS LOCATION OF . . . ?

THE JADE
BUDDHA

THE MARS
MUSHROOMS

3 WORKED TOGETHER

DISCOVERED BY

2

PROFESSOR
HOMER
PINKERTON

5

KILLED BY

CLAUDE FONTAINE
(TIGHTROPE WALKER)

7

WORKS FOR

LORELEI
VON LEYDEN

STOLEN BY

10

THE LUCITE
KEY TAG

11

"An unblabby person . . . like an agent, you mean?" said Clancy.

"Yes, like an agent," agreed Ruby. "Maybe the plan is to, I don't know, kidnap someone from Spectrum and make them talk, but since no one seems to have a clue as to what any of this is about, it's hard to imagine what useful thing they would say." She picked up a card. "And as far as we know, the cyan scent would also come in handy. Used correctly, it could draw a person out of hiding, same as luring prey to the wolf. You could lure your victim or bait to a location without them really understanding they're being lured."

"I don't think it would work on me," said Clancy. "I *know* the scent — I know what to smell for."

"Same here," said Ruby. "I think I might be cyan-scent-proof."

Clancy picked up one of the cards from a side stack, the one that had the word "Oidov" printed on it.

"Still drawing a blank on Amarjargel Oidov?"

Ruby sighed. "Why try to kill her? Why not just *steal* the snakes if it was the snakes this creep was after?"

"Because maybe it wasn't about the snakes," said a voice.

Neither of them had heard Baker come in.

"Boy, you move quietly," said Clancy.

"Must be the training. I'm Bradley." he said to Clancy. He stepped carefully over the cards. "These snakes are rare and ancient and amazing to look at, but I don't think the attempted murder of Oidov has much to do with reptiles."

"So what *does* it have to do with?" said Ruby.

"So there are a few thoughts I've been mulling over," said Bradley. "Two weeks ago you came into my store asking if I had ever read anything about so-called Mars Mushrooms, which I'd never heard of but later learn you read about in those confidential Spectrum files — a discovery of this Pinkerton guy, right?"

Ruby nodded.

"So I asked SJ, and she filled me in on Pinkerton's findings, told me how these Mars Mushrooms enhance your memory — by a pretty big factor, by the way; they also extend your life by quite a number of years, but you know all this, right?"

Ruby nodded again.

"So what did you conclude?"

"That if anyone got their hands on these mushrooms, they could pretty much name their price," Ruby said.

"Exactly," Baker said. "Which brings me to these rare and ancient mushroom-eating snakes. Have you noticed how everything keeps coming up mushrooms?"

Ruby and Clancy were staring at him.

"So I went to meet Consuela. . . ."

"Consuela Cruz?" said Clancy.

"Yeah," said Bradley, "we're old friends."

"When?" said Ruby. "I mean, when did you meet her?"

"Just now," said Baker.

"You said you were going to Penny's Books."

"That's where I met her," said Baker.

"Oh," said Ruby.

"What's Consuela got to do with anything?" asked Clancy.

"She's researching the snake mushrooms," said Ruby slowly.

"Yeah, she's been analyzing the mushrooms that the yellow snakes feed on, so we cross-checked her findings with Pinkerton's Mars Mushrooms, and guess what?"

Ruby looked at him, suddenly knowing what he was going to say. "They're the same," she said.

"Precisely," said Baker. "So I took it a little further and I began to wonder why a person would want Oidov dead when she appears to be the only one who knows where these snakes who eat mushrooms live, or rather where these mushrooms the snakes feed on grow." He looked at her. "And then I thought to myself . . ."

"Maybe someone wanted Oidov dead because she *wasn't* the *only* person to know where these mushrooms grow," said Ruby.

"My thoughts exactly," said Baker. "So what if . . . I mean, think about it before you fall over laughing — what if the Jade Buddha has something to do with all this? What if whatever's embedded in those eyes, written there, encoded or what have you, what if it's a location? Coordinates telling you where to find the Mars Mushrooms?"

"That makes a lot of sense," said Ruby. "The legend . . . look into the eyes of the Buddha at midnight and *double your wisdom and halve your age.*"

"That's what I thought," said Baker. "It's telling you where to go if you want to discover the secret to immortality — or something approaching it."

"Ah," said Clancy, "so the looking-into-the-eyes part doesn't automatically make you either smart or youthful. . . ."

"That would account for my dad's unchanged state," said Ruby.

It felt like a breakthrough, and as Ruby rearranged her clue cards she saw that the puzzle was fitting together.

Bradley Baker excused himself. "I might take a nap. This memory-recall stuff really knocks it out of you."

They had been working flat-out for several hours, and it really was time for a snack.

"You want to go ask Mrs. Digby if we could have one of her Digby clubs?" said Clancy.

"You got legs, why don't you go ask?" suggested Ruby.

"I'm totally wiped," said Clancy. "I can't even move."

"Well, tough, I'm busy."

"I know," said Clancy. "I'll get Bug to ask — I'll get him to do the 'go find' trick."

"Good luck with that," said Ruby. "He only does it when he's in the mood."

Clancy looked at Bug asleep on the floor and tried to discern if the husky was in the right frame of mind to perform this most useful of tricks. He wrote Mrs. Digby a sandwich order and tucked it in Bug's collar, then he said, "Go find Mrs. Digby."

But the dog just stared up at him.

"Go find Mrs. Digby," he repeated.

And the dog lay down and closed his eyes.

"Why won't he do it?" moaned Clancy.

"Because you're saying it all wrong," said Ruby. "You have to say it with energy. Bug, go find Mrs. Digby!"

Immediately, the dog got to his feet and pushed his way through the door and downstairs to the kitchen.

Seven minutes later, Bug returned carrying a basket of clementines in his mouth.

"This isn't what we ordered," complained Clancy.

"You'll have to go make them yourself," said Ruby. But before anyone could do anything, Mrs. Digby arrived with a plate of Digby clubs.

"I got your message," she said, "and it's your lucky day that I happen to be feeling so generous spirited. Tomorrow you can fetch your own darned sandwiches."

An hour later, once Clancy was gone, Ruby went to find Baker. She felt she had better say what had to be said.

"Look, you're probably wondering how come I'm discussing all this confidential stuff with Clancy. I mean, this is strictly not allowed. Spectrum's rule number one being *keep it zipped.*"

"Is that so?" said Baker.

"Yeah," said Ruby. "I mean, I would most definitely get

kicked out of Spectrum if they knew I was discussing cases with a civilian."

"So why do you?" he asked. "Discuss this stuff with Clancy, I mean."

"Because I can't not," said Ruby. "I can't lie to him — he knows everything. Don't ask me how, he has a sorta sixth sense — he looks at me and he can just tell if I'm lying, like he can see into my head."

Bradley Baker nodded. "Yeah, I think I used to know someone like that." He gave her a sideways look. "So anyone else in on your secret?"

"Just Hitch," said Ruby. "Him, me, and Clance — that makes three of us."

"So now it's the four of us," said Baker, "and it's your lucky day because I'm good at keeping secrets."

CHAPTER 41
What We Know

WHEN RUBY GOT HOME FROM SCHOOL THE NEXT DAY she found the Spectrum 8 boss standing on the stoop.

"Have you come to see Bradley?" asked Ruby.

"Well, I'm not here to see your mom and dad," said LB, "charming as I'm sure they are."

The door was opened before Ruby could reach for her key.

"Howdy ma'am, do come in, let me take your coat." Mrs. Digby performed the coat-taking with such speed and vigor that LB was yanked sideways.

"Don't worry, one of my arms is still attached," said LB, steadying herself. "Thank you."

The housekeeper turned to Ruby and said, "I've baked. I've toiled. I've put snacks on a plate and drinks on a tray. I trust you can manage the rest yourself."

Then she turned back to LB. "Delighted to meet you, ma'am. Relax, enjoy, use the facilities."

With that, the housekeeper disappeared down to her apartment.

"Does she have some peculiar condition?" asked LB.

"It's TV bingo night," said Ruby.

"I have no idea what that is, but it obviously isn't good for the soul," said LB.

They walked upstairs to the kitchen, where they found Hitch cutting sandwiches.

LB looked at him. "Is this really what Spectrum pays you for?"

"I can assure you it's money well spent. I can make a pretty good Digby club sandwich now."

"Well, I'm glad the job seems to be challenging you," said LB. "And where's Baker, vacuuming the dining room?"

"Watching *Crazy Cops*," said Hitch.

"I sincerely hope that's not true," said LB.

"*Crazy Cops* is actually a pretty good show," said Ruby.

"I'll take your word for it," said her boss.

LB and Hitch went up to find Bradley, Hitch balancing the various plates on his arm, waiter-style. Ruby fetched the drinks prepared by Mrs. Digby and followed.

When she teetered in with the tray, it struck her how surreal it was to have the three most important members of Spectrum 8 sitting there among her records, books, phone collection, assorted objects, and — rather mortifyingly — strewn laundry.

Baker, of course, was not watching *Crazy Cops*. He was working on the case and had been for a straight twelve hours — no breaks.

"So what do we know?" asked LB.

Ruby gave her a quick breakdown of where they were:

"The Australian was an actress who went by the name of Marnie Novak; she was the protégée of the Count and she was and *is* loyal to him and him alone. She had a child named Lorelei who became the Count's apprentice, learning the art of disguise to an extraordinary level. Lorelei is still out there giving everyone *including* the Count a big headache."

LB: *But you don't think Lorelei's part of this?*

RUBY: *No, she's just a disrupter — a dangerous one.*

LB: *And the Count's motivation — are we any clearer on this?*

BAKER: *We have theories. It could be the promise of* Hypocrea asteroidi.

LB: *Pardon me?*

BAKER: *Mars Mushrooms.*

LB: *Ah, yes, the professor's discovery.*

BAKER: *Homer Pinkerton was once a friend of the Count's, and it's conceivable that Pinkerton told him about the life-giving properties of the mushrooms, and now the Count can't think about anything else. Problem is, he is unable to get them without enlisting the help of this other character, the evil genius who seems to be pulling the strings.*

HITCH: *But we can't know any of this for a fact?*

BAKER: *That's right. It's just a theory.*
LB: *So any theories on who might be pulling the strings?*

"I think it's the child from the rapids," said Ruby.

"Casey Morgan?" said LB.

"Why?" asked Hitch.

Ruby told them about the chalk message. "It fits," she said. "It all makes sense."

LB: *But no one knows who Morgan is?*
HITCH: *Not a clue.*
RUBY: *Other than it's someone in Spectrum.*
LB: *Hardly narrows it down.*
HITCH: *And this Larva pin — we still don't know how it came to be outside Pinkerton's house?*

"It couldn't have been Baker," said LB. "He lost that pin over thirty years ago, when he almost drowned at the rapids."

"I don't think it was lost," said Ruby. "I think the kid Morgan stole it, which means the adult Morgan dropped it."

BAKER: *Maybe.*
HITCH: *So if the Larva pin was dropped by Morgan, then it's more than possible that Pinkerton's dog was stolen by Morgan.*
BAKER: *That would seem logical.*

LB: *And the point of stealing his dog would be?*

RUBY: *To hold Pinkerton to ransom, I guess.*

LB: *So what did Casey Morgan want?*

HITCH: *It could be many things. Pinkerton knew a lot of Spectrum secrets.*

BAKER: *Whatever it was, we know he didn't get it; we know this because the Count told Ruby that he's still looking.*

LB: *OK, so I have another question. Why make a second attempt on Baker's life so many years after the first?*

RUBY: *Two reasons: the first was a grand plan to bring down Spectrum.*

HITCH: *Have LB shoot down Baker, thus killing Spectrum's finest agent. LB is finished, Spectrum destroyed.*

BAKER: *A neat plan that didn't pan out.*

LB: *And second?*

HITCH: *The second was purely emotional. Baker had everything Casey Morgan wanted: he was a successful agent, he had made Larva, and now he had just fully enrolled in the Spectrum Space Encounter Program — qualified the month he was shot down.*

"You know," said Baker, "I think there's one other reason."

"What's that?" asked Hitch.

"I think maybe I knew who he was," said Baker.

"You remember him?" asked LB.

"No," he said, "but if I was trying to get a message to you when that guy found me dying on the road, then I must have figured it was Morgan who was behind it all." He looked at her.

"So let's start looking for Morgan," said LB. "Begin by finding out where he sprang from, where he was born, where he grew up." She looked at Hitch. "We don't have time to sit back and wait for him to come to us."

"Understood," he said.

CHAPTER 42
Chasing a Shadow

HITCH DID AS HE HAD PROMISED: a talk with an elderly retired agent was how he found it, a lucky chance. The agent had remembered the boy talking about Colwin City and how much he loathed it there, and, as it happened, the agent agreed; he had grown up there too and knew exactly the district, the street, the house in which Casey Morgan had lived.

A day later, Hitch and Ruby were flying down to Colwin City with Agent Zuko, Hitch's pilot friend. They'd been lucky to catch a ride; he was officially off duty. The plane was a tiny single-engine craft: an uncomfortable flight, but a thrilling way to travel.

"Take all the time you like," said Zuko. "I've got nowhere to be — I'll just twiddle my thumbs until you get back."

They picked up a car at the airfield and drove on to the city, a gray industrial town with sprawling suburbs that seemed to stretch for mile upon mile across the flat landscape. There was nothing inspiring about the place, just a lot of ugly telephone poles marching toward infinity.

The trip was unrewarding. There was no sign of the Morgan house, nor the street where the building had once stood. The whole suburb had been bulldozed long ago to make room for a highway intersection. If the Morgans were still alive after all these years, then no one seemed to know about it, and all record of them seemed to have disappeared.

Hitch stared up at the concrete mass of overpasses and shrugged. "Looks like we're back to square one."

They got into the car and contacted Blacker back at HQ and told him the news.

"So what did you dig up?" asked Blacker.

"Squat," said Hitch.

"Huh?"

"Not a darned thing," said Hitch. "Not one person can give us any kind of description; not one person can remember ever meeting the boy Morgan. It's like he never existed. We're chasing a shadow here."

"So what's your next move?" asked Blacker.

"We're coming back," said Hitch. "Out."

A message beeped up.

›› ZUKO REQUIRED ELSEWHERE: ALTERNATIVE TRANSPORT
PROVIDED. SPECTRUM X NOW STANDING BY AT COLWIN
AIRFIELD, DUE TO TAKE OFF IN TWENTY-ONE MINUTES,
HASTE IS APPRECIATED.

"What's *Spectrum X*?" said Ruby.

"You're going to love it, kid."

They arrived at the airfield with forty-nine seconds to spare, no time to go greet the pilots or do anything more than buckle up before they were airborne.

"This is quite a plane," said Ruby. "A lot of closet space."

"There's a lot of equipment," said Hitch. "Equipped for nearly every eventuality."

"Is that so?" said Ruby.

"Speaking of equipment," said Hitch, "LB wanted you to have this." He reached into a bag and took out the little white fur parachute cape.

"You're kidding?" said Ruby.

Hitch shook his head. "As far as LB's concerned, you found lost gold; and for that remarkable feat, you get this."

Ruby had only seen the cape displayed inside a cabinet in the Spectrum gadget room. Now, holding it in her hands, she realized what an incredible thing it was: super light and super warm, and totally discreet. It was impossible to see where the chute was hidden.

"I might try it on," said Ruby.

"Be my guest," said Hitch. "In fact, take a look around, kid; you might as well enjoy the ride, get something out of this whole bust of a trip."

It wasn't often—actually it wasn't *ever*—that a Spectrum

senior agent suggested that a thirteen-year-old trainee have a good root through the high-tech gadgetry.

It didn't take Ruby long to discover the flight equipment room: a narrow tube of a space that contained parachutes, survival gear, and flying suits suitable for subzero conditions. The suit that particularly appealed to Ruby was gold, gold as in the color *of,* but actually glimmering as if made from gold leaf. It was the same exact suit she had seen in the photograph on LB's wall, only perhaps a little smaller. Over the top? Sure it was, but when did one ever get to dress like an old-fashioned superhero in an outfit that actually could make you become super? *Might as well try it on,* she thought. *You can't miss this opportunity, Rube.*

Unlike the Superskin, the flying suit was easy to get into and what was more, it felt pretty comfortable.

She caught her reflection in the polished aluminum door. The effect was dazzling. It must have been even more so when one was diving to earth at great speed. She took the little parachute cape and clipped the harness to the suit.

"Hey, kid," called Hitch, "you better not be trying on any of that gear."

"Why would I do that?" called Ruby.

She pulled her snow parka on, grabbed a snurferboard, and stuck her head around the door.

"See?" she said.

"I believe you, kid. Plenty wouldn't." Yawning, he stretched his arms and stood up. "Fix yourself a snack if you want—the kitchen's back there. I'm just going to check in with the pilot. The weather conditions aren't looking so good."

Ruby thought a snack might be a very good idea. She had a feeling that Mrs. Digby's chicken surprise was going to get eaten without them.

Hitch stepped into the cockpit and was surprised not to recognize any of the crew.

"What happened to Sasnik?" asked Hitch. "Doesn't he usually fly *Spectrum X*?"

"Oh, they didn't tell you? They switched us; don't ask me why. I'm Matthews, by the way."

"Good to meet you, Matthews," said Hitch.

"Could you take over for a tick? I just have to make a stop at the restroom."

"Where's your copilot?" asked Hitch.

"She's just checking something in back."

They were flying over the snow-capped mountains of the northern peaks when something altogether unexpected occurred.

A hand reached around Hitch's throat, and before he could consider his next move, a voice that did not belong to the hand said, "Stay right where you are, sweetie."

The voice belonged to a woman, an Australian. She stepped forward so she was standing next to him, and he felt the sensation of something cold and metal on his temple. It suggested she had a gun.

"Apologies, sweetie, this flight is being diverted. I hope you won't decide to make a fuss about it or Mr. Matthews will have to eject you from the plane." She made a show of glancing out the window. "And I'm sure I don't have to tell you, without a parachute, it's a long way down."

HITCH: *Is Mr. Matthews here planning on strangling me? And if not, then could I trouble you to ask him if he might loosen his grip? It's interfering with my ability to keep breathing.*

THE AUSTRALIAN: *Of course. But try to refrain from doing anything stupid.*

HITCH: *What would add up to stupid?*

THE AUSTRALIAN: *Any sudden movements; that wouldn't be smart, sweetie.*

HITCH: *I'll try to keep my nervous twitch under control.*

THE AUSTRALIAN: *I'm impressed by your common sense.*

HITCH: *I'm impressed by your gun.*

THE AUSTRALIAN: *Good. It sounds like we're going to get along just fine.*

HITCH: *So how can I help you?*

THE AUSTRALIAN: *Just keep flying the plane.*

HITCH: *So what's all this about?*

THE AUSTRALIAN: *I want the girl.*

HITCH: *Why? What good is the girl to you?*

THE AUSTRALIAN: *That's my business.*

HITCH: *No, I'm afraid that's my business. You see, I'm here to make sure nothing happens to her, and forgive me, but I don't think you have an exemplary track record when it comes to keeping people alive.*

THE AUSTRALIAN: *Oh, I think you've misunderstood my motives; I'm not about to do her harm, far from it. My associate wants her alive and kicking.*

HITCH: *Your associate — would that be the man who models himself on Count Dracula?*

THE AUSTRALIAN: *I wasn't aware you'd met.*

HITCH: *We haven't, formally. Who's he working for these days?*

THE AUSTRALIAN: *Someone who goes by the name of Casey Morgan. Are you familiar?*

HITCH: *I've not had the pleasure, at least I don't think I have, but I'm getting the impression that old Casey keeps a low profile. I had hoped to have the chance to look him in the eyes before handing him over to the FBI.*

THE AUSTRALIAN: *A voice on a telephone is the closest you'll get.*

HITCH: *What a pity; you just can't beat seeing the whites of a person's eyes.*

THE AUSTRALIAN: *I'll leave you in the capable hands of Mr. Matthews while I fetch your precious Ruby.*

Ruby was unaware of this high-stakes conversation, busy as

she was fixing herself a bagel with cream cheese while attempting to tune the radio to something approaching music. Mr. Matthews had his eyes firmly trained on Hitch, and Hitch was intent on flying the plane — the weather was getting unsettled and the mountains closer. No one at all was aware of the figure, clad in a black bodysuit and mask, emerging from one of the equipment crates. By the time they were, the shadowy form had karate-chopped Matthews and left him unconscious. Hitch ducked three well-aimed kicks, and the plane began to dive.

"Lorelei! Is that you?" snarled the Australian.

Ruby, still in the cabin kitchen, stumbled, her face making contact with something hard. She staggered out, nose bleeding.

The ninja and the Australian were furiously throwing things at each other, whatever they could grab and fling.

"Back off, Lorelei. The girl's useless to me dead!" shouted the Australian.

"Ruby, get your parachute on and get out of here!" shouted Hitch from the cockpit.

"What about you?" yelled Ruby, her nose now pouring blood.

"Grab a parachute!" he yelled. "I got this under control."

Doof!

"That's not what it looks like from where I'm bleeding," shouted Ruby, but she did as she was told.

"You have to get out of here, kid. Switch on your locator," he bellowed, "that way I'll find you." He ducked a second unidentified object.

Ruby looked at him. *You're gonna be dead* is what she was thinking.

"Trust me, kid."

Doof! Another blow as a flight box made contact with his shoulder, followed by a kick to his leg.

"No!" shouted Ruby.

"Jump! Redfort, that's an order!"

Ruby wrenched open the plane door.

But too late. For there was the ninja, blocking her way.

"Don't mind me, bubble-gum girl — you go ahead and jump," said Lorelei von Leyden. Yanking off her ski mask, she smiled. "Jump? What am I saying? Fall is what I mean." She tore the parachute from Ruby's back. "Oh, take this instead." She laughed, throwing her the first-aid kit. "A good Girl Scout always travels with her survival kit — I'll bet there's a Band-Aid in there for when you go splat!" Lorelei was laughing so hard now she appeared demented. "Oh, don't forget your little snurferboard — you can use it to mark your grave. So long, bubble-gum girl."

Lorelei grabbed one of the hand grips on the ceiling, swung her body forward, and kicked Ruby into the air. Her laugh followed Ruby as she tumbled into the sky, the snurferboard twirling behind her.

Ruby counted as she fell: 1,000, 2,000, 3,000.

What do you do if you find yourself falling through the air at 53 miles per second without a parachute?

Answer: Close your eyes and hope for a miracle.

Ruby did neither of these things, nor did she panic.

For what Lorelei von Leyden didn't know was that Ruby had a plan B.

She tore off the snow parka and watched as it was snatched up by the wind and whirled away. The golden suit twinkled like a disco ball as she plummeted. Around her shoulders was the white fur parachute cape. There was no backup—if the cord snapped or the chute tangled, then it would be good-bye, Ruby. She looked beneath her at the snow-capped mountain moving fast toward her, and yanked the parachute release.

She felt the amazing jolt as her body stopped hurtling toward the ground and instead began to float, a little gold canopy above her, which she was able to steer until her toes touched the mountaintop. Her landing was good. Wasting no time, she detached the chute. The plane had already disappeared from view, but when she looked to the sky she saw one small figure zigzagging to earth. One survivor . . . friend or foe? What were the odds that this skydiver was Hitch? One in four? No, the odds were not as good as that. Three maniacs trying to kill one agent. He had a chance, but it was small.

First retrieve your backpack and snurferboard. She had kept an eye on them, had watched them spinning to earth, and she found both easily. She wasted no time hopping on the board and grabbing the strap. Snow had begun to fall, large sticky pieces, making it hard to keep an eye on the parachutist.

She flipped up the viewing lens on the wrist binoculars

attached to the cuff of her suit and scanned the horizon until her eyes locked on the figure in black. Whoever it was seemed to be orienting, looking for someone. Her?

Hitch, is that you? She checked the locator for his signal, but there was none.

She aimed the search-and-find locator directly at the figure, but nothing came back, no signal. No blink of a light. Was the responder not functioning or was the skydiver not Hitch?

The figure was motionless for a moment, and then it seemed to sight her, and then slowly, very slowly began to move toward her.

Spectrum gadgets are 99.999 percent reliable, isn't that what Hal had said?

Go with instinct.

Not Hitch, she thought.

Get out of here fast.

She took off down the mountain, taking the fastest route.

RULE 43: IF YOU'VE GOT THE ADVANTAGE — MAKE SURE YOU KEEP IT.

Lose whoever was tailing her.

If Hitch was still on the plane, then . . .

Would he make it back alive?

She didn't need to wait long for her answer.

The explosion boomed across the mountains, and the sky lit up red with the flames of a huge fireball.

The plane and whoever it still carried — all gone.

She stood for a minute staring up at the sky, mesmerized, until she suddenly became aware of a rumbling sound and turned to see a huge slab of snow break away from the mountain and begin to cascade toward her. Her fear of the likely *human* killer was completely subsumed by her fear of *nature's* killer. She needed to move diagonally out of the avalanche's path and get herself across to the pines if she was to have any chance of survival; so long as she didn't smash directly into a tree, of course.

Go!

She was ahead of it, she was fast, she was making it out of there, she was going to beat it, outrun it . . . but then a second rumble, a second slab of snow began to slide, and there was nowhere to go.

Swim, Ruby, swim.

She worked her arms as fast as she could, breathing snow and losing direction; she was caught, tumbling, falling like a piece of debris. She pulled her hands in to make an air pocket around her face, no point raising her arm, no point trying to be seen, no one to see her.

The world went entirely white and then, just as suddenly, entirely black.

CHAPTER 43
WHAT TO DO IF YOU ARE CAUGHT IN AN AVALANCHE

1. Let go of your heavy equipment. *You want your body to be as lightweight as possible, so let go of your backpack and other heavy equipment you may be carrying. This raises the chances that you'll be able to stay toward the surface of the snow. It goes without saying that you should not let go of survival equipment, such as a transceiver and probe or snow shovel; you'll need these if you get buried.*

I have no survival equipment, **thought Ruby. She had let go of the first-aid kit.**

People searching for you later may be able to find you if they see some pieces of equipment on the surface of the snow, so you could let go of a glove or something else that's light to increase the chances they'll find you.

Who thought up these rules? **If she had had the chance to pull a glove from her hand, then maybe she would have, but as it was, she was mainly concentrating on not breaking her neck. Plus it** had to be considered that the person most likely to find her was the person who had least interest in keeping her alive.

2. Start swimming. *This is essential to helping you stay near the surface of the snow. The human body is much denser than snow, so you'll tend to sink as you get carried downhill. Try to stay afloat by kicking your feet and thrashing your arms in a swimming motion.*
a) *Swim on your back. This way your face is turned toward the surface, giving you a better chance of getting oxygen more quickly if you get buried.*
b) *Swim uphill. Swimming up will get you closer to the surface of the snow.*

This she did attempt. Whether it would make a jot of difference to her final resting place, she had no idea, but rules is rules, and when you are in dire circumstances, you might as well grab for them.

3. Conserve air and energy. *Try to move once the snow settles, but don't jeopardize your air pocket.*

Make an air pocket, make an air pocket, get air, you need air.

If you're very near the surface, you may be able to dig your way out, but otherwise you aren't going anywhere.

You aren't going anywhere.

Don't waste precious breath by struggling against the snow. Remain calm and wait to be rescued. If you hear people nearby, try to call them, but don't keep it up if they don't seem to hear you. You can probably hear them better than they can hear you, and shouting just wastes your limited air supply.

Try to remain calm and wait to be rescued.

Try to remain calm and wait to be rescued.

Try to remain calm

Try to remain

Try to

Try

CHAPTER 44
Buried Alive

AS THE SNOW PACKED TIGHTLY AROUND HER, so did the dawning realization that following the rules didn't make the slightest bit of difference when it came to facts.

And just because one raised one's arms above one's head as the snow cascaded down, or threw off heavy equipment, swam one's arms, yelled and screamed, that didn't change the fact that she was buried alive under about a ton of snow — maybe it was eight tons, who was there to weigh it? Who was there to care? Hitch was almost certainly dead, Bradley Baker was about one hundred miles away, no doubt chatting with Mrs. Digby and eating fresh-out-of-the-oven gingerbread. Everyone else was having a good time playing in the snow, except for maybe Clancy, who, wherever he was, was too far away to even have a hunch that anything might be wrong.

And another thing — what was the point of the subzero survival training when she wasn't even going to get the chance to try survival? How many people had rescued themselves from avalanches — a handful? She was going to die.

These were all the thoughts Ruby would have been thinking, had her head not been buzzing with white noise, the sound of panic, white cold panic.

I'm buried alive, I'm going to die,
I'm buried alive, I'm going to die,
I'm buried alive,
I'm going to die . . .
I'm going to die.

Perhaps she passed out for a few seconds, because something changed and her breathing slowed and she could see the faces of her mom and dad: they were smiling, really smiling. And then a voice, Mrs. Digby's voice in her head, crystal clear: "You don't want to be scared of this, child, this is nothing. *This* you can deal with." It was almost a memory, the way the voice talked to her. "I'm here and I'll dig you out, sure as eggs is eggs, I'll hatch you out of there. No one buries my little Ruby alive."

I must be delirious. But just the vision of her parents, the thought of Mrs. Digby, the remembered sound of her voice, were enough to calm her, and when she was calm she was able to think.

She slowed her heart down, focused her mind on surviving.

RULE 20: NINETY PERCENT OF SURVIVAL IS ABOUT BELIEVING YOU WILL SURVIVE.

So no one's coming to rescue me.

Think.

So I have to rescue myself.

What do I have with me that might help me get out of here?

Think.

She felt for her wrist — and then hope welled up within.

She hadn't lost it, it was still there: the Bradley Baker Escape Watch.

You have the watch, you have a chance.

Now it was a matter of figuring out which of its functions might best serve her predicament.

How long have I got? she wondered.

She had created an air pocket around her face and she figured that she had maybe fifteen minutes. Pressing the winder so the dial now glowed, she tapped the rescue button. Two words flashed up on the screen:

    >> STATE PREDICAMENT

She clicked through the numerous options until she reached:

    >> SNOW BURIAL

She clicked YES.

The watch began calculating the depth.

    >> APPROX SIX FEET, it read.

"Perfect," muttered Ruby, "I'm in a snow grave."

>> CALCULATING AIR SUPPLY—22 MINUTES

>> ORIENTING > VERTICAL

>> SUGGESTED TOOL > SNOW DRIVER

"OK." She took a breath.

>> GO

The folded blades opened inches from her eyes and formed a perfect propeller. With an efficient and comforting whirr, the Snow Driver began to tunnel above her, forcing a path upward through the dense and heavy snow. Within two minutes she became aware of air and light. She heaved herself from the Ruby-sized hole, spluttering and spitting snow. She was alive and hardly able to believe it.

CHAPTER 45
Cold Comfort

RUBY ALLOWED HERSELF A MOMENT, lying there on the cold surface. The soft, fat, sticky flakes were coming down fast, and it was pretty much impossible to determine where the sky began and the earth ended. It was like looking into nothing.

She supposed that whoever had been tailing her had either been caught in the same avalanche and was now buried and dead *or* had witnessed *Ruby's* burial, presumed she was dead, and returned back to their cave of evil or wherever it was these villains hung out. Either way, the human factor was no longer a problem. It was *nature* that might finish her.

She needed to get off the mountain as quick as she could. She was free, but she would soon be frozen if she didn't find some shelter. She used the wrist binoculars, setting them to blizzard conditions. They allowed her to see through the blur of snow and make sense of the landscape. Head for the trees.

It was tough going, but she made it, and once there, she set about fixing herself some makeshift snowshoes. She made a mental note to thank Sam Colt for the hours of misery he had put her through teaching her these "dumb tasks." Boy, was she ever wrong.

The snowshoes worked pretty well, and she trekked as far as she could, heading through the fir trees to the west. The forest already provided her with a certain degree of cover, but she needed to make camp, gather wood, build a fire.

She was lucky. She found a partially fallen tree that created a perfect angle to clad in fronds of fir, and there was plenty of fuel for a fire.

For now, all her energy and reserves were devoted to this one task. And what's more, Colt was right, it was good to be alive: enjoy the here and now.

RULE 24: STAY ALIVE LONG ENOUGH TO FIGURE OUT YOUR NEXT MOVE. She pulled the hood down over her face, closed her eyes, and slept as well as she had slept in a long time.

Ruby's very next move was to wake up. *Not bad,* she thought, especially considering what had happened the previous day. The sky was clear and, despite the minus 10 temperature, the day looked like it might be a good one. She set about the task of rebuilding the fire and making sure she had enough fuel to keep it alive, even if a blizzard hit. She tried not to think about Hitch.

RULE 21: DON'T THINK BACK; DON'T THINK AHEAD; JUST THINK NOW.

That meant keeping warm, finding food, and figuring out a plan. She had learned a lot about survival from her spring training camp. She had put herself in grave danger by striving to reach base camp as quickly as possible, rather than assess the situation and keep herself healthy. Once the tasks aimed at keeping her alive were completed, she had time to think. She needed to get help, needed to alert LB to what had happened. Only then did it occur to her that LB would already know the fate of the *Spectrum X*. No doubt her team was searching for the plane wreckage right now.

But they wouldn't know about her; they wouldn't have any idea that she was still alive and holed up alone in the middle of the Northern Mountains.

She sat staring at the Escape Watch for a full ten minutes, her finger hovering over the FIND ME button, before she came to the inevitable conclusion that this was not a smart move. Someone back at HQ was rotten, and though she could send a message directly to Blacker or LB, there was no way she could be certain that this message wouldn't be intercepted. Someone, or some kind of device, had tipped off Marnie Novak. Somehow, Novak had known that Hitch and Ruby would be flying from Colwin City—who had tipped her off? Who had sent Zuko on another errand? Who had arranged for *Spectrum X* to fly them home? What had happened to the Spectrum crew? Someone was pulling the strings here. So if it wasn't LB or Blacker, then who? Froghorn? Ruby doubted that. He disliked her, sure he did, but he didn't *hate* her, at least not enough to lose his mind.

Hitch? Of course not Hitch, because Hitch was . . .
Don't think about Hitch. Gotta stay focused, Redfort.

She cooked up what food she'd managed to forage, and when she'd eaten she decided to turn in early.

Get some sleep, and head off at dawn.

She stoked the fire, making sure there were enough red-hot embers to see her through the night, then she lay down on her makeshift bed and felt the warmth beneath her. She was almost comfortable. She tucked the parachute cape around her and, with the fir fronds on top, she thought she might just stay warm.

She had slept for no more than an hour when something woke her.

She felt hot breath in her ear, an animal sound, snuffling, a lick to her face.

She shrieked, leaped to her feet, grabbing a stick, and . . .

"Bug?" She stood there breathing hard.

The dog barked.

"How did you get here?" She dropped to her knees and pushed her face into his fur. "Dog of mine, is it really you?"

She looked past him to see the figure of a man trudging toward her, his hand raised in greeting.

"Found you!" he said.

"Bradley Baker?"

"So I'm told."

"What are you, some kind of tracking genius?"

"I am pretty good," he said, "but actually, I cheated."

"How?" asked Ruby.

"I attached a transmitter to your pack."

"You did?"

Baker tapped his head. "You know, peace of mind and all that. Turns out I worry. It must be the Mo Loveday part of me."

"So why didn't you let me in on this transmitter secret?"

"I didn't want you to rely on it. I wasn't sure it was going to work—I'm kinda rusty on all this secret-agent stuff. It's been a while."

"I guess it has," agreed Ruby. "Even so, that bump on the head obviously didn't do as much damage as everyone thought."

"It's all coming back to me, slowly but surely." He looked around. "You built this?" said Baker. "I'm impressed."

Ruby followed his gaze. "Me too, actually. Hard to believe I flunked survival training, huh?"

"You must have paid better attention than you thought," said Baker. "Look, I don't mean to undermine your efforts or anything, but I'm pretty sure there's a cabin down in the valley above the lake, and it might be a tad more comfortable."

"You have to be kidding me," said Ruby. "You're saying I could be sitting fireside in a snow cabin?"

Baker extinguished the fire while Ruby gathered her things then, hoisting her backpack onto her shoulders, they set off.

"So Spectrum found the pilot," said Baker. "He's alive but pretty shaken—he was tied up back at the airfield; he was unable to identify the hijackers."

"Marnie Novak," said Ruby. "Lorelei was also on board, but she wasn't part of the plan."

"OK," he said.

Ruby looked at him. "No word from Hitch?"

He shook his head. "No word," he said. "But don't give up hoping. There's none better than Hitch — that's what I'm told. So until we know otherwise, then he's alive." He looked Ruby square in the eye. "Agreed?"

She nodded. "Agreed."

He handed her a pair of skis and a couple of poles, and they were soon off at some speed — Bug chasing behind them.

The cabin wasn't exactly the Grand Twin hotel, but there were dry logs in the wood stack, and once the fire was lit, at least it was something approaching warm.

"You must be pretty hungry," said Baker.

"Ah, you forget I got my Spectrum foraging badge."

"So not hungry?"

"No," said Ruby, "I'm starving."

Once she'd eaten and thawed through, Ruby realized how cold she had been before.

"So tell me what's been going on," said Baker.

"Well, it's been eventful," said Ruby. "I got kicked out of a plane, buried alive, and almost froze to death, but at least I didn't end up dead like you."

"I didn't do so badly being dead; look, I started my own grocery business, became an expert in edible fungi, and, I have to say, I ended up with some pretty nice friends — quite a few of them too."

"From what I hear, you were never short of them in your previous life either."

"That's good to know."

"So does anyone actually have any idea that you're here?" asked Ruby.

"Just LB."

"Are you sure?"

"Could we have been bugged, is that what you're asking?"

Ruby shrugged. "It feels like there are ears everywhere."

"LB and I met face-to-face and in a mole-free zone. I can assure you, no one was listening in. I'll meet her tomorrow at the rendezvous just a half-mile to the east, bring her back here."

"There's something I'm curious about," said Ruby, "and there's not a chance that LB's gonna fill me in, so I wondered if you would?"

He shrugged. "Try me."

"OK, so I mean I get that LB rescued you from crocodile-infested waters and all, but how did she end up here? How did she go from the northern territories of Australia to Twinford, USA? How did . . ." She stopped midquestion. "I forgot—you probably don't remember, right?"

"Actually," said Baker, "turns out that recall of SJ's does indeed restore the memory—and I *do* happen to know the answer to your question."

"So are you allowed to tell me?" asked Ruby.

He shrugged again. "It's not such a secret, it's just LB's not particularly talkative. You may have noticed this." He smiled. "I doubt that there are more than a handful of people who know anything much about her."

He stared into the fire for a minute. "It seems she was quite a kid, that Loveday Byrd; saved my life more than once, actually. But on that first occasion at the rapids I had three ways I could have died. If the rocks didn't kill me and the river didn't drown me, then I guess Casey hoped the crocodiles would make a meal of me."

"But you were saved."

"Loveday was there, she was a local kid, knew the area inside out, and saw the whole thing unfold."

"She's Australian?" said Ruby. "She doesn't sound Australian."

"I guess she lost the accent over the years. She's been living over here a long time," he said. "Anyway, she did this incredible thing, I mean, I watched her, this tall skinny girl, jump down about twenty feet, land on a shelf of rock no bigger than my two hands, and then she leaped across the boulders until she reached me. I can't tell you how she pulled me from the water because the last thing I remember is meeting a pretty big rock head-on, but if it weren't for her I'd have sailed right over that waterfall and I doubt if they'd ever have found my body — the crocs would have seen to that."

"I'm guessing you have no idea what the kid version of Casey looked like?"

Baker shook his head. "No memory of that, and I heard there is no filed record in the Prism Vault, is that true? I mean, you've been in there."

"The only mention of Casey is in that account of your almost demise. LB never met him, and Samuel Colt said he wouldn't be able to pick Morgan out in a lineup."

"Not forgetting that he's gonna have changed quite a bit by now; it's a lot of years ago," said Baker.

"And if SJ's right about her theory and Casey Morgan *did* seek out the Count, then it's quite possible that Morgan's learned the technique of complete transformation."

"Which would explain why not a soul knows who he is," said Baker.

"Except perhaps," said Ruby, looking at him, "you?"

CHAPTER 46
Run

RUBY HAD NO IDEA at what point she fell asleep, whether it was while *she* was talking or *Baker* was talking, but when she woke up he was gone.

It was the sound of the door closing that woke her. Ruby looked around, but there was no sign of anyone, just a note pinned to the cabin door.

```
Gone to meet LB, stay put, back soon.
```

Ruby yawned, stretched her limbs, pulled on her boots, and went outside to greet the day. Bug was lying warming himself in the sun, but got to his feet when he saw her.

He followed close by while Ruby gathered some wood and built the fire. She was thinking of boiling some water for tea when she noticed a light flash in the corner of the cabin. It was shining through the pocket of Bradley's backpack. She picked up the bag and searched through it until her hand closed around a mini locator. Its signal was flashing violet.

Hitch, is that you? Are you actually alive?

What to do next, she wondered.

Should I go and find him right now? Or should she wait for Baker and LB to arrive?

She thought for a minute. If he was in bad shape, maybe he wouldn't last another hour. . . . She should go.

She left a note telling them where she was headed and, since she had no way of contacting Baker directly, she pinned the transmitter to her suit so he could track her that way. She did not send a message to LB—the watch transmitter she was wary of.

She wasted no time, grabbing just the essentials: gloves, hat, goggles, and first-aid kit. Once her skis were on, she checked the locator—it was telling her to head northwest. She whistled for Bug, but he stood his ground.

"Oh, come on!" she said. "Hitch could be dying."

But Bug just barked.

"OK, have it your way, Bug, but I have to go."

She had gone no more than fifty yards when the husky caught up with her.

"I knew you'd come around," she said.

LB climbed out of the chopper and set about snapping on her skis. Due to weather conditions, she had touched down a mile east of the meeting point, but it would take her no time to ski the final stretch. She held the binoculars to her eyes and searched the horizon. Baker was a good way there already. She was about to set off when her eye was caught by another figure, smaller and clad in gold . . . and what was that following behind?

"Is that a dog?" she muttered. "Redfort, where are you off to?"

LB watched as Ruby and Bug headed toward a low ridge not so far from the frozen lake.

Where is she going? thought LB.

She panned across the landscape to see what might be drawing Ruby that way. She counted three figures, crouching low in the trees. She focused in closer and saw a fourth, a woman, sitting on a sled. *Marnie Novak?*

It didn't take LB long to figure what was going down here.

She radioed. "Bradley, we got a situation; the kid is headed due northwest and about to hit trouble."

"How many?"

"Four."

"I'll be there."

But it was LB who reached the ridge first.

Ruby was still a ways off when a shot rang out. The surprise of it caused Ruby to lose her balance and she fell awkwardly, losing her ski.

More shots.

Through the trees Ruby could see movement, blurred figures zigzagging in the woodland. Then she heard a distant voice.

"Run!" shouted LB. She yelled from far across the valley, and Ruby began to run, harder than she had ever run. Bug at her side, she ran through the dense woodland where the snow was less deep. They ran downhill toward the frozen lake and they didn't look back.

Baker arrived at the ridge to find three guys unconscious on the ground and LB searching the trees for the woman.

"Where did she go? I didn't see her go." LB's own blood drip-dripped onto the pristine white snow.

"You're hit," said Baker, placing his hand on her bloodied leg.

"I'm alive," she said. "Just save the kid."

He looked into her eyes, pressing his hand to hers. "You can count on it," he said.

He kissed her and then he began to run.

"Don't die!" shouted LB.

He turned, just for a split second. "I never do!"

And he was lost in the trees.

"I'll make it back," he called.

"I know it," she said. But her face said something quite different, and her eyes turned glassy. Her sixth sense was telling her something, and she tried to blot it out.

"Don't die!" she whispered.

But the voice told her he was not coming back.

CHAPTER 47
On Thin Ice

GIRL AND DOG STUMBLED OUT OF THE FOREST and tumbled down the makeshift path slick with frozen snow. Ruby part-fell, part-slid down to where the lake met the rock shore. From the corner of her eye, Ruby saw a dogsled swiftly gliding across the flat snowscape to the edge of the trees. She got to her feet. She was standing on the lake now. Several inches of ice separated her from the death-cold water beneath. Nowhere to go but across the expanse of frozen lake, vast and exposed. All she could do was keep going. So she ran, across the iron water, skidding and falling and scrambling and running, and all the time Marnie Novak in her six-dog sled was gaining on her.

"I see you, sweetie; you've got nowhere to run, you can't hide in plain sight."

Ruby turned, tripped, and fell; all hope seeped away.

"Even your dog has deserted you."

She looked around. It was true. *Where is Bug?* She had been running so hard she hadn't noticed him fall. Then she saw him in the distance, limping toward them.

Marnie Novak, dressed in fur, stepped from the sled, casting a shadow that fell over Ruby and trapped her where she lay.

"I believe you have something for me?" said the woman.

"I have nothing," said Ruby. "What do you think I could tell you, what do you think I know?"

"More than you realize," said the woman. "It's time for you to come with me. Casey Morgan would like to look you in the eye and find out what you know."

"Why don't you look *me* in the eye instead?" said a voice.

The woman spun around, a face of fury and next, sheer puzzlement.

"Who . . . what are you . . . how . . ." she stammered.

"Hello, Marnie," he said. "Long time no see."

Slowly, she smiled. "Back from the dead, Bradley? How original."

"It's easy to pull off if you keep breathing."

"I guess that's true, sweetie, but for how long will that continue?"

She fired shots at his feet and there was a cracking as ice split, and a crash as Baker fell into the lake below.

"No!" Ruby screamed.

And then there was Bug. From nowhere he appeared, leaping into the air, knocking into the woman, who lost her footing and went skidding toward the black abyss.

Almost traveling in slow motion to where the water lapped up through the ice.

Her eyes wide with terror, her mouth a silent scream as she disappeared in.

She would not be found until spring.

Ruby began to yell Baker's name.

"Bradley! Bradley! You can't do this!" She only left off when Bug began to bark and she saw Baker pounding at the ice beneath her feet.

She knew what to do.

The laser function on the Bradley Baker Escape Watch made easy work of the ice, and in under thirty seconds Ruby and Bug were pulling at him, heaving his exhausted body from the oil-dark water. Ruby's strength came from that superhuman place of life and death. As he emerged from this underworld, she let go of his hand and sank to her knees. She had saved Bradley Baker as he had saved her. And the Australian? She was gone.

"You gotta get warm," Ruby said, and she began peeling off his coat. "It will kill you, you have to get warm." She snatched the reindeer furs from the dog sled. "You gotta wrap yourself in these."

He didn't move.

"You have to," she said, her face so earnest he smiled.

"It's not funny," she said. "You'll die."

"I know," he said.

He didn't look so good. He really didn't.

"This is my fault," said Ruby. "If I hadn't tried to find Hitch, you would not be here now."

"Oh, that's baloney, Ruby. That's not how it is — you know that, right? Tell me you know that."

She was silent.

"My dying has been a long time coming, so if my last breath was taken saving you, then it was worth dying for."

Ruby began to speak, but Bradley Baker stopped her.

"Listen, Ruby," he said. "These people, well, they aren't people at all, they're monsters, and they will track you down until they have what they want, and what they want above all else is you."

She looked at him like she didn't understand.

And she didn't understand.

He grabbed her arm and closed his fingers hard around her wrist.

"Wake up, Ruby, you gotta see, open your eyes; you start blaming yourself for any of this, then you can't win. LB did what she had to do, and she was right. I would have done the same."

He seemed to catch sight of something way above him, his eyes tracking this imaginary thing as if there might be something floating across the blue. She followed his gaze, but there was nothing there.

"*You* have the answer. You're the only one who can make sense of it."

He looked very pale, the blood gone from his face. He was dying, she could see that.

"You're not making any sense," said Ruby. "Tell me what

you mean!" She was shaking him now, this man almost gone, this agent of old, the only one who could unlock the past and cast up the future.

"What are we without memory?" he said. "Lose memory and lose ourselves."

"What are you saying?" she pleaded.

"It's in you" was all he said.

"*I* have the answer? Me? Ruby Redfort? Is that what you mean? Stop dying and tell me!" She shook him. "What answer?"

"You," he said. "*You* are the answer."

She looked at him, the breath leaving him now, the life almost ebbed away.

"You can't die. LB will never forgive me if you die."

"Yes," he said, "she will."

"I will never forgive me if you die."

"There is nothing to forgive." He smiled. "Ruby Redfort, you made my life better than it *was*," he whispered. "Close your eyes and see the truth." He closed his own and was gone. And Ruby laid her head on his heart and sobbed.

CHAPTER 48
Sorrow

THEY SAT TOGETHER ON THE ICE, the child, the woman, and the dog. They sat there because their grief would not allow them to move.

The woman held his hand in hers and pulled it to her cheek and felt his touch for the last and final time. A single tear fell from her eye and landed near his own, and they shared the sorrow, one dead, one living, both loves cut short.

And when she *did* speak, she turned to the girl and said,

"I must thank you, Ruby Redfort. I must thank you twice, once for bringing Baker back to me, and once for freeing me of my guilt."

And Ruby put her arms around her and hugged her tight.

CHAPTER 49
We Wish You a
Merry Christmas

RUBY HAD FELT ADMIRATION FOR MANY PEOPLE in her lifetime, but none perhaps so great as the admiration she felt for LB that day. LB had lost him twice, this friend, this colleague and treasured soul, but she did not cast around for someone to blame. Instead she did what had to be done, made the calls, gave instructions, and flew him home. But the more remarkable thing was the way she took Ruby in hand. Two days after the tragedy at the lake, Ruby and LB met.

LB, dressed in a white hooded coat, was sitting on the bench under the oak on Amster Green. The sun was setting and a delicate snow had just started to fall. She had contacted Ruby and asked if she would meet her *here,* "not at Spectrum," she had said.

LB looked up as Ruby approached, and, raising a hand, she smiled.

"How *are* you?" asked Ruby.

"Full of sorrow," said LB.

They sat watching the snow until LB spoke.

"I will always be in your debt," she said. "You found Bradley Baker."

He's dead, thought Ruby, *and that's because of me.*

"It's not your fault," said LB, as if she could read her mind. "Baker came to find you in the Northern Mountains because you were part of his team; it's what any agent would do. His death is due to Novak. We know Novak's instructions came from the Count and the Count has been working for Morgan. So if you want to direct your loathing at anyone, let it be those three, and more specifically the two who are still out there. Do not waste valuable energy beating yourself up — it's no good to Baker and he wouldn't like it."

Her face was set firm: nothing to be negotiated.

On the issue of Hitch, the Spectrum 8 boss was equally clear. "Until we know otherwise, Hitch is considered missing, not dead, and we will concentrate on what needs to be done."

What needed to be done was the partial shutdown of Spectrum 8. Only a skeleton staff was kept in situ, and there was no question of Ruby walking into the subterranean headquarters any time soon.

But Ruby had also had other things to occupy her mind, concerns *outside* of Spectrum and the drama of Casey Morgan and the Count and whoever or whatever might be lurking in the shadows. The most immediate being: Would arriving back home having been so long away spark a series of impossible questions? Would her parents wonder where she had been all this time? Would Mrs. Digby have called in Sheriff Bridges and filed a missing-person report? And Principal Levine? What would he make of this three-day absence? Would she return to Twinford Junior High only to be faced with a series of detentions?

But she needn't have worried. It had been quite clear when she walked into the house that Hitch had done his job; he'd had it all covered. Ruby was supposedly on some snurferboarding trip that her parents had clean forgot about. All excuses made ahead of time, no need for explanations. He had even made provision for himself, explained his own absence in a brief letter to her parents.

An unforeseen personal situation has called me away, and I have organized for someone to cover for me while I am gone. In the unlikely event that I am unable to return to my post as house manager, I will have the agency make provision for a permanent replacement. I apologize for the doubtless inconvenience caused, and I deeply regret the short notice.

There was a short list of things to pass on to Mrs. Digby, a long list for Sabina, a message about the new alarm system, and a word of assurance in the form of a P.S. —

You will find my replacement supremely capable.

He was some house manager, some secret agent, and one very remarkable man.

The Bug injury was harder to explain, since Hitch had not been aware that the dog would play a part in any mountain rescue, but Ruby was a quick thinker and she came up with a more than adequate story.

When Ruby, returning from her meeting with LB, walked into Green-Wood House and upstairs to the living room, she found her mother standing in front of the huge picture window, looking out at the snowflakes that were dropping lazily from the sky. The fire was lit, the tree trimmed, Christmas cards decked the piano, and all in all it was a very pretty sight.

Maybe it was looking upon this cozy scene, or maybe it was the fact that Ruby had looked into the eyes of a legend as he had faded away. Maybe it was LB's ability to survive his death, maybe it was something to do with being buried alive, maybe it was because it had been her parents' faces she saw when the snow packed in around her. Maybe it was because it was Mrs. Digby's voice that had reached her in her most desperate hour, maybe it was all of these things, but when Sabina Redfort held out her hand and said, "Rube, how about you and I grab ourselves a nice chicken dinner at Pollo's?" Ruby found herself saying, "I'd like nothing better," and she meant it.

Pollo's was the perfect place to be on a winter night. A lot of people had had the same idea, and the restaurant was busy. They had left Bug sleeping downstairs in Mrs. Digby's apartment, his leg now encased in plaster. It was a bad break, but it would heal just fine.

"So did Bug *really* save your life?" asked Sabina.

"Uh-huh," said Ruby. "My snurferboard landed me in a hole, and if he hadn't pulled me out, then I would have died for sure." She looked at her mother. "I feel just dreadful about his leg; it was on account of me he broke it."

"I knew those snurferboards were a bad idea," said her mother. "Why anyone would want to hop on a piece of wood and head full-tilt down a mountain I will never know."

They talked of school and Mrs. Drisco's annoyance at Del for proving her wrong about the corridor rules. Principal Levine had conceded that since roller-skating was not mentioned on the long list of prohibited corridor activities, Del Lasco could not be punished with litter-picking duty. That said, she had better not do it again or she would be on litter-picking duty for the rest of her days.

"I'm glad Principal Levine saw sense — that Mrs. Drisco should think about retiring," said Sabina sympathetically. Also discussed were: Vapona Begwell's decision to sing in the carol concert (*"One can only imagine the sound that kid's voice is likely to honk out"*) and Clancy's struggles with his French exam (*"I guess I could help him. My French has gotten pretty good now. Est-ce que vous avez la taille en dessous?"*).

"Yes," agreed Ruby, "I am sure Clancy will find phrases like that very handy."

And then Ruby's father arrived.

And so they talked of the approaching holiday and the big New Year's Eve party to be held at the old Eye Hospital.

"I've got some incredible news for you, Rube," her father said, ruffling her hair. Ruby put her hand up to straighten her locks and realized something was missing—the fly barrette was gone. With all that had happened, she simply had not noticed. She was sure she'd had it when she'd returned from the lake, *yes, definitely*, she remembered Clancy asking her if Hitch had tried to contact her on the tiny transmitter. So where was it?

"Are you OK, Ruby honey?" asked her father.

"Yeah, sure, I just lost my barrette is all," said Ruby. "What were you going to say?"

The news was that Brant Redfort, who was owed more than a few favors by party hosts Mr. and Mrs. Hassensack, had acquired several extra invitations.

"This means you and Clancy can cheer in the New Year with everyone—Mouse, Elliot, Red, *and* Del—you're going to have a blast," said Brant.

"They'll need to start thinking about costumes," said Sabina.

"Your mother and I want you and your pals to have the greatest time," said her father. "You really deserve it. I took a look at your grades, and you are just about acing every class."

"I don't know where she gets her brains from," said Sabina, "but it's more likely to be you than me."

"Nonsense, honey," said Brant. "You're smart as a whippet."

"Whip," corrected Ruby. What she didn't say was that all she really wanted to do was stay home, turn the locks in the doors, hunker down, and pull the covers up over her head. But instead she just said, "Geez, thanks, Dad!"

When dinner was just about finished, Sabina sighed and said, "Boy, do I ever wish Hitch was here."

"We all do," said Brant. "But he'll be back."

"What's more," said Sabina, "I miss Mo too. There was just something about that man that made you want him to stick around."

"I agree," said Brant. "You couldn't meet a nicer fellow."

"I had hoped he might want to spend the holiday with us," said Sabina. "Do you think there's a chance?"

Ruby shook her head. "I don't think he's coming back this way."

"A pity," said her father.

"But I know for a fact that he would have liked to," added Ruby.

"Shame," said her mother, "but he left me just the nicest note."

"A note?" said Ruby.

"Yes," said Sabina, taking it from her purse. "See?"

Dear Redforts,
Thank you for your warm hospitality. I loved every minute of the time I spent with you. I am only sorry it couldn't have

been a lot longer. Please forgive me for not saying farewell
in person, but where I had to be just couldn't wait.
Yours with affection, Mo
P.S. Look after that kid of yours, she's one in a million.

"And you know what?" said her mother. "He's right, Rube,
you really are the most incredible kid."

"So say all of us," agreed her father.

Hitch was being missed for a whole lot of reasons. Though he
had provided more than adequate cover: house manager Luke
Philips (or, to those in the know, *Agent* Philips from Spectrum 1)
was indeed *supremely* capable. Things moved like clockwork in
the Redfort home, every household issue was attended to, and
though no one was aware of it, their security was monitored and
every safety procedure followed. But life seemed dull without
Hitch. His replacement had little interest in engaging with
Sabina's whims and fancies, Brant gave up attempting to chat
with him about his day at the office, and Mrs. Digby felt a little
affronted that this man never ate seconds of her home-cooked
nourishment. Ruby crossed her fingers, and then her toes for
good measure, and hoped that Hitch would surprise them all
and walk through the door before Christmas.

But the only surprise that walked in that Christmas came
through the doors of Twinford Junior High. No one believed
she would turn up, no one imagined she would actually climb

onto the stage and stand there in front of the entire school, but she did. Vapona Begwell not only got up onstage, but she sang a solo *and*—biggest surprise of all—she had a voice that left her audience teary eyed for all the right reasons.

"Simply looking at the kid could just about scare the pants off a person," commented Sabina, "but when she hits the high notes, I mean, who could care less about pants?"

And then came Christmas, and Mrs. Digby cooked her goose and five different vegetables and served eggnog and cookies and cake and ham and so on, and *still* Hitch did not walk through the door.

And Ruby, she began to give up hope that he ever would.

CHAPTER 50
Even the Mundane Can Tell a Story

IT WAS ONE DAY DURING THE WEEK between Christmas and New Year that Ruby stumbled across something very small and not particularly thrilling. It was as she was pulling notebook 114 from the stack that the whole pile of yellow books toppled and slid untidily between the joists.

"Darn it," Ruby muttered. She didn't want to have to waste time getting them all back in order; she lifted them out, a few at a time, and stacked them there on the floor, as far as possible keeping them in their correct position. She did this by turning them facedown so the most recent books were on the bottom of the piles and the earliest on the top. As she picked the last remaining notebook from the hole in the floor, she revealed something she had no memory of at all. She reached in and pulled it out. It was yet another little notebook, but this one was not yellow. Instead it was blue and had an illustration of a little fluffy dog on the cover, a cartoony thing with big eyes, the sort of image Ruby might once have considered cute. She opened it, flicking through the pages, only a little curious to see what they held.

There was a date, November 1962, though it was spelled Novmember 1962, written in her own little-girl handwriting, which wasn't bad considering she had still been a few months shy of three. She remembered *studying* handwriting from a calligraphy book she'd found in the library, and the first few pages were just filled top to bottom with the alphabet as she practiced her joined-up letters. But as they went on, little sentences appeared.

```
    we have a new white couch, mom says no
eating food any wher near it

    misses Beesman has 50 cats and 3 mor new
ones.

    mom took me to see misses Humberts new
baby it is named Quent he looks very pink and
makes a bad noise

    mom and dad said we can not have a dog
you are to yung.

    misses digby made pancakes I ate 12.
```

It was pretty riveting stuff and it continued in that vein.

```
    spilled banana milk on the couch it would
```

```
not rubb off but I moved cushons on top so it
is gon
```

But then it got more interesting.

```
    mr pinkoton has left he did not say
goodbye.
```

OK, so her three-year-old self *had* noticed the old man's departure.

But it was this line that really grabbed her.

```
    misses Beesman has a dog in her yard I
herd it barking.
```

```
    the dog has been barking for one hole
week and one day.
```

The eccentric lady who kept all those cats in her yard now had a dog? That was strange; strange because Mrs. Beesman didn't like dogs, strange because as far as anyone knew she had only ever kept cats. Ruby turned the page to see what else she had noted.

```
    mom moved the cushons she got very mad
when she saw the banana milk stain.
```

There was nothing more.

Ruby was called down to eat her supper, and while she was chewing on her slightly overcooked lamb chop, she asked Mrs. Digby if she could remember Mrs. Beesman owning a dog.

"A long time ago," said Ruby, "like maybe when I was about two and three-quarters, going on three?"

"Are you out of your mind, child? That old lady can't abide hounds, never could; she sees a hound, she crosses the road."

"She doesn't cross the road when she sees Bug," countered Ruby. "She doesn't seem to dislike *him*."

"That's different," said Mrs. Digby. "No one dislikes Bug. He's more than a dog."

But the note about the barking lodged there in Ruby's brain; it might seem of little consequence, a barking dog in the cat woman's yard, but **EVEN THE MUNDANE CAN TELL A STORY**. It was **RULE 16**. So what story was *this* mundane piece of information trying to tell her?

By the next day, Ruby decided that she really, really needed to know. In fact, she thought she might creep into the old lady's yard if that's what it took, and in the end that's exactly what she did.

The yard gate had long since been secured with nails and screws to prevent any unwanted visitors, which actually meant *anyone,* but there *was* a way in if you knew exactly where to look, and Ruby *did,* because for many years she had watched cats come and go this way. A couple of the fence slats were secured by just one nail and so could be pushed to one side to create a gap big enough for a medium-sized animal to crawl through, or a particularly small thirteen-year-old girl. Once she was inside, the problem became about finding whatever it was she was looking for, and to be honest she had no idea what that might be.

Ruby had stood in Mrs. Beesman's yard only once before. It was back in April, when she and Clancy had helped to clear the junk, which was piled up so high it was getting to be a health hazard. They had shifted quite a lot of it but had only worked to clear the area nearest to the house, where it was at its most precarious.

The junk seemed to be growing again, and it wouldn't be long before it would be back to how it had once been. Ruby looked around her. *What a dump,* she thought. *And where exactly do her cats hang out? Poor creatures.* Ruby couldn't see any of the seventy-four felines Mrs. Beesman was rumored to have. Then, as she poked around, she noticed a narrow channel between stacked-up crates and she edged her way through, expecting to find another wall of garbage. But what she actually found was another gate, this one unlocked, and when she levered it open, she found herself in a garden. Not a formal garden, or even a well-weeded or -maintained garden, but it was certainly a garden. A garden with colored bottles suspended from trees and tin-can sculptures and a broken-crockery mosaic path; a beautiful garden, even in winter. So struck by it was she that Ruby began to walk along the twisting mosaic walkway that snaked around the trees and plants. The land to the back of the house was a lot bigger than she'd ever realized; she had just never seen beyond the junk.

At the far end, Ruby saw another little work of art in the form of tiny rows of colored boards all decorated with words and numbers, all sticking out of the ground. She moved closer and read: Fred, Billy, Giggles, Fluff, Bertrude, Rolly, Puddle . . .

Cat graves! thought Ruby. *Here lie Mrs. Beesman's cats. . . .*

And the names went on. Hubert, Flip, Fester, Kimble, Mnemosyne . . .

Ruby stopped. The same name as Mr. Pinkerton's dog. A coincidence?

But Ruby didn't believe in coincidences, not when they were as big as this.

She looked at the name again. This *had* to be Mr. Pinkerton's dog. There were hardly likely to be two animals called Mnemosyne, not on the same street, probably not even in the same city.

The date said November 1962. It made sense, this had to be the dog whose barking she had heard, the date matched. But why had it arrived here, and why had Mr. Pinkerton never come back to find it?

Ruby did not hear the footsteps as they neared, she only became aware of the hunched figure behind her when she felt a hand on her arm.

"I see you got your coat back."

Ruby shrieked. "Jeepers, Mrs. Beesman!"

"I found it in that alley; you ran off pretty quick," said Mrs. Beesman. "Looked like you had taken fright."

Ruby had never heard the old lady say so many words all at once. And her voice was not the voice Ruby had imagined, not gruff as Ruby had expected, but softly spoken and perfectly clear.

"It looked warm," said Mrs. Beesman. "Too good to lose."

"*You* returned it?" said Ruby. "It was *you* who left it on the stoop?"

The old lady didn't seem to hear. "So you're the child," she said.

"Uh, well, yeah," said Ruby. "I'm the Redfort girl." She pointed unnecessarily toward her house across the street, as if the old lady hadn't observed her day in and day out for the past thirteen years. But Mrs. Beesman just nodded.

"Thank you," said Ruby, ". . . for the coat." She hesitated. "You're probably wondering what I'm doing here?"

"You're looking for Homer Pinkerton."

Ruby nodded. "Well, yes," she said, "I guess I am."

"He hid for a long time, years and years he hid, and then one day they found him — came and took his dog," said the old lady.

"Who?"

"I don't know," said the old lady.

"Why did they want his dog?" asked Ruby.

"They knew he would do anything to get her back," said Mrs. Beesman, "and what *they* wanted, *he* had."

"What was it?" said Ruby.

The old lady shrugged. "He told me one day someone might come."

"He did?" asked Ruby.

"He said he had something that people wanted and when they figured out he still had it, they would find him and make him give it to them."

"So he did?"

"I don't know; he never came back," said Mrs. Beesman.

"But his dog did. Mnemosyne came to you — why?" asked Ruby.

"Mr. Pinkerton trained her to find people — a smart dog, that mutt. He called it the 'go find' trick. If he told her where to go, then she would go."

Ruby thought of Bug. Bug could do that trick, but only when he was in the mood.

"Were all his dogs as smart as Mnemosyne?"

"He only had one," said Mrs. Beesman. "He lived for her — had her for forty years, you know."

"What?" said Ruby. "That isn't possible. A dog's life span is twelve years, fifteen maybe."

Mrs. Beesman shrugged again. "All I know is what I know — that dog lived forty years. He said he kept her healthy, but I think it was something to do with those mushrooms he fed her."

"Mushrooms," mouthed Ruby.

"Mushrooms." Mrs. Beesman nodded.

"What kind of mushrooms?" asked Ruby.

"He said they came from Mars," said the old lady, "but I don't know about that. The dog died two weeks after Homer Pinkerton went missing, call it a broken heart, call it what you will, but that dog couldn't do without him."

And then, without word or warning, Mrs. Beesman picked up a spade and began digging in her yard, pulling up a rosebush with her gnarled old hands.

Was that it? Conversation over? Ruby was unsure if she should stick around, so she turned, walked through the gate, and headed back toward the fence.

She was halfway through the gap, one leg out on the sidewalk, when she felt a tap on her shoulder. She looked up to see Mrs. Beesman, her hands muddy. In her grip was a dog's chew toy, a bone made of blue rubber all covered in dirt. She pushed it into Ruby's hand and looked at her with an expression that Ruby had never seen before and would never see again.

"He said you might come," she said. Then she tottered away and seemed to disappear into the pile of junk.

Ruby walked slowly back toward her house, clutching the bone in her hand.

She went up to the kitchen, poured herself a banana milk, sat down at the table, and wrote down everything Mrs. Beesman had said. She looked up when she heard Mrs. Digby open the door.

"Where did that come from?" asked the housekeeper, her eyes trained on the muddy chew toy.

"You won't believe me," said Ruby.

"Well, that's more than likely," said Mrs. Digby, "but I'm willing to take a chance."

"Mrs. Beesman gave it to me," said Ruby.

Mrs. Digby picked up the dog bone. "That poor old soul, she really has lost the plot."

But Ruby was beginning to wonder if Mrs. Beesman was the only one to have any sense of what the plot might actually be.

CHAPTER 51
The Fly Barrette

BACK IN HER ROOM, Ruby sat at her desk and stared at the bone.

What did it mean? Was it a clue? And if it was, then what exactly was it trying to tell her?

The telephone started ringing, and Ruby reached for the lobster.

"Hey," she said.

"Rube, where are you?"

It was Del.

"What do you mean, where am I? You just called *me*—I'm at home, bozo."

"You're the bozo, bozo."

"How do you figure that?"

"Because you're supposed to be at Red's place checking out space costumes for the Eye Ball, *remember*?"

This had completely slipped her mind.

"Oh," said Ruby.

"Yeah, you got that right," said Del.

"I completely forgot," said Ruby.

"I figured," said Del. "You did this last time. Halloween, remember?"

"Sorry," said Ruby.

"Everyone's here waiting for you."

"Sorry again," said Ruby.

"So are you coming over?" asked Del.

"Sure," said Ruby, "give me five minutes and I'll be there."

"Redfort, there's no way you're going to be here in five minutes," said Del.

"OK, so maybe six," said Ruby. She put down the phone, picked up the blue dog bone, and stuffed it in her laundry basket. It was as good a place as any to hide it. Then she pulled on her boots, grabbed her coat, and ran out the door.

Once on her bike, she rode as fast as she could down Cedarwood onto Amster, and when she met Dry River Road she hit the hyper-speed-boost button and the bike suddenly accelerated and Ruby tore down the road.

She arrived at Red's house exactly as she had predicted, six minutes later.

Red's mom, Sadie, had brought home a selection of space-themed costumes, pretty good ones too, so it took a while for everyone to pick and choose, but once they had, Sadie pinned them on and made alterations where alterations were required. They were just waiting for the pizza delivery guy to arrive when Clancy yelped, checked his watch, and began to flap his arms.

"Six seventeen! I gotta split," he said. "I promised my mom I'd be back to watch Olive."

He was pulling on his coat and already halfway out the door. "I'm going to be late," he said, sounding more than a little panicky.

"I'd drive you there, Clancy," said Sadie, "but the car's got a flat. Let me order you a cab at least."

"It's OK," said Ruby, "I'll take him. Jump on the back of my bike, Clance; you'll be home in four minutes, I swear."

When they reached Ambassador Row, some three minutes thirty-nine seconds later, Clancy was clearly impressed.

"Boy, that's some bike," he said. He looked both impressed and relieved. His mother was very committed to punctuality.

"Yeah, I mean, I could almost forgive it for being red," said Ruby, "but I'm going to respray it as soon as I have a minute."

Ruby was about to head off when Clancy remembered something.

"Oh, I forgot, I found your scarf, the striped one," he said. "Come in for a minute, I'll get it."

They stepped into the house and immediately a voice called down from the second floor.

"Clancy? Is that you?"

"Just a minute, Mom!" he called.

"Now!" called his mother.

Clancy gave Ruby an exasperated look.

"Don't worry, Clance, I'll get it," said Ruby.

"It's down the hallway," he said. "Coming!" he yelled as he made for the stairs. "I'll see you tomorrow, Rube, OK?"

"Sure," said Ruby.

She found the scarf draped over a chair at the far end of the corridor and was just turning to leave when she was confronted by Olive, who was coming the other way. She was pushing Buttercup in a tiny stroller and talking to her as she went.

"Now, Buttercup, I don't want to hear another peep out of you or you will have to go right to bed without any tomatoes."

Olive was dressed in her mother's (no doubt very expensive) pink blouse, which trailed down past her knees. On her feet were a pair of Lulu's high-heeled shoes, and she made for a strange sight as she shuffled along. What made her look even odder was that she had pinned one of her mother's hairpieces to her own curly head, and it was secured in place with approximately thirty assorted barrettes. Some of them looked to be Minny's, since they were printed with words like "puke" or decorated with skulls and other gothic images. Others, Ruby suspected, were Lulu's, since they twinkled quite a lot, and Lulu was a fan of things that twinkled.

"Nice look," said Ruby as she approached Olive. "They your sisters' barrettes?"

"They're not barrettes," said Olive. "They are wig *j-e-w-e-l-s*."

"Right," said Ruby, trying to step past the little girl.

"This one's an emerald and this one's a diamond, probably," said Olive, pointing first at a snot-green hairclip and then at one covered in gold sequins.

"Well," said Ruby, "don't look now, but you have a fly in your hair."

"That's not a fly," said Olive, "it's a spider."

"Wait a minute," said Ruby, moving in to take a closer look, "that's *my* barrette."

It was too.

"Olive, I'm gonna need that barrette back."

"It's not a barrette, it's a wig jewel," said Olive.

"Whatever," said Ruby.

"You'll have to pay me," said Olive.

"Why should I pay you for something that's already mine?"

"Finders keepers," explained Olive.

"Olive, do you have many friends?" It wasn't really a question.

"Buttercup's my friend," said Olive.

Ruby sighed. "How much d'ya want for it?"

"Five hundred dollars," said Olive.

"I'm not giving you five hundred dollars," said Ruby.

Olive frowned. "Twenty-five . . ."

Ruby gave the kid a hard stare.

"Cents?" suggested Olive.

Ruby reached into her pocket and pulled out a quarter. "You drive a hard bargain, Olive Crew."

Olive smiled and as she tugged the barrette from the hairpiece, she took a chunk of the fake hair with it. Olive would have trouble coming her way when Mrs. Crew made it downstairs.

Ruby slipped the fly barrette into her hair and walked off down the corridor and out the front door.

Ruby was attempting to cycle while also winding her scarf around her neck. It wasn't easy because the breeze kept catching it and whipping it away, and the bag with the space costume kept banging against her side. Eventually, she saw sense and came to a halt on Everglade, leaned the bike against the wall, and attempted to untangle it. Suddenly she felt a hand grab her and pull her away from the streetlight's glow and into black.

She would have certainly yelped had it not been for the palm pressed over her mouth.

"Don't scream," hissed a voice. "I am not in the mood for screaming."

The hand let go.

"Don't look so alarmed, Ms. Redfort. I am not the Grim Reaper — not today, at least."

"S-so . . ." stammered Ruby, stepping back a pace, "what *do* you want?"

"I want the key tag," said the Count.

"The key tag?" said Ruby. "But you already have it. You took it when we were on the roof of the Hotel Circus Grande; you must remember?" Her heart was pounding.

"I gave it away," he said bitterly. "A mistake, as it turns out."

"Who did you give it to?"

He didn't quite answer; instead he said, "Someone who started off as a little fly in the ointment but over the years seems to have grown into a spider. I had this apprentice once, you see, but he has gotten quite above himself, and now I find I am rather at his mercy."

"It must be very embarrassing for you," said Ruby.

"It *is* irksome," said the Count with a wave of his arm. "Little Casey Morgan sought me out when just a tiny rat of a boy, begging me to teach him the dark art of disguise, real disguise, you understand, transformation of face and voice so convincing that if you mastered it, your own mother wouldn't know you."

"Homer Pinkerton taught you. . . ." said Ruby.

"Oh, so you know about dear Homer. Such a friend until he became an enemy."

"An enemy you killed?"

"No, no, why would I do that when he held such a secret? No, Casey Morgan killed him — the fool."

"Doesn't that make you the fool?" said Ruby. "You trusted him."

"I'll admit it was poor judgment on my part," he said. "I trusted him to find me the one thing I had been seeking for so many years."

"A soul?" suggested Ruby.

The Count clapped his hands. "Very witty, Ms. Redfort. . . .

No, I'm not interested in souls; they are ten a penny. No, it's long life and wisdom I am after."

"The Mars Mushrooms?"

"*Hypocrea asteroidi,* exactly so," said the Count. "I set little Casey Morgan the task of finding where they grew, and thirty-three years later he did indeed find what I so desired. Encased in an iceberg north of Alaska."

"In the eyes of the Jade Buddha of Khotan . . ." said Ruby.

"Oh, congratulations, you figured it out; or was that dear dead Bradley? My, what an agent he was; what a shame he had to die all over again." The Count made a mock sad face before continuing with his tale.

"Morgan betrayed me, reneged on the deal, which is why I find myself doing his bidding." He tutted to himself. "A word to the wise . . . *if* you ever make it that far—which of course you won't—never impart knowledge that might bring about your own downfall."

"But it was you who looked into the Jade Buddha's eyes," said Ruby. "Why give what you saw there to Casey Morgan?"

"Alas," said the Count, "I do not have your talent for deciphering code, and the eyes held a code that only Morgan could solve." He looked at her sadly. "It seems I am now the prisoner of my protégé."

"Don't expect me to feel bad for you," said Ruby. "This problem is yours."

He gave her a pitying look.

"I don't think you are seeing the big picture here," said the Count. "Such blinkered vision. The reason you *should* feel bad, very bad indeed, is because, Ms. Redfort, Casey Morgan is very much *your* spider too, and he's creeping closer and closer across his web, and, forgive me for noticing, you seem to have your wings all tangled."

"Then tell me who Morgan is," said Ruby.

He gazed down at her with a puzzled expression. "You really don't understand, do you, little Ms. Redfort?"

There was brittle anger in his voice, and her heart began to thud. "Understand what?" she asked. "Understand what?"

"That I have no idea who Casey Morgan might be."

In her surprise, Ruby began to laugh, an involuntary reaction not of her choosing.

"While you delight in my misfortune, you might want to think of your own." He peered into her eyes and said, "Remember, Morgan is coming for *you. The spider is getting ever closer.*"

And he turned on his heel and disappeared into the dark, his footsteps accompanied by his final words:

"My advice: look closer to home, very close to home."

CHAPTER 52
Instinct

IT WAS ONLY AS SHE WAS PARKING HER BIKE to the side of the house that Ruby realized she no longer had her space costume. At some point she and it had parted company, and who knew where it now was? She had no desire to go back out there, no desire to leave home ever again. She climbed the steps, and before she could reach the front door, it swung open and there was Hitch.

"Hey, kid, it's been a while."

She looked at him, really looked at him.

"You're not dead?" she said. "I thought you were."

"If I was, then I seem to have made a full recovery," said Hitch.

"But the plane crash?"

"I jumped."

"But where have you been all this time?"

"I've been busy," he said.

"But that's good," said Ruby, "that you're not dead. Great, I mean."

"Why ever would he be dead?" said her mother, appearing from her room. She shook her head and kissed Ruby on the cheek, and she and Hitch walked upstairs and into the living room.

"It's swell to have you back," said Brant, raising a champagne glass. "Mrs. Digby has cooked a delicious chicken surprise in your honor—you completely missed the last one."

Hitch turned to Mrs. Digby. "So what makes this chicken such a surprise, Mrs. Digby?"

"The fact that you actually bothered to show up and eat it," said the housekeeper. She gave him an irritable look, and he gave her a kiss on the cheek and she immediately forgot her grievance.

The dinner that followed was indeed delicious. It was also full of mealtime chatter, and Sabina and Brant spent the evening firing questions at Hitch.

SABINA: *Where did you get that suit?*

HITCH: *London.*

SABINA: *How chic.*

BRANT: *Why London?*

HITCH: *I have a tailor there; he makes very hard-wearing suits, and I need my suits to be hard-wearing.*

SABINA: *Of course, I see, house-managing must play fast and loose with one's clothing.*

HITCH: *You'd be surprised.*

SABINA: *I'm sure I would.*

HITCH: *The last thing one needs is for a suit to rip at the seams.*

BRANT: *You must give me the name of your tailor.*

And when they were done quizzing him, they filled him in on the latest Twinford gossip.

SABINA: *The Eye Ball is going to be magnificent; you will come, won't you?*
HITCH: *I'll think about it.*
BRANT: *What's to think about? It's the only party in town.*
SABINA: *No, honey, it's not the only party in town; it's just the best party in town.*
BRANT: *That's what I meant, darling, the best party!*

There was little chance to talk to Hitch alone, and though of course Ruby should have told him about the Count encounter there and then, the evening was so perfect and everyone seemed so happy that she just couldn't bear to spoil it.

I'll tell him tomorrow. Tomorrow I can face it, but not now.

She climbed into bed and switched off the light.

She lay for a while just thinking about things. The best thing had happened, almost a *miracle:* Hitch had returned. When she thought of Marnie Novak and Lorelei, the plane crash, it made her shudder. The odds of Hitch surviving all that seemed so slim, so unlikely. It really was *something* that he had survived.

She stared at the tree shadows as they waved their spindly arms. What was it that was gnawing away at her? Because *something* was. Something ugly was lurking in the very darkest part of her mind, and every time she tried to drag it into the light, another thought blocked it.

At exactly 3:33 a.m. Ruby woke up. She was drenched with sweat and finding it hard to breathe. She sat up, reached for the bedside light, knocked over a glass of water, and stumbled out of bed. Bug woke too, his eyes fixed on hers as he got awkwardly to his feet, his plaster-cast leg tap-tapping as he followed her to the bathroom.

Ruby ran the faucet and splashed her face with water. Bug was standing next to her, his ears alert for danger.

Ruby was muttering.

How did Hitch survive that plane crash?

Who booked that plane? Well, Spectrum had. *Who told her to jump?* Hitch. So had he actually wanted her to plummet to earth? She thought about it. Without the parachute cape, she would have been splatted over the mountaintop.

He had given her the parachute cape, a gift from LB, so he *hadn't wanted her to die.*

She thought again: no, he hadn't wanted her to die *falling from the plane,* but had he set her up for what came later?

What if Hitch had been the one to call in that request to Zuko, what if he had scheduled the Spectrum jet — tipping off the Australian, allowing her to get on board, bringing with her her own henchman?

No, this is stupid, thought Ruby. *Hitch was punched by those guys, he was all beaten up.* She pondered on this, and another horrible thought spread. *But what if that was staged?* All part of the plan, right up until Lorelei appeared, then things had gone wrong. *Lorelei wasn't supposed to be there,* thought Ruby. *Lorelei wanted me dead and Marnie for some reason needed me alive.*

Was *that* why Hitch had told her to jump? He knew she had a chute, knew that she could make it out of there in one piece. *The plane was supposed to land safe and sound, but it didn't, couldn't.*

I got down to earth, but I might have died afterward. No one could have known she would survive. *Not only that,* she thought, *but no one could have known they would find me.* In fact, they *hadn't* found her, *she'd* found them, so there it was, an accident, a cruel twist of fate; *if I hadn't picked up that signal on Hitch's locator, if Marnie Novak hadn't taken Hitch's locator, then I would never have followed the signal. . . . Oh . . .* another bad thought. What if Hitch had handed his locator to the Australian knowing that this would be the way to lure Ruby, knowing that if Ruby got Hitch's signal, then she would come and find him? What if he'd planned all this, faked his own death and then disappeared for a while so he could do whatever he needed to do without anyone asking tricky questions?

Ruby slept fitfully, as you might expect someone to sleep if they had a probable murderer sleeping three floors below them.

But by the time the light began to creep into her room, her suspicions faded and the very notion that Hitch might in some way be implicated in her capture seemed ridiculous.

❋ ❋ ❋

When Ruby came down for breakfast she found her parents dunking croissants into bowls of coffee while they perused *Paris Match*. There was no sign of Hitch.

"He might be in his room," suggested her mother, "though he said he was going out for the day, so you may have missed him."

Ruby went down the two flights of stairs to the ground-floor apartment and knocked on his door. There was no answer, so she tried again, a little harder this time. When she knocked the second time, the door sort of drifted open. She peered in. She knew she shouldn't, but she couldn't seem to help herself.

"Hitch?" she called.

No answer.

She stepped into the room; it was tidy as always, but today there was a file on the desk. It was very unlike Hitch to leave anything like that lying around; his desk was always clear, save for a glass paperweight, a black fountain pen, and a pad of white paper. She walked over to see what this file might be. As it turned out, it related only to the house, the new alarm system and security devices, nothing of any consequence. As she slid the file back to the center of the desk, she noticed his document case. It must have slipped off the chair, because it was lying on its side and some of its contents had spilled out onto the floor. She picked up a little metal card. It was a Spectrum swipe key, with his name, date of birth, and his agent code.

"Child! Where are you?"

Ruby ran to the door and slipped out into the hall and up the stairs.

"Here!" she said. "I'm here!"

Mrs. Digby gave her a look. "I'm not gonna ask what mischief you've been getting into because I know I won't like the answer." She handed Ruby a stack of envelopes. "You can mail these on your way out."

CHAPTER 53
Nothing Is Completely Safe

SHE MET CLANCY AT THE DONUT, just as they had planned.

Once they were seated she told him about Hitch's return, how she'd arrived home and there he was.

"But that's great," said Clancy.

"I know," said Ruby.

"So why do you look like someone stole your sneakers?"

"That's it, Clance, I don't know."

Then she told him of her spiraling paranoia.

"It's understandable," said Clancy.

"Yeah, but you haven't heard the worst," said Ruby.

"What?" asked Clancy.

"I actually went into his room."

"When he wasn't there?" whispered Clancy.

"I know," said Ruby, "it's bad, isn't it?"

"You're lucky he's not Minny," he said. "She'd kill you if you stepped inside her room."

"Maybe he will," said Ruby. "He's bound to have some little trip wire system."

"So what did you see?" asked Clancy. "A dirty mug, cookie crumbs on the floor?"

"Nothing that extreme," said Ruby. "Just his Spectrum identity card."

"So what was on it?"

"Just 'Hitch,' his agent code, and his date of birth," said Ruby.

"So how old is he?" asked Clancy.

"Forty-two, like he said," said Ruby.

"So what's the big deal here?"

"Nothing, other than I have his ID and I need to get it back into his room before he realizes it's missing."

"You're kidding!"

"I know, it's bad, I'm losing it, super losing it."

"You're not *losing* it, Rube, you're just trying to fit a puzzle together, trying the pieces, some of them fit, some of them don't," said Clancy.

"You're right," said Ruby.

"And some of the pieces are missing," he added.

"That's certainly true." Ruby sighed.

"And maybe some of the pieces belong to a different puzzle," he said.

"OK, stop with the puzzle metaphor, you're overdoing it, Clance."

"The point is," said Clancy, "there's a lot to juggle."

"You got that right," said Ruby. "But what am I *doing* putting Hitch in the frame? He's saved me from a forest fire, he rescued me from Baby Face Marshall, Nine Lives Capaldi. Jeepers, he's saved my bacon more than a *few* times, so it seems a little unfair to even *imagine* he might be trying to kill me," she said. "I mean, if I were him, I would want to clonk me on the head just for being so darned ungrateful."

Clancy shrugged. "I think Hitch would understand. Like I said, sometimes you have to allow yourself to think the worst..." He paused. "And let's face it, the thing is, well, lately ..." Again he stopped as if not wanting to finish the thought.

"What?" said Ruby.

"Well," Clancy said, "he *has* been acting kinda odd. I mean, where has he been all this time, why didn't he try to contact you? Put your mind at rest and ..."

"What?" asked Ruby.

He looked at her. "You're in danger, and he hasn't been there for you." His eyes were round and scared as they looked into hers.

"It's OK, Clance, really it is." She could not tell him about the Count, not now.

"But you're worried," said Clancy. "You're wondering if you can trust the person you need to trust most."

She stared across at him,

"And what's your instinct, Clance?"

He said nothing for a long moment, but when he finally did, he looked Ruby straight in the eye and said, "You have to go with *your* gut feeling. You have to trust in your own sixth sense because deep down you know the answer."

When she arrived home there was still no sign of Hitch, which was good because it meant she had an opportunity to slip back down to his apartment and replace the identity card on the floor where she had found it. She was busy trying to position it exactly where she'd picked it up from when she saw the corner of something almost hidden but not quite. It was just poking out from under a low sideboard, and when she slid it out she saw it was a passport.

Curious, she opened it. As one would expect, there was a photograph of Hitch, recently taken, and his date of birth, which corresponded with his ID card. It was his name that troubled her: Art Hitchen Zachery, the boy from the rapids.

Her mind began to process this information.

So he had *been in the Larvae Program.*

But he'd told her he hadn't been.

But he would have undergone SME, *so how would he know?*

That's right, SJ had told her so, the Junior Space recruits had all undergone Specific Memory Extraction —"*some of them as young as ten years old.*"

She looked at his date of birth . . . *Now, that doesn't seem right.*

Forty-two in 1973 meant he was . . .

s*even* when he was in the Larvae Program.

No memory-zapping for Hitch.

So why would he not be able to remember being a Junior Space recruit?

Because he was lying, that's why.

She quickly slid the passport under the sideboard, slipped through the door, and closed it quietly behind her, but as she turned to climb the stairs she heard a voice.

"Why were you in my apartment?"

But she found herself unable to speak.

"*Come* on, kid, I'm sure you can come up with some explanation — *some* plausible reason — for snooping."

Still she couldn't find a single word.

"No?" he said. "Should I be worrying about what team you're rooting for?"

"I saw your passport," said Ruby. "You're Art Hitchen Zachery; you were in the Larvae Program. You told me you weren't, but you *were*."

"I had no memory of it. I told you the truth as I knew it."

"*Really?* That's weird, because you didn't undergo SME — the only kids who did were ten or older — SJ told me."

"And did SJ tell you *why*?"

"You were too young?" said Ruby.

"I went into shock — getting chomped by a crocodile will do that to you. I remember nothing about it, nothing about that training week, which by the way is when I joined; I only know any of what I'm telling you because last night I took a look at my file, and it didn't make for pleasant reading — turns out Casey Morgan threw me to the crocodiles; apparently I caught him launching Baker into the rapids."

"*Oh,*" said Ruby.

"Yes," said Hitch, "*oh* is right."

"Sorry," said Ruby. "It's been a tough week."

"It certainly has," said Hitch.

She looked at him, her face full of regret. "I'm sorry," she repeated.

He sighed. "It's OK." And he extended his hand.

"Do you forgive me?" she asked.

"Nothing to forgive," he said.

They shook on it.

"Will you be coming to the Eye Ball thing tonight?" she asked.

"I'm not sure, kid, depends where I need to be."

"I thought it was your night off," she said.

"House managers don't have nights off, don't you know that?"

"So you *are* a house manager, and there was me thinking you were a secret agent." She smiled.

"Secret agents definitely don't take nights off—they'd wind up dead if they did."

She paused. "I'm not sure I want to go," she said.

"Did something happen?" he asked.

"The Count. Last night I met the Count; he was waiting for me."

"You didn't think to *tell* me this?" Hitch looked bemused.

"I'm telling you *now,*" she said. "He said all the usual Count stuff, it was creepy like always, but nothing was so creepy as what he said when I asked him who Morgan was."

"What did he say?" asked Hitch; there was something different in his voice, less even perhaps, unlike himself somehow.

Ruby looked up at him. "He said, 'I have no idea who Casey Morgan might be.'"

Hitch held her gaze for several seconds. He said nothing and then,

"You can't stay here; you have to go. You'll be safer surrounded by all those people, you *all* will."

"Wouldn't I be safer here?" suggested Ruby. "With all these alarms and security features? It's completely safe — you said so."

"Nothing is completely safe, kid. Go to the Eye Ball with your folks; try to have a good time and forget about spiders just for one night."

Some chance, thought Ruby.

"I'll be there," said Hitch.

She smiled. "You will?"

"Sure I will; you can count on it," he said.

Ruby went up to find her mother, who was talking to her father about the car and the driver and her outfit and a whole lot more.

She caught sight of Ruby, standing in the doorway. "You'd better get changed, honey; we have to leave in a half hour."

Ruby ran upstairs to her room and was surprised to see her laundry strewn across the floor.

What's going on? she wondered. There was a strange gnawing sound coming from the bathroom. She found Bug chewing on something.

"What have you got there?"

She peered at him and then she saw it.

"Bug! Drop it! Will you drop it!"

He let go and the blue rubber bone fell to the floor.

"Jeepers, Bug, what's got into you?" She picked it up and saw that the husky had chewed right through it.

There was something inside: a piece of paper.

What's that? she wondered. She found some tweezers and pulled it free.

CHAPTER 54
All Systems Are Down

THE PIECE OF PAPER was a note written in a wobbly hand.
It said:

Dear Ruby Redfort,
   I chose you because you are the smartest child I
ever knew and I predicted that one day you would grow
up and achieve great things.
   Many years ago I developed a way of extracting
memories, an invention intended for good, but lately I
have begun to fear it will be used for ill. For this
reason I encoded the formula, split it in half, and
hid it in two places. The first is a Lucite rectangle,
disguised as a key tag. If the Lucite reaches freezing
point it will reveal the image of two eyes.
   The second part of the formula is hidden in the
pattern of your irises. I don't need to explain to you
how all eyes are unique, much like a fingerprint. If
these Lucite eyes are placed directly over your own,
what's embedded in the tag can be perfectly read.

It is essential that if the code tag gets into
the wrong hands you deactivate the code—this you
can do by wearing the contact lenses hidden in this
container.

Once in place, these lenses will ensure that whoever
looks through the tag into your eyes will be given a
scrambled reading, though they will believe it to be
accurate. I cannot stress how vital it is that you use
the lenses if you fear the tag is stolen.

Ruby picked up the blue rubber bone and peered inside.
There was no contact lens blister or jar or tube or pouch, nothing.

She looked at the husky and rightly concluded that Bug had
eaten them.

"Great, just great, Bug."

Hearing his name, he pottered over to where she sat, a little
piece of paper hanging from his mouth. She took it and, unfolding
it, saw that it was another note. This one said:

In case of emergency and these lenses fail you or
become lost, there is a second pair. I asked SJ to put
them in the Ghost Files, in a folder marked "Blink."

Ruby turned and ran, right down to the apartment at the
bottom of the house, as quickly as her legs would carry her, but
when she got there, there was no sign of her protector.

"If you're looking for Hitch, he left ten minutes ago," shouted her mother. "He said he'd received an urgent message and he had to go — he didn't say why."

Ruby's heart began to race. "He just left us?" she said.

"It's a shame, I know," said her mother, "but it won't spoil your evening — you're going to have a high old time."

Ruby couldn't believe it. What kind of bodyguard did this? What kind of agent was he? She was alone.

Don't panic, she told herself. What she needed to do was act quickly, make contact with someone at Spectrum. She ran up to her room and clicked on the Escape Watch and set it to transmit — maybe she could bring him back. But when she clicked "contact" nothing happened; it just wouldn't connect.

She tried SJ too, but it was the same story.

This can't be happening.

It was the same with LB, and Blacker and Gill. She began randomly pressing buttons, but to no avail.

Finally, in utter despair, Ruby triggered the emergency bluebottle SOS symbol — still nothing. Her agent locator had been deactivated. She felt for the fly barrette and pulled it from her hair and clicked the radio transmit switch but found it wouldn't engage, and when she took a closer look she saw why: it had gotten bent out of shape, probably due to Olive's manhandling.

That kid is nothing but one big pain in the derierre, she cursed.

And then she had an idea. She wasn't sure if it was brilliant or totally stupid, but it was the only one she had — and good ideas were getting hard to come by. She pressed the HQ call button, held her breath, and waited.

Would the call go through?

"Yes," said a voice.

"It's me," said Ruby.

"Yes," came the reply.

"I need your help," said Ruby.

"Why?"

"Because I can't reach anyone else," said Ruby.

"All systems are down."

"I figured that," said Ruby, "which is why I'm calling you — you're the only one who can help me."

Silence.

"Look, I mean, I know we've never actually really gotten along or anything. . . . OK, so you probably don't actually like me, I mean, do you *like* anyone? But could we just let bygones be bygones? OK, how about just for today, just this one day, try to be interested in what I have to say — after that you can go back to being totally bored."

Silence.

"Look, I'm begging you, I need your help, OK, simple as that. What I need to know is in a file called 'Blink' — it's hidden in the Prism Vault." Ruby paused before continuing. "Only the thing is, I can't get inside the Vault because I can't make contact with anyone, but you can."

"I don't have the authority to enter. I need a written request or good reason."

"I have good reason!" said Ruby. "The reason is, if we don't figure out how to obscure the code that I hold, then it has a good chance of getting into the wrong hands. If you want an instruction in writing, I'll gladly write it down. Could you at least try to be helpful?"

She was getting desperate now, pleading, almost begging.

"You gotta see, this isn't only about me, it's about you, it's about Spectrum and Twinford and maybe *everything*. If Casey Morgan gets his hands on this code, then . . ."

"Who is Casey Morgan?"

"That's the thing," said Ruby. "I don't know, no one knows, how can you avoid someone if you don't know what they look like?"

Silence.

"Are you there? Will you help me?"

Pause. "All right," came the reply, "I will look for this file. When I find it, I'll contact you — where will you be?"

"The Eye Ball," said Ruby.

"I'll come find you."

"Thank you," she said. "Thank you, Buzz."

She was no longer alone.

CHAPTER 55
Make Like Bananas

HER MOTHER WAS CALLING.

"Ruby! Are you changed? We're about ready to go. Mouse and Elliot are already here."

Ruby looked at herself, standing there in her jeans and T-shirt, the word *swat* printed across it.

As her space costume was lost somewhere between Everglade and Cedarwood, she would have to come up with an alternative or her mom would be on her tail. She pulled out the black jumpsuit and correctly predicted her mother's reaction.

When she arrived downstairs, Sabina looked at her and said, "Ruby, what on earth are you wearing?"

"Don't you mean, what *in space* are you wearing?" said Elliot.

"Well, if I do, then I can't imagine what she is supposed to be," said Sabina, looking at Ruby's all-black clothes.

"I'm infinite space," said Ruby. "Isn't that obvious?"

"Not to me," said her mother. "So I'm wondering: (a) are you actually infinite space or (b) is infinite space just an excuse to wear that black jumpsuit I told you I didn't like?"

"Quite a heavy question," said Ruby, "but I swear it's option a." Ruby really didn't want this conversation; wearing the right party outfit was way down her priority list. Tonight, pleasing her mother came a long way behind moles and madmen and mushrooms.

Mrs. Digby was all dolled up and wearing one of Cousin Emily's hair ornaments. It looked a little dangerous, precariously sticking out of her bun at a troubling angle: a long jeweled silver chopstick.

"So what are you dressed as, Mrs. D.?" asked Brant.

"I'm an earthling," said Mrs. Digby. "An earthling who works all the hours God sends and doesn't have time to waste trying to cobble together some crazy costume." She turned to fetch her coat, almost taking Ruby's left eye with her.

"Yeeks! Careful with that, Mrs. Digby, you almost got me with your killer chopstick." But Mrs. Digby wasn't listening; she was checking the rouge on her cheeks.

"You'd be safer wearing your glasses," said Mouse. "That way she wouldn't be able to prong you in the eye."

"I'm trying to make my mom happy," said Ruby. "She's not a fan of my glasses."

"It's because you have such beautiful green eyes," said her mother. "A girl needs beautiful eyes, and it's such a shame to keep them behind those big black frames."

"What are you, some kind of Victorian?" exclaimed Ruby.

"You do know we are on the cusp of 1974? What happened to all your feminist talk?"

Sabina looked torn. Ruby had a point. She sighed. "You're probably right; wear whatever you like."

"Actually, Mrs. Redfort, I really like Ruby's glasses," said Elliot. "I think they are kinda cool. They give her an edge, you know what I'm saying? They make her eyes look big—like when you look at fish in a tank."

"Thanks," said Ruby. "You're quite the smooth talker. Maybe I'll stick with the lenses."

Mr. Redfort clapped his hands. "So are we all ready to go, folks?"

"Where are Red and Del?" asked Sabina.

"We're picking them up on the way," said Mouse.

"OK, so let's make like bananas and split," said Brant.

Sabina looked concerned. "Bananas?"

"Let's get out of here, let's go!" explained Brant.

"Wait a minute," said Ruby, "I just have to get Bug."

"For the last and final time, we are not bringing Bug. Mrs. Hassensack is allergic," said Sabina.

"I'm not leaving him on his own," said Ruby. "The vet said he needs to be reassured; she said don't let him get anxious."

"Why would he get anxious?" asked Brant.

"New Year's Eve," said Ruby, "and you know what that means?"

"Champagne and caviar?" said her mother.

"Fireworks," said Ruby. "Bug *hates* fireworks. We can't leave him alone; he'll totally freak out."

"But he's been alone before," said Sabina.

"Yes, but he's suffered a trauma," argued Ruby. "He's vulnerable, and if he freaks out with this injury, then he could really do himself some damage."

"I know Bug broke his leg," said her mother. "That's awful, of course, but I don't see what that has to do with fireworks." She looked confused. "Bug has never liked loud noises, but he'll just lie under the table like always, won't he?"

Ruby would have liked to have explained, make her mom really understand what Bug had been through, but that would mean telling her about the incident in the Northern Mountains on the edge of the frozen lake, and how could she do that? So instead she just looked at her mom with her most pleading expression and said, "You do know Bug saved my life?"

She knew her mother would be unable to say no to *that*.

"Brant, what do *you* think? Ruby's concerned about leaving Bug and maybe she's right—that poor hound has been through the wringer."

"I'll square it with the Hassensacks," said Brant. "Bring him along, Ruby, on one condition—don't let that dog leave your side. Got it?"

"I swear on my life," said Ruby.

Eleven years earlier . . .

he could only hear the voice; his blindfold prevented him from seeing his captor, but he knew who it was, he knew without a single word being spoken — his sixth sense told him.

"You?" he said. "Of all Spectrum, it's you?"

"You are surprised?"

"Who would have thought you capable?" said the old man.

"Of murder?" said the voice.

The old man shook his head. "No, of deception. I saw you many times at Spectrum, but never once did I ever consider you a risk. What a clever disguise."

"You have no imagination," said the voice.

"Perhaps you are right," said the Professor, "or perhaps I saw someone I could trust."

"People see what they want to see."

"That's true," said the old man. "Sometimes you have to close your eyes to see the truth."

"And sometimes you have to look beyond the face to see the man — you disguised yourself well," said the voice. "It took me years to find you."

"And was it Victor von Leyden who sent you searching?"

"The Count — yes, it was his idea to seek you out, but the dog-napping, that idea was all mine."

"Where is she — where is Mnemosyne?" asked the old man, anxiety in his voice.

"Oh, so that's its name. How wry — you named your dog after your life's work. How old is the mutt, by the way — thirty, forty?

Such a long time to own a dog, you must be very attached to her, very attached indeed."

The professor felt a pang to his heart.

"Is this what it's all about? You want the location of the *Hypocrea asteroidi*? I'm afraid I no longer know, plucked out that memory, but you'll find the answer you're looking for in the eyes of the Jade Buddha of Khotan."

"It's Victor who wants to prolong life and stave off senility; my only interest in the so-called Mars Mushrooms is to see him beg. His time is marked; he's greedy for life."

"So what do you want?" asked the old man.

"I want the power to wipe memories," said the voice, "to destroy the only things we humans can truly hold."

"For without memories, what are we . . . ?" mused the old man.

"Nothing," replied the voice. "Without memories we are no one, we are lost."

"Poor little Casey Morgan, did life deal you an unfair hand?"

"Just tell me what I want to know, and save your little dog's life," hissed the voice. "I'm afraid I will not be able to promise you yours."

"I will tell you what you ask, but first you must free Mnemosyne."

His captor laughed. "Your wish is my command, old man. What use have I for some wretched hound?"

The dog was fetched and the old man reached to stroke her head and then bent to whisper something in her ear.

"Go find Mrs. Beesman," he said.

And the dog licked the tears from the old man's cheek and, with one last lingering look, turned and ran.

"How touching," said the voice. "Now tell me where it is, this SME coder."

"You'll find it in two parts: the first is in a Lucite tag. The second is hidden in the eyes of a child."

"And how do I find this child?" asked the voice.

"You need to find the man who holds the tag."

"And who is this man?" said the voice.

"The man you killed," said Professor Pinkerton. "Your nemesis — Bradley Baker."

CHAPTER 56
The Eye Ball

THERE WERE MAYBE TWO HUNDRED CARS inching along in
double rows down Third Avenue, all waiting to pull up in front of
the City Eye Hospital. It had been billed as "an exclusive event,"
but it looked to Ruby as if the entire city had been invited. It felt
like the Eye Ball really was the only party in town. The gowns
were phenomenal and the costumes suitably out of this world.
Some guests had taken the space theme on wholeheartedly:
Freddie and Marjorie Humbert, for example, who had come
as the constellation Gemini. They were dressed elegantly in
black. Freddie's suit and Marjorie's gown were threaded with
fiber optics so when they stood against a dark backdrop, you
saw the little white points of light denoting the arrangement of
stars. Other guests just nodded to the theme, with a subtle hair
decoration or patterned tie or item of jewelry.

Brant and Sabina had opted for glamour, Brant sporting a
silver tux, Sabina stunning in a gown embroidered with silver

sequins — when the light caught her, she beamed so brightly that it was possible to imagine that, were she floating in outer space, she might just outshine the planet Venus.

"I swear there are more people dressed as stars than there are stars in the whole galaxy," said Sabina.

"That would be somewhat impossible," said Ruby drily. "I mean, considering there are more stars in the sky than grains of sand on the beach."

But her mother wasn't listening, she was too busy taking in the scene.

"How do you even *know* that?" asked Elliot.

"She reads stuff," said Mouse.

"Yeah, but how do the people who write stuff *down* know this stuff? I mean, has anyone actually gone into space and counted *every* star?"

Ruby rolled her eyes. "It's an estimate," she said. "There are approximately 100 to 400 billion stars in a galaxy. There are estimated to be around 100 billion galaxies in our universe, which means that there are approximately 10 sextillion stars in our universe. Maybe around 8,000 grains of sand can be packed into one cubic centimeter, 10 sextillion grains of sand could create a sphere with a radius of 10.6 kilometers. Some say there are give or take 700 trillion cubic meters of beach on our planet, which could hold approximately 5 sextillion grains of sand. So basically it means there are twice the number of stars in the sky as there are grains of sand on the beach — give or take."

They all stood looking at her like she had just beamed down from the planet Zuton.

"Anyway," said Mouse, "the point is, your mom's got a point. There are an awful lot of stars at this party."

The group made their way up to the thirty-third floor, taking one of the eight elevators.

When the doors opened, they were greeted by a woman in a gold dress and an elaborate hairdo, a tiny satellite sticking up out of her brunette curls. She checked their names against her list and directed them to the cloakroom, where they shed their coats and wraps before moving into the main ballroom. The ballroom opened into a whole series of other rooms, which in turn opened out onto balconies and terraces. It was "some party," as Brant Redfort correctly remarked.

Ruby was not surprised that the first person she ran into was not exactly the kid she was looking to spend the evening with, but that of course was the whole thing about parties — they were unpredictable.

"Hi, Ruby!"

Ruby looked around to see a slice of Emmentaler smiling at her.

"It's me! Quent! I'm moon cheese."

"You can say that again," said Ruby.

"Is that your dog?" asked Quent.

"Well, it's not my grandmother," said Ruby.

"He's got a broken leg," said Quent.

"Yeah, I noticed that too," said Ruby.

"I wanted to bring *my* dog, Dorothy, but my mom said it was strictly humans only, which is a shame because I was going to dress her up as Laika, the first dog in space."

"Well, that's *tragic*," said Ruby.

"Why?" asked Quent.

"Because Laika never made it back to earth."

Quent's face fell. "No one told me that."

"Sorry to burst your bubble, Quent, but it was no fairy-tale ending for that poor dog. Laika just went around and around in space until . . ."

Ruby stopped midsentence when she saw that Quent's lip was beginning to tremble.

"You know, Quent, maybe I got that wrong. Maybe I'm thinking of something else. . . . You know what, it was probably that film *Moon Mutt,* or *Space Spaniel* or something space-dog related."

Quent dabbed his eyes with his cheese sleeves and smiled. "Well, that's a relief." He took a closer look at Bug. "So what has your dog come as?" he asked.

"I don't know," replied Ruby. She glanced down at the husky. "Pluto, I guess."

"Doesn't Pluto have big droopy ears?" said Quent.

"OK, the Dog Star," said Ruby.

"But then shouldn't he be silver — like a star?" suggested Quent.

Ruby shrugged. "So he's a Martian."

"He doesn't look like a Martian," said Quent.

"How would you even *know*?" said Ruby. "Have you ever been to Mars?"

"Uh-uh, but I'm pretty sure Martians are green."

"Why? Why are you pretty sure they're green?" asked Ruby.

"Because that's what people say," said Quent.

"Do you listen to *everything* that people say?" asked Ruby.

"Not *everything*," said Quent. "But a *lot* of people seem to think Martians are green."

The conversation was going nowhere, and Ruby was relieved when Red joined them. She was dressed head to toe in green, with a radio antenna waving about on her head.

"So what are you?" asked Quent.

"I'm a Martian," said Red. She tried to catch a look at herself in one of the many mirrors. "Don't I look like a Martian?"

"You look *exactly* like a Martian," said Quent.

"I should," said Red. "This is the original costume from the film *The Missing Martian of Manhattan*."

Quent looked at Ruby. "You *see*! I *told* you they were green."

"Oh, brother! Look, speaking of Missing Martians, has anyone seen Clancy?"

"*I* saw him," said Quent. "He arrived the same time as me, and all these gazillion girls were with him."

"His sisters," said Ruby.

"They looked kinda grumpy," said Quent.

"His sisters," said Ruby.

"Hey, look, that's them." He was pointing at the Crew family, who had a whole bunch of cameras pointed at them, and photographers were rattling off shots while the ambassador's family attempted to say "cheese" and look like they meant it. The only people who seemed truly happy about it were Ambassador and Mrs. Crew. Amy had the fakest smile it was possible to make, Nancy was looking weird, Minny looked annoyed, and Lulu looked bored, while Olive had her cardigan over her head—there was no sign at all of Clancy.

"Excuse me, Quent, I'll leave you to orbit on your own for a light-year. I just need to check in with ground control."

Ruby weaved her way through the crowd to where the Crew girls stood. "Hey, Minny, is Clancy around?"

"He was," said Minny, "but Olive dropped her stupid Buttercup doll when she got out of the car, and Clancy volunteered to go down and get it."

"Because he's nice," said Amy.

"He's not being *nice*," argued Nancy. "He just didn't want his picture taken is all."

"Who can blame him?" said Lulu.

"I don't see why *he* should get out of it," said Minny.

"I'll bet he's gone looking for that astronaut guy—what's his name?" said Lulu.

"Dave Scott Mackintosh," said Ruby.

"Yeah, that's it," said Lulu. "He's kinda obsessed with this whole space thing. I'm telling you, he can be quite a bore about it."

"Well, he's come to the right party," said Ruby. She could see Del waving at her. "So, Lulu, when your brother finally decides to make it back to the thirty-third floor, can you tell him to come find me? I'll probably be over by the chocolate fountain."

"There's a fountain of chocolate?" said Lulu.

"Yeah," said Ruby.

"Don't tell Nancy," said Lulu. "She'll stick her face right in it."

Clancy was beginning to wonder if he wouldn't prefer to be smiling for the cameras after all. This whole Buttercup errand was taking him a lot longer than he had anticipated, and he was eager to get back to the party — it looked like fun. Plus he wanted to see Ruby, and if he was honest, more than anything he wanted to see Dave Scott Mackintosh. He had specially brought along his silver indelible pen, the one that worked on pretty much any surface or any fabric. Clancy was going to ask Dave Scott Mackintosh to write something on his shirt. He had decided against his Jupiter costume and instead worn black: black shirt, black suit, black everything — it felt more spacey. It was a most un-Clancy-like thing to do to have his shirt signed, but this *was* Dave Scott Mackintosh, and having him sign one's actual shirt was the best space-themed outfit one could wish for. His mom would naturally be livid, but how often do you find yourself in the same room as a real-life spaceman? Actually, for Clancy that would be twice.

Rats, he thought, *I'm wasting valuable minutes.*

He just hadn't foreseen that he'd have such a hard time locating his father's limousine, but it wasn't an easy task: the underground parking lot was crammed with limousines, and one limousine really looked pretty much like another. When at last Clancy found the Crew car and the doll lying on the ground next to it, he grabbed the doll, stuffed it in his jacket pocket, and lost no time wending his way through the lot toward the elevators. He was a few yards away when he got the funniest feeling, like there might be someone else lurking in this underground place, some*one* or some*thing.* He got down low and crouched behind one of the shiny black vehicles, holding his breath and trying to determine what this thing he sensed might be. There was a sound of a car door opening just a couple of rows over, and then the sharp *tap tap tap* of good-quality shoes walking purposefully across the lot. What *was* it about that sound that suggested something bad? What was it about the waft of cologne that caused goose bumps to appear on his arms? Clancy kept very, very still. He didn't twitch so much as an eyelash until he heard the elevator's *ping* as the doors opened and then the soft *thunk* as they closed. He watched the numbers light up as the elevator car reached level 1, 2, 3, and kept on going, 14, 15, 16, and on until it reached 34.

The next thoughts that went through Clancy's mind were very conflicted.

Get out of here, Clancy, get out of here right now, go home. . . .

You have to follow him. . . .

You know what? It probably wasn't actually him. . . .

Are you crazy? Of course it was him. . . .

Let someone else deal with the problem; I'm just a boy. . . .

Don't be a coward, Clancy Crew. You have to find out what he's up to —just follow him, would you!

Oh, brother, I hate myself. . . .

Clancy of course had a sixth sense for this kind of stuff; he'd always had it.

And now a voice told him: *Something bad is going to happen, and it's Ruby it's going to happen to.*

Sometimes he really wished he didn't get these hunches; it would save him a whole lot of grief if he were more like Del—no intuition and no sensitivity . . . If you were Del, you saw trouble, you met it head-on, and you punched its lights out. But unfortunately for Clancy, he wasn't Del, so instead he hurried over to the elevator and stepped inside, thumped the button for floor 34, and when the doors closed he leaned back, breathing hard.

What to do, what to do?

He watched as the numbers blinked up: 30, 31, 32, 33 . . . 34.

Ping.

CHAPTER 57
A Man About a Dog

SABINA AND BRANT were sipping green martiantinis and chatting with the Humberts.

"I only wish they had managed to finish the roof garden in time; the view's spectacular from the top of the building."

"They won't let you up there," said Freddie.

"Never mind," said Marjorie.

Sabina looked longingly at Brant. "Oh, but I had my heart set on popping a few corks and sipping champagne in the light of that giant eye."

"I know you did, sweetheart," said Brant.

"Why the roof of the Eye Hospital?" asked Marjorie.

"It's where we got engaged," said Sabina. "We sat on that eyeball and knew we were for keeps."

"How did that come about?" asked Freddie.

"It's a long story," said Brant.

Clancy was standing face-to-face with Victor von Leyden, Count of all darkness.

"How sweet of you to make it all so easy, Master Crew. I must confess I thought it was going to be so much more difficult, but now that I can enlist your help to bring Ms. Redfort to me, most of my work is done."

"W-w-w-what do you mean?" stammered Clancy. "What's Ruby to *you*?"

"What is she to me?" mused the Count. "She's bait, a little fly tangled in a web. She will bring the spider out of its lair; if I dangle her from the roof, it will come." He smiled. "You see, she holds a secret right there in her eyes, and I know someone who wants it."

"What someone?" asked Clancy.

"I must say, he had me guessing," said the Count, "but once I saw it, I knew it had to be true, it's so wickedly perfect."

"Who?" whispered Clancy, fearing the answer.

"Her so-called guardian angel," said the Count. "Trust makes you vulnerable, leads you into trouble, the same sort of trouble *you* have just walked into, but at least *you* have a way out — bring Ruby Redfort to me and I will spare your life."

"Never," said Clancy. "I would never do that! You can throw me to a pack of wolves or feed my toes one by one to a bunch of crocodiles, but I will never do that!"

The Count fixed him with his black shark eyes. "It would be my pleasure, if only wolves or crocodiles were to hand, but alas there are none, so please know that I *will* without qualm drop you from this rooftop if you refuse me."

"Then that is what you'll do," said Clancy, looking back at

him. Without a blink or a tremble, he held the man's gaze. "But I will not betray Ruby Redfort."

The Count smiled at that.

"I do believe you speak the truth." He circled the boy, stepping around him, his eyes fixed firmly on Clancy's. "You know, it is *rare* that I admire another human soul—you almost move me. What loyalty, what a friend, what a waste."

And from his black coat he took a vial of indigo, exquisitely inky blue, and, unscrewing the top, he took the dropper and squeezed it full.

"Do you recognize this?" he asked, holding it to the light.

Clancy kept his mouth firmly shut because he *did* know what it was and it frightened him more than crocodiles, more than wolves.

"The serum of honesty," announced the Count. "It will make you talk, and whatever you say will be the truth, the whole truth, and nothing but the truth, so help you, wretch.

"Open wide," he said, his hand pressed hard on Clancy's windpipe, forcing him to gasp for breath, and when he did, the Count dropped six pretty tears of indigo-blue on Clancy's tongue. He slid his gold watch from his pocket and waited for the hand to tick around once and then he sighed.

"Now, you tell me how I bring your pal, your friend, your kindred spirit, to *my* little party." The words were hissed out, full of hate. "You'll tell me now because you have no choice."

Clancy shook his head and the Count laughed.

"Get ready to blab." He made a snapping motion with his hand. "And look," he said, "not a crocodile in sight and all your toes intact."

The party was going very well, and it seemed everyone was having the time of their lives, except for Ruby, who was anxious. Where was Clancy? He couldn't still be down in the parking lot. She and Bug did a quick circuit of the main room and then went back to ask the coat check girl if she had seen him, and then the party greeter, but they shook their heads.

Ruby and her husky circled back and rejoined the friends by the chocolate fountain, Elliot transfixed by the bubbling gloop.

"No sign of him?" Ruby asked.

"No," said Mouse, "but I just saw Hitch."

"When?" said Ruby. "Where is he?"

"He said he was going to see a man about a dog," said Red.

"I have no idea what that means," said Del.

"It's English for *mind your own business*," said Elliot.

"I thought the English were supposed to be so polite?" said Mouse.

"It's a myth," said Elliot.

"Is Hitch English?" asked Red.

"Where did he go?" said Ruby. "Can anyone tell me?"

"Hey, look, there he is," said Mouse.

He was making his way through the party people, his face serious and his stride purposeful.

Where are you going? thought Ruby.

She called out to him, but he didn't hear her and continued snaking his way through the crowd.

She hurried after him, but he seemed to evaporate into the mass and she was left zigzagging this way and that in an effort to spot him.

"Darn it!" she muttered. "I need you." And then she had an idea.

"Bug! Go find Hitch." She reached to stroke the husky's neck but found he wasn't there. "What? You gotta be kidding me."

The Count pointed to a telephone. "All I'm asking you to do is make a call to the front desk and tell the greeter that you urgently need to speak to Ms. Redfort, that she must come to the phone, and when she does and she asks you where you are, you say, 'I'm dangling out a window on the thirty-fourth floor; please come to my assistance as fast as your little legs will carry you.'"

"But I'm not dangling out a window on the thirty-fourth floor."

"Give me a minute — it's easy to arrange," said the Count, and he smiled. "So what do you say?"

"OK," said Clancy.

"OK, what?" asked the Count.

"OK, I'd be happy to," said Clancy.

"Why?" said the Count, furrowing his brow. "Why would you be *happy* to tell her that?"

"Because," said Clancy *truthfully,* for there was no other way for him to tell it, "she'll know right away that something is up. She'd know I'd never put her life in jeopardy like that; she won't believe me—not for a second; she'll assume I'm kidding around."

The Count frowned as he considered this hiccup in his plan, and then he said, "So, Master Crew, tell me, what *will* bring Ms. Redfort running? Tell me what is her so-called Achilles' heel when it comes to the tugging of her little heartstrings?"

"Bug," said Clancy without hesitation.

"Bug?" said the Count. "Who is Bug?"

"Her dog," said Clancy. "If Ruby's here tonight, then Bug's sure to be here too; she wouldn't leave him home on New Year's Eve, and if Bug wanders off, she'll go find him."

"And why should she care about a dog, pathetic creatures that they are?"

"Bug is not pathetic. Ruby is crazy about that dog, she would do anything for him, plus he's injured, so she's feeling very protective, won't let him leave her side."

The Count clapped his hands. "Music to my ears! So let's get that hound to come to us."

"If we do, she's sure to follow," said Clancy.

Ruby had hoped that the dog would have moseyed back to the group, but there was no sign of him.

"Mouse, have you seen that dog of mine?"

"I thought he was with you," said Mouse. "He's probably sniffed out the buffet room."

"You better not let Mrs. Hassensack see him," said Elliot. "She's not so crazy about canines."

"It's because she has allergies," said Quent. "I have allergies, but I love dogs so much I don't care."

"Actually, she is phobic about dogs," said Red.

"Is there such a thing as a phobia of dogs?" asked Elliot.

"Cynophobia," said Quent.

"That's a big word for a small kid," said Del.

"I know everything about dogs," said Quent.

"So how do you know that Mrs. Hassensack has cyno-whatever?" asked Mouse.

"My mom designed her costume," said Red, "and they got chatting. Turns out Mrs. Hassensack has issues."

Suddenly, bringing Bug to this crazy party seemed like a very bad idea. There would be a scene, her parents would be mortified, Ruby would be in the doghouse, and all in all it would be a very bad start to 1974.

"I better go find him before we both get sent to the pound." Ruby sighed. "Look, if you see that Crew boy, tell him he's royally late."

"Where shall I say you are?" asked Elliot.

"I don't know, tell him I'll be on planet Mars — which is where I wish I was, by the way."

"Sure," said Elliot.

"You want me to come with you?" asked Mouse.

"Nah, I won't be a minute. I'll bet he's gone to find Consuela. She's a soft touch when it comes to Bug."

Ruby began to weave her way through the party, making sure to avoid her parents, who were in the middle of a highly animated conversation with the planet Neptune and a flying saucer, or *some* unidentified flying object, it was hard to say.

"Bug!" hissed Ruby. "Where are you, you horrible husky?" She looked in the rooms on either side of the grand corridor. There were people everywhere, elegant gatherings clustered here and there, some sitting, others standing, all of them chatting, but no Bug.

"Hey, anyone seen a husky?" she called.

Barbara Bartholomew turned around when she heard Ruby's voice. "Oh, hey, Ruby, I *did* see Bug, and you better catch hold of him before Mrs. Hassensack sees him. She's not a fan, if you know what I mean. She has allergies, and that thing, what's it called?"

"Cynophobia," said Ruby.

"That's the one."

"Thanks, Barbara. Could you grab a hold of him if he comes this way?"

"You can count on it, honey."

Ruby lingered a second. "Would you maybe not mention it to my mother?"

Barbara gave a theatrical wink. "I'll keep it zipped; no reason to ruin her evening."

"I appreciate it," said Ruby.

She continued on until she reached the staircase. She wasn't certain why, but if she had to guess, instinct told her to go up rather than down. As she climbed the stairs, the chatter and laughter receded, and once she was on the thirty-fourth floor, there was just a gentle hum and burble. She cocked her head and listened, and then she thought she heard the sound of Bug's plaster cast tapping along the marble floor. She quickened her pace, rounded the next corner, and then she saw him.

"Bug! What in jeepers are you doing?" The dog stopped, turned to look at her, paused for just a moment, and then walked on.

"Bug, you come back here!" But he wasn't listening. This was odd, super odd. Bug was one very well-behaved dog — at least he was on just about any other day.

"Hey, what's got into you? Geez, Bug, you choose *this* moment to give up on the whole command thing?"

It was then that she became aware of the air. It wasn't the smell of candles, perfume, and food that she now breathed. It was something far richer. It was different from the other delicious smells that were coming at her from all directions and everywhere. This scent was intoxicating. More exotic than jasmine, more heady than roses, more . . .

Cyan, she thought.

She knew that scent. The last time she had smelled it, she was on top of Wolf Paw Mountain, nose to nose with its fearsome creator, the blue Alaskan wolf. Cyan. The rarest perfume in the world, a scent designed to lure prey.

"Bug, come back here!" she whispered. But the dog wouldn't be called.

When she turned the next corner, she saw him standing there at the far end of the hallway. He paused just a moment and then he was gone.

Her instinct was to follow, but she knew this was a trap. Whoever was luring Bug was actually luring her. *Don't follow. If you do, whoever is around that corner will kill you and then they will kill your dog. You live, Bug lives.*

She could hear footsteps coming her way. She backtracked, slipping through a half-open door. The room was dark. The footsteps moved quickly.

A man? And then she heard a voice. It was hushed, but there was no mistaking who it belonged to: *Hitch.* She was about to step out from her hiding place, when his words caught her. He was speaking into some kind of radio device.

"I'll find her," he whispered. "She's here in the building. I saw her come up; she'll be lurking somewhere in the shadows. She's smart, but I can outsmart her." He stopped almost directly in front of the door behind which she hid. "I know we want her alive," he said, "but that all depends on whether I reach her before our friend the Count does." He sniffed the air. "I smell cyan—

he's here already, and he'll kill her if he gets the chance." The way he spoke was matter-of-fact, urgent but without emotion. "At least with her gone, it would bring everything to a close."

He began to walk, his footsteps heading off down the passageway.

Ruby didn't move. *Stay still until you are absolutely sure the coast is clear.* Was that a rule? She couldn't remember.

It was while she stood there as still as the walls that the Escape Watch flashed red.

A message from HQ.

>> YOU ARE IN DANGER!

This word message was followed by a picture message. A black-and-white photograph appeared on the screen, a boy of about six, maybe seven.

She stepped backward as if the small white teeth of the boy might take a bite. For the eyes that stared back at her were the eyes of the Redforts' very own house manager, the eyes of Spectrum Agent 192.

The image dissolved and the following words appeared:

THE FACE OF
CASEY MORGAN

CHAPTER 58
No Rule 81

THE MESSAGE WAS FROM BUZZ and was followed by the words:

> `>> I AM COMING TO FIND YOU, STAY WHERE YOU ARE,`
> `KEEP AWAY FROM HIM.`

It was hard to be exactly reassured by this.

It was good to know that someone was on the way to rescue her from mortal danger, but if Ruby could have picked anyone to come to her aid, it would not have been the woman who sat, mushroom-like, surrounded by telephones, picking up messages and passing on instructions. Of all the people in Spectrum 8, Buzz seemed the least likely to be capable of saving her. But it was turning out to be that kind of day, since Ruby had to admit that of all the people she had worked with, Hitch seemed the least likely to be the one to try and kill her.

RULE 81: WHEN YOUR MOST TRUSTED ALLY TURNS OUT TO BE A PHONY

But the answer was not in Ruby's little magenta rule book, because for most of her life, Clancy Crew had been her most trusted ally and so she had never once had to contemplate the thought.

Clancy Crew, meanwhile, was trying to recall any one of Ruby's rules in the vague hope that it might perhaps give him even the faintest clue as to what he should do next. Bug had been shut behind a door, the Count obviously didn't trust this injured husky not to take a bite, and so Clancy alone stood staring into the eyes of Count von Viscount, unsure of what his next move should be.

"So, Master Crew, we have managed to acquire a dumb animal but failed to lure the smart girl."

"Yes," agreed Clancy.

"Why is that?" asked the Count.

"She didn't follow," said Clancy.

The Count looked at him with cold disgust. "She did not."

Clancy said nothing.

"You lied to me," said the Count. *"You lied."*

Clancy looked back at the man. "How could I? You gave me a truth serum and I told you the truth."

The Count's eyes were boring into him; he could almost feel their stare. "What do you think I am, some kind of fool? An imbecile?"

"A bear," said Clancy.

The Count looked puzzled.

"Do you know what I'm capable of?" he snarled.

"Anything," whispered Clancy. "You're capable of anything."

But the Count didn't hear. His attention was caught by another sound — footsteps moving fast, two people, but not together. He let go of Clancy, who stumbled, his head hitting the edge of the sill, a nasty thud.

"I'll catch up with you later," said the Count. "You might as well stay where you are. No one can save you now."

I think that might be true, thought Clancy as he watched the man walk away, his shoes *tap tap tapping* on the cold marble floor.

WHAT TO DO IF YOU MEET A BEAR — WISH YOU HADN'T!

As Clancy lay there, he thought about the unsolvable problem, the problem that had no answer — bears. The only thing he and Ruby had always agreed on was who in all the world might save you should you have the misfortune to meet one.

"Mrs. Digby," he whispered, before passing out.

As Ruby turned the corner, she saw him and, more to the point, he saw her.

"Ruby!" called Hitch.

She turned and ran.

"Kid, where are you going?"

But she didn't reply. She just tore down the passageway as fast as she could. She made it to the back staircase and quickly sprinted down the zigzag stairs to the thirty-third floor. She was relieved to be back where the party was, where all the people were. She ran along the deserted east corridor until she reached the big wooden doors that led to the grand hall. She could hear the hubbub on the other side. She reached for the handle and pushed down hard, expecting the doors to swing open, but they didn't — they were bolted shut. She hammered hard with her fists, but no one was going to hear her, not with the racket of the music and the dancing and the laughing and happy chatter.

Where is Buzz? Darn it, where is Buzz! She pulled at her hair and slapped her hand to her head several times. *Keep calm,* she told herself. *Focus, Ruby, stop freaking out and focus.*

She closed her eyes, took a breath. And just like that an idea popped into her head. She remembered that conversation — her mother talking about the party, the little catering elevator, a sort of updated dumbwaiter that was going to be installed to carry food and dishes from the newly built kitchens all the way to the grand dining room on the thirty-third floor. If Ruby could find that, then she could climb inside, she was certainly small enough, and once in the elevator, she would be able to travel to the basement level and grab a cop or a passerby. She really wasn't feeling choosy.

If only she had paid attention to her mother's chatter; if only she had, she would have known why this plan was simply not going to work. Two minutes later she found out. The room was an empty shell of a space, a building site. There was no dumbwaiter, just one desperate girl.

She could hear Hitch, his footsteps clicking along the marble corridor. How had he known she would come this way? Could he read her mind? Was it some Spectrum intuition? And as she lifted her hand to her head, she found the answer: the fly barrette; she must have triggered the locator. It was not broken, just jammed. Hitch knew exactly where she was because *she* had told him. She began barricading the door with ladders and construction workers' tools and anything that might possibly buy her one more second of time.

RULE 44: WHEN IN A TIGHT SPOT, BUY YOURSELF SOME TIME: ONE MINUTE COULD CHANGE YOUR FATE.

Now what? Wait for help to arrive? *Buzz, you walking mushroom, where are you?*

She could hear him outside, trying the handle.

"Kid, I don't know who's spooking you, but you've got this all backward."

She kept quiet, as if silence was a good way to fool him, make him think she wasn't there.

Not a chance.

Clancy came around and realized he was very uncomfortable sprawled there on the floor. Something rock-like was digging into his hip. He reached a hand under his side.

"Buttercup?" he said, pulling the doll from his jacket pocket. "Oh, boy, I forgot about you. Olive's going to be mad at me, Mom and Dad are going to be mad at me, and where am I? Flat on my back doing nothing about nothing." He looked sadly at the doll. "Why don't you go get help, Buttercup? I'll try crawling off to find Ruby while you find someone to save us." And then he remembered the last thought he'd had before he'd slipped into unconsciousness. It had been about Mrs. Digby and bears, and he wondered, *was it possible that* she *could save Ruby?*

He groped for his indelible pen, he still had it in his back pocket, and he scrawled a silver message on the doll's face.

It said:

Follow me back to Clancy

Then he sort of half-walked, half-staggered to the door that held Bug.

The dog wagged his tail, pleased to be released, pleased the frightening man in the long black coat was gone. Clancy stroked the husky's head.

"OK, Bug, you gotta do this one thing; think you can?"

The dog wagged his tail some more.

Clancy held the doll out to him. "Go find Mrs. Digby?"

The dog's ears pricked up when he heard her name.

"Here, go find Mrs. Digby." But Bug just stood looking at Clancy and the trickle of blood running down his cheek. "Bug, go, you have to go, OK?"

But the husky did not move.

"Bug, you know this game, you're really good at it." Clancy

threw the doll and said in his most commanding voice, "Bug, go find Mrs. Digby!"

The dog stood still.

Clancy was getting desperate, his voice losing hope. "Bug, for jeepers' sake, you have to go get Mrs. Digby, you have to or Ruby will die, you understand? I need your help."

And the dog *did* seem to understand. He picked up Buttercup and he turned and he ran back down the corridor toward the staircase.

"Kid, open the door; you've *got* to open the door."

"I don't gotta do anything. I'm not listening to you; listening to you is how Bradley Baker wound up dead."

"I don't know what you're talking about, Ruby."

"Your *picture* is what I'm talking about. It was found buried in the files, the files you tried to hide."

"Kid, you're not making any sense."

"You've been lying to me!" she shouted. "But you're good at that, aren't you? Because that's what you are, just one big lie."

"You're all mixed up, kid — open the door and we can talk."

"If you think I'm gonna open this door to you, you must be crazy. Oh, I forgot — you *are!*"

"You *have* to let me in, Ruby!"

"Never!"

The noise that followed was of Hitch's shoulder thumping

into the door. The barricade was beginning to give. There was no way out. Except via the window. She was a long way up; what was this, the thirty-third floor? Another story and then the roof.

She went to the window — a broken latch, no way to open it.

"Ruby?" A small voice came from the watch. "Ruby? Are you there?"

"Buzz, is that you? Where are you?"

"I tracked you, I'm in the next room; can you make your way to me?"

"How?" said Ruby. She was feeling straight-up panic now.

"There's a ledge. Do you think you could get yourself to me?"

"Maybe if I can get out the window." She looked around; there was a fire extinguisher in the corner. She heaved it from the wall and ran at the window, smashing it into the glass, tiny fragments exploding into the air.

Jeepers, Rube, is this how you want to die?

Ruby peered out and looked to the sidewalk below.

Oh, brother, she thought.

"It's a long way down."

"I see that," said Buzz, "but you can make it, I'm right here."

She saw Buzz's hand beckoning her. Six yards, maybe eight, and she would be safe.

"You can do it, Ruby."

Buzz was right, she could do this; she'd done it before. It was just that back then, a few months ago, when she'd taken a walk along the outside of the Sandwich Building, there had been no ice-cold wind, no ice, and, more to the point—no psychopath trying to pluck her from the ledge.

Don't think about that.

She stepped through the window and out onto the narrow stone shelf.

Behind her, there was a crashing sound as the door finally gave and Hitch sort of tumbled into the room. He righted himself, looked around, wondered where she'd gone, ran to the shattered window, and then he saw her. "No!" he shouted. "Don't do that!"

"Get away from me!" she yelled. "I know who you are, don't you see?"

"Whatever you think you know, you got it wrong," said Hitch, his voice steady.

"I know what you did. I know who you are."

"And who's that?" asked Hitch.

"You're Casey Morgan," said Ruby.

CHAPTER 59
Follow Me

MRS. DIGBY FELT A NUDGE to her leg and looked down to see Bug.

"Well, where in the dickens did you come from?" said Mrs. Digby. "You're supposed to be with Ruby."

The dog nudged her again, and the old lady's drink, a precarious sort of red cocktail, splashed from its glass onto her dress. "Well, now look what you've gone and done," she said, tottering to the nearest table and wiping at her skirt with the edge of the elegant white tablecloth. The dog followed her, butting her leg with his head. "Stop it, would you, you're making a scene." She bent down to grab his collar and for the first time registered what Bug had in his mouth.

"What is that horrible thing?" She reached for Buttercup. "Where did you get this?" The dog looked at the old lady and *she* looked more closely at the big round face of the baby doll, and the silver words scrawled across its face.

Follow me back to Clancy

Mrs. Digby looked at Buttercup's round green eyes staring unblinking back at her, and then she looked at Bug.

"You got something you want to tell me, dog of mine?"

Bug wagged his tail, sensing she had finally understood.

"Come on, then," she said. "You take me to Clancy."

Ruby was losing her nerve. Safety was too far away. She was still several icy steps from the window where Buzz stood calling to her.

"Be careful. Don't slip, Ruby, just focus," Buzz urged. "LB is on her way."

Ruby tried not to think about what would happen if LB didn't show.

"Kid, you're making a big mistake, the biggest of your life. Who fed you this information?"

"It doesn't matter who told me, because I just heard you talking to your accomplice not ten minutes ago. I know you want me dead! As soon as you have the code, I'll be toast!"

Her fingers searched for something to grip, to hold on to.

"Kid, that wasn't *you* I was talking about! That was —"

"He'll kill you, Ruby!" Buzz warned. "Just like he tried to kill Bradley Baker, that day at the rapids, just like he tried to kill little Art Zachery."

"Not true!" yelled Hitch. "The boy who almost got *chomped* by a crocodile was me."

"Well, forgive me if I don't take your word for it." Ruby yelled.

"Wanna see the bite? It's ugly, took an awful lot of stitches to put me back together."

Ruby felt her foot slip on ice and she barely managed to steady herself.

"Ruby!" cried Buzz. "Hold on, keep moving—focus on me."

"Focus on her and you'll wind up dead," shouted Hitch.

"Don't listen to him, Ruby! He stole someone's name and plotted murder."

"Speaking of names," shouted Hitch, "do you know what *Buzz* stands for, kid?"

"Of course I know," cried Ruby. "Brenda Ulla Zane. What's that got to do with anything?"

"Nothing," shouted Hitch. "Not until you know what those initials *really* represent: **B**aker, **U**ggerlimb, **Z**achery, all the agents Buzz wants dead. Baker, the boy who was better than her, and the two who tried to save him—oh, and you can add *your* name to that list. Once she has obtained that code, you really *will be* toast. You can stake your life on it."

"You're actually trying to tell me that an HQ *administrator* is part of this?"

"Not *part* of this—the whole deal, the one who's been pulling the strings all this time."

"*Buzz* is Casey Morgan? You're out of your mind if you think I'm going to believe that!" yelled Ruby.

She was looking at a piece of jutting stonework, trying to figure out how to get past it.

"He's a liar and deep down you know it, Ruby," yelled Buzz. "Ask him where he's been all this time, where was he this evening, for instance — why didn't he answer your call?"

"Want to know where I was? I was on a wild-goose chase, that's where — and someone cut my line."

"It was you who shut down transmission, you!" yelled Buzz.

"Why would you do that?" shouted Ruby.

"You're missing the big picture here, kid."

"That's funny, the last time I heard those words they came out of the Count's mouth — friend of yours, is he?"

She was grappling to find handholds; her feet kept slipping on the ledge.

"The Count's a friend of no one, you know that. Ask Buzz, she used to be his apprentice, didn't you, Buzz?"

"You're the assassin!" shouted Buzz. "After all, it was *you* who took her up in that plane! *You* who handed her to Marnie Novak! *You* who went missing without contact! Abandoning her to all that danger! It was you!"

"I was left for dead in the back of beyond!" yelled Hitch.

"Don't listen to him! He's trying to save his own skin."

"Believe me, Ruby, you're about to grab the hand of Casey Morgan!"

"How could Buzz be Casey Morgan? Casey Morgan was a boy!" yelled Ruby.

"No, kid, Casey Morgan was a girl who *disguised* herself as a boy in order to become Larva — no women in Spectrum, not back then, that made little Casey mad, it wasn't fair, and it *wasn't*, was it, Casey? It was most definitely *not* fair — but instead of proving herself, little Casey here decides to take out the competition."

"If I'm so smart that I can outwit all you brilliant agents with all your training, then how come I'm sitting surrounded by phones, taking calls and passing on messages?"

"It's true," shouted Ruby. "How could a mushroom like Buzz be some evil genius!"

"Because she's not a mushroom, she's a toadstool, sitting there attracting flies."

"He'll say anything to make you believe his lies."

Who's lying, who's lying, who's lying?

RULE 29: JUST BECAUSE A LION SAYS IT'S A MOUSE DOESN'T MAKE IT A MOUSE.

Just because an agent says he's a house manager doesn't make him a house manager.

Just because an agent says he's one of the good guys, doesn't make it true.

Just because a toadstool looks like a mushroom, doesn't make it any less dangerous.

Who's lying?

She was stuck halfway between Hitch and Buzz, her back to the building, the snow gently falling, with no idea which way to go.

"He's playing you, Ruby," said Buzz. "You've been working for him, feeding him information."

"All this time," said Hitch, "it's been Buzz, sitting right there in the corner of the room, so obvious we didn't see her, like a spider spinning a web, catching flies, catching agents."

It was Ruby's mind that was beginning to spin. . . .

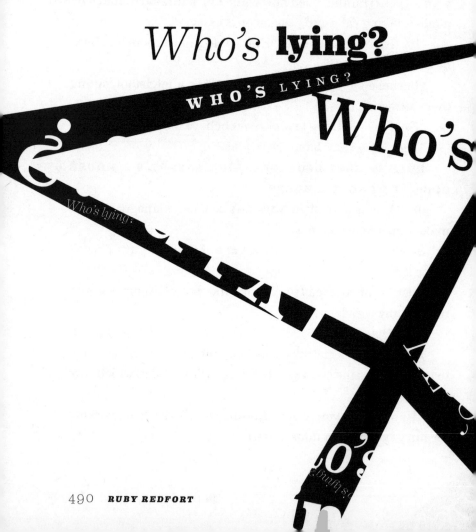

Who's **lying?**

WHO'S LYING?

Who's

Who's lying:

She looked up and saw the great blinking eye at the top of the old City Eye Hospital.

Who's lying?

Who's lying?

How to know?

Who would know?

Clancy would know . . .

She closed her eyes. "Clancy, where are you?" she yelled. And to her great surprise, a voice came back to her.

"I'm here, Rube! Up here!"

Ruby looked above her to see Clancy's small face looking down from the roof of the building.

"Climb up to the sign," said Clancy. "Get up on the roof! I'll be here for you!"

Get up on the roof!

And Ruby began to climb, away from Buzz, away from Hitch, and up to safety. She looked down; she could no longer see Buzz, but out of the corner of her eye she could see Hitch. He was at the far edge of the building and climbing.

"Keep going, Rube," urged Clancy, "just keep going."

She was moving fast. Though the snow was falling and the ironwork was slippery, she was already halfway up the sign.

"You've nearly made it," said Clancy. "Just grab the eye and you're almost there."

"I can't, I'm caught on something," she screamed. "My shoe is caught!"

"Don't panic, Rube, take it easy, just try and wriggle free."

"I don't know who to trust, Clance," she cried.

"Rube, what do you do when you meet a bear?"

"Wish you hadn't," whispered Ruby.

"No," shouted Clancy. "You go with your gut instinct, tune in to your sixth sense."

"I don't have one!"

"*Everyone* has one! Who is it telling you to trust?"

Ruby closed her eyes.

"Hitch," she said.

CHAPTER 60
Hanging on by an Eyelash

IT WAS HITCH WHO REACHED THE ROOF FIRST. He looked around for Ruby and saw a figure crouching near the parapet, just caught by the light.

"Clancy, is that you?"

Clancy got to his feet. "Yeah, it's me."

"Where is she?" asked Hitch.

"On the sign!" said Clancy. "Her shoe is caught."

Hitch ran to the edge. "Stay there, kid, I'll get you."

"You gotta save her," said Clancy. "The Count—once he figures she's up here he'll follow. You have to save her!"

"You can bet on it, kid, but you have to hide, no heroics, do you hear me?"

Clancy nodded.

"So go hide in the shadows; no one will see you in that black suit."

Clancy did as he was told, and Hitch began to lower himself over the parapet.

Too late he heard the *tap tap tap* of Italian shoes.

Too late he turned to see the silhouette of Victor von Leyden.

And he was too late to save himself from what was to come.

The Count didn't hesitate. He aimed and fired — not a bullet, but a dart of paralyzing parasol poison, and Hitch felt its sting as he reeled backward, arms flailing as he grappled air.

The Count picked his way carefully to the roof's edge and peered down to see Hitch hanging on by an eyelash, quite literally clinging to one of the giant iron eyelashes that surrounded the vast neon eyeball.

"Let's hope it doesn't blink," said the Count, looking at his watch. "It blinks and you die." He laughed.

Hitch was trying to grab on with his other hand, but it wouldn't move, the venom having already taken hold.

"Want to strike a bargain, Casey, dear fellow?" called the Count. "I'll give you the girl — if you give me the location of those Mars Mushrooms."

"I'm afraid I can't help you with that," shouted Hitch.

"You don't have long," warned the Count. "Once that paralyzing poison takes hold, *you* will no longer be able to — those parasol fish really are quite deadly."

"Like I said, I can tell you nothing," yelled Hitch.

"They'll be no use to you once you fall, and you *will* fall."

"I don't have the location," yelled Hitch.

"Don't lie to me. You betrayed me, Casey Morgan, and I want what's mine."

"Oh, I'm not Casey," called Hitch. "You've got the wrong guy."

"Of course you're Casey," hissed the Count.

"No, Casey would be the woman standing right behind you."

As the Count turned, Buzz kicked him hard in the back of the knees, and the Count lost his balance, pitched forward, and fell headlong into the sky.

And at the very same moment, Hitch lost his grip; the poison took hold, but as his hand let go of the lash, his jacket caught it. The dark gray fabric of his Savile Row suit was the only thing between him and the great abyss.

And next they heard Clancy's voice, yelling from the darkness. "Over here, I'm over here!"

The distraction bought them time. Buzz ran to the shadows but could not see the boy; his dark suit blended with the night.

"Ruby!" yelled Hitch. "Kick off your shoe and climb! Get out of here!"

"What about you! She'll kill you!"

"Get out of here! That's an order!" he yelled.

She yanked her foot and the shoe came away and she began to move, hand over hand, reaching for the top. She stretched out her arm and felt for the stone, but instead of stone it found . . .

"Buzz!"

"Call me Casey," she said.

CHAPTER 61
Blink and You Die

THE WOMAN FORMERLY KNOWN AS BUZZ was much stronger than Ruby would have ever guessed. Her grip was so strong that Ruby was held there, struggle was futile.

Casey Morgan pressed the 8-key key tag that had once belonged to Bradley Baker into the snow, and slowly the etched eyes appeared. Then, very carefully, Casey Morgan held the Lucite eyes over Ruby's own.

"Blink and you die," she growled.

She peered into green, trying to align the pattern in the Lucite over the pattern in Ruby's irises. But something was wrong. The code was blurred. And then she realized why.

"You're wearing lenses," she hissed. "Pluck them out or I'll kill your friend."

In the darkness Ruby could see Clancy creeping up. All he had to do was push.

Suddenly Buzz flung out her arm and Clancy went sprawling across the roof.

"I don't think he'll be getting up from that," she snarled. "Lose the lenses or I'll pick them out myself."

And so Ruby did.

Buy yourself some time: one minute could change your fate.

And while she waited for Casey Morgan to read the code, through the blur Ruby thought she could see a figure, two figures, one human and the other animal . . . a dog.

The human figure crept slowly and quite silently.

Casey Morgan heard not a footstep. The figure drew something from its hair; it glinted in the moonlight.

And then with one sudden move the figure jabbed it into the rump of Casey Morgan. The shock caused her to let go of Ruby, and as she twisted around to face her attacker, Casey lost her footing and tumbled away into darkness.

Her scream could not be heard because at the very moment of her falling the bells began to ring, announcing the arrival of 1974.

CHAPTER 62
1974

THE FIGURE LEANED DOWN to help Ruby up, and Ruby saw the silver chopstick glinting in her hand.

"Mrs. Digby?" said Ruby. "What are you doing here?"

"Just looking out for what's mine," said the old lady.

"You know you saved my life?"

"All part of the service," said Mrs. Digby. "No one messes with my Ruby."

Then she hurried over to tend to Clancy, who was lying flat on his back while being licked vigorously on the face by the husky.

A searchlight panned across the rooftop and suddenly there shone the brightest silver light, brighter than the Venus star, so bright it seemed it could almost blind.

Ruby watched as the silver thing moved quickly toward her.

"Ruby?" came a voice. "Look, Brant, it's Ruby!"

Sabina's dress had become a mirror ball, and as it moved the light danced around it.

"Honey, you're much too close to the edge, you could fall," said Brant.

"Yes, that occurred to me too," said Ruby, taking her father's hand.

"Oh, and Mrs. Digby!" said Sabina.

"Howdy," said the old lady.

Clancy opened his eyes. "Happy New Year, Mrs. Redfort," he groaned.

"Are you OK, son?" asked Brant.

"How jolly!" cried Sabina. "How *tout à fait joyeux!* Our own little party! What a way to welcome in 1974."

"I don't suppose you could give me a hand?" The call came from somewhere not quite on the roof.

Mr. and Mrs. Redfort peered over the edge of the building to see their house manager dangling precariously, hooked on a single eyelash of the giant eyeball.

"Hitch, whatever are you doing?" asked Sabina.

"I lost a cuff link — I was just reaching for it when this happened."

"Cuff links," said Brant. "They're a terrible liability."

"Thank goodness for a good suit," said Sabina.

"You can always rely on Guy and Hills," said Hitch.

"I think you should unhook him," suggested Ruby.

"Yes," said Hitch, "I'm afraid my arms have gone rather numb."

"That's from the cold," said Sabina. "Help him up, Brant, darling, his seams might go."

And just as Hitch was hauled back onto the roof, a helicopter hovered overhead and two figures began to descend, a woman and a man.

"At last," said Hitch, and they all watched as Loveday Byrd and Agent Blacker touched down.

"Have we missed anything?" yelled LB.

"No," shouted Ruby, "I'd say you're just in time."

"Gee, how exciting," exclaimed Sabina.

"What a show!" said Brant.

"Is it a show?" asked Sabina.

"It's hard to say," said Ruby.

"Well, *something* just happened," said Sabina. "What do *you* think, Mrs. Digby?"

"You know what, Mrs. R.," she said, looking up at the glittering figure with a placid expression. "It's like I always say: ask me no questions and I'll tell you no lies."

Two Lucky Escapes

IT WOULD SEEM Casey Morgan had been attempting to track down the child with the code in her eyes for the past eleven years. She had set elaborate traps, hoping to draw the girl to her, though only two of these plots had come close to succeeding.

The first was printed on the back of a Choco Puffles packet, and although Ruby had spotted it, solved it, and even filled in the coupon with her name and address, the information had never reached its destination. This was due to her father's forgetfulness: he had neglected to mail his daughter's envelope and in so doing had undoubtedly saved her life.

The second lure was a yellow balloon printed with a smiley face and tied to a long pink ribbon attached to a brown paper tag. Had Ruby thought to look, she would have seen that there was a puzzle contained inside that smiling yellow sphere. But instead she carefully detached the balloon from the ribbon and then let it go, watching as it climbed high into the fall sky before completely disappearing.

Heroics

From the **Twinford Hound . . .**

NEAR FALL AT THE EYE BALL
It was high-rise mayhem last night at the
Eye Ball. The New Year extravaganza, dubbed
"the only party in town," hosted by Twinford
millionaires Mr. and Mrs. Gerald Hassensack,
was brought to an early close when an
intruder was spotted climbing up the side of
the building.

Detectives suspect that the woman, Brenda
Ulla Zane, was there to rob guests of their
jewels and valuables. She was challenged
by plucky thirteen-year-old Ruby Redfort,
who in a hair-raising turn of events had to
climb for her life in a daring effort to
escape the robber.

Art "Hitch" Zachery, house manager to the Redfort family, came to the teenager's rescue but was pushed from the rooftop by an as yet unidentified man. Mr. Zachery was saved when his suit jacket became hooked on the Eye building's landmark giant blinking eye. When asked to comment on his heroics he said, "I would just like to thank my tailor at Guy & Hills."

The incident was brought to a close when housekeeper and senior citizen Mrs. Myrtle Digby bravely confronted Zane, who in an attempt to evade the law, leaped and plummeted 34 floors to her death.

Brant and Sabina Redfort, parents to Ruby and employers of both Mr. Zachery and Mrs. Digby, said they were "relieved to have everyone home in three pieces."

The Oak on Amster Green

THE SIX FRIENDS had spent the afternoon sitting in the Donut Diner, eating pancakes and catching up on the previous night's events, but it was now time to head on home.

"Rube, are you sure that butler of yours is actually a butler?" asked Elliot as he pulled on his hat.

"He's a house manager," said Red.

"Yeah, but he behaves like some sorta secret agent," said Del Lasco.

Mouse turned to Ruby. "Hey, maybe you should become a secret agent; you might be good at that stuff."

"What, with my eyesight?" said Ruby.

When the others were gone, Clancy and Ruby climbed up the old oak on Amster and sat for a while looking at the passing traffic and chatting.

"So how did Olive react to you scribbling on her doll's head?" asked Ruby.

"Surprisingly well," said Clancy. "She was very excited about it; she thinks Buttercup is trying to communicate with her."

"Because she has the words 'Follow me back to Clancy' scrawled all over her face?"

"Exactly," said Clancy.

"People will believe anything," said Ruby.

"Tell me about it." Clancy sighed. "Now she's following me around like I'm some kind of superhero."

"You're welcome to come and stay with us any time you like," offered Ruby.

"Great," said Clancy. "I'll get a moving company to bring over my stuff."

They sat there until the stars came out and it was time to say good-bye.

"Hey, Clance," called Ruby, "thanks for saving my life!"

"Any time!" shouted Clancy.

"And I forgive you for blabbing!" she yelled.

"I never blabbed!" shouted Clancy. "I was truth-serumed!"

"I know! Don't get your underwear in a bunch — I was kidding."

"You could dangle me over a pit of wolves . . ."

"Feed your toes to crocodiles," added Ruby.

"And I still wouldn't blab," shouted Clancy.

"And you know why?" yelled Ruby. "Because you're some friend!"

"It takes one to know one," shouted Clancy.

A Badge of Approval

WHEN RUBY WALKED into Spectrum 8 she was greeted by a friendly wave from the young man sitting in the middle of the round telephone desk.

"Go on in, Ruby," he said. "LB's expecting you."

Ruby entered the office to find her boss sitting there in white, her feet shoeless. The only color in the entire space: the red of her toenail polish.

LB took no time getting to the point.

"Spectrum is very appreciative that you didn't give up the code."

"That wasn't really up to me," admitted Ruby. "It's thanks to our housekeeper."

"Yes, and how exactly did she come to be there at precisely the right moment?"

"You'd have to ask Bug," said Ruby.

"You're suggesting I talk to your dog?"

Ruby shrugged.

"So this housekeeper of yours, can we trust her?"

"I think you can trust her with your life," said Ruby.

"She won't blab?" asked LB.

"Not a chance," said Ruby. "But if you want to keep her sweet, then send her a subscription for *Poker Chips Quarterly*."

They discussed the case, the events, the outcome.

The Lucite tag had been recovered, but it was now nothing more than a key tag; its fall from the rooftop had damaged it beyond readability. As for the Count, there was no sign of him at all. He had quite simply vanished.

"Is he alive, is he dead?" mused LB. "I guess we'll just have to wait and see."

And just as Ruby thought the debrief was coming to a close, LB threw her a curveball.

"You seem to have a hard time managing rule number one. Why is that, Redfort?"

Ruby was caught off guard. "Are you talking about Clancy?"

"I am indeed talking about Mr. Crew."

"The thing is," Ruby began to explain. "The thing about Clancy is he knows things without knowing things; he has this sixth sense." She looked up at LB. "Do you know what I mean?"

"Yes," said LB, "as a matter of fact I do."

"You're saying you knew about him," said Ruby. "That I talk to him? How come you never said anything?"

LB held her gaze, unblinking. "I had a best friend too. I know how it is."

"But you stuck to the rules," said Ruby.

"Quit looking at me like a dog who's lost a bone, Redfort."
She reached into the drawer of her desk and pulled out a circle
of white tin. "Here, it's yours, you deserve it."

"Deserve what?" asked Ruby.

LB held out her hand. "You made Larva, kid, the second
child to ever make the grade."

"But I thought I broke rule number one."

"Let's not be dramatic, Redfort. After all, rules are just rules,
and I think we all know, rules are made to be broken."

Team Players

HITCH WAS WAITING for her when she exited the ice rink on Bowery.

"How did it go?" he asked.

"I got a pin," said Ruby.

"For good behavior?" he said.

"Something like that," said Ruby. "By the way, sorry for mistaking you for a psycho."

"Perhaps it was my cologne that was throwing you off."

Hitch was surprised that she had not figured out the part he had played in getting her into the Prism Vault. The access to Froghorn's code maps, the scytale cylinder, the clues he had given to her.

"What do you think that trip to the planetarium was all about?" he asked.

She shrugged. "I thought you just liked it there."

"Kid, I'm beginning to think you might be losing your edge."

Ruby wondered why he hadn't just told her. "Why be so cloak-and-dagger about it?"

But he only replied, "I had to keep it all under the radar. I kept an eye on you, though."

"I felt like someone was watching me," said Ruby.

The other surprise was how Hitch had come to realize that Buzz was Morgan.

"You know it was Froghorn who figured it all out. If he hadn't gone into the files that night and put two and two together, you would have been toast."

"I underestimated him," said Ruby. "I guess I owe him one."

"I guess you do," said Hitch. "Give him a break, why don't you, buy him a donut or something."

"I might just do that," said Ruby. "I might even give him the whole box."

"That's the spirit," said Hitch.

And as they pulled up in front of Green-Wood House, Ruby said, "You know, Hitch, you're some agent."

And he gave her one of his winning smiles and said:

"Right back at you, kid."

Crime Pays

Mrs. Myrtle Digby and Ms. Ruby Redfort are all the richer for appearing on the hit quiz show *Thirty Minutes of Murder.* The pair achieved an unprecedented perfect score when they answered every single question correctly.

"I was raised on horror movies," said thirteen-year-old Ruby, by way of explanation, "and I was watching TV Crime Night before I could run."

The big check was presented by the show's producer Jovis van Straubenzee in front of an excited studio audience. Myrtle commented, "Like my old pa always said, crime does pay."

A Note on the Prism Vault Codes

by Marcus du Sautoy, super-geek consultant to Ruby Redfort

Ruby has to break several codes in order to gain entry to the Prism Vault, all of them set by her adversary at Spectrum, Miles Froghorn.

The grid

Ruby is faced with two 10x10 grids of black and white dots. So how does she figure out that the grids encode a four-digit code number? Here they are:

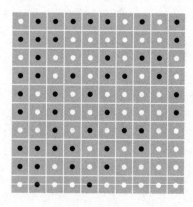 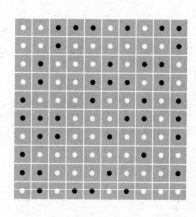

What she spots is that the grids have a rather interesting property, which reminds her of a book she saw in Froghorn's office about error-correction codes. Ruby notices that if there is an odd number of black dots in the first nine boxes of each row, then the last dot is black. If there is an even number, then the last dot is white.

The same is true of the columns. If there is an odd number of black dots in the first nine boxes going down a column, then the last dot is black. If it is even, then it is white.

For example, there is an odd number of black dots in the first nine boxes of the first row, so the last box in that row contains a black dot. But there is an *even* number of black dots in the first nine boxes of the first column, so that last box at the bottom of the column has a white dot.

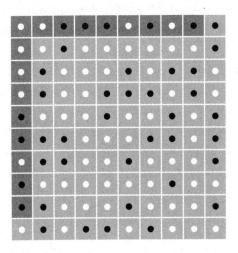

This type of code is called a *parity bit code*. It belongs to a family of codes known as error-correcting codes, which are used by computers to detect errors that might have crept in when they are sending messages via the Internet or beamed between satellites. Error-correcting codes like this are used in everything from encoding digital photographs to helping you talk to your friends on the Internet.

You've probably experienced, when trying to talk to someone on a phone, that you can't always make out everything the other person says. When computers talk to each other, they have the same problem, but using clever mathematics we've managed to come up with ways to encode data that can get rid of this interference.

In real life, due to its simplicity, the parity bit code in particular is used extensively in computer-to-computer communication where large amounts of data are being transmitted.

This is because computers send most information in the form of binary data—a sequence of 1s and 0s. Parity bit codes are attached to these streams of data, telling the receiving computer whether there should be an odd or even number of 1s or 0s in the message. If the parity bit says odd but there is actually an even number, or vice versa, then the receiving computer knows that something has gone wrong.

That property of the parity bit code is key to how Ruby cracks it. Like a computer receiving a transmission, she notices that there seem to be mistakes in the grid: in one of the rows and one of the columns. Can you spot which row is wrong?

Look at the fourth row. It has an odd number of black dots in the first nine boxes, but the last box has a white dot. It should be black! Also, the ninth column is wrong because there are an odd number of black dots and again the last box has a white dot.

Ruby realizes the mistakes are deliberate and are telling her that the first two digits of the four-digit code are 4 and 9.

Can you work out the other two digits from the second grid? Which row and which column are wrong?

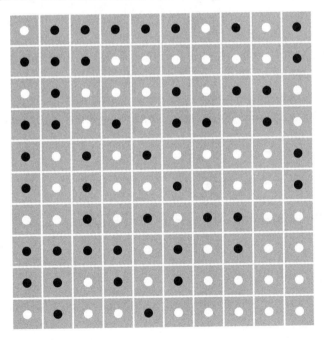

The chromatic code

Later, Ruby is faced with a code that involves listening to a sequence of musical notes, then playing a response on a keyboard.

The input device she sees looks like this:

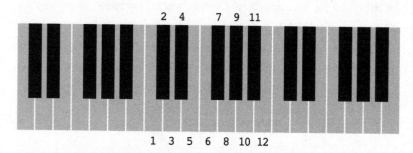

This code relies on the fact that there are twelve notes in a chromatic scale: a sequence of 12 white and black notes on the piano that are repeated.

If you number them from 1 to 12, then what Ruby hears are the notes:

6 7 5 8 4 9 3 10

She realizes that the four missing notes are:

2 11 1 12

Which she has to play on the keyboard in order to access the files.

But how does Ruby know which notes to play? Well, in this case, she has noticed that the notes she heard belong to a famous mathematical sequence and that the last four are missing.

The permutation of numbers is in fact a well-known card shuffle called the Mongian shuffle. If you have a pack of twelve cards numbered 1 to 12 in your right hand, then by continually taking top and bottom cards and placing them on top of a *new* pile of cards in your left hand, you get this sequence:

$$6 \quad 7 \quad 5 \quad 8 \quad 4 \quad 9 \quad 3 \quad 10 \quad \mathbf{2} \quad \mathbf{11} \quad \mathbf{1} \quad \mathbf{12}$$

Having identified what she is hearing, all Ruby has to do is play the four missing notes, shown here in bold.

This sequence of notes was used by French composer Olivier Messiaen in his piano piece "Ile de Feu 2." Interestingly, Messiaen, like Froghorn, was synesthetic: he experienced musical notes and chords as particular colors and used this in composing his music. Perhaps this is why Froghorn thought of him when setting his chromatic code.

Acknowledgments

I have been working on the Ruby series for the past seven years and have been extremely lucky to be surrounded by so many generous and inspiring people throughout. First I would like to thank some of those who worked directly with me to create the books and to produce, promote, and sell them:

AD, Ruth Alltimes, Carla Alonzi, Tanya Brennand-Roper, Martin Brown, Mary Byrne, Kate Clarke, Emily Faccini, Rachel Folder, Thomas Gardner, Nick Lake, Alice Lee and the ID Audio team, David Mackintosh, Kerrie McIlloney, Lily Morgan, Phil Perry, Alison Ruane, Sandro Sodano, Marcus du Sautoy, Rachael Stirling, Geraldine Stroud, Sam Swinnerton, Nicola Way, Danny Webb, Sam White, and all the HarperCollins team.

I would also like to thank the many booksellers, librarians, teachers, and reviewers who have been so supportive.

Many friends contributed ideas, gave me feedback, or generally helped me to get on with things. There are more than

I can thank here, but in no particular order, thank you: Marcia, Natalka, Neyla, Ilona, Aneta, Abi, Cress, Maisie, Jo, Quincy, Pete, Trisha, Simon, Ben, Richard, Conrad, and Enzo.

Special thanks to the following for being readers: Lucy Grosvenor, Lucy Lardle, Georgie, John, Molly, Delfina, Bay, Louis, Lorelei, Matilda, Alice, Peps, Inaara, Isaac, Sarah, Stanley, Claudia, Albie, Vincent, Hal, Sasha, Beatrice, Josey, Sophia, Nell, Rachel W., Jenny, Cousin Lucy, Cousin Phoebe, my father, my mother, and, especially, Tuesday, who although too young to read or listen to the stories, still tells me she enjoys them.

Most of all, thanks to you for reading the books. I am very touched and grateful that you do. I have had some lovely letters about Ruby and seen some inspired Ruby T-shirts, drawings, phrases, and further adventures, so thank you.

Finally, huge thanks to my publisher, AJM, the LB of HC.

Hey, Buster!

How many times can Ruby Redfort defeat the villains threatening Twinford?

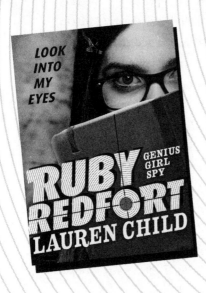

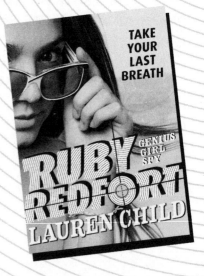

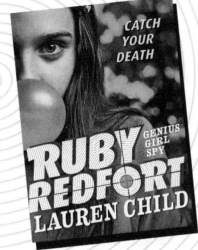

CATCH YOUR DEATH

RUBY REDFORT
GENIUS GIRL SPY
LAUREN CHILD

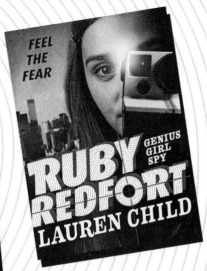

FEEL THE FEAR

RUBY REDFORT
GENIUS GIRL SPY
LAUREN CHILD

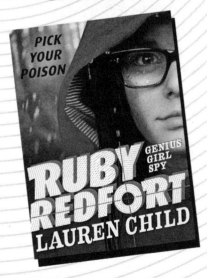

PICK YOUR POISON

RUBY REDFORT
GENIUS GIRL SPY
LAUREN CHILD

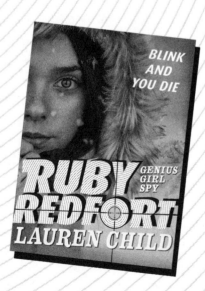

BLINK AND YOU DIE

RUBY REDFORT
GENIUS GIRL SPY
LAUREN CHILD

LAUREN CHILD, the U.K. Children's Laureate, first introduced the character of Ruby Redfort in her three award-winning, best-selling CLARICE BEAN novels. Since then she has been inundated with letters from fans asking for RUBY REDFORT books. Those letters worked, because this is the final book in the six-book series.

Lauren is also the creator of the CHARLIE AND LOLA books, as well as associate producer on the TV show of the same name. Her books have won many prizes, including the Smarties Prize (four times), the Kate Greenaway Medal, and the Red House Children's Book Award.

The RUBY REDFORT series features codes and puzzles created with the help of super-geek consultant Marcus du Sautoy, Simonyi Professor for the Public Understanding of Science at Oxford University and all-around genius.